Fragile Heart

Fragile Heart

JILLIAN RINK

For every person who has had to start over.
Better days are ahead. I promise.

Playlist

Out of Oklahoma
Lainey Wilson

The Prophecy
Taylor Swift

Silver Lining
BLÜ EYES & Ryan Nealon

Sure Be Cool If You Did
Blake Shelton

Dance Again
Selena Gomez

Blue Healer
Birdtalker

Kiss Me
 Ed Sheeran

Annie's Song
 John Denver

Say Don't Go (Taylor's Version) (From the Vault)
 Taylor Swift

Nobody but You
 Blake Shelton

Before You Read

Fragile Heart is a story of finding yourself after immense loss. While Brielle and her Alphas have a happy ending, please note that there are discussions that may be concerning to some readers including suicide, cheating, and death of a spouse.

You can find a full list of content warnings at the back of the book.

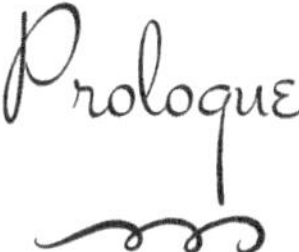

Prologue

ETHAN

The front door of the farmhouse slams behind me.

"Brandon, you ready to head out?" I call up the stairs.

There's a muffled grunt from upstairs.

Melissa sits on the island, her hair pulled back and tucked under a simple blue ball cap that coordinates well with her brown glasses and gray hoodie. She glances up as I walk deeper into the house, not bothering to toe off my boots.

They're mostly clean.

She eyes them, her lips pursing, but doesn't say anything.

"Hey, Mel," I say, wrapping an arm around her shoulders and pulling her into my side. She hums, loosing a deep breath. "How was your trip?"

"Good. Denver is always pretty, especially the mountains," she says. "We got to see Vail, and I've never seen it not buried in six feet of snow. I think it's even more impressive with the aspens full of leaves."

Her voice slowly lightens the more she says, and she smiles, just a little. I high-five myself. She hasn't smiled much recently, not since her dad died in May, right during her last round of finals in college. Without any more comment, she picks up her breakfast and dumps it in the trash, loading her dishes into the lower level of the dishwasher. Once the kitchen is tidied, she blows out a breath.

"I'm going to take Lizzie for a ride, I think," she says, though I'm nearly positive she isn't really talking to me. After a minute, she nods. "Yes. A ride will help."

"Be careful. That fire's burning hot right now, and today's winds might send it over the ridge."

Caleb had made sure I wasn't going to be moving any cattle over Fool's Bluff today because of it.

She glances over her shoulder, a rueful smile gracing her lips. "Brandon should be down any minute."

And she disappears out the sliding door that leads to the backyard—and the detached garage.

I glance around the kitchen, trying to keep myself occupied while I wait for Brandon. A piece of paper catches my attention, the black flowing script standing out in the rustic-leaning home. I take a step closer until I can read what it says, and then I wish I had just let my curiosity lie for once.

Brielle Jones and Brett Ashford request your presence to celebrate their love in a wedding...

I turn around, trying to get the damn words to scrub from my mind.

It's been three fucking years. Of course she'd have moved on.

That *thing* inside me rumbles its disapproval, its possessive-ness still an overwhelming wave all these years later. It didn't make any sense. It was a simple summer fling, something that had been doomed from the moment it began. And I'd been the one to make sure it didn't turn into some half-assed long distance abomination that fizzled after two months. No, there's no reason for my breath to catch and my stomach to drop out at the thought of her fucking someone else—knotting someone else. And so I shove it all down until I can hardly feel it.

Brandon comes down the stairs at last, dressed similarly to me, a worn flannel overlaying a simple white T-shirt and faded dark wash jeans that have seen better days. His boots are even more worn, but he doesn't mind. Not much is more comfortable when you're in the saddle for ten hours moving cattle than the worn boots you've spent the last four seasons breaking in.

As we head out the same door as Melissa, he tucks his hands into his pockets and looks out over the mountains. There's just a bare layer of snow coating the highest peaks, the spring runoff well and truly finished. Not that there had been all that much. Caleb had been gone the last five weeks, fighting multiple fires across Wyoming and Montana. He'd even been called in to help with a nasty one running along the Canadian border in Washington.

"You think about it?" Brandon asks, not looking at me. He grabs Phoebe's saddle and heads toward her stall.

My stomach clenches, but I shove that reaction down, too. She'd moved on. So could I.

I nod and grab Martini's bridle. "Let's do it. If we get the paperwork done by the end of the summer, we could be at the October gala."

His shoulders relax. "Think we'll get matched the first time?"

I shrug, focusing on getting Martini ready for the hard day ahead.

"Yeah, probably not. I think I read somewhere that the average pack takes three galas to match. But that still puts us before next year's fire season, so at least Caleb won't be up a creek."

Brandon continues on about the Council and our registering as a pack. I keep my mouth shut, not willing to ruin his good mood or hopeful disposition.

We set out toward the far field, but I can't quite manage to get the damn invitation out of my mind.

Chapter One

BRIELLE

The GPS chimes for the third time, notifying me that I've managed to miss the turn. Again. I blow out a breath and pull over to the shoulder, easing the car into park and turning on my hazards even though I haven't seen more than a handful of cars the last fifty miles on this two lane highway.

What is wrong with me today? It's not like I've never been to Melissa's family ranch. Granted, it's been a few years. But could so much have changed that the turnoff is now impossible to find?

I close my eyes and lean my head against the headrest, trying to get my bearings. My eyes burn with tears, but all I've seemed to do the last several weeks—months, really—is cry, and I'm freaking over it. It doesn't help that I've been in this stupid car for the better part of twelve hours. My legs hurt, my back hurts, and I can't seem to find a way to keep one hip or the other from going numb at the most inconvenient and frustrating intervals. I tap my toe, counting to ten. My phone pings, but I ignore it.

I can do this.

Finding this ranch couldn't be as hard as finding those damn messages on his phone. Or having to face down *that woman* while I was cloaked in the black dress that made me out to seem like a mourning wife. And certainly not as hard as shaking her damn hand while feigning ignorance over her being more than just his coworker. That's how everyone else knew her, at least. No one in his family knew that she'd been his mistress. Not until a month later when she announced she was pregnant and sued me, trying to force the estate to settle with her instead. As if that was how estate laws even worked in Colorado.

So instead of his mistress getting his millions, I have it all—along with the daily waffling between smug satisfaction knowing she got fucked over by him just like I did and guilt that I have his money when he clearly cared about her more than me.

My breath lodges in my throat, and I force my thoughts away from the entire mess. I can't think about any of that right now, not when I'm already knee-deep in panic over finding the ranch. The road is long and flat with copses of trees appearing every few hundred feet before the long green prairie grasses overtake the land again. The mountains seem small here, even though I know they're just as tall and majestic as the ones I hiked in Colorado the last decade. Everything is green and tan and contrasts against the bright blue, cloudless sky.

It's beautiful. And I can't manage to appreciate it.

That anxious bubble swells in my chest, and I shake out my hands.

"You can do this," I whisper, trying to believe it this time.

I glance down at my phone and can't help but smile at the text message from Faedra.

We're rooting for you!

And then she sends a picture of the twins on her lap, and I laugh, the sound wet with my tears. Each girl holds a sign. Iris's bright smile is in contrast to Rose's more sober expression, though her eyes are happy. Iris's sign says "Luv You Ant Brielle!", and it's done entirely in blues and purples. The "r" is backwards, and none of the letters are anywhere near the same size, but it warms me anyway. Rose's is simple, a heart with my name in the middle.

Faedra sends another text.

Rose wants you to know that she made the heart purple just for you even though hearts are actually red because she knows it's your favorite color.

I laugh. I can't help it. Of course that's something Rose would need to clarify. She may be the spitting image of Logan. But personality? She could have been Jude's clone. I've never seen a five-year-old be so stoic in my entire life. It's freaking *wild*.

They're perfect. Tell them thank you!

She doesn't immediately text back, so I drop my phone and focus on the road again. It's only a matter of time before someone notices I've traveled the same three miles on this blasted highway and calls the cops. I wipe my hands across my cheeks, ignoring how they come away wet.

Won't that just be the fucking cherry on top of this whole mess? Nothing quite like needing a damn police escort to your best friend's place because the turnoff isn't where you remember it being and the sign you always used as your marker is nowhere to be fucking found.

"Come on, Brielle. You can do this," I say. I reset the GPS

and prop it against the display screen of the car. "If you can face down that bitch, you can find Melissa's place."

When it no longer feels like I'm half a second from losing my mind, I ease back onto the narrow highway, turning so that I'm heading the opposite direction. Going significantly slower than the posted speed limit, I manage to notice a gravel road right where the map promises there should be a turn off, though there isn't any sign like there was last time. Large trees that were little more than saplings last time I was here tower on either side of the road, blocking view of anything but what's directly ahead of me.

How fast do trees even grow in four years?

"Melissa, I swear to God, you're putting in a damn sign at the road if it's the only thing I manage to do this summer," I mutter.

A couple hundred feet from the highway, hidden by the trees, a large metal arch spans the road. The poles on either side are large and the same black metal as the gates attached. The gates are currently pulled open and held with serious-looking locks on each side. In bold letters, the name of the ranch arches over the road, following the simple arc of metal above and below it, dark against the pale blue afternoon sky.

Misty Mountain Ranch.

She hadn't changed the name after all.

Breathing deeply, I follow the curve, my anxiety easing away. The turn off might have changed—dramatically—but the view when I crest the hill and the valley opens below me is the same. The mountains tower in the distance, the peaks still snow-capped. The valley sprawls away from the road, reaching so far into the distance that the details blur into a singular sage green. It's perfect today, the wind nonexistent for once, and the sky clear of any smoke from the wildfires I know are burning farther north in Idaho and Montana. It makes the scene something out of a magazine. Or maybe a postcard, something that can be sent to beckon someone home.

Wyoming was never my home except for the summer I spent with Melissa after freshman year when Mom ended up back in rehab and I had no home to return to during the break. But I've always felt that, maybe, this would have been the perfect place for me.

At least back then. And, with any luck, now, too.

Something boils in my chest, something I haven't felt in far longer than I care to admit, and certainly not since handing *him* the divorce papers on Christmas nearly five months ago. It feels suspiciously like happiness, but I refuse to name it.

My smile is wide as I navigate the road down into the sprawling prairie and ease the car to the right when confronted with the fork that splits it maybe half a mile from the turn off, following Melissa's directions. I can't help but glance toward the left, though, curious how much her family home has changed since I was here last.

There are more buildings than last time, three barns instead of one and a series of cabins painted a bland middle brown that somehow manages to blend well with the light green and yellows of the prairie grasses as well as the dark forest that sprawls along the mountains rising in the distance. I love the high-rises of the city, but there's something special about these mountains. Can I put a name to it? Not really. It's not like Denver has a shortage of mountains. It has the most fourteeners of any state—and by a landslide. But seeing this stretch of the Rocky Mountains lightens my chest until it doesn't quite hurt to breathe.

It has nothing to do with the mountains. That voice nudges me, but I try to tune it out. I've done really damn well not thinking about what moving out here might mean for running into *him*. It's been ten damn years. It won't mean anything.

The road widens, and I pull off, heading toward the largest of the buildings, following the brown and white signs that label it as the Main Lodge. It's painted that same sepia tone as the cabins

I'd seen from the road, though the roof is more complicated, a series of black clay shingles rather than the simple metal sheets that reflect the light back. The open space that functions as the front lawn is landscaped with a beautiful set of wildflowers that are planted just close enough it exudes carefree intentionality. The pinks and blues and whites complement the warm feel of the building. Large flagstones carve out a pathway leading to the railed-in porch that wraps around the far side, groups of chairs clumped together.

As soon as I ease the car to a stop in the unpaved parking lot beside the house and turn off the engine, I lean my head back and let my eyes close, breathing carefully through my nose. Another well of emotion chokes me, but I manage to breathe through it without dissolving into a second round of tears.

Made it.

Chapter Two

The front door opens as I stand from the car, my legs unhappy about the long hours I've spent behind the wheel. I shake them out, trying to get feeling into them both, as I duck back into the car and grab my phone from the passenger seat. I slide it into the back pocket of my shorts and then sling the small purse across my body.

There's a bright, happy squeal as I'm turning back toward the building. I manage to catch a flash of blonde hair tucked under a simple brown cowboy hat before Melissa's slight weight slams into me, knocking me back against the car. Her happiness is like a drug, and I wrap my arms around her, laughing despite all the mixed up emotions rolling through me. Her coffee scent surrounds us just as quickly as her laugh.

"You made it!" she says, her chin tucked against my shoulder and her grip still tight where she holds her wrists against the small of my back. "I got worried when you didn't text after lunch."

I take a moment to soak in her touch. It soothes that bone

deep ache that's been building since last fall—though I don't dare name it now. With any luck, being with Melissa will be enough for it to stop digging its thorns into me.

I gently push her away from me, taking her in. Her glasses are larger than last time, the rims thinner and a happy rose gold that accents the cool pink undertone of her skin. She's dressed in a practical pair of light wash jeans that flare at the bottom and a pink shirt with the words "Omegas Do It Better" written in a frilly black script across her chest. Though I can't see it, I know I'll find the symbol of our Omegas exclusive sorority scrawled along the back.

We joined together freshman year, over a decade ago. Seeing it makes my heart lurch. We were so young, practically untouched by the world. In comparison to now, at least.

"You still have it?" I ask, running my hands down her arms.

She shrugs and twists our fingers together, like she can tell I need the touch. "You know how attached I get," she says.

I did. It's a trait we share. Just like most Omegas, really. We're creatures of comfort and stability. We attach to objects significantly more often than others. The small box tucked under my passenger seat flashes through my mind, but I ignore it. Should I have gotten rid of every last item my cheating bastard of a husband owned? Yes. Was I actually able to? No. Not yet, at least.

"By the time I was willing to think about decluttering, everything happened with Brandon and then again with Kayla." Her blue eyes are bright but haunted, and her smile doesn't quite make them light up the way it used to. I change the subject, steering us away from the absolute mess those six months had been.

"It took me three tries to figure out where to go," I say after a minute. "Why the hell isn't there some kind of sign? I thought I was just disappearing into the freaking mountains, girl."

She flushes. "It's been a bit of a problem this year," she says. She sounds... ashamed?

Before I can ask why missing a sign is cause for her own shame, the door opens again, not as violently, and Melissa takes another step away from me, turning toward the person stepping onto the porch. The woman's honey brown hair is long and stick-straight, reaching nearly to her hips. Her brown eyes are light enough they could pass as hazel—or amber if we were in a romance novel. She wears a simple gold chain around her neck, a star pendant resting in the hollow of her throat. She looks like she belongs here.

She's stunning. She'd look just as much at home on the runway during fashion week. I force a swallow, trying to gather my thoughts. I'd expect nothing less of Emily Monroe, though. She'd been studying abroad when I stayed here that summer. Thank goodness, too, since it meant that the only people who knew about my fling with her brother were Melissa and Olivia— and I'd sworn both to secrecy when the thing went up in flames.

"Hi, Brielle," she says, offering a wide smile. Her eyes crinkle around the edges as she does. She holds out her hand. I take a step toward her, taking her hand in a light grip. That gnawing ache settles nearly at once—practically all evidence of my becoming touch-starved fading away.

I don't realize I'm taking another step toward her until her vanilla scent weaves around us both.

Oh.

Melissa never mentioned Emily had designated as an Alpha. And I hadn't really interacted with her when I'd come for Brandon's funeral.

"Sorry," I offer, blushing. Scenting random Alphas isn't something I do. Ever. Brett was too jealous to let me near them. Yes, I know that's super toxic. You don't notice sometimes until it's too late, you know? "I'm, um, newly off suppressors, and the adjustment is more intense than I expected."

I threw them out the same day I handed Brett the divorce papers, damn what the doctor had said about tapering the dosage to avoid a reaction. I needed a clean slate and that included with my designation.

She shakes her head.

"Don't worry about it." Then she glances over my shoulder, her lips pursing. "You want to get everything unpacked first? Or grab something to eat?"

My stomach rumbles, answering for me.

She smiles. "Dinner first then. We'll go to Lefty's. They have the best burgers."

Melissa groans. "Oh my gosh, yes they do. I'm so excited."

"Sounds like a plan," I say with a smile. "Thanks again for letting me stay in your guest house. I'm hoping to find a small place in town once the tourist season dies down a bit."

I can afford the prices as they are now. I could buy any of the four large ranches for sale along this stretch of highway, actually, without making much of a dent at all in the estate's assets. But I want a chance to get a sense of the town and surrounding land before committing to something. It's been ten years since I called Creek Falls my temporary home. I wanted to make sure I chose the right place to make my permanent one.

And if the prices go down in the winter, I won't complain about it.

"No rush." She waves off my offer. "It's not like it was getting a ton of use anyway."

Melissa loops her arm through mine. "I'll ride with you. I left my car at Emily's this morning anyway."

Which is how I end up back in my car following Emily's bright teal Jeep down the highway. Melissa's ranch is one of the furthest from town. I used to hate the drive, always so impatient to meet up with *him*. Now, the distance didn't bother me in the slightest—outside of my legs protesting being stuck behind the wheel again so soon.

The speed drops off when we get to the town limits, and not long after buildings start to line both sides of the road. Mostly quick and easy things for the tourists passing through: a gas station, a grocery store, and a smattering of novelty shops sporting a variety of Wyoming blazoned items.

"Turn up here," Melissa says, pointing to the next stoplight. "It's tucked back behind the hardware store."

"This wasn't here last time," I say.

"Hudson opened it a couple years ago." She taps her fingers on the door. "Ethan helped him strip out all the old wiring and stuff. It took them an entire summer."

Somehow, I'm not quite ready for the lurch my heart makes at hearing his name after all these years. I swallow and focus on the other person she mentioned.

"Wait. I don't think I know Hudson."

"Oh, right. Yeah, that's Caleb's youngest brother. I think he was still enlisted last time you were here," she says.

Last time I was here was for her brother's funeral, nearly exactly four years ago. She takes a quick breath, and her fingers tap faster.

"And that whole weekend is kind of a blur if I'm being honest, so I'm not sure who all you even met."

Her voice wavers. I grab her hand and squeeze it. After a minute, she blows out a breath.

"Sorry," she says.

I shake my head. "No apology needed. To be fair, I don't remember most of that weekend either. Brett was ridiculously overbearing. If he's an Alpha, I doubt I met him."

She guides me to the little restaurant. It's a converted house, the gables painted a bright white while the rest of the building is a dark navy. It almost reminds me of the little Cape Cod houses that litter the coast in New England. I ease into the spot next to Emily and turn off the car.

"This... doesn't feel like Wyoming at all," I say.

Melissa chuckles. "Oh, yeah, he caused a fuss when he painted it. But according to him, it reminds him of his favorite place."

She closes the door, and I scramble to follow her.

It's surprisingly busy when we walk in, a wall of chatter hitting us the moment Emily opens the door. The hostess glances up from where she rolls silverware, and then her cheeks flush.

"Hi Emily," she says.

"Hey Mallory." Emily offers a smile. This one, though, doesn't light her eyes. "There's three of us tonight."

She nods and marks something on a laminated sheet and then grabs a handful of menus. As we settle into the table tucked into the back corner of the restaurant, she gives me an odd look, almost like she's sizing me up.

The girls don't say anything, though, so I keep my mouth shut. Small towns thrive on gossip. The last thing I need is to end up in the rumor mill sooner than absolutely necessary.

"Is the Rustic Roast still here?" I ask.

Melissa's eyes light up. "Yeah, Joan still runs it. You remember her, right? Being a grandma has made her even sweeter. We should swing by. I bet she'll be so excited to see you!"

There my heart goes, lurching again.

"She's closed already," Emily says. "But she makes cinnamon rolls fresh every Sunday."

"I'm excited to have them again," I offer.

Joan's cinnamon rolls are one of those things that have stuck with me. They're *that* good. I steer the subject away from anything relating to Ethan, though, not sure I can keep up my feigned indifference for much longer. I'm exhausted from the drive, and Emily being an Alpha means she'll pick up on more subtle changes in my scent and body language than Melissa will, even with my scent blockers.

"You still all right with me shadowing you tomorrow?" I ask. "I know I'm not a paid stable hand, but I'd love to help out where I can."

Melissa nods and pushes her glasses up her nose. "Oh, definitely. The stable hands don't help with our private horses. I'm happy to show you around the barn. Maybe we can even go riding!"

I manage a smile. "Sounds perfect."

Chapter Three

CALEB

Ethan doesn't say a word as he strides into the kitchen, heading straight for the coffee maker tucked against the far wall. He's already dressed to work on the ranch—dark jeans and a black tee overlaid with a light blue plaid flannel. I glance at the microwave's clock before raising an eyebrow. Ethan never wakes up before six in the morning of his own volition. And certainly not on a damn Saturday.

The ranch is more than successful enough to have hired hands to run the day-to-day, so weekends were spent with the three of us, a leftover tradition from before Kayla and Brandon died that we couldn't manage to find the stomach to cut off.

"Thought you were letting the hired help run everything today," I say. "Something happen?"

He nods but doesn't offer anything more, going through the motions of getting a cup of coffee ready. When he's added the creamer, he turns toward me, leaning against the counter.

"Dad texted last night saying the stream up north is dry.

Need to get the cattle moved closer so they have access to the water troughs until another storm rolls through."

Ah. He never lets them move cattle without him there. He scowls and takes a long drink.

"Not that I'm expecting anything soon," he mutters. "This has been a dry-ass lead-in to summer. Not even the spring run-off has been enough to offset it all."

That's an understatement. There's been a handful of fires up and down the range with a particularly nasty one running along the western slope in Colorado. I'm honestly shocked that I haven't been called into one of them yet. Probably, Sam's been running interference and calling other pilots first. He knows I'm not hurting for the hours—and every day Camden gets older.

Like it's been summoned by my thinking, my phone alerts me with a text. I pull it from my pocket, cursing as I set it on the counter.

> Official Notice. Report by 1100. Southwest of
> Boise. Exact location incoming.

"Fuck," I mutter.

"That the call?" Ethan asks. When I nod, he grunts and pulls out his own phone. "I'll text Mom and see if she can take Cam for the day."

A few minutes pass, and then he breathes out a sigh. He takes a drink of his coffee, focusing on me, his gaze inscrutable. I flip the pancakes onto a plate. Ethan is really good at those looks— something he learned from his dad. Sometimes he follows them up with a question, sometimes he continues on with his day. Most of the time, I prefer when he goes on with his day.

"I didn't realize you went on a date," Ethan says.

Yep, definitely prefer when he just moves on with his day.

I pour another pancake into the pan, making sure to not meet his gaze. The last thing we need right now is a full-on brawl, and even if the blonde woman from last night was nothing more than a one-time hookup, it doesn't stop the instinctive rage at having my territory and decisions questioned.

"It was my night off." It's not really an explanation. Ethan grunts. I blow out a breath, trying to find some semblance of calm, and add another pancake to the pan.

"And?" he asks when I don't offer anything else.

"And I had a date," I say, giving up and looking toward him. His scowl is firmly in place, his eyes an interesting mix of angry and betrayed. "I didn't propose to her. I bought her dinner and fucked her in my truck. I'm not expecting to have a follow-up. Stop freaking out."

He ticks up one eyebrow.

"You know I'm not ready," he says.

No shit. You weren't ready for Kayla, either, fucker.

I swallow down the urge to say just that, but his eyes darken, and I know it must be written all over my face. The downside of raising a kid with your best friend—a best friend you once shared a bonded Omega with—is that they get really damn good at reading you, even when you'd rather they didn't.

I flip the first round of pancakes onto a plate before turning to grab Camden's plastic dishes and getting his breakfast ready. Ethan steps up beside me, seamlessly taking over without putting down his coffee. Grabbing the spatula, I focus on pouring the next round of pancakes.

"She was different," he says after an extended silence.

I don't bother to comment on whether Kayla was different. It won't diminish the urge for change that's starting to claw its way under my skin. I recognize it from the last time I felt it, over eight years ago: it's the need to find an Omega and knot her until we're so connected I can smell her in my dreams.

Footsteps patter down the hallway, breaking me out of the thought before it can manage to leave me with an annoying hard-on. I twist away from the stove just in time to see Camden come rushing into the room. He scans the living room before focusing on the kitchen. His eyes land on Ethan first, and he crosses the room, slamming into his legs before Ethan can put down the mug of coffee.

"Good morning, kid," he says, some of the cynicism melting away from his voice.

"Morning," he says, his voice muffled against Ethan's jeans. "Riding today?"

Ethan nods. "Beau and I are moving cows."

Camden grins, showing off his dimples. Damn, he looks like Kayla when he smiles like that. My chest tightens at the thought.

I'd thought the grief would get more manageable with time. Sure, I don't think about them every single waking moment anymore. But when the moments come? They seem to cut deeper than anything I've ever experienced.

Making breakfast doesn't erase the pain, but it's certainly something I know how to do, something I'm *good* at doing. Knowing I'm caring for and protecting my Omega's son settles the grief lodged so deep I feel it in my bones. Even after four years —nearly—of her being gone.

So, pancakes.

I flip the second batch onto the plate and pour the final group.

"Go with you, Daddy," Camden says, suddenly serious. I frown. It wouldn't be the first time we've taken him. Except it's always been us. Mostly me, to be honest. I saddle up Maple because he can handle the extra weight, and Cam rides double with me.

Ethan shakes his head and herds Camden to the table, grabbing the plate of food on his way out of the kitchen. "You can't this time. Papa has to go to a fire."

He sighs but nods. "Nana?"

"Yeah." Ethan kisses his temple as he helps him into his booster seat, setting the plate full of food in front of him. "She said she has flowers to plant today. You want to help her with that?"

Camden smiles again, appeased by the available option, and then attacks his breakfast with a ferocity that has me mildly concerned for when he becomes a teenager. I'll have to ask Mom how she managed all three of us during those years.

As soon as the final pancakes are finished, I dump them onto the plate and clean up. I kiss Camden on my way toward my room, running my hand through his blond hair. He glances up at me, his eyebrows furrowed enough there's the little line between them, exactly how Brandon would get it.

"Love you, Papa," he says around the pancake, garbling the words.

I grin and hug him, wrapping my arms around him. "I'll see you soon, all right? You have a good time with Nana today and be a big helper with Daddy during the week."

Camden nods without pulling away from me, his cheek brushing my shirt.

I kiss his temple again as I pull away.

"Be safe," Ethan says, as serious as ever.

I nod before heading to my bedroom, shutting the door quietly behind me. It only takes me a few minutes to throw on a new shirt and grab my go bag. I sling it over my shoulder, shoving my phone into the pocket of my jeans. I keep the lights in the garage off, working off muscle memory as I situate myself in my truck and ease it out of the space. Another text from Sam comes through as I'm heading away from the modest house.

> Pulling in the LATs for this one. Just bring
> yourself.

The sun is just cresting over the horizon, its rays a pale orange today, as I nudge the truck onto the highway, heading north toward Jackson and the small, private airstrip where I keep both of my planes in a private hangar.

The itchy *need* just under my sternum doesn't lessen, though, and by the time I'm prepping my Cessna, I'm fighting back the urge to pull up the dating app I downloaded last week in desperation. Fucking that Beta last night clearly hadn't been enough. I resist the urge, though. It's not worth the fighting with Ethan.

Doesn't change the fact that I clearly need something to change, though.

Chapter Four

ETHAN

Pivoting to being the single parent takes more time than I'd hoped to lose this morning. By the time I have Camden and his three favorite cars packed into the backseat of the truck, the sun has already crested the horizon. And my bad mood has soured and petrified into something dark and oozing. Emily's teal Jeep sitting in front of our parents' place adds the fucking cherry on top that I absolutely do not need.

It's such a happy color to be the omen of everything going wrong. Because, without fail, if Emily is at our parents' place before me on a work day, something is guaranteed to go wrong. And while Saturdays aren't typical work days for me, I have no hope that it will fare any differently from typical. Facing several long hours in the saddle moving cattle, it's enough to have me cursing.

Camden perks up in the backseat, looking up from his cars.

"Is Aunt Emily watching me?" he asks. "But you said Nana."

I frown. "I'm not sure, kid. Grandma said she was going to watch you. Maybe they're working on a project together."

It would at least mean that she wasn't here at the literal sunrise to bother *me*.

Camden doesn't say anything, and I focus on getting the truck parked beside the Jeep and getting him unbuckled. He holds my hand as he climbs down. His blond hair just passes his ears, needing another trim. His cheeks are starting to thin out, the last of the baby fat fading with every passing day.

God*damn* he looks like Brandon. He has Kayla's bright blue eyes. But everything else? You could misconstrue him in pictures for his father.

The moment his feet touch the ground, he's bolting up the porch steps. His happy shriek as he gets to the front door alerts everyone in the sprawling farmhouse that we're here.

Mom and Dad's house sits on the western portion of the ranch, nestled against the rolling hills that gatekeep the larger peaks to the north. In the same clearing, scattered far enough apart to not feel overly crowded, stand two barns, a large detached garage, and an independent workshop that doubles as an office if I really want one. Our bookkeeper and administrative help maintain offices in town, though there'd be room here if they wanted it. The buildings combine together into bookends to the sprawling farmhouse.

It's a large enough meadow that it's easier to drive to any of the buildings than actually walk. Sometimes I still opt to walk, though, needing the time to clear my head. Especially if I'm prepping to be in the saddle all day.

I'd thought this discontent would have gotten better over the last year. Instead, it seems to grow with every week that Cam gets older. And knowing that Caleb is happily fucking strangers again just adds a stab under my ribs that makes me want to punch something. I heave a sigh and look toward the barns.

Beau waves at me once before disappearing into the barn nearest the workshop, already working to saddle up Megara where he keeps her stabled with the other ranch hands' horses—a perk of employment here if they want to utilize it. The other one, the one that's closest to the farmhouse, is for our own private horses. Nearly all of us have at least one personal horse, though Caleb and I have several each. Even Melissa keeps her horses here rather than the semi-public barns that house the recreation ranch's trail horses.

The door opens, and Mom steps onto the porch, snapping me out of my thoughts. She's swapped her typical gray robe for a set of black sweats and a pale blue cardigan, but her hair is still in rollers. Her morning coffee is held carefully in one hand, and she holds it away from her body to keep it from spilling on Camden as he slams into her.

"Good morning," she says, hugging him.

"Morning!" he says and then rushes by her, slipping into the house. No doubt he's on his way to the toys we keep here, needing to find the perfect companion options for his cars today.

I grab his bag from the passenger seat. Mom meets me at the top of the porch stairs. She hugs me, her slight arms wrapping around my waist.

"Thanks for the help," I tell her as I pull away.

She waves a hand. "Always happy to watch Cam, you know that. Beau's already been by to grab a thermos of coffee. He mentioned you guys will be out for a few hours at least."

I nod and cross the porch, following my son inside. I toe off my shoes, not missing Mom's eagle-eyed glare from where she stands just behind me, holding open the screen door.

"They're all the way out on the Forest Service land. It'll take a while to get them in. Hoping to be done in time for lunch."

Camden looks up from where he's building a ramp out of

blocks for his cars, using the armrest of the couch as a starting point.

"Water flowers, Nana?" he asks as Mom closes the door and moves around me, heading toward the kitchen.

Mom and Dad's house is the definition of sprawling. The main area is large and open, the living room on the left with the dining room on the right and the kitchen in the far back, anchoring the space. A hallway exits both sides of the kitchen. The one to the left leads to the main bedroom as well as an office and bonus space they've recently converted to a home library. The other leads to where my sister and I slept as well as an extra couple bedrooms that our friends would use when we were teens. It's all done in the light whites and beiges and tans of modern farmhouses.

I head straight for the coffee pot that's still half-full, grabbing one of Mom's travel mugs and filling it to the brim, not bothering with creamer or milk.

As I pour the coffee, she says, "You ready to water the flowers, Cam?"

"Can we watch the bees?" he asks.

She laughs. "Yes, we can watch the bees, too. Let's get out there before it gets too much hotter."

The bees were three hives that sat nestled in Mom's large cut flower garden. They started as a single hive as an extra credit project of Emily's in highschool. But when she went to college, Mom took it over. And then promptly added two more hives when she discovered how much she enjoyed the hobby, too. Now her honey sells in a small Artisan market in downtown Jackson— and she can never manage to keep it in stock.

Mom and Cam leave out the front, Cam running over for another hug.

I lean over him and kiss the crown of his head.

"Love you," he says into my legs.

"Love you, too, kid," I say. "Have a good time with Nana, all right?"

He looks up at me, his grin so wide it lights up his entire face. It's another small thing of Kayla's that he has, too. A hard, twisting stab of grief steals my breath. Nearly four goddamn years without her. Without my bonded Omega. Would we have more kids now? Or would she have decided Camden was enough on his own? Would Caleb still be working fires? Or would he have decided to opt for a business that kept him closer for more of the summer?

The questions come too fast, drowning me between one heartbeat and the next. I force a swallow, wetting my dry mouth.

"I think the bees are already awake," Mom says. Camden drops his arms from around my legs. I kiss his head one more time, and then he sprints out the front door, letting the screen door slam behind him.

Mom focuses on me. "You be safe out there."

I nod. "I always am, Mom."

She purses her lips, and I can practically hear her thoughts across the room. Brandon had promised to be safe, too. That didn't stop the bull from goring him, though. Today, though, she decides to leave it alone. She closes the front door behind her, the clicking of the doorknob quiet.

Not that it would matter because Emily walks out from the right hallway, her hair pulled back and tucked under a University of Wyoming ball cap. She has a pair of her old riding boots, the toes worn and the tread practically nonexistent, tucked under her arm.

I cock an eyebrow as she focuses on me, her lips pursing in a dead-ringer for our mother.

"What do you need?" I ask. Does she want to move cattle today? I figured she'd be hanging out with Melissa and her friend. Didn't she just move in yesterday?

"You all right if I saddle up Phoebe today?" she asks. Straight to the point, that's Emily. It's something we both inherited from our father. "I know you always take Cottonwood out when you're moving cattle, so I thought I'd get her out for a bit today."

I frown. Emily *never* rides Phoebe. She's too... tame for my sister. She prefers the easy pastures and simple trails rather than the hard rides through the forest that Emily loves most. And she's absolutely shit with the cattle unless they're in an arena. She'd been Brandon's roping horse, and she'd won him enough money to get him through college in Laramie when he had no other way to make ends meet.

Emily arches one eyebrow when I don't offer an immediate answer.

"You have a sudden desire to learn roping?" I ask.

She smirks. "Not that kind, no."

I groan and tilt my head back. "Too much, Emily. Too fucking much." She cackles, and I sigh. "Fine. I have no problem with it. She could use the work, to be honest. I'm sure she'll be easy for you."

She smiles. "Thanks!"

And then she's disappearing out the front door, too, her hair swinging with her bounding steps. I push off the counter and follow her, heading toward the barns. Beau already has Cottonwood saddled beside him.

"Let's get this over with," I mutter.

He laughs. "Happy Saturday to you, too, Ethan."

Chapter Five

ETHAN

The sun is bright and warm where it hangs nearly directly over us. There's not much breeze, and the sky is clear of any kind of cloud. We've been in the saddle nearly five hours, moving two separate herds of cattle to more favorable places for finding water. By all accounts, I should be exhausted. But riding with Cottonwood always manages to clear my head. Give that horse an hour and some open space, and she'll have me feeling in control again.

"Hudson and I are going to The Outpost after the evening crew gets to the restaurant. You want to grab drinks tonight?" Beau asks from where he rides beside me, his hat low over his eyes. He's ditched his flannel just as I have, leaving him in a dark blue tee.

"Caleb's out on a fire," I say, shaking my head.

Cottonwood misses a step, and I run my hand along her shoulder, easing farther back in the saddle to help her manage the climb down the mountain.

Beau grunts. "That explains why you stopped at the house before saddling up. I thought you had just forgotten your own coffee."

I roll my eyes and change the subject.

"I think Mom's making lunch for the masses, though, so you're welcome to stay."

Beau legitimately *moans*. "Hell yes. I hope it's her mac and cheese. She makes the best I've ever had." He turns to me, pursing his lips. "Don't tell Hudson I said that, though. He'll spit me over a fire."

I laugh, the sound rusty, and pull my phone from my back pocket.

On our way back. Should be there in ten.

Mom's response is faster than I expect.

Perfect. Mac and cheese will be done in about five.

I glance over at Beau. "You sure you don't have some sixth sense that tells you what Mom's planning?"

He's never guessed wrong about whatever Mom is making. Ever. I learned to stop betting against him by the time we were sixteen and I'd lost a couple hundred dollars over it.

"Hell yes. That just made my entire Saturday." He whoops, fist-bumping the air.

After a few minutes, I offer, "Emily mentioned she's taking Phoebe out today."

Beau frowns, shifting the reins to his other hand. "She mention why? Phoebe doesn't like riding the way Emily always wants to. She's too calm."

I shake my head. "Nope. And when I pressed, she made it awkward."

"That sounds right." Beau grins. "Well, at least that saves me from needing to come out tomorrow and work her. I'll get back on a better schedule with her now that calving is done."

We settle back into silence, just like we have the last several hours. I love working the cattle with Beau. He's damn good at it, yes, but he also doesn't force conversation. He's content to let the quiet of the pasture and mountains around us fill the space between topics. It's probably something to do with him being a Beta when the rest of us—Hudson, Caleb, and I—are all Alphas. So are three of our permanent hired ranch hands. Beau is just... calmer than everyone else. It helps on days like today, when I'm so on edge I'm ready to jump out of my damn skin.

Just as the clearing opens up around us, the barns on the far side of it, Beau says, "Heard Caleb had a date in Jackson last night."

"How the hell did you find that out?" I ask, instantly defensive.

"Hudson heard a couple of the girls at the restaurant lament about it last night," he says, keeping his voice light. "They've been eyeing him up apparently."

Goddamn small towns. I stretch my neck, trying to keep myself from falling back into that festering rage that's been eating at me. It bubbles up anyway. Cottonwood tosses her head as I choke up on her reins unintentionally. I force a deep breath and relax my hands.

Shit, maybe it's time to consider a rut suppressor. At least until Camden is in school. Maybe by then I'll be ready to talk about moving on from Kayla.

And Brielle, that voice whispers.

I urge Cottonwood faster, trying to outrun my thoughts. Beau sighs but keeps pace.

"Didn't realize it was a no-ask subject," he mutters.

I ignore him. He doesn't understand, not the way his brother does. Which is probably why Hudson shared the gossip with him and not me. Being a Beta, Beau isn't inclined to have a territorial hissy fit over finding out someone's gossiping about their best friend's fucking.

Not that that's what I'm having. I'm too goddamn old to be having piss fights. That's what stupid Alphas just out of high school do. Not thirty-three-year-olds with a child.

I force another deep breath and start toward the barns, ready to have a quiet afternoon with my son. There's an unfamiliar car parked in front of Mom and Dad's place alongside Emily's Jeep. It's an impeccable dark green Land Rover. As we get closer, dodging around the tended area immediately surrounding the front of the farmhouse, the simple Colorado plates become more obvious. I frown.

Who is here from Colorado?

Beau grunts as he takes in the car. "Wonder who that might be. You didn't hire anyone new, right?"

"Nope. Everyone stayed on from last summer. Didn't even need to put out an ad this year."

Beau frowns. "Weird. Wonder what someone from Colorado wants with your parents. Or maybe they're wanting something with you? You haven't had anyone call about the ranch this year, have you?"

"Not since the investor last November. I think I made it clear enough to scare off most people." I better have, at least. I was born here, and I had every intention of dying here, too. If Camden didn't want it by then, he could decide what to do with it all.

Emily's leaning against the entrance to the primary barn, her head tossed back as she laughs. Beau pulls away, heading toward the second barn. He tips his hat at Emily as he passes her. She offers a wave, then turns away, walking into the barn.

I ease off Cottonwood, grabbing her lead rope before she can decide to follow Beau. My legs are stiff, but I don't show it as I guide Cottonwood forward. She hesitates, shaking her head.

"Let's get you a snack. That all right with you, pretty girl?" I say, keeping my voice low, running my hand down her nose. She stomps one foot and then nuzzles into my shoulder. I can't help but laugh.

The sound catches in my throat, cutting off all at once, as the shadows in the barn clear as my eyes adjust. Emily and Melissa stand with a third woman, both of them helping pull equipment from Phoebe.

"That was so much fun," Melissa says, her bright voice filling the space. "I've missed having you here."

Emily nods. "Phoebe and you were great. She'll be happy to have someone other than Beau to work with."

The third woman doesn't respond, her eyes locked on me. The brown of them slam into me, a thousand memories tied to them, and I can't fucking breathe. What is she doing here? And why the *fuck* is she holding onto Phoebe's bridle while Melissa eases off the saddle Brandon used to use? Her face is pale, like she's seen a ghost. God knows mine probably matches.

Emily glances at me.

"Oh, hey," she says. "You're done early. Mom says lunch is ready."

I should look at her. I should say something. I should do literally anything other than just stare at Brielle. But fuck if I can't manage it. She's still stunning, and it brings my body— unresponsive to literally anyone over the last four years—back to life between one second and the next. Her jeans hug her hips, her boots a new, shiny black and sporting a designer label I don't recognize. Her shirt hugs her curves, the deep vee of the neckline just showing the swells of her breasts. Her brown hair is pulled away from her face, highlighting the delicate line of her jaw.

There are too many smells in the barn, and I'm sure she's

wearing some kind of scent blocker, but my memory fills in the gaps just fine, supplying the smell of her perfuming—lavender, like a damn English cottage. The need to pull her away from Emily, to mark her and surround her until my scent is the only one anyone can smell on her skin, slams into me with the force of a damn stampede.

My pulse races in my ears, and my palms are sweaty.

Cottonwood ducks her head, nudging my shoulder. I tighten my hold on her lead rope, trying to figure out how to move her without actually closing the distance between me and the Omega that's haunted my dreams for the last ten years.

Emily frowns, her gaze bouncing between Brielle and me. It's only a matter of minutes until she realizes it, until the last decade of my summer fling being a faceless woman no one knew goes up in flames. The secret Melissa and my mother have guarded with their lives, knowing nothing good would come from the town knowing her name, her face, her designation. Certainly not with Kayla being our matched Omega—our *bonded* matched Omega.

And now she's here, standing in front of me.

Mint floods the barn as I lose the fight with my body. Brielle swallows, the column of her throat moving, and the palest version of her lavender scent overlays everything else happening in the barn.

Holy *fuck*.

Memories of the last time I smelled that, smelled *her*, overwhelm me. Her hand laced with mine, her knees straddling my hips, her hair brushing over my chest. My scent grows even stronger. And I can't do anything to curb it, struck motionless like I've been hit with a damn bolt of lightning.

Melissa grabs Brielle's hand, and it steals her attention, breaking whatever the fuck moment was just happening. I can't help but drop my eyes to her fingers, needing to remind myself of the mark that sits there, that confirms she's not mine and never will be again.

There's no fucking ring. Not even a simple gold band like the one and only time I saw her in the last decade.

What in the actual hell is happening right now?

"Emily, could you let Phoebe out to the pasture?" she asks, not looking away from Brielle. "Bri and I will put away the equipment really quick."

Emily raises an eyebrow but takes the lead rope and ties out Phoebe. Before I can figure out how to make my legs work again, Melissa has Phoebe's bridle off and in Brielle's hands, and they're ducking into the second storage room on the far side of the barn, the one with the equipment that isn't used as often.

I finally manage to move, and I get Cottonwood tied out so I can get the saddle off and her brushed through.

"You going to explain what the hell that was?" Emily asks, her arms crossed. "Or am I cornering Melissa later?"

There's no way she'll actually wear Melissa down. She's kept the secret for a decade, just like Mom. One night of pestering from Emily won't cause her to break down.

I work through getting Cottonwood cooled down and then turned out to the pasture, ignoring my sister the entire time even as she mirrors me, turning out Phoebe at the same time. Melissa comes out of the storage room as we're walking back into the barn. I ignore her, too, trying to get my body under control, and focus on grabbing my saddle to put away.

"Bri's going to head back to her place," she says to Emily, ignoring me completely. "She said she needed a shower and to work on unpacking."

Unpacking?

Holy fuck. *Brielle* is the friend that's moving into Emily's guest house? The one that's a widow needing a clean start?

Emily's been talking about her for weeks, her eyes bright with excitement. The entire damn town knows about the newcomer.

A lot of the guys at The Outpost have been putting bets on who can manage to snag a date with her first. Just the thought is enough to have me scenting again, the edge of it sour with my festering rage that's entirely unexplainable.

Emily's eyes bore into me, the curiosity so strong they're practically drilling through me. I don't bother to acknowledge her at all.

"Let's go," Melissa says, her voice wavering, responding on instinct to the change in my scent. "Lynn's got lunch ready."

Melissa pulls Emily from the barn as I disappear into the primary tack room. When I finally manage to leave the barn and start toward the farmhouse, the green SUV with Colorado plates is gone.

Chapter Six

I set the steaming cup of tea on the wooden railing beside me, watching as the surface ripples. With a sigh, I focus on the rising sun. Today, it paints the sky in purples and oranges, casting a warm glow on everything it touches. It turns the snow still clinging to the highest peaks an odd shade of silver. The prairie that surrounds the guest house sways in the early breeze. I tuck my nose into my sweater. It might be the beginning of June, but mornings are still chilly.

Three days I've been hiding out in my temporary living situation. Three days of Melissa checking that I'm really all right while Emily bursts at the seams from wanting to know what had clearly happened between me and her brother. Sure, I'd explained it away to Emily as just wanting to settle in. But it's just a matter of time until she walks across the clearing and asks me how I know her brother.

Had I used the time to unpack and find places for the small amount of things I brought with me? Yes. Had I spent an entire afternoon doing the online equivalent of shopping until I dropped? Absolutely. But neither of those were the reason I hadn't come up with the courage to venture past the cleared pasture immediately surrounding the guest house.

Goddamn, it should be illegal for him to have become *more* attractive over the last ten years. Seeing him in jeans and that black tee was a far cry from the formal suit I'd last seen him wear. And the barn where we were unsaddling our horses was just about the opposite of the funeral where I'd last seen him—with his newborn son in his arms and a delicate, shattered-looking strawberry blonde woman clinging to him as people offered their condolences for Brandon's death.

And the fucking *tattoos*? He hadn't had a single one that summer I'd been tangled up with him. Now both his arms are complete sleeves, the black ink mixing with earthy tones, twisting around his skin in patterns I want to learn and trace and memorize.

Lavender explodes around me, thick and overwhelming, but I ignore it.

No, the reason I've been hiding out has everything to do with the man I convinced myself I had gotten over when he broke up with me ten years ago. Not even convinced, really. I *had* moved on from him. Met someone else, married them, and built the urban version of the white picket fence and everything.

"All the good it did you," I mutter. I palm the mug and sit on the railing, leaning against the support beam wedged up against the house. "At least his heartache was a clean break."

Didn't doctors say a clean break was better for healing?

Of course, not much really could be worse than the absolute bullshit that Brett put me through. Sighing, I close my eyes and let my head drop back. Fuck, I need to think about anything other than Brett. Half of why I moved out here was to move on from him, find a place that had never been touched by him, poisoned by him.

Against my better judgment, I let the picture of Ethan in the Monroe barn fill my mind again, trying to remember the details of his tattoos. At least it's better than thinking about Brett fucking *her*. Except all it seems to do is highlight that deep need sitting just below my skin, ready to overwhelm me with its itching intensity.

The aroma of my scent turns acidic, and I swallow the lump in my throat, letting the thoughts of Ethan fall away, too. Someone clears their throat, and I glance over my shoulder. And then blush when I realize it's Emily. A young boy with bright blond hair holds onto her hand, his eyes a deep blue that reminds me of sapphires. His hair is nearly identical to Melissa's. It doesn't take a rocket scientist to figure out who he must be. I wait to be introduced to him, though, just in case.

"You good?" Emily asks, leaning against the porch's support column.

When I shrug, her eyebrows furrow and she frowns.

Before she can say anything, the boy pulls away from her and waves.

"Hi, I'm Cam," he says. "I'm four. Aunt Emily said we were going hiking today while Dad looks at the horses."

I offer a smile and say, "Nice to meet you. I'm Brielle."

He nods. "Aunt Emily said you're Aunt Mel's friend even though you're staying with her and not Mel." He frowns, his eyebrows furrowing, a line appearing between them. It's so cute, I can't help but smile again—without forcing it this time.

"Melissa doesn't have a guest house," Emily says, humor lighting her voice. "Brielle's waiting until the fall to find her own house."

The boy doesn't say anything to that, his head tilting as he stares at me for a minute longer. Then he shrugs and drops

Emily's hand. He takes a couple steps away before picking one of the wildflowers blooming in the open valley. I let my smile drop away, the fleeting moment of happiness already ebbing away from me.

The breeze picks up just as she steps onto the porch, pushing my scent away from us both, hiding my secret for a bit longer.

Thank. God.

She sits on the swinging bench seat, her eyes watchful as she focuses on Camden. I want to ask about him, but it seems insensitive.

"You can ask," she says, like she can read my mind. I raise an eyebrow and play ignorant.

"Ask what?" I keep my voice light.

She cocks an eyebrow as she looks over at me. Camden grabs another flower before sprinting several feet away. "About him."

I purse my lips, and she laughs.

"Or don't. Just figured I could relieve your curiosity while Melissa's busy. But you're welcome to ask her about him, too, if you'd like. Just not around Ethan. It's still..." Her lips twist, and she shrugs. "Just don't ask about Camden in front of him."

I tuck away that bit of information. "He was Brandon's?"

I don't know why that's the question I start with.

"Yep," Emily says.

"Do you normally watch him during the week?"

She shakes her head. "I'm third option," she says, keeping her voice low enough the little boy doesn't seem to hear her. "My mom's first, then Joan. But Mom's in Jackson with Dad today, and Joan had someone call out at the coffee house."

She glances at me before focusing on Camden again, like she knows the scrutiny makes me uncomfortable.

Damn, it's an adjustment being around an unbonded Alpha again. Especially now that I'm not suppressed. I run my fingers through my hair.

"And that setup only happens during fire season when Caleb's getting called out with little notice. During the year, Caleb typically has an open schedule. I think he's planning on taking on some more off season work this year when Camden starts school, but it hasn't become family official."

"Family official?" I ask.

"Meaning they've announced it to the family," she offers. "Once something is family official, it's the mark that they're serious about whatever it is. Mom is..." She hums. "Not really sure there's a term for it. But if you tell her something is happening, she'll throw herself into it with everything she is. So we don't mention things to her until we're sure they're happening. Family official."

That made sense. I haven't actually seen Lynn since moving back. But the woman I spent a decent chunk of time with that summer certainly didn't give half of herself to a project. She was all or nothing. I don't suppose time would have changed that, really.

Thinking of her reminds me of Ethan. Again. Nerves settle in my belly.

Will Emily ask about him this time?

I can't quite manage to remember how to breathe as the silence stretches longer. Eventually, she shrugs.

Her voice is louder, carrying across the meadow when she says, "Anyway, Camden and I thought you might want some company."

Camden glances up from the small bouquet he's managed to gather, a mixture of yellow and white flowers pressed into his palm. He grins and starts toward us, the foraging forgotten.

As he gets to the stairs of the porch, he says, "Here."

He holds out the flowers, a dimple flashing in his cheek as he smiles. I drop from the railing, landing on mostly solid legs, and cross the porch.

"Brielle?" He trips over my name, the vowels merging and the "r" not quite sounding right.

"You can call me Bri," I offer.

"Bri." He still mangles the "r" just a bit, but I don't say anything. As I take the group of flowers, he asks, "What's your favorite color?"

"Purple."

He frowns. "Oh. Sorry these aren't purple."

I shake my head. "It's fine. Want to help me put them in a vase?"

He nods, smiling, though his eyes are still serious. He follows me into the small guest house. Emily stands and closes the door behind him. Her eyes track over me, assessing me in one quick, unnerving sweep. I ignore it and focus on filling a small decorative vase from the living room with water. Camden puts each flower into it, his tongue sticking out in concentration. I can't help but smile.

When they're all arranged, he nods and asks, "Do you like hiking?"

"I haven't hiked in a long time," I tell him. "Let me get my shoes on, and we'll go find out."

Chapter Seven

"Did Emily bother you about Saturday?" Melissa asks.

I chance a glance at her, but she's swiping through her phone with a blank face.

"No," I say.

Hiking with Emily had been more enjoyable than I'd expected. She'd been quiet and reflective, a perfect balance to Camden's happy-go-lucky adventurous spirit. I'd expected her to drill me about the awkward as hell runin with her brother, but she didn't bring up anything about him or the ranch. Nothing beyond doubling down that I'm allowed to ride Phoebe whenever I'd like.

Melissa nods. "Good, then she actually listened to me for once."

I raise an eyebrow. Melissa shrugs and readjusts her glasses.

"You know how Alphas are. Even when they're your friends. Sometimes the need to protect overrides the friendship, you know? I told her it was just you reacting to an Alpha after coming off the suppressors. But I wasn't sure she would just leave it alone."

She points to the stop sign a few hundred feet ahead of us.

"Turn left here," she instructs. "And then it's the second one on your right."

We're spending Friday night going to The Outpost, a bar unofficially known as the locals' hangout space. It's an unassuming building a few blocks off of Main with a single story, flat-roofed shape and brick facade. Its large double doors are painted a dark brown, probably to look like wood. The windows are large but little light makes it through them, probably from a film they've put over the glass for privacy. It's clear the building is older, but there's no neon signs or overly western touches that I'd expected.

A majority of Creek Falls makes money from the tourists traveling north to Grand Teton and Yellowstone. And tourists *love* cliche. So much so that sometimes even the more local spots end up being infected with it. The only concession is the name itself. Calling a bar "The Outpost" is practically right out of the Old West.

The parking lot is nearly full, so I slide into one of the only open spots in the farthest corner. Melissa adjusts her dress as we head toward the building. As she gets her small clutch situated on her wrist, I take a moment to mess with my own outfit, making sure my shirt is tucked into the black skirt and laying flat.

Inside, it's more of the unassuming design. Simple dark hardwood floors and sporadic landscape photographs on the deep navy walls. The bar runs the entire length of the wall to our left, barstools a simple black with low backs. Smaller tables line the far wall and the one to our right, carving out a large space in the middle for dancing. The only nods to cliche evident inside are all of the people wearing jeans and cowboy hats. Some are bedazzled, some shimmer under the low lighting. I'm the only one without one.

I glance down at my outfit—a metallic black skirt that flares away from my hips and falls mid-thigh and a mostly see-through dark purple top that shows off the lacy black balconette bralette I'm wearing underneath it. It's something that would have been considered appropriate for a night out at most of the more informal bars in Denver.

I glance at everyone around me and seriously consider just turning around and heading back to the guest house to hide.

"You're fine, Bri." Melissa loops her arm through mine and guides us to the bar, sliding into a seat.

"Hey, Mel." The woman behind the bar greets Melissa, her voice warm and a large smile lighting her face. "What has you out on a Friday?"

Melissa smiles and gestures toward me. I slip into the chair beside her, crossing my ankles and tucking my small, crossbody purse into my lap.

"Devynn, this is Brielle," Melissa says over the din of the music and crowd.

The woman turns to me and offers a hand. "Nice to meet you! There's been tons of buzz the last week about you. What would you like to drink?"

I keep my face a happy, empty smile. I'm not surprised the gossip about me has made it to the bars despite it only being a week since I moved into Emily's guest house. It's certainly all over the Rustic Roast—despite Joan not encouraging it at all as far as I can tell. Each time I've swung by since Emily coaxed me out of hiding on Tuesday, there's been more eyes on me than when I ran the high stakes executive meetings at Hawkins Corp.

"Nice to meet you," I offer. "I'll take a Cape Cod."

She raises an eyebrow even as she nods. "You want your normal, Mel?"

When she nods, Devynn turns away to make the drinks.

"Sorry," Melissa says.

I shrug. "I figured there'd be people talking. I spent an entire summer under the microscope, remember?" Melissa worries at her lip, messing up the gloss she reapplied in the car. I palm her knee. "Really, Mel. Don't worry about me. We came out to have some fun, so let's do that, all right? People are going to talk, whether I'm here or not."

Devynn comes back as I'm reassuring her, and she murmurs her agreement.

"Shiny object syndrome. Give it a couple weeks, and it should settle down."

I slide my ID across the bar to start a tab, and Devynn shakes her head. "No need. I'll make sure you pay out. Or make you deal with Marcus."

Her eyes fill with humor, and I tilt my head.

"Marcus?" I ask.

Melissa giggles. "Her Newfoundland. He won't hurt you. Not intentionally, at least. But he'll get enough drool on you that you'll wish you'd just done whatever Devynn asked of you."

Devynn smiles and shrugs before moving farther down the bar, responding to someone's wave. I tuck my ID away and take a sip of the cocktail, letting the bite of the vodka steal my focus. Melissa leans her head against my shoulder, and I can't help but smile.

"Just like you to order something so fancy," she says, a smile in her voice.

I laugh. "It didn't occur to me until I'd already said it that she might not know what it is."

"Devynn grew up in Boston," she says.

Surprise lights through me. She doesn't have the accent. Melissa must see my reaction because she sits up and takes a drink of her cocktail.

"She went to school in Jackson the same time we were going to school. She met Brandon while there, and they ended up friends. She moved here when she graduated and set up The Outpost." Melissa's voice wavers a bit, but she takes another drink to hide it. I grab her hand. "Anyway, she says she's been here long enough to drop the accent. But, really, I think she just hates sounding like an outsider. Things like that are a big thing in a little town."

I trace the rim of my drink as I force a deep breath. Melissa squeezes my hand. The song changes, but I ignore it, trying to let my mind empty out. Before I can quite manage it, Devynn clears her throat. Melissa straightens, dropping my hand, suddenly incredibly focused on the drink sitting in front of her.

"The guy at the end wants to buy you a beer," Devynn says when I look at her. "As I'm not one who likes to waste beer or money, I figured I'd ask you before opening it."

Melissa glances down the line before I do. Her nose scrunches before she hides it behind her cup. I try to keep my look more subtle, just in case he's watching. Turns out, he isn't. What kind of guy doesn't at least watch while the bartender delivers their number?

He's maybe a year or so younger than me and seems vaguely familiar. His red flannel shirt hangs open, revealing an unassuming white tee underneath. His cowboy hat is ivory and looks brand new—not a single sun spot or discolored patch from sweat.

Do people here have a specific hat they wear when they go out? Like the women I used to hang out with had specialty dresses for when they were going to spend a night on the town? The thought makes me giggle, but I don't let it out of my mouth.

"No, thank you," I tell Devynn.

Turning him down might make for more problems than I really care to deal with. But it's leagues better than being stuck talking to someone all night when I have no intention of dating for the foreseeable future. And I'm not one for casual hookups. I'm not built like that. From what I've read of other Omegas, it's a trait many of us share.

Devynn nods. "Figured as much. I'll handle it."

"Thanks," I offer as she turns away.

Melissa sighs. "Sorry."

I shake my head. "I'm the pretty new toy. It's fine, Mel."

She doesn't seem convinced, but she doesn't push me, either. "To be honest, I'm shocked it's Calder that made the first move," she says, a little of her wry tone coming back.

I scratch at the tattoo behind my ear before running my hand through my hair.

"Who did you think it would be?" I ask.

"Brody," she says without hesitating. "He's in the far back corner, chatting with the Baileys."

Without even looking over my shoulder, I know it's not someone I'm remotely interested in knowing. The Baileys have been on my metaphorical shit list since I lived here ten years ago. I pretend to gag, and she laughs.

And then the first name she mentioned catches up to me.

"Calder?" I ask. "As in Calder Dean?"

That small bit of guilt I felt for not accepting the beer bleeds out of me. Like hell do I want anything to do with him. Or his brother.

Melissa hums before taking a long drink.

"Yep."

The one word conveys an entire lifetime of conflict. The Deans—and the Baileys—hate Melissa. Technically, they hated her dad. But small town politics meant that that hate transferred to her as if she was the original aggressor.

Devynn turns to the wall of liquor, and I chance a glance down the bar. The man's laughing, his head thrown back. He's a far cry from the lean teenager he'd been the last time I'd knowingly seen him. He's bulkier now, the last little bit of youth gone from his face.

After a moment, he throws down cash onto the bar top and then joins that same group of guys Melissa mentioned. I just manage to duck my head as they focus on where we sit.

"Trish quit," Melissa says, her voice quiet and somber. Then she slams the rest of her drink, emptying the cup in a single gulp. Devynn glances over, an eyebrow cocked, but turns back to the woman in front of her.

I frown. "Why?"

Trish has been the office manager for Misty Mountain since Melissa owned it with Brandon. She loves the ranch just as much as Mel does. She's not the type of person to just suddenly quit.

Of course, neither am I, and yet I'm sitting here in Creek Falls with my best friend rather than a condo in the heart of Denver.

"Her mom called. She's apparently been sick for a while but didn't bring it up. To Trish, I mean. She didn't tell Trish she was sick." Melissa traces the rim of her drink. "Stage three lung cancer. It's really bad. Trish was a mess."

Oh no.

"I told her she can have the job back if she ever wants it, no questions asked. But she's not sure how long she'll be gone." Melissa sighs. "Emily and I talked it over. I'll take over the day-to-day things, and she'll juggle the larger items. If it becomes too much for the both of us, then we'll see about finding someone new."

Her lips curve down, and she bites at her lip again, betraying her nerves. I bump her shoulder with my own.

"I'll take over the animals," I say.

She has an amazing staff that cares for the trail horses at Misty Mountain. But she takes care of the chickens and goats—

and her personal horses. She tenses like she's going to fight me, so I grab her hand and squeeze it.

"It'll keep me busy."

The resistance fades away from her, and her shoulders drop. "All right."

A man sits down beside me, and Devynn turns to him. Her posture changes, though it's subtle. Her shoulders stiffen, and the corners of her mouth gain a tension that tightens her smile. Whoever this guy is, he doesn't have a fan in Devynn. Men who piss off bartenders aren't anyone I want to hang out with.

Just as he's turning toward me, his intention clear in the set of his shoulders and practiced smile curving his lips, I stand from the stool and drag Melissa with me.

"Let's get going."

She doesn't argue, letting me pull her from the bar before the guy manages to say a single word to me.

Chapter Eight

Camden sprints to the porch of the farmhouse the second the truck's doors unlock. I sigh and grab his bag from the back seat, scooping the tractors he'd dropped onto the floor in his rush to find Mom. She steps out onto the porch as I'm starting up the stairs, a mug in her hands. She's dressed in jeans today, and her hair is already styled.

"You're later than I was expecting," Mom says as she hugs Camden. Her eyes are on me, though. "I already watered the garden."

Camden doesn't seem to mind, holding tight to her leg as he looks up at her. "Can we make brownies? Aunt Emily mentioned brownies on our hike yesterday. And you make the best ones, Grandma."

She laughs and guides him inside, holding the door for me, too.

"Sure, sweetie. Want to help me grab everything?"

Camden nods as he pulls off his shoes, and then he's running to the kitchen. Mom and I are slower to follow him. My phone vibrates in my pocket, and I pull it out, already scowling. Anyone texting before seven in the morning has bad news. It's an unspoken rule about ranching. I swipe open the text from Beau.

> Triston says the creek is running, so we shouldn't need to move cattle until next week. Friday at the earliest.

Well, that just opened up my day.

> Great. Have him organize it for Monday. We'll double check conditions Friday and then again Sunday just to be sure.

"Dad said you're having to move one of the herds again," Mom says, pulling me away from my phone.

"That was the plan, but Triston says we're good to wait a bit longer." She sets a mug in front of me before pulling ingredients from the pantry. I slide into one of the seats perched at the island. "So now my day is magically free."

At least until guilt gets the best of me and I finally sit down to do some admin work while Camden is distracted with screen time this afternoon.

Camden looks up from where he's moving the step stool over to the counter.

"Daddy doesn't have to work?"

I shake my head. "But you can still hang out with Grandma, kid."

God knows there's a thousand things that need to be done for the ranch—just none of them pressing enough to be labeled dire at the moment. He races around the island, abandoning the step stool.

"Can we ride?" Camden asks, leaning into my leg, wrapping his arms around it. His eyes are wide. "Please, Daddy?"

"I thought you were going to make brownies with Grandma," I say.

Camden frowns as he pulls away from me until he can see Mom. She's leaning against the island, her coffee back in her hand, a small smile playing at her lips.

"Sorry, Grandma," he offers.

Her smile widens. "We'll make them next time you're over instead."

He giggles and then races for the door, all thoughts of staying inside forgotten.

I sigh and set the mug of coffee on the island before following him outside.

I'm not as good at riding double with Camden as Caleb is. Partly because Maple doesn't like me as much as some of the others in the family and partly because I don't have the same level of patience for being uncomfortable as Caleb. He's used to being stuck in a small ass cockpit where he can't stretch his legs. Even when on horseback for several hours, there's ways to stretch. Not when you're riding double, though. And the elbows in my side and stomach aren't a selling point, either.

"You want to work with Nyx in the arena?" I ask once we're walking toward the private barn.

He tilts his head, biting his lip. It makes his single dimple show up. My stomach twists.

I hate that my stomach does that. I hate that sometimes when I look at my son, all I feel is grief and anger and heartbreak. I shove the feelings down before Cam realizes that something's off. Kids are so fucking perceptive to things like that. I never want him to think I regret him. I don't.

I just never expected to see him grow up without Kayla involved.

My phone rings, cutting my pity party short, and I dig it out again.

"Cam, kid, it's Papa. You want to say hi?"

He smiles, the question of riding Nyx instead of going for a trail ride forgotten for the moment. He runs back toward me, and I scoop him into an arm, propping him on my hip, before answering the video call and handing Cam the phone.

"Hi Papa!" he says the moment Caleb's face comes into view.

I tune out their chatter and focus on crossing the pasture. The green SUV is back, parked a small distance from the private barn. My steps slow without me meaning to. I've seen that car enough around town to know exactly who it belongs to.

Fuck me.

I've managed an entire fucking week without seeing her, not since I walked into my own goddamn barn and was confronted with the ghost of a life I had ten years ago. Consider it good luck... or tactful avoidance. Either way, the last thing I need right now is to be confronted with Brielle Ashford's sumptuous body and take-me eyes. My dick twitches, but I ignore it.

"Ethan?" Caleb's voice draws me back to the call.

"What's up?" I ask.

"Should be home late tomorrow or early Thursday."

"Sounds good," I offer.

Setting Camden back on his feet, I cross the last ten feet to the barn's entrance before I lose my nerves.

Because there's not a chance in hell I'm nervous. There's no goddamn reason for me to even *be* nervous. She's just a woman.

A woman that I fucked.

A woman that I spent an entire summer fucking.

A woman that's haunted my dreams for the better part of the last decade.

There I fucking go again.

Camden grabs my hand, wrapping his fingers around one of my own. He holds up the phone to me.

"Here, Daddy."

"I'll text if anything changes," Caleb says once I've taken the phone back.

We say a quick goodbye.

Camden runs ahead of me, straight through the open barn doors and into the building. I take a bit longer.

I'm not hesitating. I'm just... collecting myself.

"This barn is private property, ma'am."

Beau's voice cuts through the quiet and has my feet moving before I feel anywhere close to ready.

A cool, steady voice responds, "I have permission from Emily."

Beau grunts.

"She hasn't—" His voice cuts off and gains a different, more worried edge. "Cam, you can't just come flying in like that. I could've had Minthe out here instead of Phoebe."

The relative darkness of the barn takes a minute for my eyes to adjust to.

Brielle stands in front of Phoebe's stall. The horse is tied out just in front of it, using the ring designed exactly for that purpose, the knot of the lead rope a bit messy but effective nonetheless. She's already saddled. The horse's nose presses into Brielle's hand as the silence extends into the territory of uncomfortable.

I force my gaze to skip over Brielle. Beau stands a few stalls down. His arms are crossed, a frown etched deeply into his face.

"I have Phoebe out," Brielle murmurs, the same collected tone.

Something a bit too close to admiration warms my chest at her easy standoff with Beau. He might be a Beta, but she's still an Omega. They crave comfort and safety. Conflict is something most of them outright avoid. It's part of the reason I took over the family ranch from Emily when Brandon died. Melissa needed an Alpha running Misty Mountain with her to keep people from bulldozing right over her. And I have no patience for tourists even on a good day.

Phoebe looks at me and blows out a huff of air, her ears pinning back.

Camden runs up to Brielle, though, and waves before I can pull him toward Nyx's stall.

"Bri!" he shrieks. "Are you riding today, too? We're taking Nyx into the arena so I can practice. I have to have Daddy pull my saddle, though. I'm still too little."

Beau starts to say something, but I cut him off.

"Beau, meet Brielle. She's Melissa's friend." I walk past Brielle, not looking at her. I work on getting Nyx's stall open and him pulled into the main walkway. "Emily's given her permission to use any of her or Melissa's horses. And I let her include Phoebe with that."

I intentionally keep my gaze away from her. She's just another woman, just another person using our barn for housing horses.

Beau's face lightens. "Oh, you're the friend of Melissa's that's been working Phoebe the last week." He closes the distance between them and holds out his hand. Brielle takes it after a moment of hesitation. "I'm Beau. Sorry for the rough start. We've just had a couple problems with people walking in here without permission. A few of the horses in here are pretty skittish."

I swallow the possessive growl that tries to rip up my throat. I force my gaze away, trying to stamp out the violent aggression being near this woman is bringing out. There's no reason for it. I can't even fucking scent her from over here.

No, it's just me caught up in memories of the past.

My movements are jerky where I focus on Nyx.

"Nice to meet you," Brielle says.

I glance over my shoulder. She's smiling, but it doesn't touch her eyes. There's that same half-beaten feel to the way she holds herself as there was the last time I saw her.

It gets harder to hold down the growl.

"I'm going for a ride today," Brielle says, her voice changing into a softer croon, focusing on my son. "But you work with Nyx, all right?"

Camden sighs before nodding. He crosses the walkway until he's standing with me, his hand pressed flat to the back of my thigh.

"Let's grab his saddle and then we'll get you up, kid," I tell him.

He smiles, and then turns to wave as Brielle guides Phoebe out of the barn. She offers him a small smile and then swings into the saddle, the movement so graceful it could be something she's done a thousand times.

She hasn't. Not unless that finance asshole decided to buy out a ranch on the East Coast. Thoughts of her husband make that rage grow hotter. I force another deep breath. And then I walk into the tack room, stilling my mind so I can actually focus on my son.

Chapter Nine

CALEB

My body aches as I pull into the empty parking spot behind Mom's coffee shop, right next to her newer Lexus SUV. I turn off the engine and drop my head against the steering wheel, trying to find the motivation to go inside. Twelve days on a fire isn't all that bad. It's certainly better than what I averaged before we had Cam. Some summers I would be gone for multiple months at a time.

But that doesn't change the fact that the hours are long and the work demanding. My phone vibrates with a message, and I pull it from the middle console.

> Camden's with your mom for today.
> Trimming Melissa's herd. Should be back for
> dinner.

Right. I forgot it was Thursday.
I send Ethan a quick reply.

Sounds good.

Knowing my son is inside helps get me moving.

The shop is bustling, practically all the tables full. Most of the people I don't recognize, tourists on their way to the national parks just north of us. One of the women working behind the counter glances up as the bells above the door ring with my entrance. She smiles, her cheeks flushing, and then waves.

I offer a single nod back. It's hard to toe the line between polite and flirting. I have no interest in her—Poppy, I think, or maybe Penelope—and God knows Ethan wouldn't approve even if I did. But things like being just a bit too polite are taken as the gospel truth in small towns, and I don't have the damn energy for it today.

Mom walks out from the back room, a small plate in her hand. She sets the plate on a table a few away from my son and disappears into the back again, not seeming to notice me. Camden is a half-step in front of her, a to-go cup in his hand, though it doesn't have a lid. Instead, there's a mound of whipped cream with a few pieces of shredded chocolate on it. His eyebrows are furrowed as he crosses the room to the far corner where a single table is open. He pushes the small red sign that states "RESERVED" in bold white letters out of his way as he settles into the seat and starts licking the whipped cream.

I drop into the seat next to him and kiss his cheek before he can turn around.

"Papa!" His happy squeal echoes around the busy cafe, and several people look up from their tables. I smile, letting him crawl into my lap and circle his arms around my neck. "You're back!"

I breathe him in, wrapping my arms around him, and close my eyes.

I love flying. I love knowing I'm helping with something larger than just myself. But, fuck, every time I leave it gets harder to justify the distance, the time away. Way too soon, Camden pushes away from me and shuffles back into his own seat, his focus on the whipped cream topping his hot cocoa again.

"Oh!" My mom's surprised gasp is just behind me. I turn in the chair and watch as she closes the distance between us. "I didn't realize you were getting back today."

She hugs me, pulling me into her belly and kissing the top of my head, like I'm as old as Camden and not thirty-five. I let her do it and then bask in her smile as she pulls away.

"Nana, can I have the muffin now?" Camden asks.

She mutters a curse. "I knew I forgot something," she says. "Give me just a moment. I'll bring you a coffee, too."

I run my hand through my son's hair, relaxing into the seat. I don't trust myself to stay awake if I let my eyes drift shut, so I focus on the cars outside, counting the number of out of state license plates as they pass through town.

I'm up to fourteen when Mom returns with a blueberry muffin and a large, steaming mug. I take it with a murmured thanks but don't immediately take a drink. As Mom sets the muffin in front of Camden and settles in the seat across from me, the smell of lavender wafts toward me. My muscles lock. It takes all my control to keep from growling in reaction.

"How was Idaho?" Mom asks.

I shrug. Words are probably not the best idea right now. I breathe slowly, trying to get the unexpected violence to drain away from me. Another trace of that lavender hits me, though, and it does the opposite.

"Something happen on the way in here?" she asks after half a minute.

"You get a new floral arrangement?" I ask instead of admitting I'm on the edge of flipping over this table, my son's pastry be damned. And for literally *no* reason. There's not an Omega in heat anywhere in here. And that's the only reason I can come up with that justifies this level of overreaction and bone deep *need* to protect that's riding me hard despite my exhaustion.

Mom shakes her head. Her gaze catches on someone behind me, and she smiles, waving them over.

"How are you, dear?" she asks. "You weren't here yesterday. I got worried."

"Decided to go for a small ride," a distinctly feminine voice says. One that I don't immediately recognize, and I recognize pretty much anyone Mom knows well enough to chat with in the coffee shop.

Curiosity gets the best of me. I look over my coffee mug. A brunette woman stands a few steps away, her hands tucked into her back pockets, her brown eyes warm and yet somehow still wary. The oversized sweater she wears is a little heavy given it's nearly the middle of June, and it drowns out whatever curves she may have, but the dark green of it makes her skin glow.

Mom smiles and hugs the woman. "I'm sure that must have felt nice after living in the city for so long."

"It was... helpful," the woman says. "I don't trust myself on long rides alone yet, though. Still trying to get the feeling of being on a horse back into me."

Mom nods. "Do you want another cup of tea?"

She's already turning for the counter when the woman shakes her head. "Thank you, though, Joan. I'm going to go help Melissa with everything at the ranch."

"Well, don't let the girls work you too hard. They both love the feel of it and forget others need to work up to the same level of stamina."

The woman smiles, but it doesn't quite touch her eyes. She runs a hand through her hair before waving at Mom.

As she turns, another small wave of that lavender scent hits me. And suddenly it doesn't feel like I've been on a fire for twelve days. My eyes don't hurt, my head doesn't ache. Even the exhaustion is gone, overloaded with the adrenaline coursing through me. Everything within my body is focused on this woman, this Omega, that isn't five feet from me.

She must be wearing a lotion to block her scent rather than the more traditional scent blocking underwear. It's the only explanation for why I managed to get even that small taste of her scent.

It takes every single ounce of my control to stay in my seat, my head ducked, my hands tight on the coffee mug as the woman leaves the coffee shop. I need to stop her, need to touch her, smell her, mark her, *claim* her. Understanding floods me, followed nearly immediately with shock so strong it takes my breath away.

Mom says something, and I nod, not even knowing what I'm agreeing to. She holds out her hand, and I offer her the mug. I turn toward Cam, not trusting myself to look out the windows and see which car is the woman's.

Holy *fucking* hell.

There's absolutely no way that this is happening right now.

Scent matches have only been confirmed to exist for a couple years. A brilliant Omega in California has spent the last half a decade studying them.

You can't open any news from the Council without seeing Violet Montegue's face somewhere in the first few pages. When her first round of research was published, it sent waves through the entire world. Literal proof of soulmates, the perfect pairings between Alphas and Omegas. Within weeks, the Council had put out a statement regarding their matching process and the ways in which they'd be integrating the newly-discovered markers for recognizing your match.

For Alphas, it's intense protection and possessiveness, even worse than when they drop into rut due to an Omega's heat. Nothing matters but that perfume, that Omega.

Fuck me sideways that mine just happens to be in my mother's coffee shop. Ethan is going to fucking *lose* it when I tell him. He was ready to fight me over fucking a random woman in Jackson that I haven't talked to since—and it's not like she's been banging on my metaphorical door begging for a second round.

When I tell him I've found my scent match?

The growl builds in my throat before I realize it's there, and Mom hesitates beside me. I swallow the sound, breathing carefully through my nose, trying to forget the lavender smell.

"What has you so up in a mess all of a sudden?" Mom says, slipping into the seat across from me again, sliding the refilled mug in front of me.

My knuckles whiten around the mug, and Mom purses her lips.

"You were fine just a minute ago," she says.

I stretch my neck again and take a long drink from the mug, focusing on the main road just outside the window, not trusting myself just yet.

The coffee's still too hot, but I don't flinch. Mom's coffees are the best in the state. Certainly leagues better than the instant crap we get while on a fire. Pilots may get better than the fighters on the ground, but that doesn't make it much more than midnight gas station shit.

I catch sight of the woman, her brown hair grabbing my attention as she settles into a Land Rover with Colorado license plates. As she adjusts, the blue ink of a tattoo flashes in the mid-morning sunlight. A butterfly maybe? Or it could be a flower of some kind.

The desire to trace it with my tongue, to see how low it goes along her neck, rides me hard, and it's impossible to stop my scent from flooding the room. I take another drink and close my eyes, counting to ten.

Mom sighs. "I promised myself when you and your brother

designated within three months of each other that I wasn't going to put myself in a situation where it's my sanity or your anger."

"I'm not angry," I say, my voice breathless. At least it's not a growl.

Mom's a Beta, just like Dad. The more subtle changes to a person's scent, the ones that give away their arousal and anger and even an Omega's heat, are lost on Betas. It's part of what makes them Betas, part of what lets them stay stable when an Alpha is ready to drop into a possessive rage.

When I focus on Mom again, her lips are pursed, and she has her chin resting on her palm. "All right. Then I probably especially don't want to know what has you scenting so strongly right now."

"Who was that woman? I haven't seen her before," I say.

"Brielle? Oh, she's Melissa's friend from college." Mom raises an eyebrow. "She moved out here end of last month. So… a week and a half? Almost two weeks, actually. She's staying in Emily's guest house until the tourist season dies down and the housing options open up a bit more."

I raise an eyebrow. "The widow?"

"Yes," Mom says slowly, mirroring my own look. "Her husband died in a car wreck over New Year's Day."

Fuck. Me.

The desire to comfort her, wrap her in my arms and block her from the harsh realities of the world, is strong enough it robs me of any response to Mom.

Wait. Did she say husband?

"Husband?" I ask.

Mom nods. "She'd been married for six years, almost seven."

Omegas don't marry Alphas. Omegas only *marry* Betas. Even unbonded Omegas with Alphas are viewed differently under the laws, though some have weddings, too. But a bona fide marriage license? That doesn't happen between Alphas and Omegas.

What had made her end up with only a Beta?

Not that Omegas can't love Betas. Tons of packs—the legal term for a romantic group that includes at least one Alpha and Omega—have Betas included. But Omegas aren't built for monogamy, not really. They're wired for multiple lovers, especially when they go into heat.

Mom frowns. "What's that look for?"

I shake my head and take another drink of coffee. I love my mom, but I'm not admitting to what's happened in the middle of her coffee shop, especially with Betty sitting in the corner reading her book. She's not quite the worst gossip in town, but she's certainly not trustworthy, either. Not unless you want everyone to know in a matter of a few days.

And, yes, that's better than what some of them manage. You say something within earshot of Molly Bailey, and you better be prepared for everyone knowing in under twelve hours.

"You don't want to know, Mom," I mutter. "Trust me."

She sighs and takes a couple of the pretzels she brought for Camden.

"She's not interested in any of that," she says. "Alex and Calder have already asked to go out as far as I'm aware. She's turned them both down."

"How do you know that?"

Mom doesn't talk to the Deans. Not since they ended up on the other side of a dispute involving Brandon when we were teens.

"Miranda and Leanne were talking about it this morning. Apparently it's the big gossip right now." She pins me with one of those looks, the one that says she's tired of my shit and that I need to listen before the really bad consequences start. I may be thirty-five, but that look still gets my heart in my throat. "You know what it's like to grieve, Caleb. Give her space."

I wish I could.

I take another drink of coffee and run my hand through Camden's hair, focusing on the road again. I don't want to lie to Mom.

"Need any help?" She lets me change the subject.

"Nope. You might text Melissa, though. One of her employees quit last week, and she's been having to cover all the work."

I nod. Camden loves going to Melissa's ranch. It'll keep us both busy.

"Thank you for the coffee," I say. Mom waves her hand, kissing Camden's temple as she heads back around the counter.

Chapter Ten

BRIELLE

By Friday, I'm not feeling quite like a drowning woman —at least in navigating the barn and going through the morning chores I've taken over from Melissa and Emily so they can focus on Misty Mountain. The jury is still out regarding everything else, though. Yesterday only three people stared at me when I grabbed some basics at the grocery store. It was down from the ten that stared at the coffee house Monday morning. And, by some miracle, I've managed to avoid Ethan since the awkward run-in Tuesday.

Combined with the chat with Faedra yesterday, it's just enough that the sense of belonging is starting to lay roots. Sunrises on the porch each morning, hanging out with Melissa and Emily most evenings. Even chatting with some of the stable hands and other employees from both ranches. It's enough to push the overwhelming loneliness down a few notches until it doesn't feel like it's a crater inside my chest.

Nyx pushes into my back, and I smile before I straighten and run a hand down his nose.

A man steps into the barn, his strides long and sure.

Who had wandered into the private barn?

I set the feed bucket into its holder and step out of the stall, closing the gate behind me before Nyx can decide to try for an escape. I move to Phoebe's stall as I take in the man while his attention is on one of the horses on the far side of the barn. Maple probably. Or maybe Daphne.

He's dressed in jeans so dark they're nearly black and a maroon shirt that clings to his chest and arms. The sleeve covers about half of a tattoo that looks like a bird of some kind, and I can see the flash of another colorful piece on his forearm as he tucks his hands into his pockets. His cowboy hat is sun faded, whatever color it had originally been now surrendered to a splotchy warm brown. There's an air of comfortability about him, like he's here often.

I rack my mind, trying to decide which person he might be. There's something in the shape of his shoulder and the lines of his face that seem oddly familiar. When he glances toward me, my breath catches in my throat, realizing at once who he must be. The high cheekbones and deep-set eyes that are the light blue color of a clear winter sky in Denver are practically identical to Beau's.

"You ride?" he asks before I figure out how to get myself out of the barn without looking like I'm bolting—which I am. I swallow, trying to dislodge the lump in my throat.

"Getting back into it," I offer. "It's been a long time for me."

He raises an eyebrow. I breathe through my nose, slowly, to keep from blushing. Why did that suddenly sound like I was talking about something very different from riding horses? He steps up to one of the stalls and runs his hand down the horse's nose. The horse presses into him, and he smiles.

"Hey, pretty girl," he all but croons. "How are you today? I haven't been here often enough the last couple months, have I?"

I glance around the barn. Is he asking me?

He turns toward me after a minute. His lips curl into a smirk as the silence stretches between us.

"Emily mentioned she was going out with a friend today," he says.

This time, his voice is all smoky honey. It rushes over me, sending a flash of heat sizzling across my skin. My thighs clench, but I ignore the sensation. Thank God I'm riding with Emily today and not Melissa. I probably wouldn't have worn the scent blockers if it were just me and Melissa. There's hardly any danger in two Omegas riding without blocking our perfume.

And that would have left me in an incredibly awkward situation right now. None of my lavender scent breaks through the blockers, though, my reaction to him hidden.

Phoebe sticks her nose out above the gate, pushing into my shoulder when I don't focus on her fast enough. I run a single hand down her nose before petting her neck.

"She likes you," he says, tipping his chin toward Phoebe. "She's pretty picky. I haven't seen her like someone in a while."

"Melissa and Emily mentioned that," I say. "Her last owner died unexpectedly a few years ago."

I hold back my flinch. Of course he would know that. He may not have introduced himself yet, but it's clear he's Beau's older brother Caleb—and the third person that made up Brandon's pack.

"He did. It was a rough time." The man's lips flick up into a half-smile that has my body responding way too enthusiastically. "She has a habit of kicking Ethan when he's least expecting it. Refuses to shod her unless someone actively stands with her even if she's tethered properly."

I don't ask why he assumes I know Ethan. I hadn't met him

at the funeral, no more than I'd 'met' Ethan. I'd stayed in the corner with Brett, helping out Melissa when she needed something.

His voice rips me out of the thought.

"So?" he asks, looking up from Maple.

It takes all my control to keep breathing.

I'd never quite appreciated what all the hubbub was regarding an Alpha's charisma. I'd seen it a couple times with Carter, of course. It's hard to avoid when your boss is a powerful Alpha. But he's bonded, so it doesn't quite... hit is the wrong word. Impact is better, I suppose. Bonded Alphas don't have the same impact. Their physical chemistry alters with the bonding bite, adjusting until all those powerful pheromones and instincts really only come out when their Omega is near them.

And that summer with Ethan? It hadn't hit me like *this*. Never once had I wanted to drop to my knees in front of him or press myself against him until his scent overpowered my own. Not that I'd needed to beg for that. He'd hardly ever *stopped* touching me those months we were together.

Had I thought that loneliness was getting better? Maybe I'd just grown accustomed to it instead. Standing here, facing this man, there's no denying that I'm touch-starved.

Being touch-starved is dangerous.

I breathe through my body's reaction, willing it to settle before he finds out my secret.

"So what?" I ask, trying for casual. It comes out a shade too breathless, and his eyebrow ticks up. Hopefully my cheeks aren't as red as they feel right now.

"I haven't seen you around here before."

I tense, ready for him to freak out on me the way Beau did last week, but instead of harping on me for being on private property, he hums.

"You must be one of the summer hires Melissa and Emily brought in. I'm Caleb Taylor," he says. "What's your name?"

I frown. What rock has he been living under the last couple weeks?

Everyone in town knows who I am, whether I like it or not. Not a single person has confused me for one of the young kids Melissa's hired to run the ranch during the busy tourist season. And certainly not on the Monroe Ranch, thirty minutes removed from the recreational ranch on the other side of town.

Mostly, I don't mind that everyone seems to know my story —at least that Brett died while we were still technically married. But sometimes it's accompanied with sympathetic glances that I could do without. Like person number three at the grocery store yesterday.

"Brielle," I offer. "I'm not a staff member, though."

Caleb tilts his head. He starts to say something, but a set of footsteps cuts him off.

"Hey, Bri, you beat me here," Emily's voice carries into the barn ahead of her. She's dressed similarly to me, dark jeans and a long sleeve tee that's thin enough to not be overly warm once the sun settles into the sky. She smiles at the man. "Hey, Caleb. Didn't realize you were home."

Caleb nods. "Got home yesterday morning."

"That one was pretty short." Emily gives him a quick hug.

Caleb shrugs and runs his hand down the horse's nose again. She presses into his touch, and he smiles. "Winds cooperated. Managed to get it nearly contained, so the firefighters on the ground had it in hand."

He fought wildfires? Was he a firefighter, then? Curiosity burns through me, but I shove it down.

"That explains why Ethan didn't ask me about watching Cam today," Emily says. She moves to the stall next to Phoebe, guiding Redwood out from where he's picking through the last of his morning oats, tying him out in the main walkway without fuss. "I just figured Joan had him."

"Papa, look!"

Camden comes running into the barn, a group of white wild-flowers in his hands. He's managed to get grass stains on his jeans, though his shirt is clean. His cheeks flush as he glances at me.

"Hi, Bri," he says, offering me a quick wave. He turns back to the others and holds the blooms out to Caleb. "Think Grammy will like them?"

Caleb smiles. "Definitely, kiddo."

Camden nods and crosses the barn. He pulls a single flower from his back pocket and holds it out to me. It's mangled to high heaven, but none of the purple petals manage to fall to the ground.

"Here, Bri," he says. "Nana let me pick it this morning."

I take the flower and tuck it into one of my braids before offering him a smile.

"Does it look good?" I ask him.

He nods, all serious scrutiny.

"Grandma called it a..." He trails off, his eyebrows scrunching. "Ra... Ranunculus," he says, separating each syllable. "Yeah, ranunculus. It was the only purple one she said I could have."

"Thank you," I say. "It's beautiful."

He nods and then runs back toward Caleb. Caleb, who's staring at me hard enough I want to double check that I don't have a stain on my shirt or something. I twist the end of my braid around my fingers, trying to keep from broadcasting just how unnerving his attention is.

Unnerving... and exhilarating.

"Oh, right." Emily clears her throat. I tear my gaze away from him. "Brielle, this is Caleb, Camden's other dad." She motions between us even as she crosses the barn. "Caleb, this is Brielle.

She's staying in my guest house for the summer while she gets settled."

"Nice to meet you," he says, though he doesn't close the distance between us. Camden grabs his leg, and he turns his focus to his son, guiding him to stand in front of the next stall.

"Stay here until I have him tied out, kid," he says.

I take the moment to pull Phoebe from the stall, interrupting her snack. She shakes her head and heaves a sigh but cooperates well enough. Emily comes out of the tack room with both bridles and Phoebe's saddle and blankets. She helps me get them settled on Phoebe and then disappears to grab Redwood's equipment.

"Papa, are Emily and Bri coming with us?" Camden asks.

"It looks like they have their own plans. You'd need to ask Emily," Caleb says. "She might not want to ride to the Arch."

Emily glances up from where she's tacking up Redwood, focusing on me rather than Caleb or his son. We'd planned on an easy ride to one of the larger ponds at the edge of the ranch and then maybe some swimming. The Arch is in the opposite direction, the name derived from a tree that had grown across the main trail leading to the summit of one of the lower nearby peaks.

Last time I'd been to the Arch, it had been with Ethan. Nerves twist in my belly.

"What do you want to do?" she asks me, quiet enough it doesn't echo through the barn.

I glance at Camden's wide eyes and then the enigmatic man carrying a large saddle. The need to submit to him, to let him mark every single pulse point of my body with his scent, is still an overwhelming urge.

"I haven't been to the Arch in a long time," I say. Camden's smile is wide, and his whole face lights up as he realizes what I'm about to say. I can't help it. The kid's a natural charmer. "Think I'll like it as much as hiking?"

He nods as he squeals. As Caleb finishes prepping the horse and helps Camden into the front of the saddle, the wind changes outside, sending a breeze through the main alley of the barn.

And then all I can smell is cinnamon, and the desire to drop to my knees in front of this man, this *Alpha* is all I can think of.

The need to feel this man's skin is so strong my hands tremble. Slick soaks my scent blockers, and I breathe through the sudden, feral urge to strip in the middle of this barn so he can put his mouth on whichever part he wants the most.

Holy hell. There's no way.

I swallow, trying to find a different explanation for my body's response. Because there's no way I'm having the reaction the Council lists as evidence an Omega has met their scent match. It's a statistical improbability. The odds of finding your scent match are so small, it's nearly akin to hitting the lottery.

The breeze grows stronger, and so does the cinnamon. I swallow a groan as my body grows hotter. Even my nipples respond, tightening to the point of near pain, something that hasn't happened in a *very* long time. It feels almost like the hours before the one and only heat I've actually ridden out. The last bits of me that were fighting the reality, were trying to convince myself my response to him is something other than an Omega recognizing a scent match, fade away.

I suck in a breath and tighten my grip on Phoebe's bridle, forcing myself to not move. I don't trust myself. If I so much as flinch right now, I'm going to be in front of that man making a complete fool of myself. After another few minutes, the wind changes, the breeze dies down, and I swing up into the saddle, keeping my eyes to myself.

Of course my scent match is Ethan's pack mate.

Chapter Eleven

CALEB

Camden twists in my lap, lodging one of his elbows in my side before I can manage to stop him. He ducks his head under my arm, focusing on where the women ride behind us on the trail. Maple shakes his head, and I loosen the reins just a bit. We're nearly to the Arch, which means we're nearly to the point where I can get feeling back in my hips and thighs.

"Bri, why do you live at Aunt Emily's house?" he asks.

"Bud, that's not really a thing people ask," I mutter. "It's not considered polite."

Camden looks at me, his eyebrows furrowed hard enough that the line is between them again. "Well that's a stupid rule."

Brielle laughs behind us. Something loosens in my chest at the soft sound. She's been incredibly quiet this entire ride. If not for the small smiles and relaxed body posture I'd noticed the few times I chanced glancing back, I would be seriously concerned she wasn't enjoying herself.

I want her to enjoy herself.

Fuck, it's been a long ass time since I felt that desire to make an Omega happy.

"I live in her guest house because I don't have a house here," she answers easily enough. The laughter is in her voice, too.

"Why don't you?" Camden asks, unabashed.

The silence is longer this time. I chance a glance over my shoulder. Brielle's head is tilted, a thoughtful look on her face. She runs a hand down Phoebe's shoulder while she thinks over her answer.

"Well," she says slowly. "I think that buying a place to live can be a little nerve-wracking. It's something you don't really want to rush into. So I'm going to stay at Emily's until I figure out where I want to live permanently."

Camden frowns before nodding. "You could live with us. There's a room with a bed that Papa and Daddy don't use."

Emily chokes on her breath, and Brielle's cheeks flush a dark red that just brings out the subtle maroon highlights in her hair. My heart picks up at the sight, a flash of need tearing through my body and making my already uncomfortable set up with Camden even worse. I ease Maple onto the side trail. Before anyone can decide exactly what to say in response to Camden's offer, I grab him around the waist and pull him into my chest as I lean forward in the saddle, doing my best to help Maple with the grade of the last climb.

Camden giggles and nestles into my hold. His head cradles against the crook of my shoulder. Affection warms my chest, and I press a kiss to the crown of his hair. Maple clears the last of the grade, and the trail levels out, spreading into a small clearing. Across it, where the trail continues disappearing through the forest, stands the Arch. Camden claps his hands.

"Yay!" he cheers. "Papa, can I go climbing, please?"

"You have to give me a chance to help you get down," Emily

says, laughter in her voice, too. She comes up beside us a few moments later and holds out her hands. Camden climbs into her arms without hesitation, and then I ease out of the saddle and walk Maple over to where Emily's tied out Redwood on a low lying pine branch a few feet just inside the clearing.

"Bri, come climb!" Camden says.

He races through the clearing a moment later, not waiting for any of us to respond. Brielle stands at the edge of the clearing, her hand tight enough where it grabs Phoebe's lead rope that her knuckles are white.

"Here, let me help," I offer, crossing to where she's standing.

Her throat ripples with a swallow, and she tucks a loose strand of hair behind her ear.

"All right," she whispers.

I ease the rope from her death grip and guide Phoebe to the others, tying her out on the other side of Redwood.

"You all right, Bri?" Emily asks.

She stands a few feet away from her, arms tucked into the back pockets of her jeans, her brows furrowed with her concerned frown. Brielle's posture is softer... and more fragile seeming, at least to my eyes. Her shoulders are slightly rounded, and her arms are crossed over her belly, almost like it's an involuntary response to something the rest of us haven't noticed yet.

She bites at her lip before tearing her gaze away from the Arch. Her lips part, but Camden cuts off her response.

"Bri, come climb!" When she looks over at him, he giggles. "Look at how far I can get!"

He's only a few feet off the ground, not even reaching the bend in the tree as it starts across the trail. But his grin is so wide, his dimple is in full view, and her eyes are bright with his laughter. Fuck, I love that my son is such a happy kid.

After another long moment, she crosses the open space,

leaning against the tree, her head tilted so she can still see Camden. Some of her nerves bleed away. I manage to relax, too.

Emily stares at me, her eyes seeing too much, but I ignore her. I pat Maple's rump as I walk past him and join the others.

Camden, just like always, is happy to do all the talking. It keeps the birds from settling in the clearing, and the deer are far enough away that I can't even see them through the trees.

Of course, if I wanted a chance to actually see the wildlife on a ride, I wouldn't bring a four-year-old. Being subtle isn't really their specialty.

"Bri," Camden says. His tongue sticks out as he works to find a way higher on the tree. His foot slips, and Brielle takes a step closer, adjusting so she stands underneath him rather than off to the side. "Bri, do you like the rodeo?"

Brielle says, "I've never been. Do you like the rodeo?"

Camden looks down at her, his eyes wide in his surprise. "You haven't ever been? Do they not have rodeos where you were before? Grandma said it was a big city. Is it big like Jackson? That's a big town."

Brielle smiles. I lean against a tree, tucking my hands in my pockets, content to watch them interact. Emily pulls a blanket she had rolled on the back of Redwood's saddle, shaking it out and then settling on it, leaning back until the sun lights across her face.

"It's bigger than Jackson," she says. Camden slips again, and he loses his hold on the tree. Brielle catches him without missing a beat before I can even push off the tree I'm leaning against. My breath catches. Three feet isn't super tall, but it can still break a wrist if the person lands just wrong. "And there's a rodeo that happens in January every year, but I never went to it."

Camden nods as she sets him down.

"Papa, do you have a snack?" he asks, looking over at me. Before I can answer, he turns back to Brielle. "I love the rodeo.

It's so fun. One time I got to ride a sheep. I don't remember what it's called. We're going tomorrow 'cuz Daddy's friend is riding bulls."

Brielle's eyebrow rises, and she glances at Emily.

"Toddlers ride sheep?" she asks, her voice as uncertain as her look.

I can't decide if she's appalled at the idea or simply surprised.

Emily laughs. "It's called mutton busting. And they wear helmets. Cam's not actually old enough to do it for the event during the rodeo. You have to be five. But Triston let him try it out behind the scenes."

"Papa, snack?" Camden asks, running up to me.

I take his hand and walk back to Maple, pulling the small snack I'd packed from the bag draped over his saddle. Camden purses his lips as he surveys the options. After a minute, he blows out a breath and races over to where Emily's laid out on the blanket, plopping down next to her with all the grace of a linebacker.

"Triston?" Brielle asks, perching on a rock that juts out of wildflowers. She picks one of the small white wildflowers growing around its base and twists it into the braid opposite the flower Cam gave her. "He works on the Monroe Ranch, right?"

A possessive growl rumbles through my chest, but I keep it locked down. I lean against Maple's rump instead of closing the distance, though, not trusting myself to be anything other than an asinine idiot.

"Oh, yeah," Emily says. "He rides bulls, too. He's trying to get enough points to get off the amateur circuit. If he wins tomorrow night and Brooks loses by at least two positions, it'll probably be enough for next season."

Brielle nods. "I hope it goes well for him, then."

Camden shoves a pretzel in his mouth and asks, "Are you going, too, Bri?"

Brielle tilts her head. "I'm not sure. Melissa doesn't really like the rodeo. It makes her sad."

"Oh, because of my dad," Camden says without missing a beat. "He liked doing something in it. What's it called, Papa? What my dad did when I was a baby?"

My throat grows thick. "Roping, bud. It's called roping. And he did it before you were born."

"Right. Roping." Every third "r" he pronounces is garbled, but it doesn't seem to affect Brielle being able to understand him. He frowns before eating a piece of cheese.

A new calm settles over us, and I hear birds for the first time since we've been here. I leave the relative safety of Maple and settle next to Camden. He crawls into my lap, smiling as he adjusts so his cheek presses against my chest.

He grabs a pretzel and holds it up, looking at Brielle.

"Bri, do you want a pretzel?"

Chapter Twelve

The clearing is quiet. Well, not really. A light breeze sways the bench swing and ripples through the prairie grasses. Several birds sit perched on the far railing of the porch, sorting through the birdseed feeder I put up last weekend. One of the smaller birds chirps happily, its yellow belly flashing each time it adjusts its stance or ruffles its feathers.

But the clearing *feels* quiet in a way the city never could.

I settle onto the swing, trying to keep from disturbing the birds. My skin feels tight, like it's somehow shrinking over my bones. It takes all my willpower to not claw at my chest and belly to try and ease away the horrid feeling.

Touch-starved. And it's getting worse.

I pull up the article from the Council's website detailing the condition, trying to find anything that gives more optimistic outcomes than everything else I've heard about the condition. Sure, some of the symptoms seem benign. Fever, mind fog, irritability.

But some of them? Some of them are *bad* bad.

Scent changes. Anxiety. Paranoia. And, to top off the happy little symptom cake, a heat-like haze that drives the Omega to seek out an Alpha's knot.

Yeah, that sounds about as appealing as being stuck in four inch stilettos for a seven-hour standing-room-only meeting.

I close the browser on my phone and drop it into my lap. Freaking out about it won't change anything. I'm not going to hop into some random person's bed just to satisfy my body's needs.

Maybe I can see if there's a doctor in Jackson able to prescribe me suppressors. Though the idea of ending up back on those is about as appealing as knotting some random stranger.

It doesn't have to be a stranger, the little voice inside whispers.

I ignore it, just like I have the last twenty-four hours since smelling Caleb Taylor's cinnamon scent and wanting to fall to my knees in front of him.

"Brielle, get it together," I mutter.

I tuck my phone under my leg to keep it from tempting me, and focus on the birds again. I let myself get lost in watching them until a light blue Subaru pulls up at the base of the driveway to the guest house a few hundred feet away.

Melissa's glasses match her dress today, the sky blue color bringing out the darker strands of her blonde hair which she wears in its natural curls. She waves as she heads toward me, and I can't help but smile.

The birds scatter as she steps onto the porch.

"Everything good at the ranch?" I ask.

She drops into the space next to me with a heavy sigh. "As good as they can be. Things will slow down once Alec is fully trained and able to take over Trish's job entirely."

She drops her head to my shoulder, and the itching sensation crawling under my skin eases just a breath.

"Thank you for all the help," she says after a minute. "I know you came out here for a fresh start to figure out what you want to do next. Sorry you've been spending all the time driving between both ranches."

"It's fine, Mel." I ease away her worries as best I can. Taking over the animals from her has been a breath of fresh air. "I needed something to do other than cosplay Betty at the Rustic Roast."

She huffs a laugh. "Joan loves having you there," she admits.

My phone vibrates. I answer the video call and prop it against the chain holding the bench swing.

"Hey, Bri. Is now a good time?"

Faedra sits on the sofa in her living room, the midday sun casting her in literal perfect lighting. It has her green eyes sparkling and her freckles popping against her fair skin. There's the low din of voices from somewhere near her. The twins must be doing something just out of frame.

"Sure," I say. I hold a hand out to Melissa. "This is my friend Melissa."

Faedra smiles as Melissa and her exchange the typical small talk greeting. After a moment, she focuses on me again.

"We were curious if you wanted to join us when we head out there in a couple weeks. I'm not entirely sure of our timeline since Carter and Jude have been planning it. But I know that we have some down time on either side of our route."

Melissa says, "Oh, I'd love to meet you all in person! And so would Emily."

Faedra laughs. And then she's laughing harder as the twins rush into the frame, climbing onto the couch before she can decide if she wants the call to include them. Rose stares at me while Iris giggles and waves.

"Are you coming camping, Aunt Bri?" Rose asks in her bright, clear voice.

"I'm not sure yet. Your mom and I were just starting to talk about it."

Iris climbs into Faedra's lap and grabs her cheeks, forcing her to look at the little girl. Faedra laughs even as she pulls her daughter's hands away from her face. "Please, please, please, Momma. Please, can she come with us?"

Logan sighs and drops onto the couch beside Faedra, wrapping an arm around her shoulder and pulling her into his side. The move is so smooth, the girls don't even notice that they've been effectively pushed off their mother's lap.

"Not on the big hike, sweetie," he says. Iris pouts. Rose sighs exactly how Jude always does. He runs his thumb over Iris's cheek. "But I'm sure we'll find other ways to spend time with her. Let Momma and me figure out the details while Dahlia is sleeping. How about you girls go play with your space set?"

Both girls nod before running out of the frame again, disappearing just as quickly as they showed up. Melissa laughs.

"Aunt?" she asks.

I shrug, not really sure how to explain just how close I am to my boss's family. *Former* boss's family.

"Brielle and Faedra have been friends ever since they met at the Christmas party of Carter's company before the twins were born," Logan says amiably.

Melissa's eyebrows furrow. Faedra clears her throat.

"Carter is one of my other partners. Brielle worked for his company."

"Oh, that's so cool!" Melissa gushes.

"So what do you think, Bri?" Faedra asks after the clatter of the girls dies down. "We were thinking maybe more traditional camping? There's a couple spots the guys know about along the edge of the Tetons."

Melissa nods. "Oh yeah! Phelps Lake, right? Or maybe Jenny Lake? It's so pretty up there."

The desire to hang out with my friend, to be surrounded by her family, is so strong I can practically taste it.

"If it won't interrupt your backpacking plans, I'd love to," I admit.

Logan's quick to assure me it won't. As he's typing something into his phone, Melissa clears her throat.

"Not to be the awkward third wheel here," she says. "Well, fourth wheel, technically. Actually, you're an Omega, right, Faedra? So it's probably more than just the four of us." She shakes her head and nudges her glasses up her nose. "Anyway, getting distracted. Do you think there'd be space for a couple more people to tag along?"

Faedra looks at Logan who nods before saying, "Definitely."

Melissa blushes. "Sorry, not to invite myself or anything."

I grab her hand and squeeze it.

"Having an Omega crash one of these is not unheard of," Faedra says, humor weaving through her voice. Her cheeks flush a dark red, and Logan kisses her shoulder. It must be an inside joke. Knowing them, I don't really want to know.

"Will you send me a list of everything I'll need? I've never camped before," I say. Faedra nods, and Melissa squeals.

"Oh my gosh, this is going to be so much fun. Thank you for letting me tag along!"

Faedra's smile grows wider.

"I'll get things finalized with Carter and Jude," Logan says before kissing Faedra's temple. "Once we have the permits figured out, we'll send you the reservation information. It'll probably be for the end of the month if that works for you. Since we're hiking our route over July Fourth."

"That sounds good," I say.

Melissa offers a quick agreement. Logan stands from the couch and disappears from the frame. Faedra's gaze follows him, her teeth biting into her lip, before she focuses on the call again.

"We'll probably have room for a few more tents, too, if there's anyone else you'd like to invite," Faedra says. "We'd love to meet everyone out there."

An odd mixture of anxiety and cautious contentment wells up in me, stealing my breath for a long moment. How long did I move through Brett's circles, trying to fit in, trying to find a footing somewhere in the groups of fiancees and wives? And yet here were two groups that seemed to truly want me, moved plans around and adjusted their own lives to make sure I have a place within it. Tears well, but I blink them away. Faedra's eyes sharpen even as Melissa squeezes my hand.

Before I can offer a response that isn't just a blubbering mess of words, a baby's cries fill the quiet. Faedra glances over her shoulder, frowning.

"You need to go?" I ask.

She sighs, and it's answer enough.

"You go take care of Dahlia. I'll see you in a couple weeks."

I tuck my phone under my leg again as soon as the call ends. Melissa's quiet beside me, content with the stillness of the clearing. It's one of the reasons we bonded so quickly freshman year. At least that one was nicer than us both having alcoholic parents. Or both feeling like we never belonged anywhere we ended up, floating from place to place without being able to build out the roots everyone says are so important for building a happy life.

Would it be possible to have roots here when I hadn't managed after seven years in Denver? I'd thought I'd had roots. Strong, stable roots that would weather any storm. And yet, they snapped under the pressure and the winds when they came.

I blow out a breath, trying to shake off the whole line of thinking.

"Bad thoughts?" she asks, dropping her head to my shoulder in silent support.

I offer a half smile. "You know me too well."

She smirks, but it doesn't touch her eyes. "It's easy when we're two sides of the same coin, Bri."

"Think I'll ever actually fit in here?" I ask. I don't really mean to ask it. I don't want her to worry over my own concerns. But we've been best friends for over a decade. Some things just slip out.

She stills, forcing the bench to stop swinging.

Her words are cautious when she says, "I think that trying to blend in is very difficult for Omegas. And probably impossible in small towns where the Karens and Mollys are more interested in the latest gossip than doing something productive and helpful."

I snort, and she chuckles. "That's a politician's answer if I've ever heard one, Mel."

"Well..." she says, her voice rising like she has a surprise.

I laugh harder. There's no way she'd ever decide to be a politician. The few Omegas that try end up on suppressors to control their reactions to the Alphas around them—and the timing of their heats. Melissa's never once even wanted to consider going on them.

"What I mean is that I think it's easy to feel like you never belong no matter where you are," she says. "You have to decide to carve out a space for yourself, a place you love and that satisfies you. If people talk, then people talk. And in small towns, there's always someone talking. You just hope that you're at least in the next room over when they start."

Some of my worry fades. I rest my head against hers.

"Thank you," I tell her.

"Any time, Bri."

"I was thinking of going to the rodeo tonight," I mention, trying to keep just how much I want to go out of my voice. Melissa freezes. "I've never been to one."

I was too busy being wrapped up with Ethan that summer to go see Brandon compete.

Melissa relaxes. "Then let's go."

We sit there for a long time, just watching the prairie around us. The bird with the yellow belly is back, hopping along the porch's banister to get to the feeder, taking a few pieces before flying off. A small herd of deer cross toward the mountains, the mothers watchful as the smaller fawns walk between them. It's not until they disappear that I break the quiet around us.

"We should probably get ready," I say. Melissa hums and sits up, dropping her feet to the porch. "What does someone even *wear* to the rodeo?"

Chapter Thirteen

The person working the parking lot waves me forward to another section of the large dirt lot. As I get closer, a young man no more than eighteen pushes off a fence post and directs me into an open parking spot, using an orange flag to signal where I'm supposed to go.

Once I've gotten the Land Rover wedged between two astronomically large trucks, I turn it off and face Melissa, and then ask the question that's been bouncing around in my mind the entire drive up to Jackson.

"Would you ever want to actually find your scent matches?" I ask.

There's no reason to lie to myself about why I wanted to go tonight. It starts and ends with Caleb Taylor.

Melissa hums in thought, pushing her glasses up her nose as she mulls over her answer. A family parks across from us, and I focus on the woman easing out of the passenger seat. Her hair is done in large barrel waves and sits nearly to her waist. Her jeans are a dark wash with a heavy flair, and her boots are so dark they're nearly black. As the others drop out of the truck, she leans back into it and grabs a white cowboy hat, setting it on her head and adjusting her hair in the side mirror.

I glance at the white linen dress and gladiator sandals Melissa helped me pick out. Nerves tighten my belly, but I push them away. I've spent the last seven years trying to be what everyone else wanted.

"I'm not sure," Melissa says, getting out of the car. I follow her, looping my arm with hers once I've grabbed my purse and crossed it over my body. It's not overly crowded, so it's easy enough to make our way to the entrance of the arena. As we stand in line, she messes with the sleeve of her shirt, adjusting the rolled hem until it sits above her elbow rather than below it. Her body sings with nerves. Guilt flashes through me. As she messes with the second one, she sighs.

"On paper it sounds great," she says, "but it's not really a get-out-of-jail-free card, you know? You might be the perfect biological match, but that doesn't mean you'll match in other areas." She focuses on me, her green eyes nearly sparkling in the fading evening light. "Would you?"

"I think," I say, trying to decide how best to admit that, short of the Council's confirming blood test, I'm positive I already have. "I think I would be, I guess."

She nods. "It would be nice in some ways, probably. Maybe it could feel like a new chance, you know? A chance to have the happy ending you thought you were getting with Brett. Just as long as you don't leave me in the dust."

A lump settles in the back of my throat, and I swallow convulsively, trying to dislodge it. A group of guys stand behind us, a bit too close for my comfort, but I keep my back straight. Melissa glances over her shoulder before taking a subtle step forward.

"You know I'd never leave you in the dust," I say, squeezing her hand. She smiles and nods.

"You finding a scent match would be so cool, Bri."

"You think so?" I ask.

I mess with the neckline of the dress to keep from picking at my cuticles. Another couple minutes, and I'm going to have a freak out over the amount of people so close to me. How the hell do Omegas function without using suppressors? All of this sensory overload is about enough to turn me into a hermit, and I used to *like* being around people.

"Of course," she says. She tucks a strand of hair behind her ear before adjusting her glasses. "Just expect me to lay down the law of not breaking your heart with them. You've had enough of that already."

An Alpha's fruity scent wafts toward us as the wind picks up a bit. My skin tightens, that invasive itchy sensation an unwelcome addition to the night. The breeze picks up after a minute, but not before the Alpha's scent has me thinking of yesterday.

The reminder of Caleb's cinnamon scent rushes through me, my body responding without me meaning to. Lavender surrounds us, breaking through my lotion so fast it's honestly a bit impressive. I don't miss the barely-there acidic bite to it, either.

My cheeks flush as Melissa tilts her head. I dig out the lotion and reapply it. It does a half decent job, but not nearly enough if I'm going to be within scenting range of an Alpha.

Crap. I'll need to put on my scent blockers once we're inside.

One of the guys behind us grunts like he's been punched. I take a step forward, too, looping my arm with Melissa's. Before I can work up the courage to just admit to her my problem, we're at the turnstiles. I pull out my phone and let the kid working the admissions scan the ticket. His gaze travels down my body, catching on my sandaled feet, before shooting back to my face. At least it wasn't my boobs?

"Have a good night, miss," he says to me, touching the brim of his cowboy hat.

The moment we're through the entrance, I make a beeline for the bathrooms. The last thing I need is my scent breaking through a second time.

How is there *already* a line for the women's side? The damn thing doesn't even start for another twenty or so minutes. I look around, trying to see if there's another option. Melissa bumps my shoulder. I blow out a breath.

"You're not allowed to panic," I say. Her eyebrow climbs high enough I can see it over the rim of her glasses. When she nods, I admit in a rush of air, "I think I already found one."

There's a long, suspended moment. Her eyes widen as what I've said sinks in. And then she spins around, all thoughts of keeping calm forgotten. Her hands shake as she grabs both of mine.

"You *what?*" she asks, her eyes wide.

I swallow the lump in my throat. "I found a scent match. I haven't confirmed it with the Council or anything, but... I mean, the Council's pretty clear about the signs."

"Oh my gosh, where? How? When?" She sputters the questions, her voice rising with each one. "I... I don't even... *What?*"

I can't help but laugh even as I cover her mouth with a palm.

"Stop screeching or someone will call security thinking we're being assaulted or something," I murmur.

She rolls her eyes but relaxes. When she pulls away and waves for me to answer, I hold up a finger, adding one as I answer each question.

"The private barn at Monroe Ranch. Total accident, I think. Yesterday."

"Holy fucking hell, Bri. It's someone *here?*"

Her eyes are so wide, it'd be hilarious if it wasn't also drawing a ton of unwanted attention.

"Yes," I say. "And I don't want anyone else to know yet."

She glances toward the bathroom, digging her teeth into her lip.

"Who? You cannot just leave me hanging here," she says. At least her voice has dropped back to a reasonable volume. "I will pull you out of this line and make you start all over again if I have to."

I can't help but smile.

"You swear you won't bring it up?"

Melissa nods. "Scout's honor," she says, holding up her pinky.

I roll my eyes. "You weren't even in Scouts, Mel. Either of them."

She shrugs as I link my pinky with hers and then let it drop.

"It's Caleb."

Chapter Fourteen

CALEB

"Papa, look! We got popcorn!" Camden's voice precedes him.

I glance over my shoulder, cutting off my response to Beau beside me, just in time to see my son stepping off the stairs and into our row of seats. Ethan holds two bags of popcorn, one larger than the other, where he walks a step behind him. Camden runs along the small pathway in front of the metal bench where we sit. Instead of dropping onto my lap, though, he focuses behind me, skidding to a stop just shy of my legs. Ethan does some fancy footwork to stop in time so he doesn't accidentally barrel over our son.

"Kid, you need to be careful," he says. He urges Camden onto the bench beside me and hands him the smaller container of popcorn. Once Camden is settled, he slides past me and sits next to Emily on the other side of Beau.

Camden twists on the bench, propping an elbow on my arm

to give himself stability, and then waves at someone behind us. I glance over my shoulder.

And then have to take an extra minute to remember how to breathe.

Melissa and Brielle stand at the top of the arena, arms locked together at the elbows. Melissa's shoulders are tense, and she bites at her lip as she looks out over the growing crowd. How had Brielle managed to convince her to come? Because there's no way that Melissa is the one that offered between the two of them. The urge to help ease her nerves rides me hard for a moment, a natural response of an Alpha to an Omega. But before I can rearrange Camden and stand, my eyes catch on Brielle beside her. She's dressed in a short white dress that hugs her curves before flaring away from her legs, landing mid-thigh. It offsets her brown hair. They're far enough above us I can't see her eyes, but I bet they pop against the white fabric, too.

"Bri!" Camden calls, giggling. His voice cuts across the din of the crowd talking around us. Both women focus on us. Melissa relaxes and starts down the stairs, pulling Brielle behind her and blocking her from my view. But not before I see her cheeks flame a bright red.

Hudson grunts from where he's seated on the bench behind me. He nudges my shoulder before smirking.

"He's made a fast friend, huh?" he asks.

I shrug and shove down the surge of irritation that rushes through me at his comment.

Camden makes friends. Don't most four-year-olds make easy friends? Besides, Brandon always had. I still do, and Ethan isn't a stranger to it. At least until Kayla killed herself when Camden was only six months old.

Jesus fuck, why the hell am I thinking about that right now?

"Bri, you came!" Camden waves at the women, and Brielle offers a small smile and wave in return.

Beau leans closer to me, dropping his voice as he says, "You should probably tell him that she's not available."

This time I don't quite manage to bury the overbearing growl. Beau hesitates beside me. Emily's conversation with her brother fades away. Even without looking toward her, I can feel her focus on me. Hudson raises a single eyebrow, his sweeping once-over seeing too much. The smirk falls away from his lips as he leans forward.

"Shut up, Beau," he says, low enough it won't carry beyond a few feet. Camden doesn't even seem to notice.

Beau's uncharacteristically obedient, dropping the entire subject between one breath and the next. Melissa pushes Brielle in front of her as they make it to our row. Her gaze catches mine, and there's a small smile on her lips I've never seen before, like she knows a secret that she's dying to share but isn't allowed to.

Brielle settles on the bench beside Camden, and he hugs her, launching himself into her arms before she's managed to get her small clutch tucked behind her feet. She laughs as he dumps half the bag of popcorn in her lap.

"Oops, sorry, Bri," he says. He tips the bag more as he attempts to pick up some of the fallen pieces.

With a sigh, I grab the bag from him.

"How about I hold this for you, bud?"

He grins at me before focusing on the mess. Brielle helps him, popping a couple pieces in her mouth despite Camden's protest. She smiles but doesn't apologize.

"Just helping with clean-up," she says with a smile. Camden narrows his eyes. She pops another piece in her mouth.

Camden starts to say something, but a high-pitched squeal drowns him out.

"Oh my gosh! I didn't realize you'd be here!"

Olivia closes the gap between us, dropping into the seat beside Hudson. He wraps his arm around her, pulling her close, and then kisses the silver scar that sits nestled in the crook of her shoulder. Brielle turns, and her smile grows larger, lighting her eyes. Olivia shrugs out of Hudson's hold.

"Olivia!" she says. The women hug each other, Camden caught on the outside. He doesn't seem to mind, though, picking up a few more pieces of his spilled popcorn and focusing as the first event gets set in the arena.

"It's so nice seeing you for something happy this time," Olivia whispers. Brielle tightens her hold even as she closes her eyes, a look of pain crossing her features. "Melissa told me what happened. I'm so angry for you. But I'm happy you're here."

Hudson raises an eyebrow. He asks the question that's perched on my tongue.

"You guys know each other?"

Olivia nods as she pulls away from Brielle. She grabs a small pill from her purse and nestles it under her tongue.

"Of course," she says after a few moments, like it's something obvious. "We spent an entire summer together when Brielle lived with Melissa while they were in school."

What the fuck? Brielle lived here before?

The conversation beside me dies down as the rest of our group focuses on Olivia. She flushes as she realizes everyone's paying attention to her.

"That... Oh gods. That wasn't a secret, was it? I thought everyone knew that." She sends a desperate look to Brielle.

Melissa cuts in. "Brielle stayed with Brandon and me the summer between freshman and sophomore year. Not a secret." She grabs Olivia's hand and squeezes it before turning to focus on the arena. "Just not something that's really brought up. It was a long time ago."

"It was." Olivia nods. "But, gosh, it was so much fun."

Brielle offers a smile but doesn't say anything.

Olivia continues, "I'm sorry I haven't seen you since you've moved back. I've been so sick, it's been hard getting out of bed."

I frown. Olivia's been sick?

Hudson chuckles. "I thought we weren't going to hard launch it."

Olivia smirks as she nudges his side.

Brielle's eyes widen. "Really?"

I frown, and Beau echoes my confusion.

"Wait, you've been sick?" Ethan asks. "Is everything okay?"

"Getting better," Olivia says. "Should be mostly back to normal in another couple weeks. That's what the doctor says, at least. Though apparently some people are sick the entire nine months. That sounds miserable."

Before I can process what she's said, Brielle and Melissa squeal in unison, reaching across the space and hugging Olivia at the same time.

"No way," Emily says, reaching across from the other side of me and grabbing Olivia's leg. When she nods, her cheeks flushed and her smile wide, it finally clicks.

"Holy shit," I say. I shove Hudson, giving him one of Mom's looks. He rolls his eyes before smirking. "You just let us all walk into that one? What the hell, man? Didn't we make an agreement to tell each other first?"

Hudson tosses his head back and laughs. "Mom's been losing it all week. Shocked she didn't spill it when you swung by Thursday, honestly."

Beau laughs, too. "Congrats, man. When are you due?"

Olivia smiles, but the announcer cuts across the speakers before she can answer. Once he's finished, she says quickly, "Christmas."

The excitement settles down as the first bareback rider loads into the chute, the coaches and a couple of the other competitors climbing onto the rails to offer encouragement. After only a few moments, he nods his head, and they open the chute. Eight seconds is extraordinarily short, and the first kid doesn't quite make it, dropping from the horse a few moments before. The audience cheers anyway, though, as the pickup men guide the horse out of the arena.

After another minute or so, the chatter builds in the stands again.

"So when does Tristan perform?" Brielle asks, her quiet voice cutting through the low din of voices.

Beau chuckles, and her cheeks flush. I swallow back the growl that wants to rip out of me.

"Oh, bull riding is the last event," Melissa says.

Olivia nods as she snuggles deeper into Hudson's side. "Yeah, he'll compete first," she says. "According to him, he drew a nasty bull. And we say they compete, not perform."

Hudson leans forward, letting his elbow rest on his knee. His other arm is still wrapped around Olivia's hips.

"If they make it the full eight seconds, both the bull and the rider will get a score of up to 50. Best total of 100 wins the night," Hudson says. "Same with bareback which is what we're watching now and also saddle bronc. The other events are timed, and the fastest person will win those ones."

Brielle's eyebrows climb as she looks back at the arena. Camden settles into her lap, and she wraps her arms around him, like it's second nature to have a kid sitting with her. Was it?

No one's mentioned her having any kids. But maybe they were killed in the same accident that killed her husband? The idea of her experiencing even more loss sets my teeth on edge, so I shove it aside.

The next rider tries his luck before I can decide what I want to say. This one makes it the full eight seconds, and Camden shows off where the score is posted on the screen positioned at the apex of the arena opposite the tunnels.

As the horse is guided into the tunnels, Cam asks, "Bri, do you want some popcorn?"

I can't help but watch as he holds up a piece from what's left in his bag. And then I can't help my body's heating as Brielle smiles and slips the piece into her mouth, not messing up a single spot of her dark red lipstick.

Fuck, I want to see what it looks like when it's smudged.

Chapter Fifteen

The night passes in a raucous blur of laughs and popcorn. Camden proves to be a wonderful tutor in all things rodeo despite only being four. He crawls into Caleb's lap during the third event—team roping—and when the team he's declared his favorite due to their obnoxious bright orange matching shirts wins, Melissa brings him an unsalted pretzel. Every so often, I catch the cinnamon scent that belongs to Caleb. The itchy feeling burying into my bones eases a bit each time, but I don't risk moving closer to him.

By the time the saddle bronc starts—a wild event that's only difference from bareback seems to be an odd saddle that feels like a hybrid between the western saddles everyone here seems to use and the low profile English saddles used in jumping—Olivia's sat down beside me, deftly wedging into the careful space separating me from Caleb. Camden's starting to crash against Caleb, his head pressed into his dad's chest and his eyes unfocused. Melissa stands as soon as the event finishes, grabbing her small clutch and smoothing her shirt. Olivia glances over and then stands, too.

"I'm tired, babe," she says, turning toward Hudson where he still lounges behind us. In the time since everything started, Ethan's joined them, and they've held various low-voiced conversations that the noise of the arena have drowned out. My chest aches as my gaze skates over him and I try to stay as unaffected as he clearly is around me. Hudson nods and stands, helping her to her feet as he lets whatever current conversation between him and Ethan drop away.

"You all right if I grab a ride with you?" Melissa asks. Olivia quickly agrees.

Oh shit. Is Brandon's event next? What had Caleb called it yesterday? Roping? There's already been two roping events but neither of them bothered Melissa.

"You okay with me heading out with them?" Melissa turns to me, pushing her glasses up her nose.

I don't make her explain herself. It's clear enough in her haunted eyes and nervous fidgeting. Instead, I stand and hug her.

"Thanks for coming with me," I whisper.

Her smile isn't as forced when she pulls away, and her eyes lose the sad feel as she flicks her gaze to where Caleb still sits behind me. "Of course, Bri." Her lips curve into a knowing smirk. "You'll tell me before anyone else, or we're not friends anymore."

I roll my eyes and smile. "Nothing's happening."

She snorts. "Yeah, sure." Olivia hooks her arm with Melissa's. "Promise me, Bri. I'll be first."

"First for what?" Olivia asks, her brows drawing close as she frowns. I sigh but nod.

"Promise."

A quick smile flashes across her face and then she turns with Olivia. "Good."

Hudson follows behind them, his hands tucked into the pockets of his jeans.

"Have a good night," he murmurs, touching the rim of his ball cap before following the women up the stairs. I swear there's a growl from behind me. But when I settle back onto the bench and the first man nods to let the chute open, quiet settles over the arena, including our little group.

The audience stands and cheers for the winners one more time. Emily whistles where she sits beside me, quietly taking Melissa's spot after she left. It's almost enough to distract me from where most of my attention has been stuck all night. Caleb doesn't clap, his arms wrapped around Camden where he sleeps, his lips slightly parted and his cheek smashed against Caleb's shoulder. He crashed before the barrel racing was finished.

Even just glancing at them has my breath catching. I've never once felt so inside my own head. Like there's a damn spotlight on me, that every small movement I make is being noticed and acknowledged. Slick coats my scent blockers, and my chest feels hot and tight in a way I haven't felt for nearly a decade. Caleb shifts next to me, and I swallow the small noise my body tries to force out.

The moment the winners leave the arena and the announcer dismisses everyone, I'm on my feet, adjusting the skirt of my dress to keep the trembling in my hands from being noticeable to anyone watching. The rest of the group stands after a few seconds, and Emily loops her arm in mine, keeping me from bolting back to my car. I bite back a sob. Honestly, I'm ready to hide away in my bedroom until the need to throw myself at Caleb lessons enough I can think around it. He turns toward Beau, and his cinnamon scent washes over me. Again.

My thighs clench, and my belly tightens.

My skin itches, and I've had to reapply the lotion twice more over the course of the night. I'm probably more sensitive to it than everyone else, but it doesn't change the fact that the acidic edge of my scent has grown stronger every time Caleb's knee casually brushed mine and his scent was noticeable. Cinnamon and the sweet bite of whatever shampoo he uses. It reminds me of Joan's cinnamon rolls.

"I'll head back with Cam," Caleb says, pulling me out of my thoughts.

"Sounds good," Ethan answers.

Fuck. Me. Even *his* voice is shooting through me right now. I need to get the hell out of here. And then I need to figure out where the charger for my vibrator is.

"We're going to go meet up with Triston and then go out," Emily says. I force my gaze to hers, trying to keep just how much of a mess I am off of my face. Why does she have to be an Alpha, too? The contact on my arm is helping, sure, but God knows she'll be able to tell what's happening with my body.

Like clockwork, her eyes skate down my body and she frowns. "You good?"

"Just tired," I offer. My voice, at least, is calm and confident. And thank God, it's an easy enough excuse to get out of having to be around Ethan anymore tonight when I'm ready to climb just about anyone like a damn tree. I haven't craved a knot like this in... well, since before Brett, really. Certainly not since going on the suppressors when we were engaged.

I run my hand through my hair to dispel the memories. "I think I'll head home instead of going out. Not really feeling up to it tonight."

"We're still going riding tomorrow?" she asks.

When I nod, she drops her arm and hugs me. The itchy feeling settles just a bit.

As she pulls away and joins Beau and Ethan, Caleb says, "I'll walk you to your car."

And there's all that hyperawareness back in the space of a single heartbeat.

Are my cheeks warm? Fuck, I think I'm blushing. Is my breathing normal?

"All right." I manage to keep my voice from trembling.

Emily waves as we start up the stairs, her eyes sharpening on Caleb. Like an idiot, my eyes stray to the man standing behind her. His hands are shoved in his pockets, a muscle in his neck ticking from his clenched jaw. His eyes are trained on Caleb, too. But where Emily's are curious, maybe a bit suspicious, Ethan's are nothing but blazing fury. I duck my head and focus on my feet, trying to settle my breathing as we leave the arena and head toward the large parking areas.

The sun is nearly set, orange streaking across the darkening sky.

Caleb is silent where he walks beside me.

Fuck, do I just straight up say it? I totally understand Melissa needing to leave before the roping, but I can't help but be a little irritated that she isn't here to help me figure out what the hell a person does when walking in the dark with their scent match. Instead, I blurt out the first thing I remember from the ride to the Arch yesterday.

"You're a firefighter?" I ask. Caleb raises an eyebrow but shakes his head.

Before I can apologize, he says, "I'm a pilot. There's not a ton of options for pilots in small towns." He adjusts Camden to his other arm and tucks his hand into the pocket of his jeans. It makes the tattoo on his forearm stand out. "So I work wildfires in the summer and help search and rescue in the winter."

A pilot. That explains why he wasn't in Creek Falls the entire summer I spent here. We get to my SUV before I manage to break the silence again.

"Thank you for walking with me," I offer. It wasn't necessary, but I can appreciate an Alpha's need to be protective.

He murmurs, "Of course, Brielle."

Lightning shoots through me at the way his warm voice wraps around my name.

"My schedule is erratic at best," he says. I take a small step toward him that I hope he doesn't notice, my body demanding more of his scent. "I could get called to a fire as early as Wednesday. But I was curious if you wanted to go for a hike Tuesday?"

My chest flushes. God, where the hell has my ability to talk even gone?

"That sounds fun," I manage. My voice is breathless, though. His gaze darkens. My lotion fails, a small taste of the lavender cutting through it despite my scent blockers. "Where should I meet you?"

"You're staying at Emily's, right?" he asks. When I offer a quick nod, he says, "I'll pick you up around ten."

When I offer a breathless agreement, the silence stretches between us. My eyes drop to his lips for a second.

"Drive safe," he murmurs. And then he turns away and starts heading toward wherever he'd parked.

I slip into the car and send a quick text to Melissa, trying to catch my breath.

We're going hiking Tuesday.

Chapter Sixteen

CALEB

I glance over at Brielle as I guide the truck onto the turn off for one of my favorite hikes. Her hair is pulled back into a high ponytail, revealing a small blue flower tattooed behind her left ear, right where a bonding mark is traditionally laid. Her gaze is firmly locked on the passing foliage, the prairie grass giving way to the pine forest as I take us farther up the mountain.

It's been three days since I've seen her. An impressive feat, really, given how small Creek Falls is. But I've been intentionally keeping out of her path since the rodeo Saturday. It sounds chivalrous, but it's really just self-preservation. I don't trust myself to not behave like a crazed teenager near her. The small moment of smelling her perfume while walking her to her car Saturday night was nearly enough to break me. If I hadn't had Cam sleeping against my chest, I would have at least kissed her. Pushed her up against the door of her fancy ass Land Rover until I could feel every single curve and line of her small body.

Even now, without a single hint of the lavender, all I want is to pull her against me and drown in her perfume. Clenching my jaw and tightening my hold on the steering wheel, I hold back the desire. I haven't brought it up, the scent match. And I'm not about to just put it out in the open with the way Ethan's been seething since the rodeo.

Not until Brielle and I have gotten to know each other better, at least. If I'm going to risk Ethan's wrath, I'm going to make sure she's interested in exploring something between us. Scent matches might mean soulmates, but it doesn't guarantee both parties being interested in a relationship.

As I ease the truck into the small space beside the trailhead, Brielle glances at me. I force my body to relax. It doesn't keep the cinnamon from very clearly filling the cab, though. For a brief moment, her lavender joins. Without a word, she eases the door open and slips out of the truck.

We're the only people here. Tuesdays aren't a huge hiking day even in the peak of summer—which is still a month or so away. Brielle's already to the small sign at the beginning of the trail by the time I grab the bag tucked behind my seat and lock the truck.

"You need anything before we get going?" I ask.

"Could I put my water bottle in your bag? I didn't think to bring my own."

I take the bottle without comment and stash it in the side pocket. As we start down the trail, she stands a few inches away from me, closer than she really has to. Another small taste of her scent reaches me. That's a good sign, right?

Inexplicably, nerves coat my throat and make it hard to breathe. I go hiking with Melissa and Emily all the time. Though they definitely aren't my scent match. And I've never contemplated eating either of them out in one of my favorite spots along the creek. Not that I'm thinking about eating Brielle out right now either. Definitely not. I have no desire to spend the day traipsing through the forest with a damn hard-on.

"I haven't heard of this one," she says once the trailhead has disappeared behind us. "I've been thinking about working through the trails Melissa keeps as suggestions for the ranch guests. I wonder why this one isn't on it."

Is it wrong to bring up Brandon?

Fuck, I'm thirty-five with a kid. This shouldn't be such a damn gray area for me.

I clear my throat and shove my hands into my pockets. I keep my gaze on the trail ahead of us as I say, "If she recommends this trail, there's the possibility of someone requesting it for a guided hike. And Melissa won't hike this one."

Brielle tenses beside me. "Oh," she whispers. "I didn't realize this was one of the ones Brandon loved."

She glances at me, like she's trying to gauge my reaction to her knowing about Brandon, but I'm not entirely sure what she's expecting from me. She's Melissa's best friend. Of course she would know about her brother. Didn't I bring him up in the barn on Friday?

"His favorite, actually. I don't think she's been up here since he was killed."

The trail grows more uneven the deeper we travel, and I grab her elbow when she stumbles over a tree root. My breath catches in my throat, waiting for her instant rejection. Instead, she leans a bit more into me before steadying herself and murmuring her thanks. I can't smell her at all, not even a faint impression of the lavender.

She must be wearing scent blockers today. Or maybe one of those lotions that I've seen some of the Omega pilots use when they don't need something foolproof. She'd used one at the rodeo. Her using a lotion would explain why I was able to smell her in Mom's shop.

I force my thoughts away from her scent, focusing on the hike.

"It's been a long time since I've spent so much time outside like this," she admits a few minutes later. "I'd like to say I'm normally more graceful, but I'd probably be lying."

I can't help but smile. "Tell me if you want to stop and head back."

She shakes her head. "I'm assuming there's a good view at the end of this one? Or a cool landmark like the Arch?"

"Something like that," I say.

One eyebrow arches as she stares at me, the first real glimpse into how she is when she isn't as guarded. It makes my dick twitch.

"There's a meadow along the edge of a creek," I say, chuckling. "I packed a lunch and thought we could set up a picnic."

The trail narrows as the grade grows more intense, and I slip behind her, a hand hovering just in case she slips again. Her breathing grows more ragged, but she doesn't utter a word in protest to the difficulty of the trail. When it splits around a large pine tree, I guide her to the right, and some tension bleeds out of her when she sees it's the path taking a slight downhill route.

"Just a little longer," I offer.

Her shoulders stiffen.

"I'm fine," she says in a tone I haven't heard from her before. It's not the calm and confident tone she used at the rodeo. And certainly not the laughter-filled one from earlier on the hike.

The path widens back out, so I move to walk beside her. I keep my own body relaxed as we traverse the last stretch of the hike before it widens into the flat meadow. The trees clear nearly out of nowhere, similar to the Arch. The creek runs through the center, maybe five feet across most places, mosses and other water-loving plants hugging the rocky banks.

Brielle's breath catches before she murmurs, "It's gorgeous."

I mentally high-five myself. She crosses the open space to the creek, standing on a large rock along the edge. I pull the bag from my back and pull out the blanket, laying it out and then setting the small bit of food in the center.

Brielle glances over her shoulder, and there's a light in her eyes I haven't seen yet today. Some of the anxious lump sitting at the base of my throat eases away. She's having fun. She might be uncertain, but she's enjoying herself. Without saying anything, she settles on the blanket, crossing her legs and braiding back her hair with quick, efficient movements. I force my gaze away and split the food up.

"There's a chicken salad and an Italian hero," I say, holding out both options.

Her lips purse as her head tips, her fingers still working their magic in her hair.

Oh shit. Is she a vegetarian? I didn't think to ask Mom this morning.

She takes the chicken salad sandwich without comment once she's secured a hair tie around the end of her braid. The urge to mess it up, to see how her hair looks splayed out along this blanket, hits me so hard it practically blinds me. The explosion of my cinnamon scent is impossible to control. I spread my legs and lean back on my elbow, ignoring the throbbing of my dick, and let my eyes close. It takes all my willpower to not make the first move, to not verify if she's as affected by this private moment as me. You'd think, with all my flight training, that I'd be more patient. I'd honestly thought I was.

"You said you made these?"

Her soft voice snaps me out of my thoughts. I tilt my head, letting it rest on my arm. The sun gilds her face. It highlights a set of freckles I hadn't noticed before, dotted along the apples of her cheeks. They're nearly the same shade as the amber highlights in her eyes and hair.

"Mom did," I admit. "My cooking is fair to average. But Mom's is fantastic."

And I want her to have the best. There's no reason to subject her to my mediocre peanut butter sandwiches on our first date, even if it's just a hike to one of my favorite quiet places. After a few minutes, she sets the rest of the sandwich aside.

"So was your plan to have a picnic in the forest and then seduce me?" she asks. There isn't any coy playfulness in her question. She's really curious if that had been my plan.

I scoff. "I might not have dated in..." I trail off and actually think back to when I last legitimately dated like this. Was it really when we matched with Kayla? Damn, that was six years ago now. I clear my throat. "Longer than I'd care to admit, actually."

Her gaze grows softer. "You haven't dated since her?"

I shake my head once and then steer the conversation away from Kayla. Talking about dead lovers is not the type of shit they tell you to discuss on a first date. Even worse is the subject of the Omega I was once bonded to.

"I still remember the rules of engagement," I say. "It's a date, not a hookup. I'm not expecting anything. Guys who expect sex on the first date are assholes."

Her lips flick up.

"Fair enough," she says.

She leans back and lets her face tip toward the sky, closing her eyes as a cloud covers the sun.

Her voice blends with the forest when she says, "It's been a long time for me, too. I haven't really had the desire to see anyone after... everything."

"I'm sorry," I say.

She shrugs and drops her head, the soft happiness bleeding away from her. She changes the subject with a finger pointed toward my forearm.

"That's a beautiful piece. Is it of a specific spot?"

I glance at the tattoo that covers my forearm and wraps around my wrist. I nod and swallow back the emotion talking about the place brings up. Holding it out for her to examine, I say, "Yeah, it's my favorite glen."

She tilts her head. "It's not this one, though, right? The trees are farther apart in that one. Like the meadow is bigger..."

Her voice trails off. She traces one of the pines along the edge of the tattoo, and goosebumps race up my arm. Is she upset I didn't bring her there?

"Is this Fool's Canyon?" she asks. "That looks like Fool's Bluff." She traces the rocky ridge that frames the upper side of the mountain meadow.

I nod, trying to remember how to form words, how to breathe, while keeping absolutely still. If I so much as flinch right now, I'm pretty damn positive I'm going to have my hands on her. She runs her finger along another of the trees.

"I've been up there once," she says. "It's beautiful. Different from here. And a lot harder to get to."

She lets her hand drop away from my arm and takes a long, shaking breath. What has her so nervous?

"I never thought I'd find my scent match," she says. Her voice is quieter, a slight waver to it. I freeze. Her throat ripples as she swallows. "It's one of those things the Council frames as largely impossible. But this place has a history of surprising me."

Her shoulders are tense, but her face is clear, her eyes only holding a soft curiosity.

"You're not upset?" I ask.

She shakes her head. "More... nervous," she says. "I spent the majority of the last decade on suppressors married to a Beta. I worry I won't be appealing to someone who's been bonded to an Omega before."

Jesus, that's a lot to unpack. I grab her hand, lacing my fingers with hers. She doesn't pull away from the touch. She doesn't scent, either. Definitely wearing a scent blocker of some kind.

I pull one thing from what she said to focus on for the moment.

"To be fair, I'm nervous, too. And we don't have to do anything at all if you're uninterested." She licks her lips. Cinnamon bleeds out from me. Fuck me, I want to kiss her. "I figured I'd take you out and get a chance to talk without distractions to see if it was something both of us wanted to explore. Perfect biology doesn't mean perfect relationship."

She smiles, her nervous energy melting away as the moment extends between us. I run my thumb along the back of her hand, and a hint of her scent wafts around us.

"Camden's a pretty cute distraction," she says, breathless.

"He is," I agree.

My phone vibrates where it's stashed in the backpack.

Fuck.

If it were any other time of the year, I'd ignore it. But summertime means it's probably Sam calling me in for a fire. Sure enough, a single text from Sam waits in my notifications.

> Fire south of Boise. Big one, just bring
> yourself. Report tomorrow 0900.

"Everything okay?" Brielle asks as I tuck my phone away, dropping it onto silent.

"Just got called to a fire," I say.

She frowns and starts to stand. "Do we need to head back?"

I shake my head, laying back down on my elbow so we're almost the same height.

"I report tomorrow, so we still have today," I whisper.

Her lips curve into a barely-there smile as she settles back in beside me. Quiet settles around us, and I don't rush to break it, content with whatever small thing is starting between us. After a while, her hand traces my tattoo, her touch feather light. I'm not quite sure how much time has passed when she speaks.

"Can I kiss you?" Her voice skates over me, a breeze that carries so much between us.

I offer a smirk as I nod once. She leans over me, and I cup her cheek. Her lips are soft, but she's anything but hesitant. She runs her hands up my arms, tracing the mountain tattoo again before palming the nape of my neck. My dick jumps, and I can't help but moan. She shudders, and then it slams into me all at once, something about her moving making her scent suddenly unfiltered.

Lavender, so strong it feels like I'm walking through a plant store. It's fucking divine, just like the first time I smelled it in Mom's coffee shop and realized what she is. This time, though, there's an acidic edge to it. A growl rumbles through my chest, the need to protect and care for her slamming into me with all the force of a damn freight train. I sit up without a second thought, keeping her pressed against me.

She freezes.

I force myself away from her, dropping my hand from her cheek to her knee. Her face is pale. Her hands shake where they still rest against my arms, and her heart is racing fast enough I can see it beating in her throat. The acidic edge of the lavender bites into me, something I've read about, been warned of, but never actually experienced.

"Brielle," I murmur.

Chapter Seventeen

BRIELLE

Caleb's nostrils flare as I perfume for him again, my arousal too strong for my scent blocking lotion to contain any longer. All I can do is pray he doesn't notice the acidic bite of it that betrays my secret. He breathes heavily, his chest brushing mine, but his hand is gentle where it palms my knee.

His Adam's apple moves as he swallows. Hard.

"You're touch-starved," he murmurs.

Oh no.

I pull my hands away from him as a blush burns my face and neck. How fucking humiliating. Everything had been... damn, it had been magical. And now my body has to ruin it. I spent so many years with a man who didn't even really *like* me, just knew he could trust me with the fortune he amassed once we graduated from college. The last thing I want is something fueled by pity. Especially with my scent match.

The thought sends a thrill down my spine even as I twist

away from him, prepping to stand and head back down the trail. I still have to survive the hike and then the drive back to the ranch with him, and that's maybe the worst part. There's no way I can even look at him right now.

Caleb makes a soothing sound, grabbing my wrist and forcing me to still before I manage more than to kneel. A shiver runs down my spine as he uses a finger under my chin to force my gaze back to him. His gaze is softer than before, the hungry edge gone.

"It's all right," he says, his voice nothing short of a croon. My knees weaken at the affection layering through the words. I run my tongue across my lip, trying to remember how to do anything other than melt into a puddle at his feet.

"I don't want your pity," I say, trying to put bite into the words. I'm only moderately successful.

His eyebrows lower as he frowns, and he squeezes my hand. "Trust me, sweetheart, I'll give you anything you want, and none of it will be fueled by pity."

He pulls me into him again, and for reasons I'm not quite up to examining, I don't resist. I don't do casual hookups. And scent match or not, I can't guarantee that this'll be anything more than a one-time experience. But does my mind care about that right now? Absolutely not.

He snakes an arm around my waist and laces his hand with mine. My knees wedge around his. His cinnamon scent surrounds me, melting into my bones. It eases the edges Brett left, smooths the wounds that never really healed and the insecurities created by realizing the man you loved didn't love you back. For the first time since finding those messages, my chest doesn't burn with the pain of his betrayal.

"Anything?" I ask, my voice breathless.

He drops my hand in favor of cupping my cheek, letting his thumb trace my lips. Warmth spreads out from my belly, and I melt into him, letting my weight collapse against him. He doesn't hesitate, taking my weight and holding me against him. He runs his nose along my jaw.

"Anything." He confirms against my ear. I can't help but shiver. "No expectations. Just pleasure. Just allowing our bodies to do what they're designed for and letting ourselves enjoy what we're hard-wired to crave."

I want to give in, want to know the way he feels surrounding me. I haven't knotted with anyone since that summer a decade ago. Is it just as overwhelming as it was then? A bolt of heat shoots through me, settling between my thighs. Caleb groans as my scent grows even stronger.

God, I want to say yes. And yet... The idea of being only temporary stings, lancing through me with the precision of a bullet.

I duck my head, trying to reel in my thoughts and cool my body. An impossible task when so much of his body touches my own. And the reality is that I *am* touch-starved.

"Tell me, sweetheart," he says.

How do I even convey the mess of everything going on in my head? I'm not about to admit to him that I don't want this to be a casual fuck when I'm not sure if ending up with anything more serious is a wise decision. He's Ethan's pack mate. That can't possibly end well.

"Brielle?" His voice wraps around my name, and I moan, the sound low in my throat. His hold around my waist tightens.

I shake my head.

"I'll tell you a truth, then," he whispers against my ear before he pulls away from me enough that I can see his eyes.

I want to cry out at the loss. His blue eyes are darker than before, so intense it sends a shiver of awareness through me. He eases me back to my knees and tangles his hand into my hair. I swallow, tracing my lips with my tongue, trying to remember how to breathe.

He doesn't continue.

"A truth?" I ask.

He nods and runs his thumb along my cheek. I can't help but lean into him, into the touch. His lips curve, a small half-smile that warms his eyes.

"All I've thought about the entire time we've been here is how you must taste," he says. "Every small catch of your scent has left me so fucking hard I can't focus. And not just today. Every time I've been near you, I'm a half-second from pinning you to a wall and burying myself between your thighs."

He drops his mouth to my jaw, running his lips along my skin before biting the sensitive spot just below my ear. I tilt back on instinct, giving him more room.

"I kept as far away as I could after you agreed to hiking today," he whispers against my skin. "Otherwise I didn't trust that I wouldn't seduce and knot you at the first opportunity."

I suck in a breath and try to turn toward him, wanting—no, *needing*—to feel his lips against mine, but he grabs my chin and forces me to stillness. He kisses the sensitive spot just below my ear, right where so many Omegas carry an Alpha's bonding mark. Right over the tattoo I got in celebration of my five year anniversary.

The reminder sours my stomach and cools my body more thoroughly than a bucket of ice water. He notices, of course. He runs a hand down my side and traces my jaw with his thumb. He croons, a voiceless, warm noise that has my knees weakening. The tension bleeds out of my body again, my body's need becoming too much for even the soured memories of Brett to force away.

Caleb pulls my head farther back, pulling on my hair, and traces his lips down my throat. His lips skate over my collarbone as he whispers, "I need to know if I can eat you better than he did."

I force a swallow. That won't be hard. Brett hated eating me out. I eventually just gave up asking for it. The thought of Caleb between my legs? Of his shoulders forcing my knees apart? My scent surrounds us in a new wave, the acidic edge still betraying my need. He groans against my heated skin.

"And then I need to hear you when you take my knot," he admits against the hollow of my throat. He sighs and bites the sensitive spot where my shoulder meets my neck. I can't help but whimper, and he presses a smile into my skin.

"We're a long drive from a bed," I say.

He laughs, low and deep, before pulling away from me again.

"No one will hear us out here," he murmurs. The corner of his mouth ticks up, a flash of humor lighting his eyes. "But I'm sure I can manage enough self-control to get us to one if you'd prefer it."

Knot him? Out here? I focus on the small creek cutting through the meadow, on the large pine trees that tower around us, on the small birds chirping all around us. He presses his lips to my ear.

"You smell like a fucking dream, Brielle."

His voice drops into a low caress, the words wrapping around me. My thighs clench, and the last bit of my hesitation falls away, the overwhelming need of my body consuming me between one breath and the next.

Chapter Eighteen

BRIELLE

I'm about to let this man knot me in the middle of the forest.

"I'm on long term birth control," I tell him. "An IUD."

He nods. "I haven't been with anyone unprotected since Kayla," he says. "And I got tested after my last hookup anyway. You're safe."

I twist fast enough to break his hold on my chin, capturing his lips with my own. He takes the move as the surrender it is. He lifts me, urging my knees around his waist. His erection presses into me, and I groan. I twist my hands into his hair, locking my ankles, trying to pull him even closer, reveling in the way our scents twine together.

He eases me lower until my back meets with the plush fabric of the blanket. He runs his hands down my legs, squeezing my knees where they're still locked around his hips.

He bites the tattoo behind my ear again, and I can't help but gasp.

"Why flowers?" he asks, his lips tracing down my neck.

I shake my head. There is no way I'm talking about Brett right now. Not on a first date. Certainly not when my body screams with so much need, I'm on the verge of begging. I haven't begged in years.

He hums and bites the pulse point at the base of my throat, pulling the skin between his teeth. I gasp and arch into him, the pain of his bite sending a lightning bolt of heat down my spine. I claw at his chest, pushing his shirt up as far as I can manage. He sits up and pulls it off, dropping it onto the backpack perched at the edge of the blanket. I follow him, scrambling out of as much of my clothing as I can manage, tossing it in the same direction as his own.

His eyes skate over me, soaking me in. For the first time in years, nerves gather in my belly and tighten my chest. It takes all my self-control to not cover my chest and hide from him. It's like he can tell, though, despite hardly knowing each other. He croons, a low, wordless sound that settles underneath my skin as his lips run down my sternum while guiding me back onto the blanket.

I reach for my panties, but he stops me.

"Those are mine," he says. "I get to pull them off of you."

He drops his lips to my hip when I let my hands fall away and twist them into the blanket. Our scents are so strong, not even the open air of the wilderness can dissipate them. They swirl around us, blending so perfectly it should be illegal. Not even the acidic undertone from me being touch-starved ruins the feeling of the mixture wrapping around me. My body aches, the need so intense it borders on pain.

"Caleb," I whisper.

He groans and guides my panties down my legs, dropping

them on top of the pile of clothes. He palms my knees, guiding them apart. His gaze is rapt on me. A hunger sharpens the features of his face and darkens his eyes. The desire to hide is overwhelming again, and I reach for him, needing him over me —*in* me—before that awful voice in the back of my head starts getting any louder.

"Brielle," Caleb growls, low and lethal, "stop trying to hide."

He lowers to his stomach and runs his lips up my thigh before wrapping his arms under my legs and pulling me toward him. He locks his gaze with mine as he pins me in place. His breath skates across my over-sensitized skin, and I can't help but roll my hips forward. He hums, and then his tongue is on me.

I drop my head back, letting my eyes close, as sensation rushes through me, my body ratcheting tighter with each flick of his tongue and swipe of his lips against me. I rub my feet along the blanket, trying to find a way to handle the onslaught. Instead, he redoubles his attention. The feelings overwhelm me. My back arches off the blanket as I moan, the orgasm cresting before I can brace for it. It's so strong that my damn fingers tingle with the aftershocks. He hums and smiles against my skin even as his touch gentles.

Before my breathing evens out, he kneels between my legs, urging my knees around his hips. I focus on him. His lips and chin glisten with my slick, and that embarrassment darkens my cheeks. He smirks, licking his lips, and then fists himself, thrusting against me before guiding the head of his cock to my entrance. He feels enormous, and that's not even accounting for his knot that's just beginning to inflate at the base.

"You're huge," I mutter.

"Don't worry, sweetheart. You can take it," he rasps. "Trust me."

He pushes in as he says it, a slow, steady intrusion that has a moan filling my throat and thoughts emptying from my mind.

He palms my stomach, forcing me still when all I want is to cant my hips and squirm against him.

"Look at you," he whispers. His gaze is locked on where we're joined, his lips slightly parted. The ring of his knot teases my entrance, just swollen enough that I can feel it. "Fuck, Brielle, seeing you stretched around me like this is a fantasy I didn't know I was missing."

The confession rumbles through him, overwhelming the sounds of the creek. He pulls out and then drives back in, harder this time. I can't help but moan, and he chuckles. Sensation races through my body, so strong it's as if the first orgasm never even happened.

Caleb lowers his head as his rhythm quickens. His lips brush against my chest before he pulls a nipple into his mouth, letting his teeth scrape across it in time with his thrusts. I arch against him, whimpering.

"Caleb," I gasp.

His knot teases my entrance, and despite the pleasure he's wringing from my body—again—nerves build in my throat.

"Caleb," I whisper.

He pulls away from me until our eyes lock. His pace doesn't falter, though, and he's hardly even winded. Like he could fuck me all day and not grow tired at all. Slick rushes down my thighs at the thought, soaking us both, and I groan. He drives into me again, and my toes curl. It steals my thoughts until I feel his knot again.

"I haven't been knotted in a decade." The confession falls between pants.

He grabs my hand and laces our fingers together before guiding it above my head.

"A decade? Not even a toy?" he asks. When I nod, he groans. "Damn, Brielle."

He drops his head, letting his lips trace along my jaw. I tilt my head back to give him better access as he pulls my skin between his teeth hard enough that I know it'll leave a bruise. And his voice? It sends a shiver down my spine.

"I'm so close," I admit. He grins against my throat.

"Good," he mutters. "Because so am I."

He lowers to his elbows, keeping his weight off my hand that's still gripped in his. And then he runs a thumb over my clit, hard, sure swipes that have no business being so incredibly perfect.

My mind empties as the orgasm rushes through me, just as strong as the last one. My voice breaks as I whimper at the overload of sensation. Caleb kisses the hollow of my throat as his pace falters. He palms my hip, keeping me still, as he drives into me one last time.

"Shit," he grunts into my skin as his knot swells, locking us together. "Brielle."

My back bows off the blanket. There's nothing but the pleasure of his knot and the weightless sensation rushing through my body. I can't help the shriek that rips up my throat and echoes through the trees. It's not from pain, though. It's from the undeniable pleasure that being with him has coursing through me. His teeth bite down on my shoulder without piercing the skin, and it just creates another wave of sensation.

"Caleb," I gasp. "Oh God. It's never..." He rocks his hips against mine, and I moan. "*Caleb*."

He pulls away from me, rising above me without moving his knot. He kisses the palm of the hand he still holds and then guides it down my body to where we're joined. I can just barely feel the base of his knot. He shudders as I trace it, muttering something I don't quite hear.

"Feel this, sweetheart?" he whispers, his eyes locked on me, the blue of them as piercing as anything I've ever known. He runs his hand down my thigh. "This is what being made for you feels like."

A lump lodges in my throat, a nervous energy stirring in my belly even as my body melts beneath him. Caleb doesn't flinch, doesn't falter. His hand covers mine and his thumb strokes my knuckles. He palms my hip.

"Is that good with you?" he asks.

I force a swallow.

"I think so," I whisper.

The corner of his mouth tips up as his eyes brighten.

Chapter Nineteen

BRIELLE

Olivia's house is tucked into a small neighborhood on the outskirts of Creek Falls. The house is as unassuming as Hudson's restaurant, the same small design touches that give both a warm and welcoming feel. As I pull up to the curb and get out of my car, Olivia opens the front door and stands in the middle of the front porch, her arms crossed and a large smile warming her face. Her hair is pulled back, leaving the silver bond scar just under her left ear visible in the midmorning sunshine.

Something uncomfortably close to jealousy twists in my stomach.

She waves as I cross the space toward her.

"How are you feeling?" I ask as she pulls me into a hug.

"Better," she breathes. "Thank goodness. I was getting pretty desperate."

She wordlessly ushers me into her home and toward the kitchen.

Melissa glances up from where she sits at the large island, a mug in her hands. Her eyes skate over me, catching on my throat, before her lips curl into a knowing grin. I'd spent ten minutes this morning trying to get the damn hickeys Caleb left covered. Are they perfect? No. But at least the average person I run into in town today won't realize I was fucked within an inch of my life a few days ago.

I raise a single eyebrow and purse my lips, trying to keep her questions from starting. Not yet, at least.

Olivia passes me as I settle in next to Melissa, pulling a large charcuterie board and small pitcher from the fridge. She sets the board in the center of the island before grabbing a glass and filling it with ice. She brings both the pitcher and the cup with her as she sits on my other side, setting both in front of me.

"Melissa said you still like cold brew, so I had Joan make some," she says in explanation.

I offer a smile and nod. "Thanks, Liv."

She smiles and grabs a strawberry. She takes a deep breath before eating it, almost like she's offering a silent prayer to the gods. Her face scrunches as she takes the first bite, though, and then she drops it and rushes to the sink.

"This is better?" Melissa asks, her voice filled with the same concern that has a frown pulling at my lips.

Olivia nods as she tilts her head back.

"Yep. I can actually keep down some foods now without medication." Even as she says it, she reaches for a small pill container resting on the window sill above the sink. After a minute, she turns around and focuses on me. "But enough about me and this dang baby that's already thrown a wrench into my life and won't even be here for another six months."

"What happened to never having a baby on a holiday?" I ask with a smirk. "And Christmas, no less?"

She sighs even as she grins. "A stupid, charming Alpha is

what happened. It didn't even happen during my dang heat. If it *had*, we'd be having a baby before Thanksgiving." She purses her lips and leans against the counter. "Hopefully they'll come late and we'll have a New Year's baby. That'll be way better."

I smile. "Yeah, we could use some good news for New Year's."

Her eyes dim and her smile falters. *Ah, crap.*

"How are you holding up?" she asks.

I shrug and focus on pouring the cold brew. I'm getting really tired of everyone asking that question.

An awkward silence stretches between the three of us, and I swallow back my frustration.

"I have some friends coming out in a couple weeks," I offer. Olivia cocks an eyebrow. "They've found a cool spot near the Tetons to go camping. Melissa's coming. I thought you and Hudson might want to come, too?"

She smiles and nods. "Mel brought it up when we were heading back from the rodeo. We'd love to join."

I take a bite of a strawberry.

Melissa bumps her shoulder against mine. "Do I get to ask about that hickey you tried to hide on your collarbone? Or the one that's almost blending in with your tattoo?"

My cheeks flush, and I duck my head, covering the flowers and adjusting my shirt to sit a bit higher. Olivia giggles and settles in the seat beside me again.

"I'd heard he'd taken you out. I wasn't sure if I could believe it though. Joan heard it from Miranda who heard it from Molly. And it's not like she's a trustworthy source nine times out of ten."

"Molly Bailey did *not* manage to find out," I say, putting down the piece of cheese I'd been about to eat. "Please tell me I heard that wrong."

Melissa laughs. "She always manages to find out."

I groan and drop my head into my hands. The last thing I need right now is Molly freaking Bailey getting into my business. It's bad enough that everyone in town knows I'm the widowed Omega. Them knowing I spent an entire afternoon with Caleb Taylor before he left for another round of piloting wildfires? I grimace as I imagine the looks I'll undoubtedly get the next time I have to run to the grocery store.

"It obviously went well, then." Melissa's voice is full of smug curiosity. When I lift my head, she's smirking and tracing the rim of her mug. "I haven't seen you covered in hickeys since college."

I grimace again and shove away all of the memories that single sentence brings up. I'm not thinking about Brett today. Not when I'm still sore from Caleb knotting me even days later.

The memory of him covering my body with his own causes my scent to explode, and I sigh. Melissa laughs, dropping her head back and letting her shoulders shake with her amusement. Olivia smiles, her eyes full of her own laughter. It fades after a minute, though, as the acrid edge of being touch-starved sours my scent. It had faded after being with Caleb, but apparently even just a few days without his touch is enough to have it getting bad again.

"You all right?" Olivia asks.

I shrug. Being touch-starved is not something I want to discuss. Ever.

"Better," I offer.

A set of footsteps cut off whatever Melissa's about to say. Hudson pauses a few steps from the landing, his eyebrows furrowing.

"Everything okay?" he asks. He's dressed in jeans and a plain black tee and looks terrifyingly similar to Caleb, even more so than when I'd seen him at the rodeo. The only real difference is Hudson's well-groomed beard—and the lack of visible tattoos.

Olivia hums in answer, and he cautiously crosses the room, running a hand across her shoulders before kissing her temple.

"Bri invited us to go camping." Olivia smiles at Hudson. He raises an eyebrow as she laces her fingers with his and presses her cheek into his chest, breathing deeply. "There's a group of us going, just south of the Tetons."

"Us?" he asks, amusement weaving through his voice.

"Yes, us," she says, pursing her lips. She pulls away from him and pokes his stomach. "You promised you'd take a few weekends off this summer. I want to spend time with Bri."

Hudson's lips tip into a barely-there smile, and the similarities between him and Caleb become even more obvious. Caleb had smiled like that when he left me on the porch of Emily's guest house, breathless and perfuming for him all over again from his kiss.

My scent surrounds me before I have a hope of controlling my body's reaction, the sour edge more intense this time. I grab the lotion from my purse.

Shit, I need to get better about wearing my scent blockers from now on. Clearly the lotion isn't enough now that I'm off the suppressors. Hudson freezes, and Olivia wraps her arm around his waist.

"Caleb didn't say anything about you being touch-starved," he says, a growl in his voice. An Alpha responding to my body's siren call of need, different from a heat but just as dangerous in the wrong crowd. A bonded Alpha, luckily, is about the least dangerous option available.

I swallow and focus on getting the lotion on every piece of skin I can see. It's not perfect, but it cuts through the worst of it, dulling the lavender until the sour feel of it isn't noticeable anymore. Not to me, at least.

"Don't," Olivia says, her voice hardening. "I'll make you take a vow of silence, Hudson Pierce."

Hudson frowns, his gaze flicking between me and his Omega. After a long stretch of silence, he nods, his eyes landing on me.

"You'll tell me if you need help," he says, not an ounce of give in his voice. "I promised Caleb I'd watch over you before he left."

A warmth spreads through my stomach. He'd told someone to make sure I was safe while he was gone?

I offer a small nod.

"Why didn't he ask Ethan?" Olivia asks. "Since they're the same pack, wouldn't it be easier for him to watch over Bri?"

Melissa grabs my hand, her grip so tight it borders on pain. I breathe carefully through my nose to keep my reaction from showing on my face.

Of course he didn't ask Ethan. Ethan hates me, has hated me for nearly a decade. I was never more than a summer fling for him, something to pass the time. No matter what I felt about him. No matter what I might feel about him now.

I shove the feelings down until I can barely feel the memory of them.

Hudson shrugs before kissing her temple again. "Not sure, darling." He focuses on me. "If you'll text me the information, I'll make sure to have the restaurant covered for camping."

He disappears out the back door before I can offer any kind of reply.

Chapter Twenty

CALEB

It's nearly nine at night when I finally pull into the garage and ease out of my truck. Gone a full week this time. I blow out a breath as I gather my thoughts, trying to find the will to get inside the house and drop into my bed.

It's not even that I'm exhausted, though I am. It's that I can't get the craving for a certain Omega's scent and taste and feel out of my mind—or my body. She might be the one touch-starved, but I need her just as intensely. If Alphas could be touch-starved, I'd bet money that I would be right now. I shove the thoughts away before my dick can get interested and open the door into the mudroom.

Camden's laugh echoes through the house as I toe off my shoes and drop my bag on the small bench that leads to the garage. Some of the stress eases away from me. A hug from my son and a chance to see Brielle, and I'll be just about back to normal.

I follow the sounds of my son, smiling as I step into the

kitchen. Camden's sitting on the island, mixing something in one of the large stainless steel mixing bowls my mom gifted us when we matched with Kayla. Ethan stands just beside him, an arm propped on the island strategically placed to keep Cam from falling. His shirt sits in a heap beside them both, sopping wet.

"Next time, let's make sure that I'm paying attention when you add the water," Ethan says, humor in his voice.

Camden laughs.

"Didn't realize you took up bread making," I say.

Camden looks up and squeals, raising his hands in excitement—and tossing a spoonful of flour onto the floor in the process.

Ethan's voice is dry. "Your family convinced him he wanted homemade cinnamon rolls in the morning. I promised I'd do my best."

I can't help but laugh. "Want me to finish them out for you?"

Ethan hates baking. I'm not overly fond of it, but I'm leagues better than him. To my surprise, he shakes his head.

"I've got it," he says. "My plan is to just make a giant loaf instead of individual loaves anyway. Like pull-apart bread."

Camden starts to stand, but Ethan stops him. I cross the room. Camden launches himself at me, the spoon hitting the side of my head as he collapses against my chest.

"Papa!" he says.

The happiness in his voice has the exhaustion melting away from me. I hope he never loses the excitement he has over seeing either of us. It's a small piece of Kayla we still have.

The thought doesn't burn as much this time.

"Papa, I got to see Bri yesterday with Emily. We played with chalk and bubbles and she let me help put flowers in a vase in her house."

Ethan's mouth tightens at the mention of Brielle. He turns

away, grabbing another spoon from the drawer and finishing what Camden abandoned. I ease Camden back onto the counter.

"I'm glad you had so much fun," I say before kissing the top of his head.

His smile is radiant.

"Let's get this mixed, kid, because it's your bedtime," Ethan says.

Camden turns away from me, scooting across the island until he's holding the large bowl again.

"You want tonight off?" I ask Ethan.

He shakes his head. "It's fine."

With a nod, I pull out my phone and send a quick text to Brielle.

> Can I take you out tonight?

I walk around the island so I can kiss the top of Camden's head again.

"I'll see you in the morning, bud," I say.

He smiles and leans into me. "Love you, Papa."

My phone buzzes with an incoming set of texts. They're all from Brielle. Nerves claw up my throat in a way they haven't in years.

> You're back? Mel said it was probably tomorrow.

> I mean, yes. Definitely.

> What should I wear? And where should I meet you?

I grab my bag from the mudroom and drop it on the floor of my closet instead, stripping out of the sweats I'd switched into as soon as I'd gotten my plane stowed away. As I'm double-checking my hair, I send a quick text back to her.

I grab my keys and head back toward the truck, smiling as Camden's laughter follows me all the way through the house.

~

Brielle crosses her arms as she bites her lip, her eyes darting between me and the half-full dance floor behind me. It makes her tits press against the low neckline of her semi-transparent black top. Cinnamon bleeds out from me at the sight, but I don't bother hiding it. Every few minutes tonight has had me responding to her on such a primal level.

Apparently going out in Denver means something different than here in Wyoming.

I'd expected to see her in a pair of jeans and a dressy top, similar to what I'd donned or what most people wore to the rodeo a couple weekends ago. Instead, she'd walked onto the porch in a black pencil skirt with a side slit nearly up to her hip and a lacy top that shows off a simple purple bralette underneath.

It's a good thing I hadn't gotten a chance to get out of the truck to open her door. Otherwise we probably wouldn't have made it all the way to one of my favorite bars in Jackson.

We've spent the last hour or so sitting at one of the high top tables scattered around the edges of the place. And now I've spent the last five minutes trying to convince her to dance a bit with me. It's not something I've ever had a woman resist before.

"You don't need to know any of the steps," I say, holding out my hand. Her gaze lands on it like it's a snake readying to strike.

"There's tons of other people just learning how to do the dances."

She purses her lips. I take a step closer to her as the music changes. I palm her waist and pull her into me until every inch of her torso touches mine. She's so damn tiny.

"I'll step on you," she says. Her voice doesn't have any fight in it, though.

"No you won't," I assure her. She cocks an eyebrow. It takes all my control to not smirk. I've just about convinced her. "A good partner that can lead makes all the difference."

An emotion flashes across her face, moving too quickly for me to identify. Her look grows more brittle than before. I cup her chin and trace her lips with my thumb.

"You'll have fun with me," I whisper. "I promise."

Her eyes search mine, and I hold my breath as I take a step away from her and hold my hand palm up again in silent request. She breathes a heavy sigh as she rests her palm against mine. I don't waste a second, guiding her until we're in the middle of the dance floor, out of the way of the more experienced dancers that'll take up the edges.

It's like the DJ knows I'm trying to convince her that dancing can be fun because the song slowly fades out, morphing into something slower and more sultry, clearly intended to have couples partnering up.

I wrap my arm around her waist, keeping her pressed against me, as I lead her into a simple two step. She relaxes into me after the first bit of the verse, the worry in her eyes melting away.

"How was the fire?" she asks.

"Big," I say. "It's been really dry this year, so it's pretty easy for them to get out of control."

She nods. I guide her into a spin, and she giggles for a heartbeat. I can't help but grin, happiness lighting my chest.

"Will you have to go back out?" she asks as I gather her into my arms again.

I shrug. "Maybe. It'll depend. My lead knows I'm not really wanting to work more than a week at a time if I can help it. Which is only something I can manage because I've been doing this for so long. Before we had Cam, I'd be gone all summer."

She tilts her head but doesn't say anything.

"So, if after my reset, it's still needing air support, I'll probably go back. But between now and then, lots can change. I wouldn't be surprised if we see several more fires start before July Fourth."

"How long is your reset?" she asks.

The song fades out, and I ease us into a dance that matches the new song's tempo a bit better. She stumbles a bit, and I apologize. She shakes her head and bites her lip.

"A week." I focus on answering her question because otherwise I'm going to have her pinned to the bathroom wall in the back of this place like she's a casual fuck and not my literal soulmate. Even the thought has my dick getting interested. I search for something else to chat about.

"Camden mentioned you hung out yesterday," I offer.

She smiles, a light in her eyes I haven't seen before as she nods.

"You're really comfortable with him." I let the unasked question hang between us.

"My closest friend in Denver has twin girls. I've known them since they were born." She shrugs. "I'm pretty used to being the aunt."

She hadn't lost a child in the wreck that killed her husband, then. Thank God.

"What about being the mom?" I ask.

She stops dead, her eyes widening. I don't push her, don't try to get her dancing again. But I don't drop my arms, either, keeping as much of my skin on hers. I trace her chin with my thumb, and her throat ripples with a swallow.

"I might be persuaded," she says after a full minute. "It's something I've always wanted, though the last six months have dulled the desire for it."

With a nod, I twist my hand into her hair and kiss her. When she's breathless and squirming against me, her hands twisting into my shirt, I pull far enough away to kiss the tattoo behind her ear.

"Come home with me?" I ask.

I don't try to calm my dick down when she nods. Cinnamon explodes around us, following us as I guide her off the dance floor and all the way to my truck.

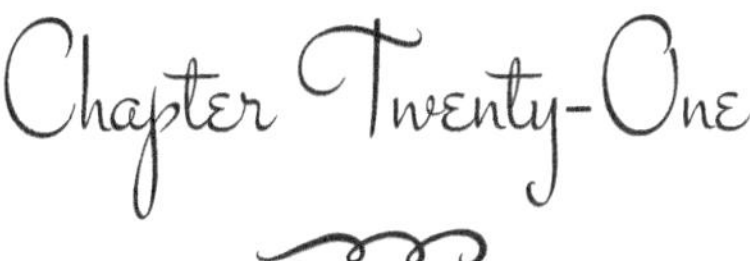

Chapter Twenty-One

BRIELLE

Caleb's lips trace over the tattoo. Again. He pulls the skin between his teeth, biting just hard enough that I gasp and arch into him, tossing my head back. He chuckles, low in his throat, and a new wave of need rushes through me as if he hadn't just knotted me and coaxed three —*three*—orgasms from me over the last hour.

"Why flowers?" he asks, his lips tracing over the sensitive skin.

I force a swallow. It's the second time he's asked about them. Nerves gather in my belly, but not nearly as strong as last week.

"I got them on my fifth wedding anniversary," I whisper. Caleb tenses behind me, his hand flattening against my stomach and pulling me closer to him. "He was a Beta. Obviously there wasn't a way for him to bond with me, so I thought it would be a nice symbol to have."

His lips trace along my shoulder.

"Forget-me-nots are often a symbol of fidelity." The words

taste like ash on my tongue. I'd never had his fidelity, not once his ring was on my finger. He played the part, though, lured me into thinking we would last for our entire lives. "And I liked how they were a small enough flower to not get lost under my hair once everything healed."

"They're pretty," he murmurs. "They look beautiful against your skin."

"I forget they're there most of the time," I admit.

And thank God for that. Every time I catch a bit of them in a mirror, my stomach clenches. I hate that he's managed to ruin part of my own body, too. As if ruining my marriage and my life wasn't enough.

"I have something to show you," he whispers after a while.

I smile and turn toward him, rolling us until I'm astride him. He raises an eyebrow as his hands settle on my hips.

"Something to show me?" I ask.

He lays hard and heavy against me, and I roll my hips to better feel him. He grunts and pushes up into me, his fingers biting into my skin. When I whimper, he pushes up without using his arms and pulls one nipple into his mouth. I suck in a breath and twist my fingers into his short hair.

"Caleb," I gasp.

He hums, the sound vibrating against my oversensitive skin. He palms my thigh before letting his thumb flick across my clit. My knees give out, my body still too sensitive for anything more than a make out session. I suck in my breath, and he lets his touch fall away.

"You had something for me," I say as he pulls away from me, my nipple hardening at the sudden rush of air against it. I can't help but shiver, and he smirks. Without a word, he adjusts me so I straddle his thighs, my weight settled comfortably on him. In the same fluid motion, he pulls a nondescript envelope from his nightstand. The seal is already broken, carefully cut open rather than ripped.

Oh shit. Had a test come back positive? I start to lift off of him, but he tightens his arm around me, keeping me pressed against him.

"It's from the Council," he says, no more than a ghost of a whisper. "I had a chance to stop by the office in Boise while on the fire."

My breath stops, catching in my throat, as nerves flare hot and bright in my chest and sour my stomach.

"It doesn't require that we register as a pair," he continues when I don't say anything. "It's just something I needed to have on file in case something happens and I need extra time off this summer."

I take the envelope in a ginger hold, as if it's a bomb ready to explode at the first incautious movement. Maybe it is. My swallow does nothing to dislodge the lump in my throat, and I lick my lips. A single piece of paper is folded inside, the Council's insignia watermarked along most of the background—the official letterhead. The words take a minute to absorb, and then something deep within me relaxes.

"You had the bloodwork done?" I ask.

Caleb nods, his gaze locked on me, his lips turned down and his eyebrows furrowed.

The reality of what I'd done for Brett, for my doomed marriage, rushes through me in a singular, overwhelming wave.

"I filed as Matchless," I admit, the whisper sitting like lead between us. "Shortly after my wedding."

Matchless meant the Council couldn't do anything about my status as an Omega unless I filled out a ton of paperwork to reverse the decision. They couldn't suggest I go to a Matching Gala, couldn't offer me time off for my heats, couldn't run my blood against the ever-growing bank of samples from willing Alphas to see if my scent match were already identified.

Matchless meant I was alone in this world with no one to help me if things got too hard. I hadn't minded that reality when I'd submitted the paperwork. Now? It was one more thing to lay at Brett's feet and his unfeeling, indifferent heart.

The corners of his mouth tighten, and a flash of something that might be hurt crosses his face before he manages to hide it.

"I'm sorry," I say.

The apology is just as quiet, just as heavy. He croons something wordless and kisses me even as he runs a hand up my spine, his touch soft and soothing. He spins us faster than I can track, pressing me into the mattress.

"It's all right," he murmurs against my skin.

"Really?" I can't help but ask. Alphas are territorial and possessive. Knowing that he can't claim me legally, that we can't have standing with the Council without a monstrous nightmare of bureaucracy? It's something that most Alphas would be incredibly angry about.

He nods, taking the envelope from my hand and setting it on the nightstand before sliding down my body, his gaze growing hot.

"I'll take you however I can, Brielle," he says against my hip. "Starting with against my mouth right now."

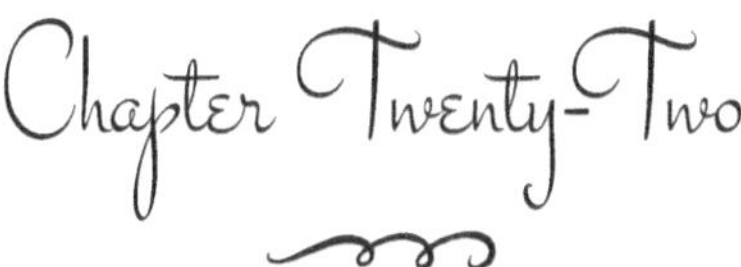

Chapter Twenty-Two

ETHAN

The cinnamon rolls aren't nearly as good as Joan manages, but Camden squeals in delight as I pull them from the oven anyway, clapping his hands where he sits at the island coloring.

"We need to give them a chance to cool before you try one," I say. Camden's eyebrows furrow as he pouts, but he doesn't directly protest. I offer him a smile and then I pull the pre-made icing Joan had handed me when I'd relented about trying to make the rolls last night. Just as I'm finishing covering them with the sticky mess, a set of footsteps echo down the hallway.

And then I hear a second set, and my heart fucking *stops*.

Brielle steps into the large open living room first, her hair messy where it falls over her shoulders, her shape drowned out by one of Caleb's hoodies. Hickeys cover her throat, and that jealous rage boils in me, hot enough it tries to claw up my throat.

I drop my eyes.

Camden screeches a heartbeat later.

"Bri!" he says. "Did you come for the cinnamon rolls? Daddy and I made them last night."

There's a stretch of silence, just long enough that my determination to not see her crumbles a bit. I chance a glance over my shoulder. Her cheeks are flushed, the bright red tracing all the way down onto the small bit of her throat that isn't covered with the hoodie and bruises.

Caleb's focus is on me, his eyebrows drawn low, a smile nowhere to be seen on his face. I scoop one of the rolls onto a plate and set it in front of Camden.

I need to get the fuck out of here before Caleb realizes I'm two seconds from losing my shit on him.

It's bad enough that he took her out a couple weeks ago, bad enough that Molly fucking Bailey found out and so now the entire town knows that he's interested in her. It's bad enough that Camden is already obsessed with her from all the times Emily's ended up having to watch him the last month.

And now he brings her *home*? Marks her and leaves his scent all over her and makes it abundantly obvious that they've spent the entire night fucking each other? All it'll take is one damn comment from Cam and the entire town is going to know that they're hooking up when Caleb's home.

This time, I don't manage to stifle the growl. It rumbles through me, low and full of anger. Caleb stalks around the other side of the island, dishing out a second cinnamon roll and handing it to her. He kisses her temple.

"Why don't you and Bri eat on the porch, bud?" He directs the question to our son, but his eyes are locked on Brielle's.

"Okay!" Camden says, climbing down from the island and then grabbing his plate.

The front door closes a heartbeat later.

Caleb traces her chin, the touch more intimate than a casual hookup demands. His body softens infinitesimally as some of the worry she holds in her body eases away. Worry I can only tell she feels because she's a goddamn Omega and her worries *call* to me like not much else can.

He kisses her, an easy mingling of their mouths. Her scent explodes through the kitchen between one breath and the next.

My growl grows louder, more violent.

Brielle pulls away from Caleb and looks at me. Her face pales, and then she ducks her head and practically runs to the front door, the small plate held in a white-knuckled grip. Caleb growls, low and dangerous. It bounces off the walls of the room. The possessive reaction stokes my rage until it's a burning inferno in my chest. The door closes just shy of a slam.

"What the fuck was that about?" Caleb asks, the growl still a dangerous vibration in his chest.

I ignore his question and cross my arms, turning so I'm not tempted to watch Brielle's retreat from our house.

"What the hell do you think you're doing?" My voice rumbles through the room. Caleb runs a hand down his face, clearly trying to keep his own reaction in check. "It's not enough to come home smelling like her? Now you need to get Camden attached to her? How the hell are we going to explain this to him in another month when you two fizzle out because you get called to a fire for longer than a week?"

"We're not going to fizzle out," he says, the words surprisingly restrained given the rage blazing in his eyes.

"Please," I scoff. "You haven't done more than fuck a random Beta since Kayla died."

He takes a step toward me, his hands clenched tight, the veins on his forearms standing out from the strain of it.

"Because you've made it abundantly clear you aren't ready for anything more. Did you ever think I've been keeping everything to the fucking shadows because you made it clear just last month that you aren't ready to move on?"

"I'm *not*," I growl.

"Then don't move on, but do not imply that this thing I have with Brielle is going to fizzle out, Ethan."

"Then stop lying to yourself about it at least," I say, practically yelling. "She's the new meat in town. You're not even the first one to pursue her since she showed up. You know that? You're probably the fourth man she's fucked here."

The thought slashes across my chest, but I ignore it, clinging to the rage instead. I ignore the possessive flavor of it, though. I haven't had her for a literal decade. I don't need her now.

"She hasn't." Caleb shakes his head. "And you better watch your fucking mouth. You've never once called a woman a whore, and I won't let you start with her."

His voice gains a lethal edge to it, something I haven't heard since Kayla first moved in with us and Alex Dean gave her a hard time. It draws me up short.

"She hasn't been with anyone since her husband, not aside from me," he says. He takes a step closer to me and then another, putting a single hand on my sternum, shoving his index finger into the bone. "I will say this once and only once. She is not the type of woman to hop from bed to bed." He scowls. "Not that there's anything wrong with that if that's the dynamic that's been established, and you fucking know it."

I clench my jaw hard enough a muscle flexes in my cheek.

"And I know it won't fizzle out because she's my goddamn scent match."

The words are a slap across the face, stunning me. I stumble a half-step back.

"What?" I ask, my voice just as shell-shocked as the rest of me.

"It's lavender. Her scent."

Yeah, I already know that. Did I not just mention that he smells like her all the fucking time? Not that I need him to remember the way her scent feels. I can still smell it in my dreams. And sometimes in the shower when I succumb to the need and fuck my hand while pretending it's her warm heat instead.

He pulls out an envelope from the back pocket of his jeans and shoves it against my chest. I grab it on instinct.

His voice is cooler now, the heat of his rage gone. "And she's my match."

He drops his hand and pushes past me, right out the front door and onto the front porch. I twist, staring at him as he closes the distance between him and Brielle where she sits on the edge of the porch with Camden. She bites her lip as he settles beside her, her eyebrows furrowed and her shoulders rolled in. A small smile graces her lips as he intertwines their fingers, and some of the tension in her body falls away.

I drop my eyes. The envelope's already been opened. I slip the single piece of paper out, my stomach dropping as I realize it's an official notice from the Council. I read the words, trying to make them change, reorder themselves.

Holy hell, he's even done the bloodwork to confirm it. They're matches. Literal soulmates. I drop the paper and practically run to the garage, intent on getting to Cottonwood before I can say something I won't be able to take back. Camden waves from where he's playing on the porch, a wildflower in one fisted hand and a piece of chalk in the other. Brielle doesn't look up as I drive past them, but Caleb's eyes are cold and calculating, the rage still simmering just under the surface.

Scent matches.

God help me.

❧

CALEB

Brielle freezes beside me as we watch Ethan disappear down the road and turn onto the main highway in the direction of the Monroe Ranch. Though he could be running off to Jackson, I suppose. Camden sets down the flower he'd picked the moment he came outside and attacks the cinnamon roll with renewed ferocity.

I don't break the silence, trying to ignore the uncomfortable edge of it and enjoy the morning with my son and my scent match. After a while, Brielle sighs and sets aside her half-eaten breakfast. She glances at me, her eyebrows furrowed, and starts to say something before shutting her mouth and looking away, focusing on the swath of mountains that jut out toward the west.

"Papa, can I ride my scooter?" Camden asks.

"Of course, bud," I say, getting to my feet and grabbing both of their plates. "You need shoes on, though."

Camden nods and follows me into the house, grabbing a set of his shoes from the basket beside the door, a pair of socks already tucked into them. I raise an eyebrow but don't fret over it. I'll just add it to my list to get done before my reset ends next weekend. As he rushes back out front, I set the plates in the sink and then head to the garage, pulling his scooter from where it's leaning against the far wall. I take the walk back to gather my thoughts, cool my body, slow the rage that's still seething through my veins.

Brielle's moved to one of the oversized chairs we have positioned on either side of the large window that looks into the living room. Her feet are tucked under her and her shoulders are rolled in, but her eyes hold an unspoken laughter as she chats with Camden next to her.

"Here, bud," I say, setting the scooter next to the stairs. He smiles and runs over, pulling the helmet from where it's looped over one of the handlebars. Instead of having me help him, though, he crosses back to Brielle.

She doesn't say anything, just helps him with a small smile curving the edges of her lips. It fades as he rushes down the stairs and starts down the sidewalk, giggling the entire time.

When I sit on the other chair, she sighs and turns to me. There's a resolve in her posture that hadn't been there before.

"I didn't want to say anything in front of Camden," she says.

My stomach clenches.

"I'm sorry," I say before she can decide that it's really her that needs to apologize for Ethan's asshole behavior. "He had no right to freak out like that."

She offers a sad half-smile and shakes her head.

"He does. I don't like it, but he does."

I frown, and she picks at the strings of the hoodie, adjusting them until they sit perfectly even.

"Ethan and I dated." The words are quiet and rushed, nearly identical to how she told me she'd filed as Matchless. They hit me harder than that admission, though. Confusion races through me.

"What?" I can't help the single word question from falling out of my mouth.

She ducks her head as she grimaces.

"When I spent that summer here during college," she says.

Oh hell, *Brielle* is the nameless Omega he was so twisted up over? I'd come home after that fire season to find Ethan doing his damn best to work himself to death, as angry as I'd ever seen him. All he'd say was that there'd been a girl—and now there wasn't.

I focus on my son, trying to keep the confusing mix of emotions roiling within me off my face.

"It started small. We'd see each other nearly every day since I was staying with Melissa," she says. "He'd swing by most mornings before he and Brandon went out to work the cattle for Misty

Mountain. We'd chat, flirt. And then it slowly morphed into something more."

I glance at her. Her gaze is locked on the mountains again, her teeth biting into her lip. She sighs.

"Anyway, I should have told you earlier instead of letting you be blindsided by him being so angry this morning." Her look is full of apology when she focuses on me, a sad tilt to her lips that's almost a smile. Almost. "The short of it is that I went back to school. He didn't want to make it long distance."

Her eyes give away just how painful it must have been even as her voice stays steady.

How in the world was this not something that was plastered across every single gossip post in town? How had Ethan—and Melissa, clearly—managed to keep the nosy asses from getting word that her and Ethan had dated? Had clearly been at least moderately serious, if her nervousness in telling me and fragile look in her eye are anything to go by?

"He'll deal with it," I tell her, reaching across the open space so I can take hold of her hand. "I'll handle it, all right?"

She nods and then climbs into my lap, tucking her head against my shoulder. Her scent surrounds us, clean and breathtaking. After a minute, the acidic feel creeps in. I wrap my arms around her and kiss her temple.

"I'm glad I found you," I whisper.

Chapter Twenty-Three

ETHAN

"How did the cinnamon rolls go?" Joan asks, a knowing look in her eye.

I cock a single eyebrow, and she laughs even as she hands me a large mug.

"They were edible, at least," I say dryly. "But that might be because of the icing you let us use."

Her eyes glint with her amusement. "But I bet Cam had a ton of fun making them," she says.

Camden nods. "Daddy let me sit on the island and stir them all together."

He looks up from the muffin Joan first handed him and sees the to-go cup in her hands. His eyes light up, but he doesn't say anything.

"That sounds like a perfect evening, then," she says, handing him the cup.

"Thanks, Grammy," he says. He licks the whipped cream before going back to the muffin he's halfway devoured.

The Rustic Roast is busier than I'd expected today—even factoring in that it's a Sunday, only a week or so until peak tourist season. Every single table is full, and only a few chairs are empty around the space. I stand next to Camden, leaning an elbow against the bar that blocks the large window that overlooks the main street. Caleb comes up behind Joan, concern furrowing his brows.

"Hey, Mom," he says. Joan turns toward him and frowns. "Miranda mentioned one of the roasters has been giving you guys trouble?"

"The one on the right. It's been overheating and I'm not sure why." Joan sighs and shrugs. "I have a call in to the manufacturer since it's supposed to be under warranty, but they're backlogged and won't be able to get anyone out for at least a couple more weeks."

Caleb crosses his arms.

She continues, "Hudson said he'd take a look at it when he gets a chance. But between the restaurant and Olivia being so sick, he hasn't managed to yet. The person I spoke to said they'd be willing to reimburse me if I found someone local to do the work since they're so behind."

I know what Caleb's going to say without even looking at him. We hadn't made any substantial plans for today, so I'm not all that worried about it. Especially since he'd drop everything to make sure my mom had help if something needed fixed at the ranch. I take a sip of the coffee and rearrange the plans I'd had for the day.

"I can take a look at it," Caleb says. "Save you waiting for the vendor to make it out from Cheyenne."

Joan relaxes, stress dropping away from her. "That would be amazing. Thank you."

He kisses the top of Camden's head and then disappears behind the counter and into the back of the cafe. The bell over the door jingles, and Joan glances over her shoulder, smoothing down the navy apron she wears. Her face lights up.

Camden looks up from his muffin and then grins, too.

"Bri!" he says, waving.

I close my eyes, trying to keep myself calm. Fuck, is there one place where she can manage to *not* show up while I'm there? First my barn. Then my house. Now not even Joan's cafe is safe enough.

Before I can stop Cam, he climbs down from the barstool and rushes across the cafe. Joan chuckles under her breath beside me.

"He really likes her, doesn't he?" she says even as she picks up the crumbs he's left behind.

I don't say anything, not trusting my voice. Being mean to Joan is like being cruel to a puppy.

"Well, I'm glad. I know Caleb's been nervous they wouldn't get on," she continues, unbothered by my lack of response. She sets the plate on the pick-up counter, and Miranda grabs it, stashing it in the sink along the back wall. "Scent match or not, he wouldn't feel comfortable with it unless Camden liked her."

Caleb told Joan about the scent match? How many other people know? Did he tell me last? Frustration wars with hurt and panic.

That panic—that fear that the entire town is about to find out that they're biological soulmates when we've not even talked to each other since yesterday morning's debacle—must show on my face because Joan rushes to explain.

"He told me just this morning before Miranda and Leanne arrived," she says. "And then swore me to secrecy. I don't think he's told anyone else. He mentioned wanting to wait until everything settles down a bit with the fire season."

I force myself to relax as I give Joan a single nod. He probably doesn't want to leave her alone while the town finds out. Kayla had enough problems when acclimating to living here—and she was a matched Omega with the backing of the Council. Despite the deep-seated pain at the thought, I can't help the reluctant satisfaction of Caleb wanting to protect her as much as possible in this gossip-filled small town.

There's squealing behind me, Camden's voice mixed with others I don't recognize. With a sigh, I push off the bar top and stalk toward my son. Brielle stands with a larger group of people taking up most of the far corner that I'd initially dismissed when we arrived. Two girls crowd her legs, their cheering growing louder than Camden's. A red-headed woman about Brielle's age steps up to her, hugging her despite the girls in the way.

Brielle's smile hits me like a damn brick to the face. It's a miracle I manage to keep walking. This smile isn't like any of the others I've seen since she moved back here—small, careful, controlled. This one is big and bright and unrestrained. It reminds me of the last time she and I were happy in a room together—a decade ago now.

Jealousy seethes through me faster than I can contain it.

"Daddy!" Camden exclaims. "Daddy, can we go camping with Bri and Aunt Melissa?"

He cuts through the crowd of people, latching onto my leg. His eyes are wide, and his lips are pushed into a pout.

"Please," he says, drawing the word out until it's practically five syllables.

I cock an eyebrow as I look toward Melissa.

"You're going camping?" I ask her. She hasn't gone in years, not since Brandon.

She shrugs and pushes her glasses up her nose. "It sounded fun. Pack Bennett got a permit for a large site on the shore of Phelps Lake."

Pack Bennett? My gaze trails to the men still seated around a table that feels much too small compared to them. All three of them are older than me and dressed in similar shorts and polos. The man closest to me, his hair and beard nearly entirely gray, holds a sleeping baby in his arms. A man with black rimmed glasses stands and closes the distance to Brielle, easing one of the girls away from her leg.

"Iris, darling, I know you're excited. But let her sit down first." His voice is a rich baritone that cuts through the noise of the kids. Brielle laughs and hugs the girl again. She tries to take a step toward the table but trips over the other girl. The man catches her with a hand under her elbow, and she falls into him.

"Sorry, Carter," she says.

He smiles and helps her regain her balance.

The growl rises in my throat too fast to tamp out. Melissa's face pales as her eyes widen. The men still at the table tense, their eyes locking on me.

"Daddy?" Camden asks, not noticing my slip up the way everyone else has. "Can we go?"

"I need to talk it over with Caleb," I say, hedging around an outright no. My voice is still too deep, carrying the jealous growl.

Stuck with Brielle in a finite space without an escape hatch? Absolutely the fuck *not*. But it's not like I can actually say that without causing a fuck load of problems.

Camden sighs but nods, pulling away from me and going back to Brielle.

"Daddy says he doesn't know yet," he tells her even though she heard me just fine. "If we can, can I stay in your tent?"

That growl rips through me again. Jesus *fuck*, I need to get that under control.

The red-headed woman frowns as she stares at me, her hand combing through the little girl's strawberry blonde hair.

"Aunt Brielle?" the girl with strawberry blonde hair says. Her voice is calm and collected, way more so than I'd expect from a kid so young. She can't be much older than Camden. "Can we see your house? Iris and I made stuff for it."

Brielle nods, not looking at me. Melissa's eyebrow is raised, though, suspicion lighting her face.

"If it's all right with your parents," Brielle says. "I'd love to see what you have."

Both of the girls look to the man with the beard.

"Why don't you all go see it? I'll head to the rental with Dahlia so she can finish her nap," he says, his voice smooth and low.

That seems to satisfy everyone. The group stands and clears out of the cafe with an impressive proficiency I've never managed with just one child—much less three. Melissa grabs Brielle's hand as she turns to leave.

"You want some company tomorrow?" she asks.

Brielle grimaces.

Melissa sighs and squeezes her hand. "All right. Text me if you need anything."

Brielle nods, and then she's gone, too, the bell over the door jingling as she leaves. Joan brings Camden's hot cocoa over to him, and he smiles as he takes it. Not a minute later, Caleb comes out from the back.

"Looks like a sensor that went bad," he tells Joan. "I have the part number. Should be an easy swap."

Joan nods and takes the small paper from Caleb.

"Thanks, Son," she says. She turns to Melissa and tucks the slip of paper in her back pocket. "If I send you with a small basket, can you drop it off with Brielle?"

Melissa nods. "Of course, Joan."

"Gift basket?" Caleb asks.

Joan shrugs. "Just thought it might help make tomorrow a bit better."

I shove my curiosity away. Not that it matters because Caleb lets his run the show.

"What's tomorrow?" he asks, crossing his arms, a frown pulling his lips down.

"Oh, it's her anniversary," Melissa says.

That jealousy surges in me again. This time, I force it far enough down I can't feel it at all.

Chapter Twenty-Four

CALEB

Brielle's sitting on the porch of the guest house when I stop the truck on the gravel drive. Her hair is down today, the strands resting along the deep v neckline of her dress, a few pieces falling across her arms as she stares out at the mountains in the distance. She's traded her typical jeans and oversized shirt for a pretty sundress, the blue linen rustling in the breeze. Her feet are bare, a small gold anklet draped around one dainty ankle.

She's *stunning*. She always is, though. She could be freshly woken up and her hair a mess, and she'd still leave me in this half-hard, breathless state of awe. And wearing only my shirt?

That might just be my favorite.

My phone vibrates with a new message, pulling me from the moment. I scowl. And then my stomach drops as I read the name. Sam is absolutely *not* the person I want to hear from today. Or the rest of the summer, really. I've never been irritated with the fire season as much as I am right now.

> Official notice, man. Another one broke out.
> They're overriding resets. Arrive by 2300.
> Northwest of Cheyenne. I'll send you the
> exact location.

I send him a quick response before shoving out of the truck, tightening my hold on the bouquet as I stash my phone back in my pocket.

Is bringing flowers to a widowed Omega on her anniversary something a new love interest should do? According to the internet, absolutely not. Though there was a dearth of information that added the context of said widowed Omega being your scent match, so I'm taking it all with a grain of salt. Besides, the reality is that the thought of her spending any part of today alone and sad wrecks me. Especially when I'm literally wired to be the perfect balance to her.

So here I am.

I pause at the bottom step. She doesn't notice me, her eyes unfocused, so I rap my knuckles against the support beam. Her gaze flicks to me. A heartbeat later, her cheeks flush. I swear I smell lavender, but the breeze sends it away from me before I can really breathe it in.

"Hey," I offer, leaning against the beam and shoving my empty hand into the pocket of my jeans.

"Hi." Her voice is shy. Her eyes drop to the flowers in my hand, and her teeth dig into her lip. "Melissa told you?"

"Mom did."

"Oh," she whispers, her eyes still locked on the flowers.

"Can I join you?" I ask.

She adjusts on the swing, moving until she's pressed up against one arm. She motions to the newly opened spot beside her. I settle next to her before handing her the flowers.

"They made me think of you," I offer when she turns a questioning gaze toward me. "And purple is your favorite color."

Her cheeks grow even darker, and she tucks a strand of hair behind her ear. She murmurs a thank you as she grabs them, her fingers brushing mine in a touch so intimate, it takes my breath away. Her chest flushes. She glances away as she lays them across her lap.

I let the silence linger, not rushing for a topic of conversation. As the minutes pass, she relaxes next to me, adjusting in the smallest increments until she's turned toward me rather than the view, her hair resting over one shoulder and her feet tucked up under her, the skirt of her dress hiding her legs.

"You want to talk about it?" I ask.

She shrugs. "I feel like all I've done this year is talk about it."

Yeah, I remember that feeling. Everyone pesters you, wanting you to just *open up* as if it's as simple as popping the lid off a can.

"I remember that part," I murmur.

I blow out a breath and spread my arm along the back of the swing, letting a piece of her hair twine around my finger. She pulls her gaze away from the mountains, her face a master class of concentration. I let my eyebrow rise and my thumb run along the nape of her neck. She shivers under the attention, and my dick twitches.

Damn, bad move. The last thing I want right now is to be stuck with a painful erection.

"That's why you always phrase it as a question, isn't it?" she asks after a while.

I offer a quiet affirmative. She nods, then lets the sounds of a ranch in the summer reclaim us. I relax into it, letting my thumb continue its light tracing of her shoulder and neck. This time, I can smell the underlying aroma of her scent, the lavender calming and arousing all at once.

I lose track of time.

Her voice pulls me from the quiet, and I focus on her.

"I hate him," she says.

Confusion fills me.

I frown. "Ethan?"

She shakes her head. "I've never hated Ethan. Not even when it would have been easier," she whispers. And then, even quieter, "His name was Brett."

Oh, fuck, her husband.

"He died in a car crash. The only person to not survive. I... I think people expected me to be distraught over that, so they didn't find it odd when I was angry at his funeral." She's quiet for a long moment. I twist more of her hair around my hand. "I'm glad he's dead."

Unease sours my stomach. Everything I've learned about Brielle over the last few weeks is at odds with her being happy over someone's death. She's so soft, so empathetic. What had happened that she's glad he was killed?

"Why is that?" I ask.

Her hand tightens around the flowers, her knuckles whitening. She takes a stuttering breath, and then her shoulders relax.

"You smell like Christmas," she whispers.

I chuckle, and she cuddles closer, running her open hand down my leg. Her scent spikes, and it has a bit of that acidic edge to it. She's still not quite over being touch-starved. I let go of her hair and trace my hand down her waist before palming her hip. Slowly, her scent sweetens again.

"He had a mistress," she says out of nowhere.

I freeze. "What?"

She swallows. "Yeah, that was my reaction, too. His business partner's assistant. It was an open secret that I was too naive to figure out. Until she texted him while his phone was on the counter right before we were about to host everyone for Thanksgiving."

I have to breathe through the rage. Her words come faster

but quieter, like she can't bear to keep them in but they hurt even as she says them.

"They were nudes. I went digging when I saw the first one. Turns out that she'd been fucking him nearly the entire length of our marriage. The first message was time-stamped three months after we got back from the honeymoon."

The growl rumbles through me before I can hold it back, and my scent gains a sour edge to it, poisoned by my rage. Brielle sits up, focusing on me.

"He married me because he could trust me with the money," she says, her eyes not straying from mine.

There's a desperation in them, like she needs me to hear the entire story even though she knows it'll only stoke the flames of my rage. I swallow back my growl, forcing it to quiet. She flattens her hand against my leg.

"We started dating my sophomore year of college. We had a class together, but he was a year ahead of me." She swallows. "We got engaged the summer before my senior year and then married shortly after I graduated. I made him move our original date because of Melissa's dad dying."

The pieces fall into place all at once.

Holy hell. Ethan had never moved on from her, not really. Not until he must have seen an invitation somewhere. Melissa's house, maybe? That was the summer he finally agreed to register as a pack with the Council so we could try our luck at being matched with an Omega. Less than a year later, we'd had Kayla.

Her nails dig into my thigh.

"I served him divorce papers a couple weeks after I found the pictures. They weren't finalized by the time he died, though," she says, skipping over her marriage. "It took me finding those texts to realize just how much I'd changed, how much I'd let him take from me."

She sighs and looks down at the flowers.

"I don't really know how to feel today. Last year, I thought I'd be starting a family by now. But all I can feel when I think of him is bitterness and anger."

"I'm sorry," I offer. Her gaze flicks back up to mine, her eyebrows furrowed in confusion. I lean into her, cupping her face, running my thumb along her cheekbone. "You deserve to be cherished exactly as you are. He was an asshole for not seeing that you're perfect."

Her lips twist into a mocking smile. "I'm not perfect," she says.

"We'll disagree on that, then." I shake my head and kiss her once.

Her lips push into a pout, and I run my thumb over them. After a minute, her body relaxes, and she gives me a real smile.

"Sorry to put all of that on you," she says. She adjusts until she's leaning against me again, her cheek pressed into my shoulder.

I shake my head. "I'm glad you told me. Now I don't feel conflicted over bringing you flowers today."

She turns her face into my chest, breathing deeply. She perfumes in the next moment, her lavender smell a siren's call to me, and I groan.

"Maybe we could make better memories," she whispers.

Before I can decide exactly the types of memories she means, she sits up and kisses me. Cinnamon explodes around us, blending beautifully with her scent. My dick is hard in a heartbeat, straining against my jeans. I hum and palm her hip again.

She smiles against my lips, and then she's crawling into my lap, the flowers forgotten on the bench beside us. She pulls up the skirt of her dress as she straddles my hips, and I see a flash of black lace against the creamy warmth of her skin. She hums, her teeth biting into her lip, as she pulls at the waistband of my jeans.

"These aren't loose enough for that," I whisper against her lips.

She whines, low in her throat, and undoes the button and zipper, dropping her hand beneath the waistband and palming my dick. I grunt and push up into her hand.

"Caleb," she says, her voice a breathless plea.

"Yeah, sweetheart?" I ask. I need to hear her say it, need to hear her ask for it.

"I need you." She palms my dick again and rocks her hips forward.

I run my hands up her sides, the fabric of her dress soft under my touch. Not as soft as her skin, though. My scent explodes around us again, and she whimpers.

"You have me," I say with a smirk.

Her lips draw into a pout as she sits back, her hand stilling against my dick. Her lips are swollen, her cheeks red, and that sad, haunted look has disappeared from her eyes.

"That's not what I mean."

It comes out a whine, and I smile. It takes all my control to hold in the laugh, but her eyes narrow like she can tell anyway. I spread my hands along her waist, letting the tips of my fingers brush the undersides of her breasts. She shivers, and her scent overlays mine, thicker than before.

God, I want to fuck her. Pull aside those panties and push up into her until she moans loud enough that Emily can hear her across the open space. But not yet. Not until I hear her ask for it, beg for it. Just once.

"Tell me, sweetheart," I say again, running my hands down her thighs and then back up, pushing the skirt of her dress up to her hips. "Let me hear you ask for it."

"I need your knot," she says, pushing my shirt up my stomach. Her lips are hard and demanding against mine, and I let her control the kiss, tasting her every second she lets me. "Please, Caleb."

I grab her thighs and stand up, pulling open the screen door even as she wraps her arms around my neck and kisses me again.

I've never actually been inside Emily's guest house. It's decorated in soft greens and yellows, the warm colors blending with the dark walnut stain that trims all the windows and doorways. The kitchen is a light oak that contrasts perfectly against the darker wood.

I cross the living room, bypassing the sofa for the promise of the bed I can just see inside the room farthest from me. This room is also done in muted earth tones. It reminds me, of all things, of Ethan's tattoos, like she took a picture of them and recreated them in linens and textures. This room has more personal touches than the living room, small pieces of artwork and a broader, unnameable *presence* that makes it feel more intimate than just a bedroom. There's no missing that this is where she's nested.

I hesitate at the threshold, not wanting to intrude.

"You all right with me being in here?"

She nods, running her lips across my jaw.

"Please," she whispers against the shell of my ear. I shiver and hold her tighter. "Mark it. Give me your scent."

I groan and close the door behind us, a byproduct of living with a preschooler. Her lips are more frantic against mine now, her tongue moving against my own in a way that tells me exactly how she wants this to go down. Lavender drowns the space, so overwhelming it's practically a drug.

She bites my bottom lip, and my control falls away from me. Cinnamon explodes around us as I drop her to the bed, burying my hands in her hair before she can move away from me and lay back on the pillows.

Chapter Twenty-Five

CALEB

Every time I'm with her, it's as thrilling as that first time she let me lay her out on that blanket and knot her in the middle of the forest. Her breaths come in short, shallow pants as I ease the dress over her head, tossing it into the corner of the small room. She pushes down my jeans and underwear, her hands wrapping around my dick the literal second it's freed from the constrictive fabric. I can't help but groan as she squeezes my base, right where my knot is just starting to inflate.

And then we're a frantic movement of bodies. Her limbs are long and lean where they stretch along the bed. I undo the front clasp of her bra, not bothering to move the straps off her shoulders before closing my lips around one nipple. She bows off the bed on a strangled cry. As I ease the fabric off of her, I focus on her other breast, giving it just as much attention. Before pulling away, I scrape my teeth across the hardened bud of her nipple and grin as she whimpers.

Her bra ends up in the opposite corner as her dress, tossed

carelessly over my shoulder. I nudge her knees farther apart with my own as I strip out of my shirt and toss it in the same general direction as her dress. Her hands twist into the bedspread above her head.

She's gorgeous. Like every fantasy I've ever had, every centerfold spread that's existed for men's eyes, laid out before me for my own enjoyment.

"You're so fucking beautiful, Brielle," I mutter.

Her throat ripples with her swallow, but she doesn't shy away from me. Instead, she tilts her hips toward me in universal question.

Her skin is smooth as silk as I duck my head and run my nose along her thigh. I press my nose into the lace covering her cunt, breathing in her scent—lavender, salt, and woman. It's like a drug, rushing through me and making me ravenous. I bite the lace panties and then pull, ripping the delicate fabric at the seams.

"Holy crap," she gasps. "You did not just rip my panties."

I chuckle, the sound full of hunger, and then trace the line where her thighs meet her core with my tongue.

"I absolutely did," I say against her skin. "They were in my way."

"Caleb," she whispers. Her hand twists into my hair, her nails running along my scalp. I nip at her inner thigh, and she rocks her hips toward me. She shudders in a breath. "Caleb, those are —were—La Perla."

Hot damn. I didn't realize she'd wear anything that expensive when she wasn't even expecting to see me. Shit like that is what women wear when they're wanting to impress the person fucking them. Had she been hoping I'd stop by? Had she worn them on the off chance we'd run into each other in town today and I'd fuck her in my truck?

The thought has my voice dropping, filling with the hunger coursing through me.

"Sweetheart," I mutter, "they could be made of real gold, and I'd rip them to shreds right now."

A rush of her slick coats her skin, and I groan. The next moment, I have my mouth on her, tasting every single inch of her I can. She's so damn *sweet*. I'll never be able to get enough, certainly not right now. Her legs start to shake, and I double down on my efforts, running my tongue across her clit while palming her knees, keeping them from closing around me. I want to be able to see her as she comes. I scrape my teeth across her clit, and she arches on a desperate gasp, her feet digging into my back.

I rise over her before she's gotten a chance to really come down from the orgasm, wrapping her legs around my hips and then twisting us. My back lands on the plush mattress as her hands splay across my chest.

"Caleb," she gasps. I grin and mess with her nipples, a feral need overcoming me as I watch them tighten into tight buds begging for my mouth.

"Ride me, sweetheart," I command her, low and fervent. She perfumes again, and I grunt, the need doubling over again. "Use me to make better memories."

Her chest shudders with her sudden deep breath. And then she's moving, her nails biting into my chest as she chases her pleasure.

Holy god*damn*, she's gorgeous. Her lips are red and swollen, and her eyes are hazy with her need. Her hair spills over her shoulders and down her front, blocking her nipples as she leans forward to change the angle. She clenches around me, so hot it's like a branding fist around my dick. I shove up into her, trying to get deeper, get under her skin the way she's under mine.

Her movements grow more unsteady as she gets closer to her orgasm. I palm her hips and take over, pushing up into her until her legs are shaking all over again. As soon as her body locks, her head thrown back on a desperate moan, I let myself fall apart, too. The orgasm races through my veins, so intense it robs me of sight for a heartbeat. My knot swells, and I pull her down tighter over me, forcing it all the way inside.

She collapses against my chest with a scream. Satisfaction roars through me. I kiss her temple and comb through her hair, easing her down from the extended bliss of our knotting. She shivers and burrows deeper into my chest, wiggling until her arms are under my body and playing with the strands of my hair.

"Thank you," she whispers.

I close my eyes, not trusting my voice. I kiss her temple again, and she relaxes against me.

"I'm going camping this weekend," Brielle says, her cheek pressed against my chest and her hand resting on my stomach. "Melissa's going, too. And Olivia and Hudson. There's a spot some of my friends know about south of the Tetons. Would you..." She trails off and takes a deep breath. "Would you like to come, too? Camden would be welcome. Faedra's girls are five, so they're about the same age. I'm sure they'd love to have another person their size."

Her words grow closer together until they run over each other, her voice rising with her nervousness. I pull her into me and press my lips to her temple. She quiets instantly, the tension in her body easing away.

"I've been called to a fire," I say, making sure my voice is heavy with my regret.

Did I think I regretted Sam's text an hour ago? I absolutely resent it now.

"Oh," she whispers. "When do you have to leave?"

"Tonight."

"And you don't know when you'll be back?"

I shake my head. "It's a small localized fire burning north of Cheyenne. So it's possible I'll be back in time. But I can't promise anything."

"That's all right," she says, offering a small smile that doesn't touch her eyes. I tuck a piece of hair behind her ear and offer the same half-hearted curve of my lips. She settles back against me, her hands tracing down my side.

I grab my phone from the side table and send a text I've never actually sent to Sam before.

> I'll be there. I have to be back by Thursday, though.

> Scent match things?

> Yep.

> You willing to file the Council's announcement? It'll get you more time off than just the confirmation info.

Goddamn, I wish I could. But I can't file anything unless Brielle does, her Matchless status with the Council making it impossible for me to make any of this official with them. Sam is an Alpha, though, so he'll understand it. Probably.

> It's on my radar. Can't do it quite yet.

> Ah. Got it. No promises, but I'll do what I can.

I send off a quick thank you and then stash it away again, running my hand along her thigh. She twists into me, burying her face in my chest. Lavender surrounds us, overlaying the older smells of our knotting. My dick twitches, but I ignore it, focusing on the feel of her skin under my hands and the brush of her hair against my cheek.

"Brielle," I whisper, turning until my lips are against her temple. She hums and wiggles against me.

I love you.

Fuck, it's too early to be saying those words. But that doesn't stop them from sitting on the tip of my tongue, ready to spill out at the first moment. I trace shapes along her hip to keep myself from being an idiot.

Her scent strengthens again, and I groan. She presses a giggle into my skin even as she traces my happy trail with a featherlight caress. My dick twitches, and I press my hips up, encouraging her lower. She gives me open-mouthed kisses down my sternum as she adjusts, rolling until she straddles my thighs. Her hair falls over her shoulder in a beautiful wave. I sink my hand into it, twisting the strands around my palm until I can see her eyes.

She glances up at me through her lashes, her hand flattening against my hip. My breath saws out of me as I nod in silent permission. Her lips brush along the underside of my dick, and I drop my head back on a groan.

A girl's laughter cuts through the quiet cabin. A moment later, a baby's cry does, too, followed by a low murmuring—a man's soothing hum. Brielle freezes, her eyes so wide I can see the whites all the way around.

Footsteps on the porch echo all the way to the back of the cabin.

Brielle squeaks as she pulls away from me. I drop my hand out of her hair before it can hurt her as my groan turns mournful. Her cheeks flush a dark red as she pulls her dress from the floor and disappears into the bathroom, though she leaves the door open. I run my hand through my hair as I sit up and pull my own clothes from where I'd left them on the floor near the foot of the bed, sliding back into my jeans and shoving my phone into the back pocket.

Once my shirt is back on, I run my hand through my hair.

Three knocks on the door have Brielle muttering a curse.

"Brielle? Is now still a good time?" a woman says. It's not a voice I recognize.

"One second," she calls. Her gaze catches on me, and she blushes again, the red tracking down her throat and onto her chest. I raise an eyebrow before leaving the bedroom, crossing the small guest house.

A woman about Brielle's age stands on the porch, two girls maybe a year or so older than Cam giggling as they run around her legs. Beside her, a blond man holds an older baby against his chest, her eyes red and her hand pressed into her mouth. The wind cuts through the house. Brielle must have opened a window in the bedroom.

The mingled scents of lavender and cinnamon waft around us, betraying what we'd been doing to anyone that isn't a Beta. The man doesn't even blink, an eyebrow rising as he takes me in.

The woman clears her throat, blushing nearly as deeply as Brielle.

"Sorry, we didn't mean to interrupt," she says. Her blush gets deeper before she groans. "Logan, save me."

The man laughs and pulls her into his side, wrapping his arm around her shoulder.

"We're supposed to be meeting Brielle for a tour of the chicken coops."

"She'll be out in just a minute," I offer, leaning against the threshold.

Not even thirty seconds later, Brielle slides past me and eases her way onto the porch. Her dress is a little wrinkled, and my scent clings to her even with her own hidden by her scent blockers. A dark bruise sits just under those damn flowers. That deep part of me that needs her to be mine, needs to claim her, settles at the sight. She'll have a new mark that won't be gone for at least another week.

The women hug as they greet each other, and both of the girls grab onto Brielle's legs.

"Is this him?" the woman asks, glancing back at me.

Brielle nods and takes a step back, not bothered by the young girls vying for her attention. No wonder she's so comfortable with Cam.

"Caleb, these are my friends Faedra and Logan," she says. "Faedra, Logan, this is Caleb."

I offer my hand and an easy smile. Logan takes it in an easy grip. Faedra runs her hand through her hair, moving it off her shoulders, revealing two silver bond scars along the left side of her neck.

"Nice to meet you," she says.

I wrap an arm around Brielle's waist and pull her toward me, kissing her before she can protest. She melts into me, and I smile against her lips.

"I'll see you when I get back," I say.

Her happiness dims as she nods. "Be safe."

I carry the words with me all the way to my truck and down the gravel drive.

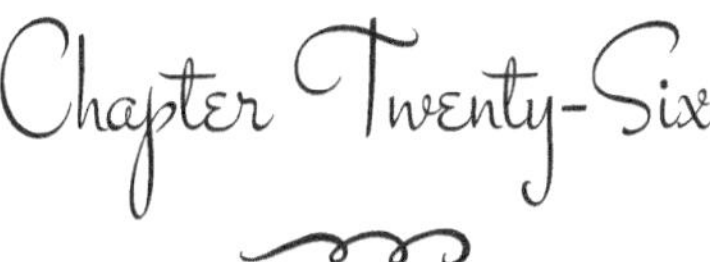

Chapter Twenty-Six

BRIELLE

Iris stands just next to me, her grip tight around the small vase full of wildflowers her and Rose had spent all afternoon picking around the guest house today. Rose giggles as she rushes past us and right off the patio. A moment later, and Jude rushes out of the house behind her, chasing her down and scooping her up into his arms. She squeals as he gives a raspberry against her belly.

"Papa, stop! Stop! It tickles!" she screams.

He laughs and sets her down. Her lips quirk, and then she's off again, running around the side of the house. Jude laughs and follows after her.

I turn my focus back to the table, smoothing out the table cloth and folding back the first corner. Faedra steps onto the patio, a roll of heavy duty tape in her hands.

"Found it," she says.

She tears off two strips of the tape and hands them to me, holding down the fabric as a gust of wind rips through the yard. I tape down the corners as fast as I can manage. Just as I'm taping the last one, someone calls through the house.

"Knock, knock." It's Melissa's soft voice.

Faedra and I look up just as she rounds the side of the house. She has two large platters in her hands, balanced carefully, one atop the other. Logan rushes to her and takes them.

"Here, I can take those," he says.

Melissa smiles and digs something out of her purse. "Here, I made labels for them, too. One is vegetarian. Olivia doesn't eat meat."

Logan takes both small cards from her without jostling the trays. As he turns toward us, Melissa focuses on me. She crosses the yard and hugs me before saying a quick greeting to both Faedra and Iris.

"Everyone should be here soon," she says. "Emily is just leaving the ranch. She had to get the horses squared away for the night after Ethan finished with them."

"That should be perfect timing. Carter planned on starting grilling right around six." Faedra smiles and smooths down the table cloth one more time. She adjusts the tape on one of the corners before turning to her daughter. "All right, Iris. Let's get that one situated and grab the other one."

Iris skips off into the house once she sets the first vase on the table. As soon as she's out of sight, Faedra leans in and lowers her voice.

"Did you get the bloodwork done?" she asks.

I shake my head and mess with the flowers in the vase. It's either that or tear apart my finger nails, and I don't really want to be dealing with cuts on my hands while we're camping and relying on hand sanitizer.

Faedra frowns. "You don't want to know?"

"Oh, he already did it," Melissa chimes in. "But that's pretty secret still."

Surprise lights Faedra's face. "He did?"

My stomach twists as I realize they're talking about different men.

"Oh, yeah. Caleb got it done, like, a week ago," Melissa says.

Faedra cocks an eyebrow, but I shake my head as subtly as I can. Please don't bring up Ethan right now. *Please.* Faedra frowns and casts a quick look toward Melissa. I shake my head in answer to her unspoken question.

"Oh," Faedra says. She takes a deep breath and then changes the subject. "Jude's going to try and have us out the door by eight tomorrow. We'll see how Dahlia does. But we should be at the campsite by ten at the latest to get everything marked off and prepped."

I smile and tuck a strand of hair behind my ear. "Perfect. Melissa and I can plan to be there by then, too."

Another couple voices carry to the backyard. I twist in time to see Hudson, Beau, and Olivia round the house, more food in their arms, too. Faedra squeezes my hand in silent support. I wave to the group as we close the distance with them.

"Hey guys. Have you gotten a chance to meet Faedra yet?" I ask, keeping my voice from betraying my nerves.

CALEB

By the time I make it back to Creek Falls, the evening air is crisp and the sun is only an hour or so away from dropping below the mountains. There's an entire hoard of cars blocking the driveway of the address Melissa gave me, so I pull up to the curb about half a block down. The house is one of the known rentals in the heart of town, only a block off of Main. I grab the grocery bag from where I had tossed it onto the passenger seat and slide out of the truck, taking a minute to stretch my neck and shake out my legs.

My phone vibrates, and I check it as I lock the truck and start down the street. It doesn't surprise me to find a text from Melissa.

Hey, are you still coming tonight?

Brielle is talking about heading out early. I'll keep her here if you want, though.

Just pulling up now. Don't make her stay if she doesn't want to.

Maybe I should have told Brielle I managed to finagle a way to get the weekend off so I could go camping with her. But I wanted to actually see her face when she found out. The downside of trying to surprise your scent match? It might not actually work. At least I am here and trying. Even if it's just a single hug as she's leaving, it'll be enough tonight. I just need to see her, feel her, kiss her.

The gate leading to the backyard is open. I slip through it, following the sounds of kids laughing. There's a large fire pit centered in the backyard, red-brown cobblestones laid in a circular pattern stretching at least twenty feet wide. There's a grill tucked near the house and a large table set up beside it, covered in a black tablecloth and mostly empty dishes of food.

Melissa notices me first where she leans against the table and crosses the space, grabbing the bag from me with a smile.

"Brielle's inside. She should be back out in a minute," she says. Then, louder, she calls out, "S'mores made it! Do you guys still have your sticks ready?"

There's a chorus of cheers from the two girls I saw on Monday as well as Camden. They grab a set of roasting sticks from a pile on the ground and rush Melissa, giggling and jumping. Everyone else looks up as I close the distance and step onto the patio. Olivia waves, and Hudson cocks an eyebrow before kissing her temple and coming toward me.

"You want something to drink?" he asks.

I shake my head. "I'm fine."

The back door opens, and Brielle and Faedra walk onto the patio.

My heart jumps.

Brielle holds her friend's baby, running her hand over the baby's fine hair. The movement feels absent, like she doesn't realize she's even doing it. My mind flashes back to when Camden was that little—younger, actually. Kayla never got to see him turn a year old.

Grief twists my stomach in a way it hasn't the last month, and it takes all my strength to keep it off my face. There's no pancakes to make tonight to tune out the thoughts. Shit, maybe I should get something to drink. It'll keep me busy, at least. Grief waves are fucking *hard*.

Brielle glances away from Faedra in that moment, her eyes lighting on me. Her cheeks flush a dark red even as a smile lights her face. Faedra looks over too, and she smirks before saying something into Brielle's ear, twisting away so I can't see her lips.

Hudson grunts. "You going to tell me what's up between you two? Because it's clearly not just casual sex like what's been floating around the gossip mills."

I tear my gaze away from Brielle to look at my brother with a frown. I hadn't heard that the consensus was she was just a hookup. Had that started after I left Monday?

"I already tried to get the story from Olivia, and she won't tell me anything. Claims it's girl business. And Mom said she was sworn to secrecy."

He gives me a flat look.

"Not tonight," I hedge.

"My money's on you guys being scent matches. Ethan's acting like it's pretty damn serious." He sighs and throws back the rest of the beer in his hand. "And you haven't risked anything more than a quick hookup since Kayla. It'd take a damn lot for you to hard launch something, not even factoring in that she's Melissa's best friend."

"I'm not hard launching shit," I grouse.

He laughs and claps me on the shoulder. "Yeah, sure. Brielle giving you 'fuck me' eyes from across the bonfire is definitely not you hard launching."

I shove an elbow into his side, and he laughs harder, letting his head drop back.

"Ethan's brought it up with you?" I can't help but ask. Ethan hasn't said much more to me than passing greetings since I brought Brielle home with me Friday night.

Hudson shakes his head.

"Nope. But he's got that look he had when you guys were first matched with Kayla." He shrugs and crushes the beer can against his leg. "He's also acting like his world is on fire, though, so not sure how much weight to put on any of it."

When I sigh, Hudson claps my back in that way guys always do to convey sympathy. My gaze drifts back to Brielle. Her cheeks are still flushed. And I can't even argue with Hudson's assessment of her gaze. It's certainly making me want to find a quiet corner and coax an orgasm from her. Cinnamon surrounds me, and Hudson chuckles.

Camden squeals, running toward me, a marshmallow barely hanging on to the end of the roasting stick.

"Papa!" he says as he runs into my legs, wrapping his arms around me.

The roasting stick stabs into my side, and I grunt. I ease it out of his hand before it can work its way through my shirt. The marshmallow, miraculously, is still holding on.

"Papa, are you going camping, too?" he asks, his eyes wide.

When I nod, he squeals again and dances in place, his arms tightening around me.

"Cam, you ready to roast your marshmallow?" Melissa asks.

Camden's excitement over having me home falls away just as quickly as it came as he rushes back to where Melissa stands with the girls near the fire. Hudson nudges me, and I glance up. Brielle stands just to the side of me, the baby still in her arms.

"Who is this?" I ask. I shove my hands into my pockets to keep from reaching for her.

She smiles. "This is Dahlia. She turns one at the beginning of August."

The baby whines in her sleep, and Brielle traces her spine, adjusting her hold as the baby relaxes further into her chest. The picture they make has me thinking all kinds of things that aren't safe right now. Like what she'd look like holding my baby—her eyes but my hair and the same chubby rolls I had.

Shit, it's a good thing she has an IUD. And isn't anywhere near her heat.

She isn't near her heat, right? Fuck, I should probably figure out a way to ask her if it's something I need to be prepping Sam about. You don't just *ask* an Omega about that sort of thing, though. It's like asking a person if they're pregnant.

If you're dumb enough to ask, you deserve the punch that inevitably follows.

"You okay?" Brielle's soft question rips me out of my spiraling thoughts.

I clear my throat and nod, not trusting myself to say anything near appropriate right now.

A man stands from one of the chairs lining an edge of the

patio and walks toward us. One of the girls looks up and smiles as he passes, and he runs his hand through her hair.

"She asleep?" he asks. When Brielle nods, he holds out his hands. "I can take her inside. Faedra mentioned you were thinking about heading out before she latched onto you."

Brielle offers the baby over, her movements cautious. Once the baby's situated against the man's chest instead, he focuses on me and holds out his hand.

"You must be Caleb," he says. "I'm Carter, one of Faedra's Alphas."

I take his hand. "Nice to meet you."

He turns back to Brielle. "If I don't see you before you leave, drive safe. I'll text you when we're on our way tomorrow morning."

Brielle smiles, and then the man disappears into the house, kissing Faedra's temple as he passes by her. The move's so graceful, it's like it's second nature.

Damn, I miss having that.

The ache is enough that I grab Brielle's hand and pull her into my side. She glances up at me, her eyebrows furrowed but her shoulders relaxed.

"Yeah, sure you're not hard launching," Hudson mutters beside me.

I roll my eyes. "Fuck off, Hudson. Your little brother complex is showing."

Brielle giggles. I press a kiss to her lips, and she melts into me.

"Damn it," Emily groans. "Now I owe Mel ten bucks."

Several people chuckle. I ignore them and kiss Brielle again. This time, she lets her weight fall against my side and a bare hint of her scent reaches me.

"I'm glad you made it," she whispers.

Yep, definitely worth whatever Ethan will rain down on me for hard launching Brielle and me.

Chapter Twenty-Seven

ETHAN

Camden giggles as he blows by me, running out of the tent. He pauses, glancing around, and then sets off to his right. I raise an eyebrow but don't comment. A second later, one of the Bennett girls races out, chasing him across the large open space of the campsite. Her lips are bunched in a serious-looking frown, and she has a quiet determination, like she's upset with whatever happened in the tent with Camden.

When there aren't any screams of frustration or crying, I focus on getting the last couple stakes set into the rocky ground so the rain guard doesn't accidentally blow away when we're not nearby. Just as I'm finishing, Caleb returns from the truck. He has two duffels crossed over his shoulders and carries a third, smaller one.

"All that's left is our portion of the food," he says, dropping all three bags into the partially unzipped vestibule, lining them up along the far side and away from the easiest path into the tent.

"I think Logan said they were still figuring out the best place to keep it all, so I figured I'd let it be until everything's settled."

I shove my hands in my pockets to keep from fidgeting. After a minute, Caleb sighs.

"We going to talk about it?" he asks. "Or are you going to keep shoving your head in the sand?"

I ignore him, focusing instead on the campsite unpacking around us.

We've arranged the tents around the perimeter, nestled up against the copse of trees a few hundred feet from the lake's shore. Emily and Beau are setting up a couple large picnic tables while the Bennett pack is moving around them with surprising efficiency, unpacking everything that isn't related to sleep in the span of a few minutes.

Caleb sighs again and walks off. It's no surprise he's heading for her tent. He eases the stake out of Melissa's hand and works on setting the remaining pieces of their rain guard. Camden comes running back into the center of the tents, the girl no longer with him.

He scans the area. When his eyes land on me, he runs over.

"Daddy! Daddy, can we go find rocks?" He wraps his arm around my legs. "Rose said she knows how to make them bounce on the water. I want to make them bounce!"

I pull him into my arms and kiss his cheek as I walk toward the tables.

"Cam wants to go work on skipping rocks," I offer.

It's not something I ever figured out, so outsourcing is necessary.

Emily grins. "Give us a couple more minutes, and I'll take you down and teach you."

Faedra and Brielle walk down the trail where the cars are parked another hundred feet away. The girl that had been playing with Camden walks with them, a small bag on her shoulders. Faedra stops at our central hub on her way to one of three small backpacking tents her pack has set up. Brielle doesn't stop, though, ducking around the group and heading toward her tent.

A taste of her lavender scent hits me.

I swallow down the unholy need to mark her, to cover her in my scent until Caleb's cinnamon is only a distant memory on her skin. Holy *fucking* hell. With a grunt, I force myself to focus on Faedra.

"Hudson and Beau both have coolers in their trucks," she says to the group at large, though her eyes are on her bonded Alpha. "Jude wants to leave the food mostly up there when we're gone and at night."

Logan nods and kisses her, a quick kiss that's so intimate a knife twists in my chest.

"Sounds good, Red. Sounds like Camden and Emily are heading down to the lake once the dust settles." He crouches in front of the girl, her blue eyes the same shade as his. "You want to go down too, sweetie?"

She nods and starts to take off the backpack—which is about the time I realize it's a legitimate framed backpack designed for intensive camping. When Emily mentioned the pack camped, I hadn't expected quite this level. Logan stops her and eases it back onto her shoulders.

"Go set your pack down at the tent, and then we'll go," he says.

Melissa calls from where she's helping Caleb set up the vestibule of her tent. "Are we going to the lake? Are we swimming or just helping the kids play?"

Carter and the other little girl walk back from the cars, their own packs on their shoulders. She holds his hand and skips beside him, a carefree grin lighting her face. She gasps and then squeals.

"Dad! Dad, can I go swimming?" she asks, loud enough that we all can hear her, too. "Please?"

She turns the word into multiple syllables.

Carter raises an eyebrow and looks toward Logan, who shrugs. Carter offers a smile to his daughter.

"Sure, darling. Let's get our packs put away and get you into one of your swimsuits."

Camden pushes away from me, and I let him down. He rushes across the campsite.

"Bri! Bri! Are you going to swim, too?" he asks, loud enough that the few people still up by the vehicles can probably hear him, too. "Or can you bounce rocks like Aunt Emily?"

Brielle exits from her tent, flipping her hair over her shoulder. A small bruise sits just under her ear. My stomach clenches.

"I think I'll stay on the shore with you. I'm not very good at skipping rocks, though. It's not something I ever managed to figure out."

Camden grabs her hand, and she doesn't discourage the touch. She smiles as Caleb comes up to them both even as her cheeks flush. Melissa joins them as they start toward us.

Beau stands back from the second table, shoving his hands into his pockets.

"About an hour or so until lunch," he says. "Someone should probably stay back to prep for it. Kids are going to be hungry if they're swimming."

"I can," I offer before anyone else can say anything. Staying back here means keeping maximum distance between me and Brielle. "I'll send a text to Caleb when it's ready."

Everyone dissipates with an impressive thoroughness over the next several minutes, leaving the campsite quiet and undisturbed. I stretch my neck and roll back my shoulders, closing my eyes to try and get the damnable need to subside. If she hadn't stayed over last night, it wouldn't be so bad. Waking up to her scent all over the fucking kitchen just about took me out.

And those damn *bruises.* She didn't even attempt to hide them. Not this morning, and not now. Like... Like she wants the world to see them, too. Like she wants what they're symbolizing. Like she wants to take his claiming bite and forge the unbreakable bond with him.

I swallow the lump in my throat.

Unease wars with dread and a primal desire I have no tools to handle. My mint scent explodes around me, so strong it overpowers every single aspect of the wilderness around me.

Yeah, it's probably time I admit that I need to go on a damn rut suppressor. I'll just consider myself lucky that the only scent I'm reacting to this poorly is *hers.* The last thing I need is to lose my shit around Melissa or Triston.

After another long, deep breath, I start toward the cars to grab lunch. The relative stillness of the campsite and mundane work of prepping food help settle me better than anything I've managed since the end of May, since that day I walked into my own damn barn and was confronted with the ghost of my biggest regret. By the time I'm grilling the first set of hamburgers, the need to find Brielle and shove her against a wall is nearly gone entirely.

As long as I don't think about the silvery scars Faedra and Olivia have. Or the way she smells like a goddamn mountain meadow in the spring.

Which I'm not. I'm *not.*

Footsteps rip me from my thoughts. And then the flash of mahogany hair with sun-kissed highlights has them slamming into me even stronger.

I hold back a groan by the skin of my teeth.

She doesn't say anything as she digs through the small piles on the other table, her hand cradled close to her chest. A small trail of red drips down her wrist, and my stomach drops out.

"What happened?" I ask.

I pull the hamburgers off the grill and stash them on the serving plate.

Her cheeks flush as I close the distance between us.

"I'm fine," she says.

I frown, watching as that trail grows and traces down to her elbow.

"You're not fine." It's a goddamn growl, and I don't apologize for it.

I grab her wrist and force her hand flat. There's a deep gash along her palm, nearly perfectly straight and spanning her entire hand. With a scowl, I focus on the trail leading to the lake. Where the hell is Caleb? There's no way he wouldn't be beside himself over her getting hurt.

"I'll be fine," Brielle repeats. She tries to pull her hand away, but I tighten my grip around her wrist. She whines, and something twists in my chest. "I just need to clean it and get it covered."

I curse under my breath and grab the first aid kit she'd clearly been going for.

"What happened?" I ask, trying to calm the fierce possessiveness that's roiling through me right now. I'm not upset that she's hurt. I'm *not*. People get hurt all the time.

She doesn't immediately answer, and I focus on pulling gauze and vet wrap from the kit while also ripping open several of the alcohol wipes.

"There was a broken beer bottle on the shore," she whispers. Her hand trembles as I cradle it in my own. "I grabbed it to keep Camden from stepping on it, and it accidentally sliced me. So I threw it away and told Faedra I'd be right back."

She hisses as I clean the gash and again when I press the gauze into the cut to gauge how quickly it's clotting. When it bleeds through before I count to twenty, I curse.

"Fuck." I press it harder into her palm. "Can you hold this? I need to find the butterfly bandages."

Her fingers brush mine, and lightning shoots up my arm.

Jesus *fucking* Christ.

I shut down my focus to just the task at hand, pulling out a few of the specialty bandages and getting them situated on her palm. As soon as I have them covering the cut, I layer a new piece of gauze over the top just in case of bleed-through and then cover it with the vet wrap. The moment it's secured, I drop my hands away.

Another damn second with her skin against mine, and I'm going to fucking lose it.

She watches me as I reassemble the kit and gather the bloody pieces of trash. The last thing we need is blood getting on the ground and attracting bears.

"Thank you," she murmurs, no more than a breath of air between us.

I close my eyes and force a swallow, trying to dislodge the lump in my throat. She sighs and turns, taking a step away from me, stirring the air between us. I'm expecting her scent but instead I get Caleb's cinnamon.

Something in me snaps.

I grab her hand, forcing her still. When I manage to open my eyes, her gaze is wide. Her cheeks and chest are flushed, and her pulse flutters in her throat. And still, all I can smell is cinnamon.

I should say something, should explain the absolute mess she's made of me the last month. The words don't come. Instead, I crowd into her, stealing the careful foot of space she's kept between us. Like we're fucking strangers. Like I've never felt the way her body clenches around my knot, like I've never heard the way she whines when she's on the crest of her orgasm, like I've never seen the way her hair sprawls out on a mattress as she gets eaten out.

Mint surrounds us, strong and fast and undeniable.

She sucks in a startled breath. Her eyes drop to my mouth for a heartbeat. Her lips fall open, but I don't let her say a word.

I slam my mouth on hers, forcing the kiss hard and deep, trying to cover every single speck of Caleb's scent that clings to her shirt like they've spent the last half hour twisted together on the shore of the lake. Maybe they have.

The thought has a jealous rage rushing through me. I bury my hand into her hair and twist us, crowding her against the table. She goes boneless against me, her curves molding to the hard lines of my body. Lavender bleeds out from her, not nearly strong enough to appease the aching need that's dug itself into my bones.

She whines, and I tighten my hold in her hair. Her nails dig into my stomach, and the touch is so familiar, so second-nature, that the decade between us falls away. I'm just the dumbass twenty-two year old who was convinced a long-distance relationship was an idiot's move.

Her little sounds grow more desperate. I loop an arm around her waist and lift her onto the table, pushing the first aid kit out of the way. Her knees bracket my hips with the same intimacy, and I groan.

"Ethan," she whispers against my lips.

Fuck, how many years did I dream of that? Of the way her voice grows breathless when she's so damn desperate? I soak it in, letting it soothe the need. I tilt her head and kiss her again, pressing my hips into hers so she can feel exactly what she's been doing to me the last damn month.

A girl's laugh cuts through the haze of lust. Brielle freezes for an endless moment. And then she pulls away, dropping her hands from my stomach and scooting far enough back on the table that she can close her legs. Her chest heaves even as she looks over her shoulder. I take a step away from the table and run a hand over my mouth.

Faedra's eyes are wide. The little girl that holds her hand is stoic, her blue eyes seeing right through me. She tilts her head, a line appearing between her eyes as she frowns.

"Oh my god," Faedra says. "I'm so sorry, Bri."

Brielle doesn't say anything as she ducks her head.

"Is she like you, Momma?" the girl asks. "She has two Alphas?"

Faedra blushes but doesn't answer her daughter's questions. The silence extends into being uncomfortable. Faedra clears her throat.

"The girls got hungry. Everyone else will be here in a few minutes," Faedra says.

Without a word to either of them, I put the second round of patties on the grill.

Chapter Twenty-Eight

BRIELLE

The campsite is quiet when I wake up.

Melissa is asleep on the other side of the tent, a careful two feet of open space separating our sleeping bags. I ease out of my own setup as quietly as possible, sliding into a new set of jeans and my favorite oversized tee—and the new scent blockers Faedra brought from Denver. I'm two seconds from leaving the tent entirely when my skin itches enough I practically groan.

With a muttered curse, I grab Caleb's too-large hoodie and pull it on. His scent drowns me in a matter of heartbeats.

The restless need settles.

Damn, I thought the touch-starvation would be getting better by now. Maybe a walk will help. At least my scent doesn't carry the acidic edge anymore. As I step out of the tent and start across the campsite, Jude looks up from his perch near the center, a small mug in his hand.

I offer a half-hearted smile.

Faedra steps off the trail leading to the cars, her gaze lighting on me before focusing on Jude. They exchange one of those looks that speak a thousand words. I cross the campsite, leaving them to it. If I don't start walking right this moment, I'm going to embarrass myself by trying to crawl into Caleb's sleeping bag. Or maybe Ethan's.

My cheeks heat, and my heart races in my ears. I shove the idea of being wrapped up with Ethan away and pick up my pace.

The lake is calm, the small breeze that lifts the ends of my hair not marring its surface. I pause and soak it in, trying to absorb its stillness into my bones. I close my eyes, focusing on the small sounds around me—a bird's high trill, the fish just breaching the surface of the water, the squirrels scuttling across the rocks. After a while, the soft footsteps of someone moving just behind me join the subtle cacophony.

I pause for a moment, waiting for the spicy cinnamon scent of Caleb to drift toward me on the light breeze. When it doesn't, I glance behind me.

Faedra stands a few feet away, her hands tucked into the pockets of her jeans. She wears a light vest in a pretty dark green that offsets her red hair and highlights her freckles. Her lips curve into a soft, understanding smile. She raises an eyebrow when I don't immediately say something in greeting.

I offer the same smile back to her. She closes the distance between us, stopping when our shoulders just brush. Her gaze is on the lake in front of us. It takes me a bit to relax into our friendship and admit the truth.

"I don't need the bloodwork," I say as quietly as I can to not interrupt the quiet morning unfolding around us. "It's..."

I force a swallow, trying to dislodge the lump that's settled in my throat. Faedra presses her shoulder harder into mine. Some of the nerves ease away.

"It's the same reaction I had to Caleb. At first, I thought it was just me reacting to seeing him after... everything. Especially since I was touch-starved." I cross my arms. "But Caleb and I have been together for a couple weeks now. And he's done his best to alleviate all the mess I've been in. And still there's this *ache* for Ethan."

She hums and leans her head against my shoulder.

"Yesterday was just confirmation for me. If you hadn't walked up when you did..." I sigh and run a hand through my hair to keep from picking at my cuticles. "Well, we wouldn't have stopped, realistically. The *need* for him..." I trail off.

Faedra says, "I get it."

I nod. Of course she does. She was one of the first Omegas to have her scent matches confirmed with the bloodwork that's becoming more common practice with each passing month.

"What has you so unsure of everything?" she asks after a minute. "It's not the time apart. I'm nearly positive. And I don't think it's Camden, either. You and him seem to be on really good ground right now."

"When I first moved back, he acted like we had never met each other."

She lifts her head and focuses on me, her eyebrows drawn low.

"And in the month I've been here," I continue, "he hasn't said more to me than a couple sentences. Last Sunday in the cafe? That's every single interaction we've had. He pretends I'm not there. And when he doesn't?" I blow out a breath and shrug. "He's always been... grumpy isn't quite right."

I pause and purse my lips.

"He's a lot like Jude, I guess. Stoic and closed off unless you're part of his inner circle," I say.

Faedra nods. "I've noticed that about him, too. He's so soft with Camden. And warm with Beau and Emily. I bet in other circumstances him and Caleb are as close as Caleb is with his brothers."

I nod. "Yeah, so most of the time he's closed off. You can't tell anything from his face at all. I don't..." I twist a strand of my hair around my finger. "Maybe all those years with Brett have messed up my ability to read Alphas. I don't know. But shouldn't my scent match be... less indifferent about it?"

"I wouldn't call him indifferent," Faedra disagrees, her voice still soft.

I glance at her and raise an eyebrow. "No?"

She shakes her head. "He seems wor—"

She cuts off and glances over her shoulder. I follow her gaze, and my stomach clenches. Beau and Ethan are on the trail, their heads close together. Neither seem to notice where we stand at the edge of the lake. Beau frowns and stops, his eyes wide. Ethan nods in response to whatever Beau asks.

"Want to walk?" Faedra asks, her voice pulling my attention.

She points toward the trail that leads around the lake. With a shaky agreement, I fall in step with her. She tucks her hands into the back pockets of her jeans and glances over her shoulder before taking a deep breath.

"Have you talked about the Omega they were bonded with?" she asks once we're a few hundred feet down the path.

"No. Caleb's never brought her up. It's... a weird gray area," I say. "I met her, just once. At Brandon's funeral."

"That was the third Alpha of their pack?" Faedra double checks. She hums when I nod.

"Anyway, since I'm so close with Melissa, I know what happened," I continue. "It feels weird to bring up something I already know." I pick at the ends of my hair. "And it wasn't like my whole dynamic with Brett at the end. They... I mean, they were *bonded*. It devastated the entire town, not just them."

"What happened?" she asks.

My answer is no more than a whisper that settles like a stone between us. "She killed herself a couple months after Brandon died."

She sucks in a breath.

"Melissa said it was awful," I say, trying to keep myself detached from it all. It doesn't stop my stomach from clenching thinking about what Caleb must have gone through. "She said Caleb was gone on a fire. Camden was four months old."

Faedra nods like I've given her some solution to a problem.

"I don't think he's indifferent," she says again. "I think he's terrified."

"What?"

I don't mean to ask the question. But Ethan? Scared? I've never once seen him scared of anything. And of *me*?

"I'm not an expert on any of this," she admits. "I've never dealt with the type of loss Caleb and Ethan carry. But I can imagine it. If I lost Carter or Jude or Logan?" She shudders. "I'm not saying that you should walk on eggshells around him or anything. You deserve to be wanted exactly where and how you are. But what I saw of him yesterday and especially in the cafe on Sunday? It was an Alpha that is incredibly possessive and in denial of it."

"Think it's something I should bring up while here?" I ask. "The kiss, not Kayla."

She shakes her head and loops her arm with mine. "I'd let him sit with it and see what he does. It's not like either of you are going anywhere."

I raise an eyebrow. "I could."

She laughs. "But you aren't. Your eyes are happy for the first time in years, Bri. And I've seen you smile more in the last week than I remember in the last *year*."

Footsteps cut across the quiet space. This time, Caleb's

cinnamon scent does greet me. Faedra looks over her shoulder with a smile.

"Good morning."

His voice draws me in like a moth to a flame. I drop Faedra's arm and turn around. His eyes are shadowed by the baseball hat he wears, a plain maroon with a vintage airplane. His lips curl into a small smile, and my heart lurches.

"Good morning," Faedra says.

"I was sent to let you know that breakfast is ready."

Faedra nods. "I'll head back and help with the girls, then."

A smirk flashes across her lips before she weaves around Caleb and starts back toward the campsite.

"Good morning," he whispers.

His voice is lower this time, and it shoots right through me.

I close the distance between us, and he wraps his arms around me, running his thumb around the shell of my ear as I let my eyes close and my cheek settle against his chest. His scent intensifies, and I go boneless.

He laughs into my hair. "We should head back before I decide pressing you up against a tree is a better breakfast."

My cheeks are still flushed as we rejoin everyone else in the campsite.

Chapter Twenty-Nine

BRIELLE

"Bri! Bri! Watch this!"

Camden looks over his shoulder, making sure I'm actually watching him, before he jumps off one of the large rock outcroppings that hug the lake. He squeals a second before he hits the surface of the lake, water splashing out from him.

Rose squeaks and scoots away from the edge of the large rock, huddling into Logan's side.

"You're going to mess up my hair!" she says ruefully. She runs a hand over the end of her braid like she's making sure it's still there.

Logan hugs her as she sighs into his side. "Momma will fix it if she needs to."

Rose pouts but nods. A second later, Camden surfaces from his jump. His eyes find me as soon as he pushes his hair out of his eyes, ignoring both of his fathers.

"Bri! Did you see?" he asks. "It was so big!"

"That's what he said," Melissa murmurs.

Caleb's laugh is rich in my ears. I can't help but grin as I nod and lean back on my hand, my arm brushing Caleb's leg.

"It was! That one was even bigger than the last one." I point to the splash marks on the rock, highlighting the newest set that's about three inches higher than the previous grouping.

He grins and then turns around.

"Aunt Emily, can I be on your board, too, now?" he calls out.

Emily looks over her shoulder, her paddle still in the water. She smiles and then slowly turns the paddleboard around, easing it closer to Camden without managing to accidentally beach it. He flops along the front of the board, forcing Emily to one knee to keep from falling into the lake.

Melissa laughs where she sits beside me, her knee brushing mine.

Iris jumps up from Jude's lap once Emily and Camden have started moving deeper into the lake.

"My turn!" she says. "Watch how high mine are!" She runs along the shore and climbs the rocks to get to the same spot Camden jumped. It's become the unofficial launching point for the kids, their new favorite way of getting into the lake.

Rose whines. "'Ris! My hair!"

"I won't splash you! Promise!" she says.

Carter's eyes are watchful as he focuses on her, his arm propped behind Faedra where she sits on the other side of Olivia. Her gaze is on Ethan where he stands leaning against another larger rock about twenty feet away, a soda held carelessly in one hand as he chats with Beau and Hudson. He cocks an eyebrow as Beau tosses his head back and laughs.

He hasn't said a word to me since lifting me onto the table yesterday and kissing me until I was ready to strip out of every single piece of clothing touching my body and take his knot until

I could practically feel it in my own damn throat. It's like it didn't even happen for him.

Well, aside from one loaded as hell look across the circle we'd formed last night while the kids watched the stars and compared them to a book Jude provided them that talked of constellations and the stories associated with them. A loaded as hell look Caleb had noticed. A look that had caused him to pull me into his lap rather than just letting his arm continue to drape over my shoulders. A look that had butterflies bubbling in my stomach for him for the first time in a long damn time.

My stomach clenches, but I ignore it.

Iris looks over her shoulder. "You watching, Daddy?" she asks.

Carter's smile is evident in his voice. "Always, sweetie."

She grins, plugs her nose, and leaps off the rock. Rose shuffles another foot or so down the edge of the outcropping, yelling as water splashes against her legs.

Caleb hums behind me before kissing the top of my head. His arm wraps around my waist as he readjusts us both, moving me with an ease that has my blood heating.

Thank God for Faedra bringing the newest scent blockers on the market with her. Mine don't work with swimsuits. Now, not a speck of my scent betrays just how easily my body melts for Caleb.

As everyone claps for Iris as she surfaces from her jump, Olivia traces the small tattoo behind my ear. A shiver runs down my spine, and goosebumps spread out along my skin.

"This is really pretty," she says.

My throat dries out. Caleb tightens his arm around my waist, pulling me flush against him, and kisses my hair again.

"Thanks," I say automatically. And then, because it's just my friends here, I admit, "I hate them."

Melissa bumps my knee in quiet support. Olivia frowns and lets her hand drop.

"Oh, I didn't realize it was from him," she says.

For some reason, my eyes wander back to Ethan. His eyes are locked on me, a muscle ticking in his cheek from how hard he's clenching his jaw. His beard is more unkempt than I've seen it over the last month. I've never been with someone that has facial hair. He didn't have one *before*. Or even when I was here for Brandon's funeral and Kayla was still alive.

Would it leave scratches behind on my skin? It had felt... really, really good when he kissed me yesterday.

Desire races through me in one hot, consuming wave. I force a swallow and drop my eyes, picking at the hem of my shorts.

"I think I'm going to get it covered," I say once I'm sure my voice won't shake.

Faedra looks around Olivia. "You've decided to do it?" she asks.

I offer a shrug. "Maybe? Probably. I'm just not sure what I'd get instead."

"What about something that reminds you of something that makes you happy?" Olivia offers.

"Or something that shows off a new start," Melissa says. "Because fuck Brett."

I can't help but laugh at the vehement fire in her voice, like she's spitting out something disgusting.

Faedra leans around Olivia and grabs my knee. "Yes," she says, just as passionate as Melissa. "Something to get him off your skin forever."

"I agree," Caleb whispers, his lips brushing the shell of my ear. "Fuck him and every mark he's left on you."

I can't help but shiver as he bites over the tattoo, pulling my skin between his teeth until I gasp. He runs his tongue over the stinging skin. Cinnamon bleeds out from him. Melissa and

Olivia both chuckle. My cheeks heat, but I let myself stay relaxed against him.

Hudson frowns and turns toward me, leaning fully against the rock beside Ethan. "Wait. Who is Brett and why do we hate him?"

Caleb tightens his hold again, his fingers digging into my side. I swallow around the lump in my throat, the panic coming faster than I've ever felt it before. It's never even really been *panic*. Why am I so nervous to have the cold reality of Brett's betrayal laid out in front of my friends?

My eyes catch on Ethan, and the nervous band around my chest tightens. His eyes are dark, his lips pulled into a heavy frown. His forearms are taut with the strength of his fisting his hands. The soda can in his grip crushes under the pressure.

I drop my gaze and mess with one of the smaller rocks still left on the shore, missed by the kids as they tried to find good stones for skipping.

I'm not ready for Ethan to know just what happened between Brett and me.

"Her asshole of a dead husband," Faedra says with the same passion as before.

The group grows still. That anxiety ratchets tighter. Caleb presses his lips to the crown of my head.

"And we hate him," Melissa continues, apparently oblivious to the sudden shift in the atmosphere, "because he was a lying piece of shit."

The silence grows charged. Somebody growls, low and lethal. I don't dare look toward Ethan this time even though it's undeniably him having the possessive, violent reaction. I run my palms down my thighs to keep from shifting in Caleb's hold. His arms tense around me. Because of course he noticed my nerves.

After a moment, his growl overlays the other.

"Momma? What's wrong?" Rose asks from her perch on the

jumping rock. She's moved back toward the edge. She kicks her legs where they dangle over the edge.

Logan kisses her head and hands her another rock as he settles beside her again. As she tosses the rock into the water, he whispers, "Just some big people things, Rosebug."

She frowns even as she takes the rock. "But growls mean someone's angry. What made anger happen? We were talking about Aunt Brielle's flowers."

Faedra and Logan share a long look, and not even I miss all the undercurrents flowing between them.

"Someone hurt Brielle, and Caleb's upset about it," Logan offers after an entire minute. Rose tilts her head, looking between her parents and the two growling Alphas. "Remember how we talked with Aunt Violet about how Alphas are very protective of the people they love?"

Love.

The word lances through me, cutting me to the bone. My breath catches in my throat. Caleb's growl grows stronger.

Rose nods. "So it's like when Uncle Dominic's brother got angry with him?" she asks.

"Not this time. But someone was mean to Brielle, and Caleb is very protective of her." Logan's voice drops even lower, nearly a whisper. Rose's eyes widen and shoot to me before looking over at Ethan. She taps Logan's hand, and he leans over her.

The sounds of Camden and Emily wading through the water cover whatever she asks him.

"Bri!" Camden calls, waving. "Emily and I found a cool spot. Can I show you?"

Bless that kid for never realizing exactly what's going on with the adults around him. I ease out of Caleb's arms even as his growl continues.

"Hold up," Hudson says. "There's a part of this story I'm

missing. Why the hell is Caleb ready to kill someone? What kind of lying are we talking about?"

Faedra and Melissa sigh in unison.

"Sorry," Melissa says, her voice contrite. "I shouldn't have said anything."

I shrug and ease out of Caleb's shirt I've been using as a cover-up. He raises an eyebrow as I drop it into his lap, his growl cutting off all at once. His eyes darken, and a new wave of cinnamon overlays the smells of the lake. Olivia shakes her head as she chuckles.

"Brielle?" Faedra asks.

With a single shake of my head, I start toward the lakeshore. The water is cold despite the warm summer afternoon. As Emily hops off the paddle board, I glance over my shoulder and focus on Hudson. It takes all my control to not let my eyes slide just a couple feet to the left where Ethan stands, his growl still reverberating through the group.

"Lying that destroyed my marriage," I say. Hudson's frown deepens.

Before he can say anything else, I turn back around and ease myself onto the paddle board, staying on my knees to keep the risk of falling lower. Camden smiles.

"You ready?" he asks.

When I nod, he turns around and points to a rock outcropping a few hundred feet to the left. I don't look over my shoulder even as Ethan's growl grows louder.

Chapter Thirty

The unsettling need that's slowly dissipated over the last couple weeks comes roaring back on the drive back to Creek Falls. By the time I've gotten out of the shower and started the laundry from the camping trip, it's bad enough I'm ready to tear apart the entire guest house. I drop onto the bed, burying my head in the one pillow that still has a bit of Caleb's cinnamon scent on it. Instead of calming me, it just sets the itchy, relentless need burrowing deeper.

There's no denying the one scent I'm craving right now. Not to myself at least.

If Ethan had been scarce before he'd lifted me onto a picnic table and kissed me breathless in the middle of the Wyoming wilderness, then he's practically gone invisible in the forty-eight hours since. Not even the small confines of the campsite was enough to get us close enough that I could try to figure out how to bring up the way my body sings for him—the hard reality that he's likely my scent match, too. Just like Caleb.

Heat surges through me, and I groan, dropping my head into the pillow.

I won't pull out a vibrator. Not yet. Not for him. Not when the only memories I have of him saying a damn thing to me are still a decade old. Even if he's meant for me, designed for me. Even if his mint haunts my fucking dreams right now.

Lavender floods the room, overpowering the purifier I have running in the corner.

Damn it.

Distraction is paramount right now.

It's like the universe hears me because the dryer's signal weaves through the cabin. I jump up and set about getting the clothes put away, forcing thoughts of Ethan and his damnable mint scent out of my frazzled mind.

A single knock on the closed door of the guest house pulls me from my thoughts—that are definitely *not* about a certain damn Alpha with tattooed arms and a beard that could be used for modeling. I drop the dress I've been putting away for the last few minutes onto the bed and cross the small cabin, adjusting my shirt dress and pulling my hair over one shoulder so that it covers the dark bruise Caleb left on it early this morning.

My thighs clench as I open the door.

Caleb leans against the threshold, his hands in his pockets, his hair still damp from a shower.

"I thought you had to go back as soon as we were done at the lake," I whisper, forgetting a greeting.

"Yeah, I do," he says. He pushes off the threshold and palms my waist, his cinnamon scent surrounding me. His voice is nothing but raspy hunger. "But I needed to say goodbye properly first."

Lavender explodes from me, and he groans. He lifts me and kicks the door closed in one single, fluid move that has slick rushing down my thighs. I'm expecting him to take me to my bedroom—my nest—but instead he lays me out on the kitchen's peninsula. The counter is cold against my skin, and I gasp, my nipples pebbling as goosebumps race across my legs. His hands are unerring, unrelenting, as he pushes up my dress and twists the seams of my panties in his grasp.

"Are these ones La Perla, too?" he asks.

When I nod, he grins. And then he rips them at the seams and tosses them across the room.

"Caleb," I gasp.

He chuckles, and another wave of need rushes through me. His tongue is warm and undeniable against my skin, drawing me into the torrent of need we share. The orgasm races through me, overcomes me, within minutes, surprising us both. He laughs against my skin, palming my thighs to keep them open even as my body ratchets tighter again.

My hands bury in his hair, my nails pricking his skin, and he laughs harder, nearly giddy.

"Three days with you feet from me," he whispers. "And that damn swimsuit that's burned into my damn mind. Three days, a swimsuit, and your scent all over my tent, and I couldn't knot you. Fuck, Brielle, that was three days too many."

He pulls my clit between his teeth, and I arch on a cry.

"Not to mention that you smelled like Ethan that first day, too."

He pushes his tongue into me, and I moan.

"Caleb," I whisper, pulling on his short hair. "Please."

He smiles and pinches my clit.

"Soon, sweetheart," he murmurs.

I can't help but whine.

It's not until he's pulled a second blindingly overwhelming orgasm from me that he lifts his head and undoes his jeans. My legs are covered in my slick, and my scent surrounds us both. Need still courses through me, so strong I'm practically choking on it. I sit up even as my fingers still tingle, needing to feel him, touch him, taste him.

"I need you," I admit as I scrabble at his shirt, forcing it over his head and then licking up his throat. His laugh is breathless now.

"You have me, sweetheart," he says, his lips brushing the shell of my ear.

He doesn't waste another second, sinking into me with a single hard thrust that has my toes curling and a moan echoing around the room. He loops his arms under my legs, forcing the angle deeper. I grab the edge of the counter to keep from overbalancing as he forces a hard pace.

"Caleb," I gasp.

"I love it when you say it like that," he says. "That little whine you get when you're so damn close to the edge. It keeps me so fucking hard when I'm flying and supposed to be focusing on other things."

I clench around him, his voice another layer of sensation I can't resist.

His hips stutter for a heartbeat, and then he pulls me into him, forcing himself as deep as he can go. He mutters a curse as he comes, and then his knot locks us in place. I fall off the edge again, my knees clenching around his waist as the pleasure turns nearly painful. My scent overpowers his, overpowers the entire cabin. He presses his lips into my throat, the smile curving them warming me even as I try to find the way back down from the sensations he's wrung from my body. He runs his hand through my hair. I collapse against him and press my cheek against his chest, letting my eyes close as he pulls me tighter into him.

"The edge is gone," he says, pride in his voice.

I can't help but laugh. "Yeah, it finally is."

I don't mention the odd need that was eating away at me

before he came by, though. Maybe it had just been an odd form of nesting.

He kisses my temple as his knot finally releases us. He pushes me back onto the counter, holding my hair until he's confident I'm steady without him. I tuck his cock back away, careful of the zipper. And then he crosses the kitchen and grabs one of the hand towels, running it under the warm water before bringing it over to me.

"What happened to using your shirt?" It's his preferred method of cleaning me up afterward.

He raises a single eyebrow. "If I use it, you'll have to wash it. Which defeats the purpose of leaving it here with you."

My cheeks heat. "I wasn't going to keep it."

He laughs and urges my knees apart. I hiss as he wipes up our combined mess, and he croons low in his throat. Once everything is cleaned, he eases my dress back down.

As he returns from putting the dirty cloth in the washer, he says, "It's either the shirt I wore in here or the sweatshirt I haven't washed from camping. And I figured the shirt was a better bet."

He grabs it from the floor and tucks it into my hands. I can't help but bring it to my nose and breathe in. The cinnamon is so strong I moan. He cups my cheek as he chuckles again. It's almost enough to ease away my growing nerves.

"We should probably talk about him and how I kissed him," I whisper.

Caleb hums. "I never expected to be exclusive," he says. "Omegas aren't built like that."

He presses his thumb into my lips.

"He hasn't talked to me since," I admit.

His mouth tightens. "Yeah, I guess that shouldn't surprise me. Ethan's phenomenal at keeping his head up his ass."

My laugh is tired.

"I'm not a stranger to being in a pack, Brielle," he says,

abnormally humorless. He moves his hand until he cups the nape of my neck. His kiss is light yet utterly serious. "All I ask is that you let me know about anyone else."

"I can do that."

"Good." He kisses me again, this one longer. "Tell Hudson if you need something, including smuggling scents out of my house. He'll understand."

He eases away from me, and I hop off the counter, leaving his shirt behind. I lace his fingers with mine as he heads to the front door.

As he starts onto the porch, I whisper, "I love you."

He pauses, his lips quirking up for a heartbeat. A lump settles in my throat. I hadn't actually meant to say that.

"Yeah?" he asks, squeezing my hand.

When I nod, he closes the distance between us and presses me into the threshold. This kiss is deeper, hotter, and it has me whining before he pulls away.

"Love you, too, Omega," he whispers. A thrill shoots down my spine. "I'll see you soon."

Chapter Thirty-One

BRIELLE

"We're about ready, little Omega," Carter says as he presses a kiss to Faedra's temple. "Much later and we'll mistime Dahlia's nap."

She smiles and looks away from the small embroidery project in her hands, focusing on his retreating form. He cocks an eyebrow as he opens the back hatch of the large SUV and adds another hiking backpack to whatever is already in it.

I tuck the small needle into the corner of the fabric before folding the project around the small hoop. Faedra organizes the various skeins of thread, wrapping them around small flat cards numbered in a thin, scrawling handwriting that is definitely not hers.

"Which colors did you need for yours?" she asks. "Ochre and amethyst, right? And one of the greens."

She sets the two colors on top of my project.

"I can order some," I say, pushing them back to her. "It's not like I'm short on spending budget."

Faedra's lip ticks up in a half-smile. "And so can I. Take them. All I have left of this pattern is the cherry red, and your snapdragons don't use it. The rest will just be taking up space in the backpacks and, honestly, will probably get dirty anyway. Not much tends to survive these long hauls."

I relent without much fight. "All right."

She grins and grabs my tote bag off the chair's back, easing the entire organizer into it along with the extra aida cloth. I tuck the project on top of it all and then hug Faedra, closing my eyes and breathing deep.

"It's going to work out," she whispers. "Trust me. If Dominic and his brothers can figure it out, Ethan can, too."

I can't help but laugh. Dominic and his brothers are practically infamous for being stubborn and bullheaded. It took a forced heat and a nasty altercation with Violet's parents for them to figure out their own dynamic several years ago. I've only met Dominic in person once, but it was enough.

Before I can dwell too much on the intimidating Italian, Iris and Rose rush onto the patio, their backpacks on and their hair done in identical french braids. Rose has a bow wrapped around the bottom of hers, a happy purple that coordinates with her no-nonsense outfit of dark jeans and long-sleeved flannel.

Both girls hug me before heading to the large car.

"Bye, Aunt Brielle!" Iris says with a wave.

Rose lingers longer, pushing a small card into my hands. "For that little spot next to our pictures in the living room," she says.

"I'll put it there as soon as I get home," I tell her, giving her a smile.

"Rosebug, you ready?" Logan asks, stepping onto the porch. She turns to him and smiles so wide it lights up her entire face.

"Have a good trip," I say. Logan and Carter nod. "Be safe."

Faedra squeezes my hand, and then I walk away from them and toward my own car parked a bit farther down the block.

"You in there?" Melissa's cautious voice cuts across the cabin.

I drop my head into the pillows, closing my eyes and pulling the blanket higher around my body. Caleb's shirt is sprawled out under me, so close I can practically taste the cinnamon of his scent. It does nothing to ease the ache in my chest or the morose mood that's clung to me the last several days since Faedra and her family left on their weeks-long trek through Yellowstone.

The front door slams closed, and I sigh.

"Brielle?" This time it's Emily.

Damn it.

Melissa might just let me stay here in my nest surrounded by every single piece of clothing I've pilfered off of Caleb over the last couple weeks. But Emily? No way in hell she will.

There's a gentle rap of knuckles against the doorframe of my bedroom.

"The parade's starting soon," Emily says. Her voice is softer than before. "We thought you might want to come."

Surrounded by people and loud noises and prying eyes? Absolutely not. Maybe the overly nosy parts of living in a small town would have started going away if Caleb and I hadn't started... whatever we're doing. Dating?

Our dynamic feels too serious to use such a mundane word. He's my scent match, not some random guy that I may or may not still be seeing in six months. But it's not like we're bonded or even living together. The thought has a thrill shooting through me, but I shove it away.

I drop my head into Caleb's shirt.

Prying eyes sound miserable right now when my skin is crawling with the need for a knot in a way I've never felt.

Before I can decide how to tell Emily to fuck off, Melissa

says, "Hudson gave me a bag with strict instructions to not open it."

Oh, hell yes.

It had taken me two full days to admit I needed something other than Caleb's cinnamon. When he'd come into the Rustic Roast to get a drink for Olivia, the request had just dropped out of my mouth. Hudson, to his credit, didn't even blink an eye. He just nodded, grabbed Olivia's caramel macchiato, and assured me he'd get something to help.

I sit up, shedding the blanket. "When did he give it to you?"

"This morning," she says. She takes a step into the room, and panic seizes me.

"*Don't.*" I scramble out of the bed and cross the room before she can get any closer and mess up Caleb's scent. I snatch the bag from her and rip it open.

Ethan's mint hits me in a single wave, and I groan. The flannel is soft and warm and smells faintly of the barn underneath his mint. I let my eyes close and breathe it in. That bone deep ache dulls into something manageable at last, and my head clears.

"You all right?"

Emily's voice has gone cautious, just like Melissa's. I focus on her without pulling the stolen shirt away from my nose. Her frown is nearly identical to her brother's.

"Yeah?" It comes out as a question.

She purses her lips and leans against the doorframe.

"If we leave now, we'll still be able to get decent seats for the parade. The sunshine will be good for you," Melissa says. She retreats as she talks, edging behind Emily in the doorway. When I frown, she raises an eyebrow and pushes up her glasses. "You can go right back to nesting as soon as the fireworks are over. And with any luck, Caleb will be back by Wednesday and you'll have the real deal again."

One of them, at least. I swallow the groan that thinking of Ethan draws from the depths of my chest. I need to feel his beard again, need to feel it against something other than my lips and cheeks. Lavender bleeds out from me.

Crap.

Melissa's right. If I stay here for much longer, I'm going to drive myself crazy.

With a sigh, I drop Ethan's stolen shirt to the bed and disappear into the closet.

"All right. Give me about ten minutes."

It won't be enough to fully erase my obsessive nesting the last couple days, but at least it won't be so obvious that I might as well hold a flashing sign over my head proclaiming I'm out of fucking control right now.

Emily's voice is lighter. "We'll hang out on the porch."

The parade is more enjoyable than I expected. Joan's coffee shop has a spot in the procession along with Misty Mountain Ranch. Camden cheers especially loud for the ranch's trail horses, each of them decorated with more red, white, and blue carnations than I think I've ever seen in one place before.

By the time we've all settled in for the fireworks at the county's fairgrounds an hour or so south of Creek Falls, my body nearly feels like my own again instead of a primal thing controlled by scents and knots.

The sunset sheds bright golden light over the mountains in the distance, and small lamps are situated every few hundred feet as a guide for the observers. I brush a bit of dried grass off the large blanket Melissa had pulled from her car.

Camden sits down next to me, a funnel cake perched precariously on a thin paper plate that looks moments away from collapsing.

"Do you like fireworks, Bri?" he asks. "They have those in your city, right?"

"Yes, Denver has lots of fireworks for lots of different occasions. And yes, I do like them."

I steal a bit of the funnel cake, grinning when he narrows his eyes at me.

"Do they have a parade?" he asks before shoving a bit of funnel cake into his mouth. Powdered sugar falls down his shirt, but he doesn't notice.

When I shake my head, he frowns.

"There's a lot of parties, though," I say. "Last year we went to the baseball game and got to watch their fireworks when it was over."

Logan, thanks to his training of two of the team's stars, had gotten us a suite behind home plate. Not that we needed the discount, but the view was perfect for the fireworks afterward. Brett had spent most of the night with his hands all over me, enough that I don't actually remember most of the game.

The thought sours my stomach, but I try to keep it off my face. My stomach clenches for an entirely different reason, though, when Camden's father settles in on his other side.

"Here you go, kid," he says before setting a glowing wand at Camden's feet. "And I got that bear you wanted."

Camden drops the funnel cake, a small implosion of powdered sugar covering us both, and grabs the small stuffed animal. It's a marbled red, white, and blue with a black cowboy hat and black shirt that says the county and year in the same alternating red, white, and blue theme.

"Thanks, Daddy!" he says, climbing onto his knees.

I grab the funnel cake before he can stick a knee into it and focus on the open field around us as Camden cuddles Ethan.

Ethan's low chuckle sends a bolt through me, and I clench my legs. Oh god. I need to figure out a way to put at least one more person between me and Camden because there's no way I can handle sitting within two feet of Ethan during this entire event.

The universe doesn't seem to hear my silent pleading, though. Olivia and Hudson sit behind us, chatting with his parents, while Beau and Emily sit on the other side of Ethan. Her parents settle on a blanket to her other side. Melissa perches next to me before I can ask her to switch, to give me just a bit of space within the confines of our group.

An expectant wave of quiet sweeps through the crowd. Camden giggles and eats another bit of his funnel cake.

And then, as if it isn't enough to be forced so close to Ethan when I want to climb him like a damn tree, a man I don't recognize comes up to the group.

"There room for one more?" he asks. He feels familiar, but I can't place him.

"Of course, Triston," Beau says.

"Here, kid, you'll need to sit on a lap." Ethan grabs Camden's light-up wand along with a couple other small items, clearing the blanket.

"Oh, okay," he says. And then he climbs into my lap without asking, clutching the bear to his chest as he looks toward the nearly darkened sky.

There's a long, heavy silence.

And then Ethan sighs and fills most of the spot Camden had occupied, giving Triston just enough room to wedge between Beau and Ethan.

A small breeze picks up in the field and carries that mint I'd know in the middle of a damn crowd right into me. My thighs clench, and a flush heats my chest. I swallow the lump in my throat and keep my body relaxed.

These fireworks can't end fast enough.

ETHAN

Emily leans around me as soon as the last firework's light fades out, practically climbing into Beau's lap to get close enough to Brielle. Beau eases back onto his hand, an eyebrow raised. Triston's breath catches in his throat as he stills beside me.

"We're going to go to the Outpost." My sister's voice isn't quite a shout, but it's a near thing. "You should come with us!"

Camden stirs on Brielle's lap and clutches the bear closer to him, though his eyes don't open. He made it through the first half of the fireworks before falling asleep against Brielle. Not even the overdone ending was enough to wake him up.

"Oh! Can we invite ourselves?" Olivia says from behind me, leaning into the space between Brielle and me.

A space that has been too damn small the entire night. Too damn small and yet a gaping cavern, too.

Emily grins and nods, giving up leaning over the others and

moving to kneel on the blanket in front of us. She pushes away the light-up wand I'd gotten for Camden without missing a beat.

"Of course! Devynn said they have a guest dancer this entire weekend, so there's sure to be fun dances happening."

The girls start chatting away, and I tune them out, grabbing all of Camden's items and shoving them into the backpack stashed behind me.

"So what do you say, Bri?" Olivia asks, pulling my attention back to them.

Brielle doesn't say anything. My gaze travels up to her face, drawn like a damn magnet. She bites her lip, her eyebrows furrowed with her frown. She glances down at my son and then pulls out her phone.

"I think I'll just go home," she says after a moment. Emily and Olivia both groan. "There's a tattoo artist that's in Jackson this weekend. She's doing a few sessions."

Melissa grins. "Is it that girl you've been following from Los Angeles?"

Brielle nods. Melissa cheers.

"Oh, yes! Definitely want to go with you. Her work is stunning. Did you already book an appointment?"

Brielle shifts her phone so Melissa can see it. Emily and Olivia lean over, too.

"Oh, I thought you were texting Caleb this whole time," Emily says with surprise.

Brielle ducks her head, her embarrassment written across her body. A growl boils up my throat, but I force it down.

"We should make it a girls day!" Olivia says. "I've been wanting to head up there and start getting things for the nursery anyway."

I get to my feet and sling the backpack over a shoulder before I do something completely stupid and mark Brielle in the middle of this field surrounded by my family and friends.

Everyone else seems to interpret it as permission to start packing up.

"Any news on when Caleb will be back?" Joan asks. She shakes out the blanket her and Mark were using and folds it away, tucking it under one arm.

"Last I heard it looked like maybe Monday, but it probably will only be long enough for his reset. Colorado's burning bad right now."

She nods and sighs. "Well, we're happy to take Camden as much as needed. Beau said you're doing second round breeding for the next week or two."

I blow out a sigh and stretch my neck before nodding. This entire next week is going to be early mornings and long days while we move around the herds so the cows that didn't take the first time get bred again. And hopefully they all take.

Mark steps around her, his eyes trained on one of the girls.

"You want me to take him, Brielle?" he asks.

I turn, scowling. Mark doesn't need to take Camden. I'm perfectly capable.

Before she can say anything, though, Melissa mutters a curse.

"I drove Brielle here. Let me drop her off and then I can meet you there," she says.

Brielle frowns and turns to her, her arms carefully caging Camden's limp form. "I'm sure I can find a different ride home. You guys go ahead. I'll text you the timing for tomorrow once the artist gets back to me."

Joan frowns. "We need to swing by the hotel and check on everything. If you don't mind waiting through that, we're happy to swing you up to the ranch."

"Mom?" Emily raises her voice. "Do you guys have room in your car? Brielle needs a ride."

Mom shakes her head. "We carpooled with the Millers."

Emily turns to Hudson, but I cut her off.

"I can take her."

The words are out of my mouth before I can keep them where they belong—in my damn head.

I've just spent the last hour with her so close to me my dick has been perpetually half-hard and aching. And now I just offer to have her in my own damn truck? Joan even said she could take her. And God knows Hudson made some deal with Caleb about watching over Brielle while he's gone. A ride to Emily's guest house would fall well within the scope of something like that.

Melissa cocks an eyebrow as she tilts her head. Her gaze cuts through me.

She knows.

Well, it's not like she didn't know the first time, either.

Fuck, what the hell am I even thinking? First time implies I'm going to kiss Brielle again, feel her curves against mine, shove my knot into her until she forgets all about her dead Beta husband. And Caleb.

Mint bleeds out from me.

Melissa's eyes narrow. I let my scowl deepen, trying to tell her to keep her damn mouth shut without making everyone else suspicious as fuck. I'm literally just giving her a ride to Emily's place. She's said nothing to me since I lost my cool while camping, not a single look or whisper that could feed a whisper of hope that she actually wants something.

"We should get going before Camden wakes up, then," Brielle says in her quiet voice that shoots right through me. The goodbyes are quick and efficient.

Once we're several feet away from the group, I say, "Here, I can take him. He's pretty heavy."

She hesitates, and I chance a quick look at her. She's biting her lip again.

"It's fine," she says. "It's not that long of a walk, and there's no reason to risk him waking up from an unnecessary transition. Getting him into the car will be hard enough."

Jealousy rises in my gut at her easy understanding of kids. The idea of her fucking that Beta gets my blood boiling. But the thought of her pregnant because of him? Of having his kids? I force a swallow to keep my reaction internal.

Fuck, I don't know what to do with any of this. The jealousy, the *need* for her, the grief and guilt at the idea of moving on from Kayla. It's all a tangled mess in my mind—and I have no tools to manage it.

She pulls the back door open and gets Camden situated while I'm still stuck in my head.

"Shit," I mutter. I slide behind her and set the backpack at Camden's feet. "I can get him buckled."

She backs away from me without comment, leaving his harness only halfway done up. My hands shake as I get the rest of it squared away. Her gaze, full of a heavy understanding and anxiety that most wouldn't notice, is on me as I close the door. A thrill goes through me that I *do* notice. I notice every damn thing about her.

The silence extends between us, that same weighted feel to it as her eyes.

Something shifts, something nameless and intangible that I couldn't describe with all the words I'm shit at using. The desire to feel her, to pretend the last ten years haven't happened and it's that first Fourth of July, overpowers whatever preservation is still in me. She turns toward the door, grabbing the handle, at the same moment I palm her waist. Her eyes are wide as her lips drop open.

I have her pinned against the truck, my mouth on hers, before she can gasp her surprise. She shifts against me, and something about the move dislodges her scent blockers. Lavender overwhelms me so fast, it's a miracle my knees don't buckle.

Her hands wrap around my neck, playing with the pieces of hair my hat doesn't quite contain. I run a palm down her thigh and then urge it around my leg, trying to get as close to her as I fucking can. I need to burrow into her, carve myself on her bones so there's no question of whether she's mine.

I break the kiss to run my lips across her jaw and then her ear, biting the damn tattoo that is another man's mark on her. Her chest heaves as she pants, pressing her body into mine so completely, it's all I can think about. Her body, her scent, her *mark that isn't mine.*

"Princess," I mutter. I don't mean to say it, have no idea why the nickname I'd once cherished and said with a smirk every damn day falls from my lips.

Her breath catches, and time suspends again. Her nails dig into my shoulders even as her body relaxes against me.

"Ethan," she whispers.

Need slams into me so hard, so fast, in a way it hasn't since Kayla. I palm her other leg and pull it around my waist, grinding into her. Her scent grows stronger, and I hum against her skin.

A loud peal of laughter cuts through our heavy breathing.

Brielle freezes.

"Shut *up,* they did not!" It's Emily's bright voice.

It's more effective than a bucket of ice water.

I let Brielle's feet drop from around me and take a step away. Her movements are jerky as she adjusts her dress. Her scent fades away with the small breeze. She gets the door open and slides in while I'm still walking around to the other side.

I catch my sister's curious gaze as I start toward the highway. Brielle leans against the door, her hands wedged under her thighs.

We don't say a word to each other the entire long ass drive to Emily's place. But that doesn't stop the words from racing through me.

Brielle's my scent match.

Chapter Thirty-Three

BRIELLE

"Oh my gosh, I haven't been here in too long," Olivia says between bites of the ravioli she ordered.

The girls chose a quaint Italian restaurant along Jackson's Main Street for our late lunch. I pick at my salad without comment. My appetite isn't quite back from the tattoo session.

Getting the skin behind my ear tattooed wasn't any more comfortable the second time around. Arguably it was worse, since she had to use more color and the piece is larger overall.

Melissa mumbles a wordless agreement with Olivia, not pausing in devouring the sandwich she picked.

"You're feeling better?" I ask Olivia.

She nods with a small smile. "Finally. My doctor said that it should be much better now until the very end." She purses her lips and takes another bite. "Though some days I still need the medication. She said that some people are just unlucky like that."

I grimace, and she laughs.

"It's all right," she says. "It's much better than it was, and it'll be worth it in the end."

"Do you want to swing by the Artisan booths before we head back?" Melissa asks. "I saw a vendor post a sneak peek on Instagram for their new bags, and they look really pretty. And I think there's a vendor or two that's selling nursery decorations."

Oliva grins. "Oh! I remember seeing them featured on the website! Bronte's Boutique, right? It stuck out to me because I couldn't figure out why someone would name their baby item shop after authors that certainly didn't write happy endings."

"Better than Stoker's Swaddles," I joke.

Melissa cackles, tossing her head back. "Oh my gosh, no *way* would that ever clear the test stages. Could you imagine?"

"I bet someone would make a bat themed one just to drive the point home," I offer, finally taking a bite of my salad. Laughter and good company are perfect for feeling like yourself again.

Emily rejoins the group, holding out a plastic bag filled with ice wrapped in a dish towel. "Here, sorry it took them a bit to hunt down a small enough bag."

I press the impromptu ice pack against the new tattoo and groan as some of the throbbing fades.

"You feeling up to it?" Melissa asks.

"Up to what?" Emily asks.

Olivia says, "Melissa was wanting to swing by the Artisan booths over on Third."

Emily raises an eyebrow but doesn't say anything.

"Sure, that sounds fun," I say.

We drop into a comfortable silence and finish the rest of the meal. Before the other girls can offer, I hand my card to the waiter.

Emily narrows her eyes but doesn't protest.

We're about a block away from the large market when Emily sighs.

"What the hell is happening between you and my brother?" she asks. Olivia and Melissa both look at her with wide eyes. "And why am I the last one that seems to know?"

"Nothing is happening," I grouse.

Nothing besides two hotter-than-sin kisses that have left me more desperate than I can remember ever being before—even with being touch starved only a month ago.

Emily crosses her arms as Olivia holds the door to the market open. It's in a large, uninspiring warehouse, the outside painted a bland gray-brown that blends with the rustic buildings that surround it. The inside, though, is anything but ordinary. Large swaths of vendors' spaces line the outer walls, each decorated and furnished independently. In the center is a large desk with several checkout lines with groups of seating clustered around it. The layout manages to not impede the large walkways that allow for getting to the stalls tucked along the back corners.

"Wow," I murmur.

Olivia laughs. "Come on, that Boutique is stall fifteen."

As she leads us around the large space that manages to feel both warm and cozy, Emily says, "Let's start with why he's always so on edge around you. I've never seen him like that. Not even with Kayla."

Olivia and Melissa split away from us, walking deeper into the small pop-up shop full of baby clothes and linens and wooden toys. I press my hand against the new tattoo to keep from picking at it.

"Ethan and I…"

Crap, did we date? Or would most people classify it as a summer fling?

We didn't really go on dates—not the fancy ones that end up all over social media but really aren't any more impressive or intimate than a night in with a movie. We mostly spent hours together on the ranch while he tended the cattle and worked on his farrier training.

"We were a *thing* when I lived here that summer between freshman and sophomore year. When I went back to school, he broke it off."

I say the words as fast as I can, in one quick rush, and then cross my arms in preparation for her anger at being left out of the information.

She doesn't immediately say anything. When I risk a glance, her gaze is contemplative. She runs a hand through her hair.

"All right. That's honestly what I expected." Her voice is lighter than I expect. "I get the feeling that you didn't really want it to end?"

When I shrug, she sighs.

"I was nineteen," I say. My voice wobbles more than I'd like. It's been a damn decade. "My mom was in rehab for what would be her final time, and I had no place that felt like mine. For that summer? It felt like I belonged here. Belonged with him."

Emily rests her head against mine in silent support.

"I'm assuming Mel and Liv knew?"

I offer a single nod. She purses her lips.

"That must be awkward as hell with you and Caleb being scent matches."

I can't help but grimace. She laughs and grabs my elbow.

"Let's go help Liv pick some outfits."

CALEB

Brielle's sprawled across my bed when I get out of the bathroom, running a towel across my hair to get it dry enough to not drip.

She turns onto her side as I come back into the room, resting her head on her hand. She's slipped into one of my shirts. It drowns out her curves and barely covers her ass.

Over a week since I saw her. Sure, we've been texting and calling, but it's not the same as having her with me, against me. Heat pours through my body again as if we didn't just knot.

"Can I see it?" I ask.

"Only if you're willing to take off the bandage." She scrunches her nose. "I tried this morning, but I couldn't get a good angle since I can't really see it."

I duck into the bathroom and grab the scent free lotion stashed in the bottom drawer.

"How did you get the first one off?"

I round the bed and kneel behind her, palming her hip to keep her on her side. Her hair is soft and still a bit damp as I ease it off her shoulder to bare the delicate tattoo. The waterproof bandage is cloudy, obscuring the details of the new artwork. I can see a couple feathers, though.

"Emily helped me," Brielle whispers.

Lavender bleeds out from her, and I force a deep breath to keep my body in check. We literally fucked less than an hour ago. And I ate her out in the shower, too. This *need* for her is so intense, though, it's nearly like those didn't happen.

I try to keep my actions gentle, easing away the bandage as carefully as possible. It gets caught on a strand of her hair, and she hisses.

"Shit, sorry," I mutter.

"It's fine," she says.

I drop the bandage to the nightstand to deal with later, my attention rapt on the small bird now emblazoned behind her ear. Not a single bit of blue from the flowers remains. Instead, black and orange and red feathers flow together, swirling around her ear and down the first inch or so of her neck.

The tail feathers are delicate enough that a bonding mark could nestle right around one of them. Cinnamon explodes around us between one breath and the next. She whines and tilts her head, showing more of her neck. I press a kiss to her shoulder even as I shove the idea of claiming her away.

"A phoenix?" My voice is raspy with heat.

"Born from the ashes," she says, closing her eyes even as another pulse of her scent surrounds us. "The artist said I'd need something darker in order to cover the blue. And I thought the symbolism was..." She trails off. "It felt like a good symbol."

She relaxes under me as I cover it with the lotion.

"They wrote about us in the paper," she whispers as I lay beside her, our noses nearly touching. "And about Ethan."

"I saw." I wrap my arm around her waist and pull her closer, twisting her legs with mine.

It wasn't a nice article. But then, it was Jessica Bailey that wrote it—and God knows the Baileys can't fucking stand Ethan's family. Getting to write a scathing paragraph or two of how Ethan and Brielle apparently kissed after the fireworks on the Fourth of July was probably her version of winning the lottery. Her comments about Brielle weren't quite as ruthless. Good thing, too, because there's no way I'd let her get away with it if she'd called Brielle a whore in public.

"At least they didn't include pictures of us," she admits, letting her eyes close. She sucks in a hard breath before sighing. "I'm going to corner Ethan this weekend and make him talk."

"All right." I trace the shell of her ear and the line of her jaw. Goosebumps rise along her skin, and I smile. "Can I take you to the Outpost?"

She opens her eyes. "You want to hard launch?"

"If they're going to talk about us, we might as well," I suggest. "I have no intention of hiding you."

Her gaze grows thoughtful. She traces my happy trail, the movement almost absent. "All right. Tomorrow?"

"Perfect."

I grin and then roll over, pinning her under me.

"Caleb!" she gasps.

And then she moans as I slide down her body.

# Chapter Thirty-Four

ETHAN

My phone rings. I pull it from my pocket before the receptionist can pin her stare on me like she did the poor teen that was here half an hour ago. Caleb's name on the screen has a ball of anxiety tightening in my stomach. Caleb almost always texts rather than calls. Unless something urgent came up. Did something happen with Cam?

I step out into the bland hallway of the Council's office in Jackson and answer the call.

"What's up?" I ask instead of offering a greeting.

"I just got called in," he says.

Shit. That's the second time this season they've overridden his reset.

There's the sound of shuffling and then a muttered curse.

Caleb's more frazzled this time. "You're still in Jackson?"

"Yeah. For another hour at least."

Because if the bloodwork comes back matching, I then get to

sit in a chair on the other side of this damn building and figure out the bureaucracy of documenting it with the Council.

And after I've finally figured that out, it's nearly an hour to get home. Two hours is too long if the frantic movements on Caleb's side of the phone are any indication.

"Shit, okay. Mom's covering at the hotel tonight." And my parents are in Jackson, too, on a date. "All right. Let me call Emily. Is Cam's bag still ready to go? By the time you get back here, it'll be damn close to his bedtime."

I lean against the wall and offer a gruff, "Should be."

Though to be honest I haven't actually looked at it for a while. Cam hasn't needed an overnight with one of our families in a while.

"Good," Caleb sighs. "That saves me time."

"Where are you going?" I ask.

"Southwest Colorado. Some jackass decided to set a bonfire in the middle of the fucking forest this morning without having anything to stop it once it was lit. It's already burned almost ten thousand acres."

Holy *hell*.

"Shit. You're going to be gone for a while."

He grunts. "Probably. Sam said we're pulling in the LATs and probably running overnights."

Fuck, he hardly ever runs overnights. The equipment is expensive and the pay is astronomical. Wherever this fire is must have the big government agencies worried.

"I need to text Brielle," he sighs.

I shouldn't ask. It's Friday, and they've been wrapped up in each other since he got back yesterday. The question slips out of my mouth anyway.

"What's going on with Brielle?"

There's a long pause, and then he blows out a breath. "We were going to go out to the Outpost tonight once you got back."

It shouldn't hurt. I've done my damnedest to avoid her all week. Discussing whatever the fuck is happening between us is too... vulnerable. Not without proof that she's my match. Fuck me, maybe not even then. I loved Kayla, adored her, *bonded* with her. Does all that just... get negated if Brielle's my scent match, the one designed biologically for me?

Could I have avoided the heart wrenching, life-altering experience of finding my Omega dead in the garage by her own doing?

But then I wouldn't have Camden. Caleb and I wouldn't have become such close friends—the brother I never had. Him and Brandon both.

Caleb cuts off the spiraling thoughts.

"I need to call Emily and get Camden somewhere," he says. "I'll let you know when I get there."

"Sounds great," I mutter and then slip my phone into my pocket.

When I step back into the waiting area, the woman who took the blood sample is leaning against the desk, a small, unmarked, white envelope in her hand. She offers it with a small smile that doesn't quite reach her eyes.

"Next steps are on the second page, Mr. Taylor."

My hand trembles as I take the envelope and she turns, heading deeper into the clinic. I don't open it until I'm back in the hallway and away from the receptionist's hawkish glare. And then every single swirling thought drains out.

The sun is setting by the time I pull into the garage. I lean my head back, trying to calm the incessant nagging voice that's been running a mile a minute since the bloodwork came back. It doesn't fucking work. They race through me in another loop.

I should tell her. She deserves to at least know. It shouldn't be anything done publicly, though. There's too many people who are obsessed with her—especially since my fuck up on the Fourth.

How the hell am I going to find a way to tell her in private?

And then what happens when I do tell her? Are we a *thing* again? Do we talk about the last decade? Do I finally bring up that sniveling, spineless asshole of a Beta she married? Ask her exactly why Melissa said he was a lying bastard?

And if we do become something, what happens with Cam? With her long term plans here?

Emily said she doesn't have a job. Honestly, she probably doesn't need one if she got her husband's wealth with his death. But does she want one? Does she want her own house?

Hell, does she move in here with us?

The idea of her living here, where Kayla lived and breathed and slept, makes my chest tighten. The rooms are all different now—mostly. And there's not a single piece of her nest that's remained aside from a few small trinkets Caleb and I kept. But just the idea of Brielle nesting in the same room has dread and guilt roiling through me.

With a sigh, I shuffle into the house, toeing off my boots and shedding the flannel I'd worn over the top of a plain white shirt. The thoughts keep swirling even as I throw together a quick dinner and then trim my beard. The light in the bathroom catches on one of my tattoos, and all that guilt and dread and confusion roar up again in an undeniable wave.

I grab my phone and text Melissa before I can talk myself out of it.

> You and Brielle doing anything tonight?

There's a god awful minute of no response before the message is marked as seen and the dots show up.

We were at the Outpost.

Were?

Ryan called and said Chesapeake went lame again, so I'm working on getting out there to see what's wrong.

Fuck me. She threw another goddamn shoe?

Shit. You need me out there tonight?

Shouldn't. Ryan didn't say it was an emergency. I'll see what's up with her feet and then send you an update.

I blow out a breath and rub my neck.

You're not a fucking coward, I tell myself. Then send her another text.

Brielle still at the Outpost?

...I think so. Let me check her location.

The dots disappear.

I grab a new shirt from my closet and my favorite cowboy hat. By the time I grab my phone from my bed, Melissa's texted me back.

Yes, she's still there.

She says she's going to dance a bit and then
head home in an hour or two when her drink
has worn off.

Why? Are you going? Did something happen
with Caleb?

I ignore her questions.

Thanks. I'll check out Chesapeake tomorrow.

I shove my phone into my pocket and slip my boots back on.
I stare at the packet still on the passenger seat like it might just
bite me.

And then I throw the truck into gear and head out toward
Main before I lose my goddamn nerve.

BRIELLE

The Outpost isn't nearly as fun once Melissa leaves, but I slowly
sip my Cape Cod and try to relax anyway. I didn't get dressed up
—first for Caleb and then for Melissa—just to end up heading
home not an hour into being here. Besides, it's not like I'm about
to drink and drive, so I have to wait a bit no matter what.

Devynn watches me from where she helms the bar. She cocks
an eyebrow, and I shake my head. I'm fine enough here. A man
sits down in the lone open chair, and she turns to him, her gaze
going guarded like that time I first met her. I go back to sipping
the mixed drink and watching the small group of women trying
to line dance in the center of the dance floor.

I'm not an expert, but I'd swear they're tourists that
somehow managed to skip both bars along Main Street that cater

specifically to people traveling through Creek Falls on their way north to the national parks. There's just a way that the girl on the left moves in the black cowboy boots, like she's not used to their weight and size and shape. I adjust my own boot-clad feet, crossing them under the barstool's foot rest. It feels criminal to be out on a Friday night in jeans. But at least I'm not sticking out here—mostly. A couple of the men gave me odd looks when Melissa and I first showed up, their gazes catching on the mostly see-through top I'd opted for, the same black one I'd worn out with Caleb a month ago.

Someone leans against the tall table, pulling me from my musings. He's an attractive man with a close-trim beard and tan cowboy hat. His blue button-up shirt is left undone, exposing a plain white tee underneath. If I'd just seen him from the side, I'd risk assuming it's Ethan—minus the tattoos. His eyes, though, aren't as friendly. He feels vaguely familiar, but I can't place a name.

"Hey, Brielle," he says.

I offer a tight smile and cover the top of my cocktail.

He leans on his elbow as he smiles back. His eyes skate down my shirt, and it takes every ounce of self-control to not cross my arms. I don't want this man to look at me at all—and certainly not like he's already imagining me undressed.

"I saw you were here alone and thought you might want someone to cheer you up," he says when I don't offer any more of a greeting. "No one wants to spend Friday night alone."

I do.

Well, not technically. But I'd rather spend it alone than with this man that makes all my alarm bells go off.

"Do I know you?" I ask, pulling my corporate no-nonsense voice from its dusty shelf. He feels vaguely familiar, but I'm nearly positive I haven't seen him since being back in Creek Falls this summer.

His grin is wider this time—and still doesn't touch his eyes. "Not yet, but you'll be screaming for me by the end of the night."

Ugh. Gross.

I lean away from him, trying to get as much distance between us without actually standing up from the table. He follows me, not allowing me to retreat.

"I bet I can guess your scent," he whispers. "Something so delicate as you probably has something that matches. A flower or maybe a fruit."

He covers my hand with his.

Oh, fuck me. Of course the one night I decide to go out on my own is the night some bastard of a creep decides I'm the perfect prize instead of the tourists still hobbling along on the dance floor.

And how in the hell does he know who I am?

"If I guess it, what will you give me?" His voice drops suggestively.

Bile rises in my throat, and I lean as far away from him as I can. He tries to follow, but a hand is suddenly on his chest and pushing him away.

"You'll get my goddamn fist in your face, Jake."

The low baritone rolls through me, and the unease that had been quickly sinking into true fear eases. The man growls, a low, dangerous thing, and shoves Ethan back.

"Fuck off, Monroe. You're just jealous she's interested in my knot instead of yours."

Monroe? He hasn't been Monroe in years. Not since they registered with the Council and were given a pack name. Who the hell is this guy?

He shoves away Ethan's hand and closes the distance between us, grabbing my elbow like he's entitled to touch me. I try to pull away, but his grip tightens.

"Let. Go." My voice shakes—with fury or nerves, I'm not quite sure.

"You should listen to her," Ethan seethes. His body is hot behind mine, a wall of warmth that has my body thinking all kinds of things that are in direct opposition to this asshole stranger grabbing me.

The man tightens his grip again, hard enough I whine.

A long, awful moment stretches between the men, and then Ethan's fist connects with the side of the guy's face. He drops his hold on me, focusing on Ethan entirely. I don't dare move.

I've heard of Alphas freaking out over an Omega. It's one of the big dangers of an Omega dropping into heat in public. But have I ever seen it happen? No. Not beyond the awkward as hell dynamic that's been developing between Ethan and Caleb.

Of course it's me that it happens to. I'm sure this article will be just as awful as the last one.

I wrap my hand around where the jerk grabbed me. The points where his fingers dug in pulse with a new ache that means they're probably bruising. And if Ethan's this ready to punch someone, him seeing bruises won't help anything.

There's shouts from across the bar a second before movement surrounds me.

"Hey! Get them out of here!" Devynn's voice cuts across the room.

"It was Brown, Dev! He started it." I recognize the voice but can't figure out who it belongs to.

A couple guys descend on them and pull them apart.

Ethan immediately drops the aggression, angling his stance to block me from the other Alpha's view nearly entirely. The guys who pulled him away drop their arms and back up a few steps, their gazes trained on the other man.

Calder Dean leans against the bar, his eyes locked on the other man, too, his lips pulled into a sneer. Devynn's frowning.

"Get the fuck out of here, Jake," a man says. "Before someone decides Miller needs to be called."

John Miller is the police chief and one of Ethan's father's best friends.

The temperature in the room drops at the implied threat.

Jake's nostrils flare, his jaw going white with the strength of his clenching it. Ethan's growl starts, low in his chest.

"Jake," Calder calls, warning clear. "You really want Pierce down here? Because he's struck a deal with his brother."

There's enough undercurrents that not even I'm quite sure of them all. Pierce is Hudson, I'm pretty sure.

This one, though, seems to be enough to make the guy back down. He shoves out of the men's holds and storms for the door, not looking back as he slams it behind him.

Chapter Thirty-Five

ETHAN

I don't move as the bar resettles around me, waiting until everyone slowly loses interest in the mess I just created. Fuck, I shouldn't have punched him. Not Jake Brown. The asshole has a reputation for a reason—namely the brutal assault charge that got him put behind bars a couple years ago.

What the hell is he even doing here? Dad hadn't mentioned he'd gotten out. Maybe the news hadn't traveled through the Millers yet. Though John not knowing about someone getting out doesn't sound quite right. He's Chief of Police, and he's damn good at his job. He keeps tabs on most of the people that might be coming up for parole.

I shake away the thoughts and breathe deeply, trying to find whatever calm center I might possess.

"Thank you," Brielle whispers.

"You all right?" I ask. I don't manage to get the gruff, possessive rage entirely out of my voice, but I don't bother to apologize for it. It was clear enough how I feel about her.

She shrugs, her hand still clamped around a small glass tumbler half-full of a pink cocktail. Her other is hiding where the bastard grabbed her. If he fucking bruised her?

I swallow down the growl that wants to rip through me. The last thing I need is to hunt down Jake Brown and give him another piece of my mind.

Instead, I grab the seat the jerk had ignored and swing it to rest beside her. Our knees just barely brush as I settle into it. Her breath catches, and she finally flicks those gorgeous brown eyes up to look at me.

Fuck, I can't believe I'm actually doing this.

"About last week..." Brielle starts.

I accidentally talk at the same time, right over the top of her. "I've been in Jackson."

She pauses, letting her half-started sentence fall away. She tucks a strand of hair behind her ear without showing the spot Jake grabbed her. After a minute, she clears her throat.

"Jackson?" she asks. "Beau said you guys were finishing moving cattle that needed to be bred again."

A flash of jealousy tightens my mouth. She must have swung by the barn after I'd already left for Jackson.

"We have been. But I left just before lunch."

"Oh." Her reply is nearly swallowed by the music pulsing through the bar.

"I went to Jackson for this," I say.

I pull the small envelope from where I've had it stashed in my back pocket and set it on the table between us. Her eyes drop to it and then her face pales, even the few freckles dusting her cheeks lightening. Even without looking at the information, it's clear she knows what it is. I suppose that makes sense since Caleb had the same blood work done last month—nearly to the day.

When she doesn't say anything, I force a swallow and try to come up with my own words.

"I'm shit at this. You'd think being ten years older would help, but it hasn't," I admit. "And it doesn't have to mean anything if you don't want it to. I just..." I sigh and mess with my hat, readjusting it, then run a hand over my beard.

Her gaze slowly rises from the paperwork she's yet to touch.

"Why do you have tattoos of the Arch and Lovers' Meadow?" she asks.

The question comes out of left field, and it takes me a second to figure out what she's even talking about. She'd noticed my sleeves? When had she gotten close enough, looked at me long enough?

Clearing my throat, I roll the sleeves of my shirt to my elbows, high enough to expose the full tattoo of Bluebird View that runs up the outside edge of my left forearm. Her eyes drink them in, every color and line that is an unspoken homage to what I threw away a decade ago but could never truly get over.

There's a couple for Kayla, too, intermixed, like the dove Caleb and I both have. And there's one of a small blue finch on my upper bicep for Camden. But most of them? Most of them are hers and hers alone.

She's unabashedly staring at the artwork.

"Ask it, Brielle," I say gruffly, needing to get to whatever that look means for this whole chasm between us. Ten years is a long time, and I'm not a naive bastard to think that the scent match confirmation sitting untouched between us will be enough to build something across it. We've both lived, both continued on, and that makes this just that much messier.

"Why the West barn?" she asks, her eyes locked on my right forearm.

I glance down at it, too. The red has faded over the years, but it just makes the piece feel more like the real building. It's one of the few reminders of it now, too, since Melissa had it torn down when she sold all the cattle and converted Misty Mountain to a recreational ranch. Now the spot where it stood is open pasture between administrative buildings for the ranch's guests.

I wonder if it bothers Brielle that the place she lost her virginity is gone. It bothered me for a long time, and I'm not wired to be the same level of sentimental that Omegas are.

I bring my eyes back to hers, and my breath catches in my throat. Her eyes pierce me, an understanding in them that wasn't there before.

"You know why," I murmur.

Her throat ripples as she swallows. The silence lengthens between us. I'm a breath away from saying something—anything —to make this whole part move faster. She grabs the envelope and pulls the information out without breaking my gaze. It's not until she has the information spread out in front of her that she glances down at it.

A mix of emotions crosses her face too fast for me to read all of them—but the worry is easy enough to see. She breathes deeply, and her eyes flutter closed. She swallows again. I spread my legs, my body deciding now is the perfect time to respond to her.

"I'm Matchless," she whispers without opening her eyes. "I haven't looked into if the scent matches are enough to overturn it."

Jealousy burns anew in my stomach, and this time I don't quell it.

That Beta asshole got this from her, too? The closest a Beta can come to making an Omega theirs without an Alpha intervening. A permanent classification—at least until that Omega figured out that scent matches were a thing. Now there's a process for overturning it, at least in theory.

"All right." My voice is surprisingly level. With a sigh, I ease to my feet and adjust my hat again. "Like I said, it doesn't need to mean anything. But I wanted to give you the information before the Council sends you some kind of notification."

I turn toward the door.

"Ethan."

Her voice stops me just as completely as the hand she wraps around my wrist.

"Do you want it to mean nothing?" she asks.

My gaze skims over her, drinking her in, every small detail that's the same and yet different. The silky brown hair, the soulful brown eyes, the tanned skin that's grown even more golden since she moved here.

The perusal stops on the just-forming bruises from that asshole. I force down the protective rage, the need to feel that fucker's bones break under my fist.

Do I want her? God, yes. I want her.

To myself—and to her—I'm done denying it. Do I want the scent match to mean nothing? No.

I shake my head, not sure my voice will work.

She stands and closes the distance between us. It's automatic to palm her waist. Her breath hitches for a heartbeat, and my body grows unbearably hot and tight. Mint bleeds out from me, filling the space around us, between us. Her nostrils flare.

"I don't want it to mean nothing, either," she whispers.

I cradle her cheek and pull her body into me until every single line of hers molds to mine. Fuck, even the way we line up is perfect. Her lips part, and her pulse ticks in her throat.

"Whatever you want, princess," I mutter.

And then I cover her mouth with mine.

Chapter Thirty-Six

W e're a mess of limbs and teeth and lips as Ethan pulls me from his truck and carries me through his house, not bothering to turn on a single light. He nips at the empty space under my right ear, pulling it between his teeth just hard enough to bruise. He kicks the door closed and crosses the large room, his mint drowning out the space by the time his knees bump the end of the bed.

"Ethan," I whisper. I dig my nails into his shoulders and try to get better leverage. I need him—his knot and his scent and his *bite*.

I groan with the force of it.

"Princess," he murmurs against the shell of my ear. He sets a knee on the bed, and then we're falling. His arms cradle me, keeping me from feeling the impact. He pushes my shirt up, baring my belly and the bottom half of the lacy bralette. His lips roam down my jaw and throat, pausing at the hollow between my collarbones. His hands tighten on my waist as he grabs the neckline of my shirt with his teeth. It pulls taut, a half-second from ripping at the seams.

Panic seizes me so fast, I lose my breath and my throat dries. He *cannot* rip this shirt.

"Don't," I gasp.

He growls. Something in my mind must be messed up because the sound has heat rushing through me instead of worry. Slick coats my scent blockers, and I clench my legs.

"It smells like Jake." His voice is low, and it rumbles through me.

Does it? All I can smell is him—his mint and his aftershave and the faint smells of the barn that cling to his jeans. Not even the spot where the jerk grabbed me smells any different.

I push him away as I shake my head and try to sit up.

"I don't care," I say desperately. "Don't rip it."

He grunts but releases the neckline, grabbing the hem of the shirt and easing it off instead. The bralette goes with it in a smooth move that has anticipation bubbling low in my belly. His calloused hands make my nipples tighten with each almost-there touch against my sensitized skin.

The moment the shirt's free of my wrists, he throws it into the corner of the room. Just like with Caleb, it takes all my self-control to not cover myself, to stay still under his uncanny gaze. But, hell, is it worth it. His breath catches as he takes me in, his cheekbones growing sharper and his scent intensifying to the point it practically drowns us both. His eyes are a wild, brimming storm, full of need and ache and unfulfilled promise.

My stomach clenches even as another wave of need rushes through me.

He attacks my jeans with the same single-minded ferocity, pushing them off my hips and tossing them behind him before palming my thighs. He crouches in front of me, his eyes locked on mine, and then pushes my legs apart, his lips slowly tipping into a smirk when I don't resist him.

My will crumbles, the need to feel his skin against mine overpowering the power I feel at having him so brazenly in want of me. I reach for him, trying to twist my hands into his hair, but he shakes his head.

"Hands flat on the bed, princess."

The name rips through me, just as strong as the first time he whispered it at the Outpost. *Princess*. I never thought I'd be called that again. Something soft and delicate flutters under my sternum, but I ignore it.

"Now," he says when I don't immediately acquiesce.

My fingers tremble as I dig them into the mattress, the first ember of unease flickering behind my navel that I'm not quite able to quell, but I purse my lips and let my legs relax more. His lips flick up in a half-there smile as his eyes drop back to the small bit of fabric covering me. With a quick twist of his wrist, his knuckles brushing my sensitized clit enough that my hips buck, he rips the panties at the seams.

I can't help but gasp.

Lavender explodes around us, so potent it's borderline embarrassing. He groans as he throws the panties toward the rest of my clothes in the corner.

"What is it with you and Caleb needing to destroy expensive panties?" I ask, breathless.

His eyebrow rises even as he keeps his eyes between my legs.

"Expensive panties?" His voice is just as breathless as mine.

"Those were scent blockers," I mutter, rolling my hips to try and get some kind of relief, some kind of pressure where I need it most. His hands tighten on my knees and force them even wider. "The newest on the market. They're just as expensive as the La Perla panties Caleb has shredded twice."

Now both eyebrows rise, and his gaze lifts to mine.

"*La Perla*?" he asks, disbelief and shock warring in his voice.

I swallow the lump in my throat and force my voice steady.

"Millionaire finance mogul, remember?"

The corners of his mouth tighten as his hands flex on my knees.

Silence stretches between us in one awful, unending moment.

And then he presses on my belly, encouraging me onto my back. His beard scratches at my thighs as he drags his lips along the sensitive skin. I can't help but tense. I twist my hands into the sheet.

My back bows with the first swipe of his tongue, and he groans against me, forcing my legs even wider.

"Fuck, I forgot just how good you taste," he mutters against my skin.

I roll my hips toward him, his breath on my clit enough to have me aching for more.

"Ethan, please," I whisper.

He hums and tightens his grip on my knees, holding me open. And then he *eats*. Every swipe of his tongue, each drag of his teeth has me twisting my hands tighter into the bed, has my moans growing louder until they reverberate through the small bedroom. He sucks my clit into his mouth, pulling until I groan, my orgasm racing through me like a wildfire across barren woods.

"Oh, God," I gasp, the words broken and breathless as he continues licking me, the scrape of his beard against my sensitized skin enough to have me hurtling back toward the edge.

"Give it to me, princess," he says without ruining his pace. "One more before you get my knot."

My body races to answer him, every single thought draining from my mind as he fucks me with his tongue. I tilt my hips toward his mouth, desperate for whatever he'll give me that will relieve this *ache* for him. He chuckles against me and then pinches my clit. My back bows, my mind empties, and I scream, loud enough that my voice breaks. His touch softens at once, bringing me back down with a practiced touch that's just as addicting as it was a decade ago.

I'm still trying to catch my breath when he stands, shucking off his clothes in a matter of seconds. The small light from the street lamp catches on a large tattoo tracing up his entire left side.

"A phoenix," I breathe.

It's red and orange with just a smattering of black, the opposite of the one that now sits behind my left ear. The color is hardly faded, though it must be a year old at least. The small lines that outline each feather are pristine, too. I can't help but trace a portion of it, the tail feathers that follow the line of his Adonis belt.

"They rise from their own death, the ashes of their demise," he says.

I nod. "They do."

Without breaking his gaze, I tilt my head just enough to expose the new tattoo covering Brett's final mark on me and my life.

His smile this time is softer, less guarded or fueled by lust. And then it's gone, and he's guiding my hands above my head, holding both wrists in his unyielding one-handed grip. His callouses catch on my skin with every slight adjustment of his body above mine. My nipples ache, and I can still feel my pulse in my clit despite the double orgasm.

"Ethan," I whisper.

I push against his hold, but he only squeezes my wrists in silent warning. He shakes his head as he sets a knee on the bed. He strokes himself slowly. And then, without warning, he wraps an arm around my leg and pulls me to the edge of the bed.

His cock presses against me, thick and hard, and I tilt my hips, squirming against his hold. He smirks, those blue eyes sharpening as he teases me with just the tip, testing me like I'm some untried virgin. As if he wasn't the one to take my virginity in that barn ten years ago.

"Patience," he says. "You don't expect me to rush this when I have all night, do you?"

He pulls away and then presses in again, the same agonizing inch of his cock giving me just a taste. Another bolt of need blasts through me. With a moan, I cant my hips, wrapping my knees around his waist, pulling him into me. He palms my belly, forcing me immobile, continuing the slow intrusion until my body trembles and I clench around him hard enough that he grunts.

I mutter a curse, and he smirks, his free hand running up my leg, pushing it into my chest at the same time he pulls out and then pushes back in. My back bows, but his hold on my wrists is unfailing as I moan.

"Please," I whimper as he continues, each slow movement of his cock making my body ratchet tighter, my pulse beat faster. I writhe under him, my mind melting under the onslaught of sensation. He finally increases his tempo, and my toes curl as my knees tighten around him.

Sweat coats his skin, dampening the hair dusted across his chest and running from his navel to his dick. His lips are turned down, his eyebrows bunched, his gaze intent on me, roving over my body with each hard thrust of his hips. In the low light, he looks like an avenging angel, intent on one purpose alone, and that thought has another lightning bolt shooting down my spine, another ragged curse falling from my lips.

"You have such a *mouth*," he says with a grin. He looks up from where we're joined. "I've never heard you say anything so crude before. Does Caleb hear this, too? Or is it something just for me?"

How in the *world* is he able to make stupid jokes when he has me so close to the edge that one small breeze across my nipples will send me over?

All I can manage is a moan, and he laughs, pulling me more thoroughly against him. He releases my hands in favor of dropping one of my legs and pressing it into the mattress, keeping me exposed to him. His callouses catch on the sensitive skin already roughed up by his beard, and I tremble, tilting my hips to keep pace with his. My noises grow with his tempo until my begging, breathless pleas drown out everything else.

"There we go," he murmurs, moving my unpinned leg to his shoulder and circling my clit with a lazy, practiced touch. "Give it to me, princess."

My mind is gone, turned to rubble under the wicked skill of his hands and body. The orgasm surges through me, taking away all thought and reality with it. I cry out, the moan a broken and breathless thing. Ethan follows me over the edge with a rough grunt. His head drops to my shoulder, his teeth biting at my skin just hard enough to sting. His hand on my thigh tightens, and then my body's overwhelmed again. His knot locks us together between one heartbeat and the next.

"Oh, fuck," I gasp. It's practically a cry for help.

I run my hands down his back, scratching long lines across his skin, trying to get closer, trying to find an outlet for the overwhelming sensations. He twists a hand into my hair and runs his lips along my collarbone and throat.

"Easy, princess," he whispers. "Breathe through it."

"Fuck, fuck, fuck." My nails bite into his sides and then I let out a wordless mewl that carries way more than just my body's pleasure.

Ethan lifts away from my skin, his eyebrows furrowed and his lips turned in a deep frown. He loosens his hold on my hair and drags his hand down my neck, letting his thumb trace the hollow of my throat. I can't help the slick that drenches us both, arousal still so strong in me. His chuckle is a little breathless this time, maybe even a bit awed.

Slowly, my body calms and my mind returns, the need to have him carve himself into my essence lessening with each passing minute. My cheeks flush as his knot releases us both, our combined mess spilling onto the sheets of his bed.

"You all right?" he asks.

I give a quick nod even as I let him take my hand and ease my body to sitting. He runs his mouth over the crown of my head, and I perfume. Again. This is honestly a bit embarrassing at this point. Maybe it's because we've spent the last six weeks circling each other without giving in to the base needs of our bodies and our scent match?

Ethan doesn't say anything, though, as he kisses my temple and urges me to my feet.

"Shower," he whispers when I wobble on unsteady legs.

Already, the need for him is rising, building in me like we didn't just knot. It's never been this intense, not even last night with Caleb. And that was borderline irrational. What in the hell is happening to me?

"Shower," he repeats, "and then I'll give you as many orgasms as you need to take the edge off."

My cheeks are bright red as he guides me into his bathroom.

Chapter Thirty-Seven

ETHAN

It's too damn hot.

How can it already be so hot this early in the morning?

I blow out a breath as I rub my eyes, trying to find the motivation to get up for the day. One last check through the separated herd to make sure they've been covered, and then prepping for moving all the cattle around on Monday to their late summer grazing spots. Hopefully the drought that's ripping up Arizona and Colorado doesn't extend any farther north, because we haven't gotten a chance to fix all the fencing that runs along the southern edge of the ranch, exactly where we'll need to move some cattle if things dry out.

I groan and scrub my face. The blanket on me moves, pressing harder into my side. Lavender floats in the air, reminding me of riding through some of the meadows in the summer.

My heart beats faster. My scent floods the room. My dick

throbs, arousal rushing through my veins in a way it hasn't in years. Fuck, I love the smell of lavender.

Wait.

Memories of the night before overwhelm me. The feeling of Brielle underneath me. The sounds she made filling the room. Her scent drowning me and all the conflicted feelings weighing down my chest. The rush of slick from her cunt soaking the sheets as I forced my knot inside her and locked us together.

My scent intensifies even as I force a swallow to soothe the lump in my throat.

Brielle whines as she presses harder into me. I snap my eyes open, scowling at the obscene amount of light coming in through the windows. Whatever has her worried, I need to fix. Whatever has that whine building into a near sob? I'm going to fucking murder it. It had taken way too many orgasms to get her calm last night, and I hate that she's already on edge again.

Not that I minded eating her out. The opposite, actually. But knowing that she was that worried when Caleb has only been gone for a day? It has unease weighing heavily on my sternum.

I run my hand down her back even as I ease onto my side, keeping her pressed into my chest with a solid palm against the back of her head. Her hair is a wild mess, brushing against my face as I turn toward her and run my lips across her temple.

I hum, low in my throat, pressing her harder into me, the bone deep *need* reducing me to instincts alone. The whine cuts off. I relax my hold on her. I can't quite manage to pull my lips away from her skin, though. Instead, I trail them down her cheek and jaw and neck, setting a soft bite in the sensitive, unmarked spot just behind her right ear. She shivers in my hold. Her hand drops lower on my waist, a finger tracing the edge of my boxer briefs.

My scent redoubles from the small touch, cocooning around us until it blends effortlessly with hers. Christ, they smell good together. I suppose scent matches would, though. She shudders against me as I bite her again. She slips her hand under the waistband, circling my dick, and I groan into her skin. She presses a smile into my chest.

"You like teasing me, princess?" My voice is gravel.

She shivers, goosebumps rising along the skin I can see— which is most of it. Her hand doesn't falter, though, and I push up into her hold. God*damn*, she feels amazing. And I'm not going to last more than a few minutes if she keeps going. My stamina is fucking shot.

"I should return the favor," I murmur against her skin.

I pull on her hair, forcing her head back, and bite at the hollow of her throat. Her breath catches, her scent growing thicker, and I grin. I need her under me. I need to taste her, feel her, breathe her in until she's all that exists around me. The purr starts before I can hold it back, not that I would in this moment. She goes boneless against me, her hand still at the base of my dick, her thumb brushing the sensitive spot where my knot starts.

"Fuck, princess," I groan.

She giggles, pressing her face into my chest.

My phone pings with a notification.

Brielle immediately moves away from me, sitting up and pulling her hair back. Her hands fly through her hair, braiding it before I can even sit up. She frowns as she looks at the base of it, like she's missing something. With a sigh, she lets go, and the bottom couple weaves come loose.

With a sigh, I sit up. My irritation at the loss of her touch fades as I take in her beautiful body.

Fuck, the aftermath of knotting looks good on her. Small bruises dot her chest, and I smirk, remembering each nip of my teeth and drag of my beard across her skin. My dick jumps, and I don't try to ignore it or downplay the effect she has on me. Her gaze flicks down before focusing on my face again. One eyebrow slowly rises as her lips bunch into a pout. I groan and reach for her. She doesn't resist as I wrap my arm around her waist and pull her toward me, sucking her bottom lip until she opens enough that I can kiss her the way I want. Lavender explodes around us between one breath and the next.

My damn phone goes off again.

She's quick to disengage, retreating to the bathroom before I can stop her, closing the door softly without a glance back. I run a hand down my face, trying to remember how mornings after when you're dating are supposed to work. We'd had to be discreet a decade ago, so we never actually left my house—or Melissa's—at the same time, intentionally staggering it just in case farm hands from either ranch noticed and said anything. Not that it was all that hard to avoid people then. We'd been so consumed with each other we hardly bothered to come up for air. It had been the best sex of my life up to that point. And last night? Easily the best I've ever had.

My stomach tightens with grief and guilt, but I breathe through it. It was probably something to be expected, just like our scents mingling so well. Biologically perfect for each other means biologically perfect, after all.

I shove out of the bed, grabbing a new pair of jeans and boxers and stepping into them, ignoring the way my dick aches at the restriction. I dig out my phone from the back pocket of the pair I'd thrown off last night. Almost nine in the morning. *Shit.*

Multiple messages from Emily have me scowling. I send a quick text to prove I'm alive and haven't left to get the milk, or whatever euphemism assholes use for walking out on their children.

> Overslept. Sorry. Be on my way soon.

Sounds good. We're hanging out with Joan.
We'll be back over in time for brunch.

And then she sends a photo of Camden, whipped cream covering his nose as he grins for the camera. I can't help but smile.

And then curse under my breath.

My steps eat up the small space as I cross the room, intent on knocking on the bathroom door, politeness be damned. Brielle opens it a heartbeat before I can drop my knuckles against it. My hand hangs suspended in the air for a moment. She walks into me and then gasps, offering a quick apology. Her eyes are wide as they look up at me, and damn if I can't quite manage to keep my hands off of her, combing my fingers through the brown strands of her hair already falling out of the haphazard braid. Her scent strengthens again, and I smirk.

Focus, Ethan.

"I didn't use a condom," I say.

No use beating around the bush. Omegas getting pregnant outside of their heats is rare but not impossible. Trust me to screw up the first hookup I've had since Kayla. Some of the light drops away from her gaze. She doesn't push away from me, though, so I let my other arm wrap around her waist. I trace shapes on her skin and twist her hair around my hand, forcing her head back far enough that I can see the small bruises I've left on her throat.

Satisfaction rips through me at seeing the physical marks. Fuck me. No wonder Caleb can't keep his damn mouth off of her.

Goddamnit, focus, Ethan. You can fuck her later.

"I can grab the Omega-specific Plan B if you want," I say, forcing my attention to the issue at hand. "And I'll take responsibility if something happens."

She presses her hands against my hips, her finger tracing the lines of my stomach.

"I have an IUD," she offers after a moment, her voice blending into the quiet of the room.

My stomach tightening over that realization is *not* out of disappointment. It can't be. Getting her pregnant would be a nightmare in the extreme. We haven't even discussed what the rest of this weekend looks like, much less the rest of the summer. Her being on birth control simplifies everything.

"I didn't put you at risk," I offer.

Difficult to do that when I haven't fucked anyone in nearly four years.

She tilts her head into my touch, a thoughtful look crossing her face. She runs her hand down the hair under my navel as she nods.

"I got tested shortly after everything happened. It was negative." She sighs. "I've only been with Caleb. I can get tested if it's something you want to double check."

I shake my head and run my thumb along her cheek. "I trust Caleb," I say.

She relaxes. I kiss her.

And then the rest of what she said catches up to me.

"Wait," I say, my lips brushing hers.

Chapter Thirty-Eight

ETHAN

Brielle freezes in my arms, her body going stiff between one second and the next. I frown and pull away until my gaze is locked with hers.

"Why would you need to get tested after your husband died?" I ask.

A shadow crosses her face, stealing the gleam in her eyes along with her seemingly good mood. She pulls away from my touch, crossing her arms over her stomach and turning to the dresser nestled on the wall between the bathroom and the closet.

"Can I have a shirt?" she asks, her voice that odd, cautious tone that she used when she first moved back here. "I don't really want to put on the jeans I wore last night yet."

Narrowing my eyes, I slip around her and open the middle drawer, handing her one of my rarely worn graphic tees. It hits her mid-thigh, and the sleeves hang nearly to her elbows. Fuck, she's so damn tiny. She blows out a breath and combs her fingers through her hair, a clear nervous gesture.

She avoids my gaze as she says, "Caleb didn't tell you? I thought maybe he would after you asked about it at the lake."

My answer comes through clenched teeth. "Tell. Me. What?"

She shivers but doesn't say anything else. Unease races through me, weighing on my sternum like a damn brick.

"Brielle, what am I missing?" I intentionally soften my voice, swallowing back the frustration. *What had Caleb not told me?*

She glances over her shoulder, like she's about to bolt from the room. I ease my weight onto the balls of my feet, intent on grabbing her and forcing whatever is causing her this much distress out in the open between us. She focuses on me and crosses her arms. The move makes her tits push against the shirt, and my eyes skate over them before going back to her face. She raises an eyebrow but doesn't quite manage to hide her smirk. Or her blush.

"Why would anyone need to test if they thought they were in a monogamous relationship, Ethan?" she asks after a moment, barely loud enough to be a whisper.

That unease crashes through me until it sits in my stomach, making me nauseous.

He cheated on her?

"You're joking," I say, my voice full of dread and shock.

She shakes her head, tears lining her lashes. She blinks them away before they fall.

Goddamn Beta asshole. That's certainly the type of lying that would ruin your life.

Rage simmers under my skin.

"Disgusting," I seethe.

She laughs, but it's hollow. "Yeah, well, that's not how most people saw it. Not in that tax bracket, at least."

I run my hand through my hair and down my neck as that rage grows hotter.

"What the hell is that supposed to mean?"

She shrugs. "You reach a certain net worth, and suddenly everyone is understanding of a husband who wanders. Because in those circles, you don't marry for anything other than securing more power and wealth. If you enter those circles with a wife? All bets on fidelity are off."

Her voice turns brittle the more she talks, less of the girl I loved visible, buried under this angry, resentful woman.

"Your wife is your eye candy to show the world you have a fantastic home life with your two children. Even better if she's an Omega you convinced to go on suppressors for 'her own good.'" Her words grow angrier as she uses her fingers to make air quotes around the words. "You're seen as powerful and important. But the woman you're actually fucking and starting a family with is your business partner's assistant."

The growl rips up my throat and through the room as I realize what she's doing, what she's explaining without actually admitting to it.

"What a goddamn piece of shit," I mutter.

Fuck, I wish he were still alive just so I could punch him like I did Jake last night.

She tilts her head, the most vulnerable look I've seen from her since she moved back flitting across her face, before she turns toward the pile her clothes ended up in. Her hands tremble as she starts picking them up.

I take a step toward her.

"Brielle," I say. "You didn't deserve that. Fuck, no one deserves to be treated like that."

She shivers, a sound dangerously close to a whine bubbling up her throat. She looks up at me through her lashes, her hands trembling even more.

After a long moment, she says, "Okay."

She scoops up her clothes and drops them on the foot of the bed, folding them with more expedience than precision. Without looking back at me, she leans over the bed, grabbing her phone where it's perched unobtrusively on the nightstand I never use.

My shirt rides up her legs, baring her beautiful thighs and ass. I'm hard in a goddamn instant, my dick straining at the zipper of my jeans.

How in the hell had that man decided she wasn't the best fucking catch of his life? How could he have possibly decided she in her own right wasn't enough to satisfy him? What stick was shoved up his ass that blinded him so completely to the reality that she's the goddamn *catch of the century*?

I close the distance between us, palming her hips and pressing my rock hard dick into the swell of her ass. She looks over her shoulder, her eyebrow cocked high. Lavender blooms around us. I skate my hands down her thighs until I reach the hem of the shirt. She smirks as I ease the shirt higher, baring her completely. When she doesn't pull away, I drop to my knees. Her legs are already soaked with her slick, and I run my tongue along the inside of her thighs, tasting every last inch of the sweet liquid. Her breathing grows choppy as her scent grows around us.

"Ethan," she whispers. I skate my lips over her clit, barely touching, and she shakes in my hold. She cants her hips back, trying to get closer to me.

Satisfaction rips through me. I bite the sensitive line where her thigh blends with her cunt, grinning as she cries out. I repeat it on the other side.

"Holy hell," she whispers. "I've never... Fuck, I didn't think I'd like the feeling of being marked like that."

It's a small mark, really. Nothing compared to the permanent claiming bite shared between an Alpha and Omega. And it's not like it's anywhere she'll have to hide it.

"You prefer your marks somewhere people can see?"

Slick gushes from her, an answer on its own. I slowly lick it up but pause when she doesn't say anything.

Her voice shakes as much as her legs. "Y-yes," she admits. "I like how public Caleb's bruises are. I... *Fuck.*" She shudders in a breath as I bruise her inner thigh. "I like how people know what they mean—the Alphas that see me in town that wanted to ask me out when I first moved back."

The growl is swift and lethal, and I don't bother to quell it.

"Don't worry, princess," I mutter. "I'll make sure they know some of them are my bruises, too."

I run my nose along her center. She shudders and whines.

"Please, Ethan," she begs. I kiss her clit, and she whines. "*Please.*"

With the first swipe of my tongue, she collapses on the bed, her hips canting back toward me. Her whimper is a fucking balm to my soul. As her legs shake with the force of her first orgasm and she buries a hand in my hair, all thoughts of being on time for getting Camden from my sister drain away from me.

Chapter Thirty-Nine

ETHAN

"Finally decided to show up, brother?" Emily stands at the top of the porch stairs of our parents' home leaning against the railing, her arms crossed and her hair pulled back. I pause at the base of the stairs, trying to gauge her mood. Her voice is neutral, but the look she pins me with is borderline hostile.

When I scowl, she just shakes her head.

"When I took Cam last night," she says with acid in her voice, "it was with the understanding that you were stuck in Jackson and wouldn't get back before his bedtime."

I cock an eyebrow and cross my own arms. "All right?"

I let it sit as a question between us.

"So since Caleb is currently flying a damn plane, you get to explain why you both lied to me and then had the audacity to show up *two hours late* to picking up your son."

"I was stuck in Jackson yesterday afternoon dealing with

paperwork bullshit." I start up the stairs. "And you don't actually want to know why I'm late, Emily."

The sight of Brielle collapsed against the side of her bed, her legs splayed and her cunt wrapped tight around my knot as I brought her to her third orgasm this morning flashes behind my eyes. Mint permeates the air around me, and her eyes narrow. I shrug but don't say anything.

"You were in Jackson?" She double checks.

I nod again, trying for patience. In reality, I want to collect my son and spend a quiet afternoon riding up to the Arch or maybe Bluebird View.

A growl rumbles through my sister's chest. I pause on the step below her.

"You going to tell me why Devynn saw you leave The Outpost last night with Brielle if you were in fucking *Jackson*?"

She doesn't move out of my way. She's tall for a woman, even an Alpha, but she's still only eye level with me from her perch above me. And every single speck of that brown that's identical to mine sparkles with rage right now.

"Probably because she saw us leave together," I say, keeping my voice low and disinterested. "I went there after I got back from my shit in Jackson."

Just in fucking time, too.

The thought of Jake touching her, bruising her, has my own rage festering.

Her mouth tightens with her rising anger. It bleeds into her vanilla scent, giving it a sour edge.

"All right. So now you get to tell me why Joan saw you drop her off at her car this morning *after* when you said you'd be by to pick up Cam."

I give her the glare that her demand really deserves. Goddamn small towns. The lack of privacy has never really bothered me— until now. Maybe because I've managed to keep my secret still secret despite the gossipers searching for the next big story. At least until Brielle moved back.

"Yeah, you know why," I tell her, "and despite what you might tell me, you don't actually want me to tell you I had Brielle laid out on my bed this morning, Emily."

Emily raises an eyebrow but doesn't move.

"Mom know?" I ask.

She narrows her eyes before shaking her head once.

Thank God. I don't have the patience to tell Mom about the scent match today. And the rest of it? Well, at least she'll understand some of it better than most. But even still, it's not something I want to approach today.

"Good," I say, trying to move around her.

Emily growls, low and lethal in a way I've never heard from her before. I pause.

"Brielle is my friend, Ethan," she says, her voice low. "Don't you fucking *dare* think about hurting her."

My patience snaps.

"So Caleb's allowed to fuck her as often as he wants, mark her and make it clear to everyone with a goddamn half of a brain in town that they're serious as fuck, but the moment I show the slightest bit of interest, you decide to have a problem with it?"

Her throat ripples with her swallow, but her gaze stays flinty.

"Caleb *wants* to move on from Kayla," she says, raising her voice.

I scoff. "And I don't? You have no fucking idea where I am in grieving my bonded Omega."

"He's her goddamn scent match, Ethan." Emily spits the words at me. "And when I cornered him after he took her out hiking and asked why he had a sudden interest in her, he was fucking *honest* about it. But you? You've done nothing but *lie to me* about her at every possible moment."

"What the hell have I lied about?" I snarl the question and force her back a step, crowding onto the porch.

"Oh, I don't know, maybe the fact that you spent an entire summer with her, wrapped up around her, entrenched enough that it broke her heart when you broke it off when she went back to school."

I pause. She'd told Emily I'd broken her heart? I open my mouth to say something, but she doesn't stop.

"Or how about when she showed up at Brandon's funeral in support of Melissa, you looked me dead in the eyes and said you didn't fucking know her and Kayla frowned because she could *tell* you weren't telling me the truth."

Her chest heaves, and she fists her hands, dropping them to her sides.

"Did Kayla know, at least? Or did she get to live in your lovely web of lies, too?"

Something snaps in me. My voice is low and venomous.

"What good would it have been to tell her? We were bonded. It's not like I was going to run off with Brielle. In case you've forgotten, I fucking *loved* Kayla. I was *happy*, Emily. She was struggling, barely surviving. I got to have a front row seat of her falling apart and having no power to change any of it." I take a deep breath, trying to get the feelings of those last few months out of my mind, out of my body, before it makes me want to punch something. "You've never been in that situation, in a pack where an Omega appreciates you all but has a special bond with one Alpha in particular, and it's not you. Kayla loved us, but she *adored* Brandon. Losing Brandon was like losing herself. All telling her about Brielle would have done is cause her to kill herself faster."

The truth of the comment rings between us. Emily's eyes widen.

"Maybe if the first time she showed back up here *wasn't* for

Brandon's funeral, it might have been different. If Kayla had asked me, I would have said something. But she didn't, and I was more concerned with keeping her alive than with airing out a relationship that had happened long before she was mine. *Especially* since Brielle showed up with the largest goddamn rock I've ever fucking seen on her finger and a piss poor excuse of a Beta playing jealous asshole the entire fucking funeral."

I suck in a breath and try to calm the trembling of my hands. *Fuck*, I want to punch something.

"Melissa knew. Mom knew. I'm pretty sure Olivia knew, too. We kept it low key because you know as well as I do that the gossip would have been orders of magnitude worse than whatever Jessica Bailey can manage now." Emily's eyes are still mutinous despite her shock at my candid mention of Kayla, my explanation not quite breaking her down yet. "When she went back to school and I cut it off, I asked them to keep it all quiet."

I take another step toward my sister, crowding her against the door.

"And just so that everything is on the table now," I bite out, my voice so low it rumbles around us like the thunder of a spring storm. "She's *my* goddamn scent match, too. So forgive the fuck out of me if I take an extra two hours with her to sort through the bullshit of the last decade to figure out if she can love me again even when all I have is half a heart and a fear of feeling my Omega's life drain away while I'm too far from her to change the damn outcome."

Not that we'd discussed any of that. Admitting that we haven't actually discussed *anything* outside of not wanting to ignore the realities of our being biological soulmates isn't something I'm going to do in front of my sister. Not when she's clearly still ready to feed me to the fucking wolves over pursuing Brielle at all.

"You're scent matches?" Emily's arms drop to her sides,

shock the only thing written on her face. All the anger is suddenly gone from her voice.

I nod once before pushing past her, opening the door to our parents' place. It takes her a long minute before she follows behind me.

CALEB

"Papa, look at this flower I found!"

Camden holds up a mangled blue wildflower too close to the camera for me to see much more than a torn petal. I settle in the chair of the hotel room and lean my cell phone against the hotel's landline. My head pounds from the lack of sleep over the last 48 hours, but I ignore it in favor of spending time with my son.

"So Sunday brunch was a success," I say with a smile.

Camden nods before frowning. "Brielle still hasn't come. Can she come next week? I want her to see how I help Nana make pancakes."

Before giving an answer either way, I focus on Ethan where he sits a bit behind Camden, sharpening some of his farrier blades. Instead of the malice or irritation I expect, his eyes are thoughtful. And then I notice the bruise just above the neckline of his shirt.

Brielle texted me yesterday morning, letting me know about her and Ethan. She hadn't given any specifics aside from his confirming bloodwork, but they weren't needed. Not yet. Seeing Ethan not bothering to hide her bruises was a good sign.

Curiosity spikes over what made Ethan drop his resistance.

"I thought you said the weekend was uneventful," I say, trying to hide my amusement.

He scowls for a heartbeat, and then it melts away.

"Figured it was the type of situation better explained in person."

There's no amusement in his voice, just a neutrality that means he's nervous about... whatever happened between them. Or what it might mean long term.

"Papa, can you invite Bri?" Camden steals my attention. Ethan goes back to sharpening his blades. "Papa, I tried but she said she needed to talk to you or Daddy."

"You all right with it, Ethan?" I ask.

I don't want to step on his toes especially if they've started figuring out something tentative between them. Ethan can be fickle as fuck over stuff like that. He drops the blade and runs his hand down his face, closing his eyes. And then he shrugs.

"Sure," he says.

"Yeah, bud," I tell my son. "I'll invite her to the next one I'm home for. Hopefully it's this next one, okay?"

He grins so bright it lights up his eyes and shows off both dimples.

Damn, he looks like Brandon.

This time, the thought doesn't hurt at all.

BRIELLE

"Bri!" Camden rushes down the porch and slams into my leg, his arms wrapping around my waist. The impact jostles the small package balanced atop my phone that I'm trying very desperately to not smash or drop.

I mutter a curse as it starts to tip over.

A strong set of hands grabs it before it manages to fall to the ground.

"Bud, you need to be just a bit more careful. If this was something hot, you both could have been hurt." Caleb's warm voice is gentle with his reprimand. Camden still blushes.

"Oops, sorry, Bri," he says. "Are you here for brunch?"

He mangles the r, so it comes out as "bunch". I smile and wrap my arm around his shoulders.

"I am. Do you think my outfit is okay?" I ask him.

He pulls away just far enough to look up at me. His brows furrow as his lips bunch into a pout.

"You wear green a lot," he says. "But purple is your favorite color. Do you like green, too?"

I smile. "I do. I feel like green looks better with my hair. Do you like it?"

Camden taps his fingers against my hip.

Caleb murmurs "Love it, sweetheart," before Camden can respond.

My cheeks and chest flush, and a wave of need surges through me. It's been a full week since I've touched him, kissed him, *smelled* him. It shouldn't have been a big deal. He's been gone on and off all summer. But this week has felt especially long. A hint of lavender surrounds us, nearly undetectable.

Caleb *purrs* as he breathes in my scent. He palms my waist and kisses my temple, ignoring his son giggling.

Damn Ethan for ripping the only foolproof set of scent blockers I have right now. The last thing I need is to be filling up Lynn and Scott's house with my scent. They might not realize what it means, but Emily will. And so will most of the people who might swing by during this brunch or later on this afternoon.

"Let me take those," Ethan says, a half-step behind Caleb. He holds out a hand for the small package attached to the bouquet of flowers.

His eyes are as stormy as they were last Friday night when he knotted me until I was damn near boneless. The bruises still haven't faded where he left me marked on my thighs. It's the only sign—aside from the shirt I wore out of his house that's now stashed in my closet—that something even happened between us. We haven't talked about it the entire week since. Nerves weigh on me, but they're drowned out by the barely constrained desire in his gaze right now. God, I need his beard to scratch me up again.

The lavender grows stronger.

So does my blush.

"Cam," Caleb says, his voice raspier, "why don't you take these flowers inside to Nana?"

He eases the bouquet off its precarious perch and hands it to his son. Camden focuses on them, letting his arms drop away from my waist.

"Oh! Nana loves roses!" He takes them as he says it, clutching them in a white-knuckled grip. He turns without so much as a word and rushes back up the porch.

"Nana!" he calls as he opens the screen door. "Nana! Bri got you roses!"

Caleb has his other hand buried in my hair and his mouth against mine before the door has closed behind his son. The small package is crushed between us as he backs me against the SUV's door. My scent breaks through my scent-blocking lotion and surrounds us. He only kisses me harder.

A car pulls up behind mine, and I pull away from Caleb. My heart races. My breathing is unsteady. Holy crap, I need Caleb to knot me. And then I need Ethan, too. Or maybe both at the same time.

Just the idea has me blushing like a damn virgin.

Caleb chuckles even as he eases away from me. His voice is breathless when he says, "I want to know exactly what thought made you flush like that."

No way am I about to admit to fantasizing about a threesome while Emily is closing her door and combing her fingers through her hair. I push off the SUV and start toward the house, tucking a piece of hair behind my ear to keep from messing with the bow I put on the unwrapped package. Ethan doesn't touch me as I approach him. He doesn't kiss me or hold my hand. But his body is a wall of heat and promise just behind me.

It's nearly as good as a kiss, I decide, as my thighs clench again.

"Brielle!" Lynn is all smiles when I step into the farmhouse.

She pulls me into a warm hug. "I'm so glad you made it. I've been asking Emily all summer to invite you."

Her eyes hop from me to Ethan and then back, her eyebrow rising in slow, unspoken question. My cheeks flush a dark red again. She laughs and hugs me again.

"Nana, can we make pancakes now? Aunt Emily is here, too." Camden pulls at her leg, wedging between us with the deftness of a sly cat. "Grandpa said I have to wait for you."

The screen door closes behind us, and Emily's vanilla sweeps through the room, stronger than I'd expected. Ethan grunts as it hits him. When I look over my shoulder, he's scowling at his sister. She shrugs, messes with her hair some more, and then moves around us, slipping off her shoes without missing a step. As she passes me, a more subtle scent wraps around me, something warm and spicy. It takes me a minute to pinpoint it.

Why does she smell like cloves?

Curiosity rises in me, but I squash it before it has me asking inappropriate questions. I'll just corner her later like she did me in Jackson a couple weeks ago. Clearing my throat, I hold out the small package of chocolate covered pretzels.

Lynn's smile is wider than before, a hint of surprise lighting her eyes.

"I couldn't find the peanut butter ones. Jackson's options aren't as varied as Denver's," I say in lieu of an explanation.

She takes them, smoothing down the silver bow.

"Oh, you're fine, dear," she says. "I didn't realize you remembered after all these years." She squeezes my wrist even as Caleb laces his fingers with my other hand. "Thank you."

With that, she runs her hand through Camden's blond hair, twirling a piece around her finger. He grins and then runs back to the kitchen. Caleb pulls me along, and we follow her through the house into the heart of it—the large kitchen. Camden's already scrambling onto an impressive-looking step stool that has three rungs and gets him nearly the same height as Lynn.

Scott looks up from the newspaper he has spread across the island, his glasses perched low on his nose. He adjusts them as he stands and approaches me. I expect a handshake, but he instead pulls me into his chest with a single arm around my shoulders.

"Nice to see you, Brielle," he says. "What would you like to drink? And I know Lynn has a fruit salad prepped if you're hungry."

"Water is fine," I say. He nods and then crosses the kitchen. I breathe deeply, trying to keep my nerves from filling my throat, and tuck myself closer into Caleb's side. Scott pulls a glass from the open shelf beside the sink and fills it with a pitcher from the fridge.

"There's a new pot of coffee just finishing up," he says. "Mom used your mug, so it's in the dishwasher right now if you want to pull it out and clean it real quick."

"Thanks, Dad," Ethan says. He moves from his position a half-step behind me. His hand just grazes my waist, and my breath catches. A thread of lavender weaves around me, and Caleb hides his smile against my hair. Scott hands me the glass, nodding as I offer a quiet thanks.

Within moments, the kitchen is abuzz with activity. Ethan and Scott chat about the ranch, rattling off horse names and trimming schedules before delving into a conversation regarding cattle IDs that I don't recognize. Emily steps up to the other side of Camden, offering a third pair of hands as they work at the large gas stove that's had a griddle placed over four of the six burners. Camden giggles as they pour the first one and he gets to wipe up the drip down the outside of the bowl and eat it.

The warmth of the family hits a nerve I didn't even realize was still raw. Mom's been dead for years, and I've had no contact with any of her siblings since she went to rehab that summer that landed me here the first time. And yet, seeing the Monroes orbit around each other, work together in such seamless unity, has an awful ball of emotion welling in my chest. I breathe through it until it doesn't feel quite so overwhelming.

Emily laughs as Lynn mutters something under her breath, a joke I don't hear over the sizzle of the batter on the griddle. Emily and Lynn are nearly twins, their dark hair and brown eyes that are a couple shades lighter than mine. Ethan's coloring is the same, too. Scott's blond hair didn't make the genetic cut.

I wonder if Ethan's kids would have blond hair, I muse to myself. And then I freeze, pain lancing through me before I can brace for it, more complicated than my sadness over Brett being a lying prick. Camden isn't Ethan's genetically, but he could have been. If Kayla hadn't killed herself only months after Brandon was gored by that bull in the pastures, would they have had more kids?

Would I have had a place to come after Brett? Or would I have ended up being the same homewrecker I left with a cold shoulder in the courtroom in Denver?

"You good?" Caleb whispers against my ear. I can't help but shiver.

I force the thoughts away and nod. He spreads his hand on my waist as I let more of my weight fall on him. He urges me into one of the chairs situated along the island and then sits beside me, his palm hot as a brand against my thigh where he grabs me in a proprietary hold.

"I was thinking of going up to Fool's Canyon tomorrow," he says, loud enough it draws the attention of the entire room. His eyes are on me, though, his chin resting on his open hand. "Would you like to go with me? We could take the horses and pack a picnic."

The room drops into a stillness so complete, you could hear a pin drop. I purse my lips, trying to understand the sudden shift in the dynamics around me. Scott raises an eyebrow, and Ethan frowns as he shakes his head, keeping his dad quiet. I tuck away the interaction to ask him about later. Maybe. After we hash out exactly what's happening between us and how it fits in with my dynamic with Caleb. And with Camden.

Yeah, maybe it'll just be something that fades into the background.

"Sure," I say. Caleb squeezes my thigh, tight enough I almost whine. "It's one meadow I haven't revisited."

Caleb's smile is bright, but it doesn't quite cover the heavy weight of the room.

I can't help but feel there was an unspoken conversation I didn't have the language for.

I make it a point to end up in the barn before Caleb. I may have gotten better at tacking up a horse over the last several weeks, but there isn't a chance in hell that I'm letting him see me struggle with Phoebe's saddle. I suppose it's probably time to admit she and I need to be seen by the local saddler and get fit for something custom to us both. Brandon's old saddle fits her great, but it's large enough to be a downright hassle for me to handle.

I mull over the best way to ask Caleb before ultimately tossing out the idea. He'd be offended at the idea of me paying for it even though I have more money than I honestly know what to do with. Scott will probably know someone, though. And he won't have the same protective, intrinsic need to coddle or provide for me.

Maybe I'll invite him and Lynn out to breakfast or coffee. The idea puts a smile on my face, and I hum under my breath as I pull the cross-under bridle Emily and Melissa taught me to use from the tack room. I also manage to grab the two saddle blankets Phoebe seems to prefer.

If you'd told me in April that horses have preferred equipment, I would have looked at you like you had lost your mind. Now here I am at six in the morning—before the sun has even fully risen—making sure the white and black chevron isn't dirty so I can use it on a morning ride with an Alpha who happens to be my scent match.

An Alpha that I've absolutely fallen head-over-heels in love with in the span of... I count back the weeks. Less than two months. I've fallen in love with Caleb in less than two full months.

Wild.

Phoebe's still quiet when I hang the bridle on the hook in front of her stall and let the saddle blankets drop to the ground. She doesn't resist when I lead her out of the stall and tie her out so I can work through the process.

My mind quiets with each step, the brushing and the placing of the blankets and the guiding of the bridle over her ears and the easing of the bit into her mouth. She shakes her head as I'm adjusting her mane so it's not caught in the bridle's leather straps.

"I know it's early," I tell her, scratching her nose. I'm not normally out to the barn until seven-thirty during the week. She pushes into my hand, and I smile. "I've been told it'll be worth it, though. If it's not, you're welcome to freak out on him."

She shakes her head again. It's not a nod, but I'm taking it as one anyway. I turn on my heel and head back to the tack room, psyching myself up for the weight of her saddle. It's just as heavy and unruly as the first time Emily, Melissa and I went riding at the end of May. I grunt as I pull it into my belly, trying to get better leverage.

I don't even manage to take three steps down the corridor

toward Phoebe before there's a set of arms wrapping around me, pulling the saddle from my grasp and lifting it over my head.

Fire licks through my core, and my scent grows stronger, quickly enough that my cheeks darken. I hadn't bothered with scent blockers. It felt... unnecessary. Though now, despite being fully clothed in jeans and a T-shirt as well as the flannel shirt of Ethan's Hudson smuggled to me before the Fourth of July, it feels like I'm standing here naked.

Caleb's purr starts up, and my flush darkens even more.

"I can handle it," I say without much fight.

Caleb's already walking into the barn when I turn around, the saddle held easily in his grasp. I take a minute to soak him in, his dark wash jeans and blue shirt that's stretched taut across his shoulders and back, the fabric hugging his skin like it's been painted on. That tattoo on his arm is mostly visible again. He saddles Phoebe faster than I've ever managed.

"Are these already set for you?" he asks, motioning to one of the stirrups as I finally manage to cross the barn. "Beau tends to work her on the weekends."

I scratch Phoebe's nose, and she pushes into my hand.

"Yeah, I'm the only one that's been riding her this summer," I say.

With a nod, he drops the stirrup so it sits against Phoebe's side and focuses on me. My breath catches in my throat.

His look... I'd burn down the world to have him look at me like that for the rest of my life. Lavender gets stronger, and he grins.

"Ready?" I ask.

He pulls me against him and kisses me, tangling a hand into my hair and running his thumb along my cheekbone.

When he pulls away, he murmurs, "Give me five minutes to saddle up Daphne."

Chapter Forty-One

I've already spread the blanket out and weighed down the corners by the time Brielle slides off Phoebe without comment, keeping tight hold of the lead rope that's been tucked into the leather strapping of the bridle during the ride. Her hands are steady as she ties it to Daphne's lead, though her legs wobble a bit.

I'm up and across the clearing, needing to make sure she's all right.

The ride into the canyon wasn't quite as smooth as I'd hoped. Phoebe isn't the biggest fan of the grade, and she spooked once when a fox went running through some of the trees.

Brielle smiles as I approach, and happiness warms me. Her eyes drop back to the lead rope she's working with, her eyebrows furrowing. I run my hand down Daphne's neck to keep from taking over Brielle's work.

"You sure this is enough?" she asks without looking up from the knot she's made. It's a bit messy, but it doesn't budge when I pull on it. "Melissa and Emily are always harping on the stable hands at Misty Mountain about making sure the horses are tied to something solid."

"Daphne's pretty solid," I say with humor. When she glances up at me under her lashes, her lips curving into a faint line, I take her hand and lead her to the picnic. "They'll keep each other company while we enjoy the meadow."

Her cheeks flush a bright red, and I laugh.

"Not what I meant," I say.

Not yet, anyway.

The thought surges through me, and my half-hard dick roars to life. Fuck, I cannot be thinking about why I invited her up to *this* meadow right now or I'm going to be a goddamn mess through this lunch. I arrange myself on the blanket, trying to take pressure off my constrained dick. Cinnamon blooms around me, conveying my arousal despite me trying to be more discrete.

Her blush grows, bleeding down her neck and onto her chest, disappearing under the neckline of her simple shirt. After a long moment, she closes the distance between us and settles onto the blanket beside me.

"Did your mom make this picnic, too?" she asks with a smirk.

I offer her the nondescript leather bag full of our lunch. She pulls out the french dip.

"Nope. I bribed Hudson, instead." I grin and grab the sandwich, unwrapping it for her before she can manage. "No way I'm letting you see how bad I am at cooking yet."

She smiles. "It is the one thing I haven't really seen you do this summer. Well, technically, I haven't seen you fly. But I know you wouldn't have the seniority with the wildfire crews if you were bad at it."

She'd looked up how my job worked?

God, she really is perfect.

"Didn't expect you to become an expert on fire pilots," I admit.

She shrugs and drops her eyes. I put a finger under her chin and urge her to look at me.

"I like it," I whisper.

Lavender weaves around us.

"So you're a really good pilot, you know your way around the horses. You probably can handle the cattle at the Monroe Ranch, too, though Beau seems to like it more than you. And that doesn't even bring up the fact you're a phenomenal dad."

Her praise shoots through me. Damn, I want to kiss her right now. I run my thumb over her chin.

She purses her lips and cocks a single eyebrow. "And yet you can't cook."

"Nope." I pop the "p". I grip her chin and kiss her, forcing myself to pull away before it can become more involved.

She giggles and follows me, keeping her mouth barely brushing mine. "Well, at least it proves you're actually human."

I hum with my amusement. My chest is light, a happiness sitting under my sternum I haven't truly felt in a long time, bolstered by her smile and relaxed body and the subtle lavender of her scent weaving around us even now.

"What kind of sandwiches did you convince Hudson to make?" she asks, pulling away and focusing on the food.

"He didn't let me pick. He said they were french dip when he dropped them off last night."

Her smirk sends a jolt down my spine, as does watching her lips part around the end of the sandwich as she takes a bite.

"This is so good," she moans.

Cinnamon floods the air, stronger than the wildflowers blooming throughout the meadow and her own scent that's still circling us. Her cheeks heat, the blush racing down her neck and onto her chest. Her throat ripples with her swallow.

Am I a masochist? Pretty sure I'm a masochist. Because there's nothing quite like the torture of watching her lips spread around the sandwich and her throat move with her eating. Holy hell, I want it to be me that's making her throat move like that.

And now I'm hard. Again.

"What's that look for?" she asks.

I don't even think to censor the thought.

"Just imagining that being my dick instead of a sandwich."

She laughs and sets the sandwich in her lap. Lavender surrounds us more thoroughly than before, its own beautifully enticing wave.

"I thought you said you didn't mean for us to enjoy the meadow that way," she says, a coy lilt to her lips.

Her eyes twinkle with her humor, and I laugh. She doesn't resist as I pull her to me, my palm flat against the back of her head and my fingers lacing through her hair. Her knees bracket mine just like that first hike and picnic. Her lips are soft as ever, and I bask in the feel of them, in the soft intimacy of having her at all.

"I liked going to brunch with you," she whispers as I pull away.

"Yeah?" I ask, dropping my hand to her neck, letting my thumb trace her collarbone. "You happy being family official?"

She nods.

"I want to ask you something," I say. It comes out breathless, even a bit nervous.

"If it's about making use of the meadow, I'm all for it," she says with a smirk.

Fuck me. I'm not going to be able to focus long enough to make this special if she keeps looking at me like that.

"It's about bonding, actually," I admit. I don't drop my eyes, holding her gaze so she knows just how serious I am.

"Bonding?" she asks, total surprise in her voice, her body. She sags against me, her shoulders dropping away from her ears. "That's something you'd want to risk again?"

Instead of giving her words, I cup her face and kiss her, long and slow and deep.

She doesn't bite back a whine as she presses into me, practically climbing into my lap. The moment it slips between her lips and into our kiss, it's like a dam breaks.

Her hands scrabble at my shirt, pulling at the hem until she has it lifted around my ribs. My body rises to her need, cinnamon exploding and intertwining with her scent until they drown us even in the open air of the meadow. Her breath stops for a heartbeat, her hands pausing in their frenzy to get my clothing off. I trace her bottom lip with my tongue, shallowing out the kiss as she pauses.

"Alpha," she whispers, low and sultry.

Every single hair on my body stands up.

All at once, her scent slams into me. The intrinsic siren call of it has me harder than I can remember, my dick aching. My mind is hazy with arousal. It takes all my self-control to not lay her out on the blanket and rip her jeans. Instead, I run my hand down her neck.

And then I pull away, cursing at the fevered feel of her skin.

"Brielle?" I ask, my voice so low it sends a shiver through her. "How close is your heat?"

She worries at her bottom lip, her gaze vacillating between focused and glazed.

"Omega." It's nothing short of a bark, all the Alpha command I can wield threaded through it. "Is your heat close?"

"I... I don't know," she admits in a whisper. Her palms press into my stomach, her nails pricking my skin. "I went off the suppressors in December and haven't had one since."

Fuck. Me.

More than six months. And she's spent at least a few weeks of them being truly touch-starved, enough that I could smell it in her scent that first time I took her out. How many of her symptoms that I'd thought were lingering effects of that touch-starvation were actually signs of her impending heat?

Her scent grows stronger, another whine building in her throat. That call weaves through me, burrowing into my bones, and my dick jumps even as my brain goes a bit foggy.

Oh *fuck*.

It doesn't matter now. The reality is that I have an Omega in heat in the middle of the Wyoming wilderness—and the only way out of this glen is by horse or chopper.

I'm on my feet before she can try to kiss me again, pulling her into me as I walk to where Daphne and Phoebe are casually grazing a few hundred feet away. Phoebe flinches as we come near, her ears pinned, but Daphne is stalwart as always. I guide Brielle's hand onto her lead rope, making sure her grip is firm before pulling away.

"Stay here," I order, that same command pushing through my voice.

She shudders in a breath before nodding.

"Yes, Alpha," she whispers.

Hell, if that doesn't send a thrill down my spine.

I pack up the picnic without any thought for the food. The moment the saddle bags are full, I'm sprinting to the horses, draping them over Phoebe's hips and buckling them onto her saddle since it'll be her only weight.

I then ease Brielle up into Daphne's saddle, forcing her up against the horn even though I know it'll be uncomfortable as fuck for her. I can't trust her to hold on to me and have the more comfortable position behind me. And I sure as hell can't trust she'll be able to ride Phoebe right now. Already, her eyes have stopped switching in and out of focus, her glassy stare landing somewhere in the middle distance.

I pull my phone from my pocket and dial Ethan.

"If you're calling now, something fucked happened or she said no," he mutters instead of a greeting.

"She didn't say no," I say.

She didn't really say anything, actually. But navigating that will be a problem to figure out after the next five days. Shit, or longer. If she hasn't had a heat since before December, this could be a hell of a cycle for her.

"Please tell me Phoebe didn't spook and throw her." Ethan's voice is both lighter and more worried than before. "She hates that path up to the meadow."

"You need to pack up," I tell him. "And then I need you at the barn."

There's the sudden clinking of metal before Ethan's saying something to whichever employee is helping him at Misty Mountain. Melissa's voice cuts through some of the noise, but I can't make out what she's saying.

"What happened?" he asks, worry overtaking his calm disinterest. "You on your way to Jackson?"

Brielle whines as I swing into the saddle behind her, my arm enclosing her and forcing her farther forward. The horn of the saddle digs into her belly, and the whine grows louder. Ethan's breathing freezes for a heartbeat, two. And then he curses.

"Tell me that's not what I think it is," he says.

Her scent surrounds me, and I have to hold my breath to keep from dropping into the haze of the rut. After a moment, the wind changes, and it blows her scent away from me.

Thank God.

"I promised you eight years ago I wouldn't lie," I say. My voice is hoarse.

Ethan curses again, and then he's calling to someone in the distance.

"You need help getting her out?" he asks.

I urge Daphne onto the nature trail at an almost trot, not risking anything faster given Brielle's fragile state. When Phoebe follows without protest, I blow out my held breath. Brielle leans her head against me, tilting until her nose is in the sensitive spot where my neck meets my shoulder.

"I can get her out," I say as we navigate the first stretch without problems. It's the worst of the grade. In theory, the rest will be manageable.

"I'll be there," Ethan says.

And then the call cuts off.

Chapter Forty-Two

ETHAN

By the time I make it through town and to my own ranch, my heart is in my throat and nerves sit in my stomach like a damn stone. Beau frowns as he steps out of one of the employee barns, his hands in his pockets. Emily follows a few steps behind him.

Shit, the last thing I need right now is another Alpha at the barns. I love Emily. She loves Brielle. But instincts are instincts.

They close the distance to me even as I ease the truck into the open space in front of the private barn. There's no sign of Caleb across the meadow, where the trailhead he's probably using dumps out of the forest. I tilt my head back and force myself to breathe, to think.

Fuck, it's been so damn long since we've had to get an Omega through a heat. Do we even have enough supplies? I count through the amount of blankets we have as well as sheets. It's likely enough as long as one of us stays on top of the laundry. Do we have an extra tooth brush? We can probably use Camden's hair brush if Caleb doesn't have one of hers stashed at our place already.

Camden.

Shit.

I pull out my phone and call Joan. She answers on the first ring.

"Hey, Ethan," she says in her happy alto. "I hope the horses didn't give you too much trouble this week. Melissa mentioned yesterday that one of them keeps throwing a shoe."

I huff out a laugh. Misty Mountain's trail horses are the literal last thing on my mind right now, even the damn palomino that's made it her life mission to go through as much steel as physically possible.

"Hey, Joan, do you still have that bag of Camden's things?" I ask.

There's a pause. "Yes. What happened? Does Lynn have Cam right now?"

I'd left him with Mom this morning, but she'd texted mid-morning saying her and Dad were headed into Jackson for a last minute issue with her booth at the Artisan shop. I focus on Emily and Beau again. A flash of blond hair runs out of the barn behind them, racing around them even as I watch.

"Emily does," I say as Camden stops to pick a flower from the pasture. I force a swallow and then say, "Brielle's in heat."

Joan curses, low and fervent. It's such a rare occurrence that I actually bark out a laugh.

"Caleb was taking her up to Fool's Canyon today." Her voice carries the same worry that's making it difficult for me to breathe.

"I know." That stone in my stomach gets heavier. "He's getting her down right now. He said he could manage."

There's a muffled sound and then Joan says something to someone else, quiet enough I can't understand it. After a half minute, she says to me, "All right. Miranda's got the cafe until close. I'll coordinate with Lynn and Emily. You need anything for Brielle?"

"I don't know," I admit. "We haven't—"

My throat closes around the words. There's a long, awful silence.

"You take care of Brielle and text me if you end up needing anything," Joan says, her voice softer than before. "I can send Hudson to Jackson if you need something from the Council, too. Everything else can wait until after."

The call disconnects, and I shove the phone into my pocket and slide out of the truck.

"What's wrong?" Beau asks.

"Something happen with Chesapeake?" Emily asks. I cock an eyebrow at her assumption it's something to do with the palomino that loves to hate me—and her shoes.

I shake my head and adjust the ball cap.

"Caleb's on his way in," I say.

Beau's frown deepens. "That's way earlier than he said. Something go wrong?"

Emily mutters an agreement. "That feels short. I mean, it's probably enough time, but still..."

She trails off.

"She dropped into her heat."

Emily curses.

"Bonding can do that?" Beau asks. He pulls off his hat and runs a hand through his hair.

I shrug. She'd been showing subtle signs for the last couple weeks. Was it the bonding that pushed her over? Probably not. But without knowing when her last heat was, there's no way to know with absolute certainty.

"Take her to the guest house," Emily says. "She's nested there, and it's a quicker drive than all the way to town and your place."

I frown. The only bed at her guest house is the one in the bedroom. If we use it, we'll have to sleep on the couch. Or in the nest with her.

Kayla hated having us sleep in her nest, especially during her heats. She couldn't stand the extra body heat when the need wasn't consuming her.

That complicated ball of emotions tries to rise again. Fuck, I don't want to deal with it, feel it, acknowledge it. I focus on something I know how to handle.

"Are there enough supplies?" I ask.

Emily frowns. "Probably not, but we can gather some and have one of the Betas bring everything over."

Beau nods. "Dad and I are happy to play runners. Get me a list, and I'll have Dad start grabbing things. You need new ones, or are things from your house all right?"

"From his house should be fine. She's already been there and smelled the laundry detergent they use." Emily takes control while I flounder with the reality that I'm about to get an Omega other than Kayla through a heat. An Omega who is my literal physical soulmate. An Omega who hasn't had more than a passing greeting with me since I fucked her boneless over a week ago.

"I'll coordinate with Hudson about getting you guys food," Emily continues. She pulls out her own phone and sends a text to someone. "I know she just went to Jackson for a fancy food haul as she calls it, but there won't be enough to feed all three of you."

My heart pounds in my chest as I nod.

Beau looks over my shoulder, and his mouth tightens.

"Here they come," he says.

I glance behind me. Sure enough, out of the trees exactly where I expected, they start toward us. Caleb pushes Daphne faster once they're on the flat ground. He's far enough away I can't see specifics, but it's obvious he has Brielle wedged in front of him, his arms holding her in place. Even from this distance, she looks like a mess.

Emily turns for Camden, picking him up and heading toward Mom and Dad's house without a glance back. Thank fuck she understood without me having to say it.

"I need you to take the horses," I tell Beau. He nods. "Emily will stay at the house until she sees us leave. And no one else should show up while we're trying to get Brielle out of here, but—"

"I'll make sure you guys are safe," he says, even more serious than normal.

It takes only a few minutes—that feel like an entire fucking hour—for Caleb and Brielle to make it across the clearing. He swings off Daphne before easing Brielle into his arms.

She's even more of a mess up close. Tears track down her face and wet her shirt. Her eyes are unfocused, her hair a tangled mass. I can't help but scan both sides of her neck, looking for his mark.

Something dark twists in my gut when I don't find one.

I start toward them, but Daphne flattens her ears and takes a step back.

"Easy, Daph girl," Beau murmurs.

He keeps up a low stream of soothing phrases as he rushes around me and grabs hold of Daphne's bridle. Once she's calmed enough, he undoes Phoebe's line and then walks both horses into the barn.

"Let's get this gear off you, and then you both can get hosed down and eat a treat," he says. "That was a hard ride."

As soon as Beau disappears, I approach Caleb. His eyes are wild as he pants, and his hands flex every few seconds where they grip Brielle's body. Brielle whimpers with every breath she takes, every movement of Caleb's body against hers. Her scent is so damn strong, it's all I can think about and breathe in even from five feet away.

"She needs help," I say, trying to keep my voice unreactive. "Now, before we go."

Every second she's like this is unfair to her. The longer the heat's triggered need goes unfulfilled, the more physically painful it becomes for the Omega. She needs to be knotted. Now.

My dick jumps like it's volunteering.

Caleb nods before groaning. "I can't. Not after that damn ride. I don't trust myself."

To not drop into a true rut and claim her while she's in heat. Fuck, he really didn't bond her. But he said she hadn't said no. I frown but don't ask.

"Emily said we should use the guest house. She's apparently built a true nest there," I say instead as I pull Brielle into my own arms and turn toward my truck.

Caleb nods. "She has. I forgot about that." He stretches his neck and groans again. "I need like three minutes to get my bearings again."

I already have the back door open. I ease Brielle onto the seat and then reach across her to grab Camden's seat. Brielle whines, shifting under me, and then bites my neck. Hard. Mint surges around us, my body responding to her fundamental need.

"Alpha," she whimpers, her voice broken and hoarse like she's been sobbing for the last hour. Fuck, she probably has.

"Can you take this to the porch?" I ask Caleb, getting my last breath of non-lavender infused air for the foreseeable future.

He grabs it with a shaking hand and then walks away.

I guide Brielle onto her back, and she whines, the sound eager in a way the others haven't been.

"Please, please, please," she begs. "Make it stop."

"I will, princess. I'll make it go away."

Her hips jerk as I palm the button on the fly of her jeans. My skin skims hers as I ease the zipper down, and she cries out, devolving into sobs, fresh tears falling over her lashes. My hands are trembling hard enough it takes me a minute to get her jeans off. Her movements grow more desperate, more jerky. Her hands dig into my forearms, trying to guide them to her cunt.

Her panties are fucking soaked, her slick sticking to her thighs and dripping to the leather seat. They're another set of La Perla, the small logo nearly undetectable. I weigh the difficulties of trying to slide them off of her so she doesn't lose another piece of expensive as fuck clothing.

Her nails bite into my arm, hard enough to draw blood, and the decision is made for me. Hopefully she doesn't hate me for ruining another pair.

The lace rips easily under my hands, falling away from her flawless skin. Somehow, her scent gets even stronger. I can't help but groan. I fumble with my own button and zipper, easing my belt loose enough to slip down my jeans. And then I wrap my arm around her waist.

"Come here, Omega," I say, pulling her into my lap.

Her knees lock around my hips. Her hand shakes as she grips my dick, guiding me into her, and then she slides down in one quick motion. Her moan is louder than mine, but it's a near thing. She doesn't pause at all, simply plants her hands on my shoulders and uses them as leverage as she moves, chasing the orgasm her body needs—both hers and mine, the one that will set off my knot and lock us together.

It takes an embarrassingly short amount of time to get me right to the edge, ready to fall off at the smallest movement.

"Brielle," I mutter.

She mewls, the sound so sad and desperate, I don't try to get her off first. She twists her hips, and I'm gone, heat shooting down my spine and through my legs. I pull her down into me. She screams as my knot locks us together, biting my shoulder.

Hard. Blood seeps into my shirt as she drops her forehead to the aching spot.

Her breathing evens out about the same time Caleb opens the driver door and slides behind the wheel. I brush aside her hair and wipe the tears off her cheek. She shivers, but her eyes don't flutter at all. Caleb rolls down the windows, and her scent slowly fades out, letting me think a bit better.

He tilts his head back and sighs before looking at me in the mirror. When I nod, he starts on the dirt road toward Emily's place.

Chapter Forty-Three

BRIELLE

The room is dark when I wake, covered in my favorite blanket and surrounded by the pillows that I usually pull off my bed before actually going to sleep. I slowly sit up, a headache forming behind my eyes that echoes my heartbeat. Is it a headache? The throbbing pulse moves lower, until my nipples ache with it.

I groan and tip my head back, trying to remember how I even got back to my nest. I'd been on a ride with Caleb, hadn't I? Lavender floods the room, and the soreness between my legs blooms into a need that's the same as the pulsating current webbing out through the rest of my body. Definitely *not* my heartbeat. It pulses in my belly, and I crumble, shrieking with the sudden ache of it.

A door clicks open, and cinnamon surrounds me.

I swallow, trying to wet my mouth.

"Omega?" Caleb's warm voice cocoons me as a set of strong hands cup my face and tilt my head. "Sweetheart?"

When I open my eyes, Caleb's blue eyes greet me, worry and heat equal measures in his gaze. That need pulses in my belly again, and I cry out, grabbing his arms to keep myself steady.

My voice shakes. "What—"

He kisses me, soft and warm and comforting. I collapse against him even as my scent surges around us. It feels like its own living thing at this point. My nipples are so sensitive, my thighs clench as they brush along his shirt.

"You're in heat, sweetheart," Caleb says against my lips, wrapping an arm around my waist and laying me out on the bed, the pillows surrounding me. They smell of mint, and it makes my need ratchet tighter.

"Heat?" I ask.

Is that what this is? The burning need through my body is way worse than anything I've ever felt—not that I've actually ridden out a heat. I've always opted to be sedated through them under the supervision of a doctor approved by the Council.

"Please." It comes out as an honest-to-God beg, but I don't have it in myself to apologize.

A haze falls over me as he pulls away and strips out of his clothes. What little sense of where I am, what I'm doing, falls to the wayside under it. Another cramp seizes me, and I whimper. I want to curl up on my side to try and hide from the pain. A firm hand on my hip keeps me immobile, though.

"It hurts, Alpha," I sob, tears spilling over my lashes. The trails they leave are hot on my cheeks.

He kisses them away as he settles over me. His arms brace around my head as his hands thread through my hair. The heat of his body has anticipation coursing through me. Like it knows the heat is what will make the pain go away, will make the horrible cramps stop. Cinnamon surrounds me, and the gut-wrenching fear fades away under its presence.

"I know, Omega," he says as he enters me, as soft and

comforting as his kiss. It lessens some of the ache low in my belly. "I'll make it better, sweetheart. Let me take away the pain."

I wrap my legs around his hips, keeping him as close as I can. My arms wrap around his neck. My nails dig into his skin. He claims me as thoroughly as he ever has, his pace never faltering. My body tightens around him. His lips run down my throat and across my shoulder in a circuit. They barely touch, but it feels like I've been branded. Need sweeps through me, a fire in winter, blazingly hot.

"*Please*." I'm not asking for his knot but something deeper, stronger. Unbreakable.

Yes, that's what I need.

My Alpha pulls his lips away, and I cry out. I dig my hands into his hair, trying to bring him back to me.

"Alpha," I sob.

His teeth scrape along the sensitive skin of my throat, just under my ear, like he's tracing something. It takes too long to remember the tattoo. Is he tracing the feathers? He grunts, biting me hard enough to hurt, and then his knot locks us together, and I'm falling over the crest of my orgasm, every irrational thought gone from my mind as sensation roars through my veins. The blistering waves take away all thoughts of pain and aches and need.

"Good job, sweetheart." His voice is a caress on my bruised skin. "Sleep now. Let it take the pain away."

His voice is so warm, so light. It's impossible to resist his quiet command. He traces my chin as I fade away into oblivion.

CALEB

The sun is just cresting the horizon when I startle awake, knocking one of the fifteen thousand pillows Brielle has to the ground. It feels like I've been hit by a damn truck, but that's to be expected when we're going into day seven of Brielle's heat. A door swings open as I slowly sit up.

Ethan's dressed in a set of dark gray sweats. Small droplets of water are splattered around the waistband. With a hard sigh, he runs a towel over his hair before tossing it into the second basket Beau swung by on Tuesday, the one we've been using for the non-essential linens. The other one is full of the last round of blankets that we haven't gotten a chance to put through the wash.

"You want anything to eat?" Ethan's voice is rough. When he looks at me, his eyes are red and there's dark circles under them. "I was going to throw something together while she's still out of it. And then maybe try to catch another nap out on the couch."

We've only been managing a couple hours between her waves. It hasn't really left a whole lot of time for sleeping or eating. It's a hell of a lot different getting an Omega through one of these with only two of us, that's for damn sure. I haven't been this exhausted since Camden was a newborn. Or maybe when he was cutting his first set of molars. That was a rough couple weeks.

"I'm good," I say with a quick shake of my head. "Go try to get some rest."

He starts toward the bedroom door, nodding once, when Brielle stirs beside me. She turns toward me and burrows into my side with the precision of a damn scent dog. Her hand digs into my thigh, her nails biting through the set of boxers I wear. And then she perfumes, the lavender overpowering the air filter we have running in the corner.

Ethan grunts and pauses, swinging his gaze toward her.

I ignore him, focusing on Brielle as she slowly rises onto her knees, her eyes half-lidded and her lips pushed into a heavy pout. Her hands tremble as she hooks her fingers into the waistband of my boxers and tries to push them down my hips.

"Alpha," she says, whining when they don't budge. She pushes again and sighs when she manages to wrap her hand around my hardening dick. "Need you."

Her voice has gone all sultry. I push up into her hold, letting my head fall back.

"You have me, Omega," I mutter.

She straddles me, and I shimmy the underwear just low enough that it frees my cock. She slides onto me, not hesitating for even a heartbeat. Her hands flex on my shoulders, her eyes still mostly closed. Her lavender envelops us, gaining even more potency.

Her movements gain a desperate edge, and so I hold her hips and fuck up into her, trying to keep her in the position she's most responsive to. Tears line her lashes after a moment, though, and my breath catches in my throat.

Oh shit. Did I hurt her?

"Brielle?" I ask, slowing everything between us. "Sweetheart, are you all right?"

She shakes her head. "Mint."

Shit. She needs more than just me. I look over her shoulder. Ethan's eyes are wide, his hand clutching the threshold of the door so tight his knuckles are white.

"You need Ethan, too, sweetheart?" I ask in a low croon. She rocks her hips and then mewls, dropping her head back. A tear falls down her cheek. I force an edge to my voice, a bite of command. "Omega, tell me what you need."

"Mint," she says again. She palms my neck and pulls me closer, shuddering in a breath when my lips trace her collarbone. "Bite."

Yeah, not a snowball's chance in hell I bite her right now. I didn't when she first dropped into her heat, and I sure as hell am not going to fuck that up now.

"Mint," she says again, her voice turning petulant.

Ethan curses, and then he pads across the room, his footsteps nearly silent. He strips out of the sweatpants, leaving them in a pile at the foot of the bed, and then eases behind her.

She squeals in sudden excitement, palming his hip and forcing him closer. His eyes are locked on me, though.

"Have you..." His voice trails off.

When I shake my head, he curses again. Brielle whines.

"Fuck. If she hasn't..." He blows out a breath. "This is not the time to try it, that's for damn sure."

"Maybe you just touching her will be enough," I offer. I hold Brielle's hips, forcing her completely still, and then drop onto my back so Ethan feels like he has more room.

Ethan kisses her shoulder, letting his teeth graze her skin. His fingers play with her nipples, pulling them until they're tight buds and her skin is awash in goosebumps. She clenches around me, slick sliding down my dick, and I groan.

"Yeah, fuck, that might be enough," I grunt.

Ethan nods and then bites her again. She shakes in our combined hold, falling forward, only managing to catch herself at the last moment with a hand splayed just to the side of my head. He follows her, easing his arm under hers until she grabs him instead of the bed sheet. Her head tilts back, her throat rippling with her swallow.

"Please," she whispers. "Oh God, please. Please."

I fuck up into her, falling into the feel of her body and the sound of her voice and the way her lavender scent wraps around me in a way that feels so fucking perfect. It blends with my cinnamon and Ethan's mint, making the entire room smell like the perfect blend of English cottage and winter forest.

Ethan wraps his free arm around her hip and circles her clit with quick, soft touches. She shakes and cries out, her body going stiff and then limp. I stop holding back the orgasm sitting at the base of my spine. I push into her, forcing my knot as deep as I can, and it rips through me, robbing me of my vision. Her voice breaks on a second desperate scream, and Ethan mutters another ragged curse.

"Shit, I haven't come like that since I was a goddamn teen," he admits.

I can't help but laugh, and it has Brielle whimpering.

Ethan guides her head back onto his shoulder, combing through some of her unruly hair. Her breathing slowly steadies as her body relaxes around my knot. After a minute, she blows out a breath and looks down at me, her cheeks flushed a gorgeous dark red.

"Oh my god," she whispers, suddenly entirely lucid. The edge in her lavender fades away even as she perfumes anew. "This is so fucking embarrassing."

Ethan laughs behind her, letting his hand move away from her clit and onto her hip.

"It's all right, princess."

She flushes. He twists a strand of hair around his finger before letting it fall across her chest.

None of us say anything else until my knot finally releases.

"Do you want waffles?" Ethan asks her, his lips brushing her temple. Her cheeks flush, and she nods once. He trails his hand up her side. "Let Caleb get you cleaned up while I make some."

Chapter Forty-Four

BRIELLE

My stomach tries to come up my throat when Caleb drops the plane toward a tiny landing strip. I can't help but ball my hands into fists where I've tucked them under my legs to keep from accidentally messing with any of the instruments on the panels in front of me. I've flown in small planes before. Brett hated flying commercially, and so I didn't put up a fuss when he'd spend the extra thousands of dollars to fly private whenever we went somewhere. But this tiny little Cessna is leagues tinier than even those jets.

Camden's giggles crackle through the headset. I twist around, and he waves at me from his perch behind Caleb's seat. Ethan's stoic beside him as he holds out an arm, keeping Camden from reaching for me.

"Careful, kid," he murmurs. "We're not quite finished yet."

Camden huffs. The plane bounces a bit as the wheels hit the pavement, and I suck in a quick gasp, trying to hide my nerves. Camden goes back to giggling, looking out the small window.

Caleb's voice cuts through Camden's laugh as he talks to whoever is manning the small airport. As he taxis the plane toward a line of much larger planes, I focus on the landscape surrounding us. It's similar to Jackson though more green. Once the plane is stopped, Caleb leans over and pulls the headset off my ears, resting it on the instrument panel between us. His lips are soft, his hand gentle, as he kisses me and holds my chin to keep me from moving away.

"Can we see the lake first, Daddy?" Camden asks.

Caleb pulls away, a smile curving those sinful lips.

"Lake?" I ask, breathless.

Camden gasps. "Oops. Sorry! I forgot Bri doesn't know!"

Apparently the surprise of where we're spending the day is only for me. Ethan laughs, and the sound sends a shiver down my spine, all the way to my toes. It's only been a few days since my heat finally subsided. I'm still sore from where they both knotted me multiple times over the course of the week. And yet... I want to find a quiet place where I can appreciate Ethan's beard and skin and scent. My thighs clench.

Thank God the new scent blockers made it while I was still out of it, lost to the depths of my heat. The small cockpit stays blissfully devoid of my scent.

"Let's start with getting a snack, kid," Ethan says. "It's been a while since breakfast, and I get cranky if I don't get enough snacks during the day."

Camden laughs. "Daddy, you're silly."

Caleb's eyes glint as he smirks. "I need special snacks, too," he whispers.

My cheeks flush, and I duck my head, pulling on the handle to open the cockpit's door. Caleb's laugh is as full as his son's.

We climb out of the plane, and I smile at both of the airport employees finalizing the storing of the plane. As we cross the tarmac and enter the equally tiny terminal, Caleb wraps an arm around my waist and pulls me into his side. I lean my head against his shoulder, watching as Camden runs ahead of us, Ethan only a few feet behind him.

"Welcome to Coeur d'Alene, sweetheart," Caleb murmurs.

Coeur d'Alene is beautiful. It's different from Creek Falls or the mountain towns near Denver. The evergreens that surround the lake are a dark green, and the trees in the parks sprinkled throughout the small town are gigantic, way taller than anything that grows naturally in either city I've called home in recent years. We stop for ice cream and pretzels shortly after getting dropped off by the rideshare a block or so away from the main thorough-fare. Caleb kisses my nose, licking away a small bit of ice cream I got on it, while Ethan sits beside his son, watching me with hot eyes that promise me *everything*. All without saying a damn word to me the entire time.

It's clear Camden's been here before and loved it. He races toward the road, promising me the best toy shop he's seen, when he skids to a stop at the corner. Caleb grabs his hand as a group of tourists come barreling by him, paying him no mind. As we turn onto the main street through downtown, we pause, too. The entire street is closed to traffic, vintage cars lining the curbs on both sides, their coats of paint sparkling in the midday sun.

"Papa, look! It's orange!" Camden points to a car that feels like it might have come from the 1980s with its super angular sides and trunk. Not that I know cars. At all. Caleb nods.

"Your favorite. How many do you think we can find?"

Camden pauses and hums. "I think five."

I glance across the cars he can't see over, taking a quick count. He's not far off, actually. I count seven that are some shade of orange. Most of them are sports cars from the last decade or so. The body shapes seem passingly familiar, at least.

Ethan stands beside me, his elbow just brushing mine. I chance a look over at him, but he's looking down the street, a frown pulling on his lips.

We haven't talked. Not really. And I didn't think the long looks counted, though they communicated plenty. Ethan's never really been one for words. I push away the unease and twist my fingers with his. He runs his thumb across my knuckles.

Caleb leads Camden down the road, weaving through the people milling around, pointing out the orange cars. And a couple of others that seem to be special or unique, though I have no idea why. Ethan and I are slower. He doesn't seem to be in any hurry, and I don't push him. It's not like I'm interested in the cars.

"Caleb's planning on asking you about moving in," he says after a while. He adjusts the ball cap that covers his head and shades out his face. He lets out a breath too forcefully to be a sigh. "We should... probably talk about this," he squeezes my hand, "before that so it's not clouding whatever you're going to want to say."

"All right." My voice is steady despite the nerves crowding my throat. I swallow around them and focus on the view of the lake visible at the end of the street.

Ethan doesn't say anything else the entire walk down to where tables are set out in a greenway, overlooking the lake. Caleb glances up as we pass him and Camden chatting with a guy standing in front of one of the bright orange cars. It looks kind of like a Corvette but more futuristic. Ethan whistles.

"Nice Lamborghini," he whispers.

Well, that explains the futuristic feel, then.

Ethan squeezes my hand again, and then we're sitting at one of the benches, his knee touching mine, my gaze on the dark blue of the lake. Breaking the silence feels impossible. And that nineteen-year-old girl inside me wants to wait until he does it first, wants to hear him say he wants me, the way he never did back then.

"What I said at the Outpost is still true," he says after a while. "If a label helps, I'm willing to put one on us."

Were labels helpful? They didn't matter to Brett. I may have been his wife, but I wasn't the love of his life. I'd rather have no labels than one that holds no meaning behind closed doors.

Do Caleb and I have a label? We've never really talked about it. We just... slowly swam deeper and deeper until there was no sign of land behind us anymore.

Besides, him bringing up the potential of bonding was more revealing of his intention and our dynamic than any label that we may or may not want to use. Bond marks are more sacred than wedding rings, more intimate than any vow we could say in front of a crowd of friends and family.

I shove the idea of bonding with Caleb away and focus on the Alpha next to me.

"Do you want a label?" I ask, my voice surprisingly calm.

He shrugs and pulls his hat off, bending it between his hands.

"We've made things official with my family. The town's already put one on us as a group." His voice is low but detached, like he's talking about one of the cattle herds on the ranch and not our relationship status. "It was impossible for your heat to stay secret with Joan having to help watch Cam the whole time."

"Okay," I say, even quieter than him. Why is my stomach in knots when he's agreeing to be serious? "A label is fine, then. It'll be simpler than trying to correct the gossip mill."

He nods, puts on his hat, and then looks behind me.

"Hey, kid," he says, his voice warming. I ignore the stab of jealousy. I'm not jealous of a four-year-old kid. I'm *not*. "Why don't you and I grab some ice cream for everyone? We can go to your favorite shop."

Camden squeals and claps his hands before running up to me. "What ice cream for you, Bri?"

His question is so earnest, I can't help but smile.

"A strawberry shake," I answer.

The line appears between his eyes as he nods, mouthing the words. He hugs me before running to catch up with Ethan.

Caleb easily takes the empty spot beside me. He wraps an arm around my waist and pulls me against him, kissing my temple and running his nose along my throat, marking me with his scent. Some of those jealous nerves fall away under his touch and attention.

"Ethan already spilled the beans," I whisper.

He laughs and tucks me into him, resting his chin on my head. "Yeah? That saves me some time, I guess."

I grab his open hand and trace his palm, letting my gaze drop from the water.

"I don't want my own room," I whisper. "I'll just end up crawling into your bed every night anyway. There's no reason to waste the space with a bed that won't ever be used. And your closet is big enough for my things, too."

Caleb chuckles and kisses my cheek. "I can live with that."

"And I think I want to ask Emily about keeping the guest house as my nest. At least for right now."

The idea of nesting in the same house as Kayla is intimidating as hell.

His countenance sobers, and he lifts my face to his with a single finger under my chin. The blue-grey of his eyes is nearly identical to the midday August sky above us. Warmth spreads low in my belly and between my legs. He doesn't say anything, simply kissing me until I'm a panting mess against him, boneless and wanting.

"All right, sweetheart," he whispers.

Chapter Forty-Five

ETHAN

"Camden wants to get something for Lynn and Mom," Caleb says, quiet enough our son won't be able to hear. He walks a few feet ahead of us toward the lake, his hand firmly clutching one of Brielle's fingers. "But Brielle's pretty overwhelmed."

I nod, shoving my hands into my pockets. I've been noticing that, too, over the last half hour or so. Her shoulders have gotten tighter, and her smile isn't as easy or as wide as it was before lunch. Just like in Creek Falls, it's only a few weeks after peak tourist season in Coeur d'Alene. I'd bet good money that the large groups of people on the sidewalk and open grass areas leading to the lake are getting to her.

Brielle pulls her hair over her shoulder, twisting her fingers into the ends as she glances both directions at the crosswalk.

"I'll take Brielle back to the plane," I offer. "That way Cam can take as long as he needs."

Caleb nods.

"She said yes," he says as we cross the street and climb the half wall that keeps the sand of the beach from spilling onto the road. "I'll chat with Dad tonight and figure out timing to get her things moved in. Hopefully it's all settled before I get called back out."

I shove the panicking, claustrophobic part of me away, ignoring it like I have since getting the bloodwork done in July. Maybe if I ignore it long enough, it'll simply go away.

"We're moving herds this week," I say. "The main pastures have dried out too much."

He nods, his look telling me he sees through the thin excuse to keep me away from the house while she invades it and makes it her own. He stretches his neck, and then he catches up to Camden and Brielle. He leans over Cam to kiss her cheek, and she blushes. He says something, too low for me to hear, and she glances over her shoulder, her eyes locking with mine.

She nods and smiles at him. I pull out my phone and schedule a rideshare for the opposite side of the park. When Brielle focuses on me, I force a deep, even breath, and close the distance between us.

"We'll only be twenty or so minutes behind you guys," Caleb says. "Just enough time for Cam to pick something out for Lynn and Mom."

Brielle finally relaxes once we're at Caleb's plane, the tension falling away from her shoulders and a small smile curving her lips. I set a hand on the small of her back and ease the copilot's door open. Her breath catches. It takes all my control to not groan, not growl, not push her into the metal of Caleb's plane and feel the soft curves of her body.

Fuck, I might still be confused as fuck over all of this, might be absolute shit at talking and comforting and calming her down. But my body? It seems to have a firm—very firm—idea of how to help ease all this horrible awkwardness between us. She leans into me, scenting me, and the urge to lay her out gets even stronger.

I don't have the self-control for this. Especially not with the bruise just starting to show up along the curve of her shoulder. Caleb must have given it to her while I was keeping Camden distracted waiting for a table at lunch.

"Brielle," I murmur. It's nearly a groan.

She squeaks. "Sorry."

She doesn't pull away, though.

I glance over my shoulder, eyeing the airport employees in charge of manning the tarmac. They seem busy enough. I follow behind Brielle without a word, encouraging her across the small seats and onto Caleb's. Then I close the heavy door behind me, shutting us away from the world.

Her eyes are clear, her cheeks flushed. Fuck, but suddenly it feels like we're in Melissa's barn, hiding from Brandon and the other ranch employees while I explore her body. Her throat ripples with her swallow.

"Ethan," she says, a wealth of understanding and history in her voice.

God, Caleb better take more than twenty minutes with Cam at that tourist shop.

With a hand on her neck, I pull her into me, kissing her with all the messed up, swirling emotions inside me. She melts against me without resistance, moaning into the kiss. Mint explodes from me in one swift wave. Brielle shudders and then whines, grabbing my hips.

I wrap an arm around her waist and bring her against me, reaching across the small gap between the front seats. She props one knee on the edge of mine to keep from overbalancing. She pulls away, breathing hard. She might be hesitant, but her eyes are full of need. If not for the scent blockers, her lavender perfume would be filling this space, I'm sure of it.

"Ethan," she whispers. "There's no room."

"It's no smaller than my truck," I mutter.

I drag her into my lap, lifting her skirt. She trembles as I run my hands up her thighs. I ease the scrap of lace to the side, and lavender surrounds us in one all-consuming wave. I can't help but grunt, my dick surging painfully behind the zipper of my jeans. She shudders in a breath as she digs her nails into my shoulders, hard enough to bite.

"See?" I whisper. "Plenty of room."

She nods. "Don't tease me, then."

My callouses catch on the sensitive skin of her cunt, and she shivers. Her scent hits me again, and she mewls in desperation. God, even after her heat she's needy and desperate between one breath and the next.

I fumble with my jeans, cursing as it takes longer than either of us really want. And then I'm pressing into her, and her slick is fucking up my jeans. She gasps. I groan. She grips me like a damn vise, so damn hot and tight. Like every single wet dream I've had since I last got her under me ten years ago. Her lips are soft and pliant as I take them in a kiss to distract my thoughts. Sensation builds at the base of my spine already.

I swallow back a curse as she rocks her hips. I skim my hands under her shirt, plucking at her nipples through her lacy bra. Her scent doubles over. I can't help but thrust into her, forcing my dick as deep as I can get it.

She whines, her nails scratching at my neck.

"Ethan, please," she whispers. "Oh God. I'm so close already."

Good. I can't resist smirking as I pull on her nipple. She clenches around me, and her hips falter. I take over, fucking up into her until she cries out, her head tipping back and exposing her throat. I run my tongue up it, ignoring that base need to sink my teeth into the delicate skin and claim her.

The thought alone is enough to send me over the edge. I come on a ragged curse, and then my knot has us locked together. She screams, so loud her voice breaks, as a second orgasm rips through her body before the first has even subsided. She collapses against me, her forehead pressing into my shoulder, as we both try to catch our breath.

"I think I like Coeur d'Alene," she whispers.

I can't help but laugh.

Chapter Forty-Six

BRIELLE

The house is quiet when I crawl out of Caleb's bed and put on one of his sweaters. It hangs nearly to my knees, and I have to shove the sleeves up to my elbows to keep them from swallowing my hands entirely. But it smells like cinnamon and the cedar undertones of his aftershave. I breathe in the combination.

Lavender bleeds out from me, but I ignore it.

Caleb stirs, his hand reaching out for where I'd been only a moment before. I freeze but blow out my breath when he relaxes back into the pillows. My stomach growls, and I cross the house, closing his door without letting the door click shut.

The kitchen is quiet, too, as I start my electric kettle and spread cream cheese over a bagel. A mug of warm tea in my hands, I lean against the island counter and watch the pair of finches that have been in the closest tree the last few mornings since I've been officially moved in. After a few minutes, one bravely lands on the new bird feeder Camden and I put on the window above the sink yesterday. Officially, Caleb was watching him. But he'd hung out on the back porch and let the two of us mostly do our own thing.

The finch sifts through the seed, dropping a few pieces to the ground, and then takes off. I sip my tea. Unease sits low in my belly, but I can't quite figure out why. Moving in had been easy, even easier than moving into Emily's guest house. Caleb had enlisted the help of his dad, Mark, and between the two of them, every single piece I've purchased since being in Creek Falls was safely stashed away in Caleb's closet and room and bathroom. A few of my pillows stayed behind as well as a couple decorations since Emily was fine with me keeping the guest house set up as a nest of sorts.

Not that I'll really need it for a while. Heats only happen every six months.

Camden was beside himself when he realized what was happening. He's been glued to my side for the last three days, walking me through every nook and cranny of the house, showing me his favorite places to draw and read and build forts. Being with Caleb every night? A woman's dream come true, honestly.

And yet... I take another bite of bagel in the hopes it makes the turbulent roiling settle.

Footsteps echo down the hallway. I palm my mug, holding it in both hands in front of my belly, almost like it's a shield. Ethan pads into the room and heads straight for the coffee bar. His hand brushes my hip as he passes me, though he doesn't offer a greeting. Mint follows him, and I breathe it in, letting it soothe the worry that's become my companion since the surprise family date to Coeur d'Alene.

It feels wrong that I'm worried at all, though.

If moving in had been seamless, living here is... not quite

perfect. But more natural than I'd expected. There's always an awkwardness in the beginning, you adjusting to the other person while they're doing the same with you. There's been hardly any of that, though, with the Taylors.

I focus on Ethan over the rim of my own mug, watching as he pulls down a travel cup and fills it with coffee and a small amount of milk. His eyes are tired, the dark circles not quite gone from the stress that was my heat last week. His beard isn't as groomed, either, longer than he typically wears it and the edges not cleaned up. It's enough to mostly hide his frown—a frown so deep, it's practically etched into his face, the small lines around his mouth becoming more permanent every day.

I haven't seen him smile once since...

I think back, and the worry tightens again. He hasn't smiled at me once.

Suddenly, the worry and the unease make sense.

I'd lived with Brett for eight years, had been married to him for nearly seven. But for the last few of those, it had felt like we'd been more roommates than partners, orbiting around each other and only occasionally meeting in the middle.

This... whatever this is between Ethan and me has the same feeling, like we're circling each other and only sometimes are near enough to touch, to talk, to have a sense or semblance of any kind of intimacy.

Ethan glances up, his frown even deeper.

"What's wrong?" he asks, his voice nothing short of a growl.

Oh shit. It's me whining like that. I swallow the sound and shake my head.

"I'm fine," I say.

Bringing up the mess inside my head when he's getting ready to work the cattle all day is asinine in the extreme. And it's probably just all in my head, anyway. Ethan's never been quick to words, but his actions have always spoken loud enough.

Even now, he closes the distance between us, his coffee forgotten in favor of cupping my face and tilting it to keep my gaze on his. His eyes search mine. Whatever he sees has his mouth tightening. He drops an arm to my waist and lifts me onto the counter, easing between my legs. He pulls the mug from my hands and sets it behind me.

All the while, his gaze never leaves mine. He doesn't smile, either. Doesn't say anything.

His lips are soft but demanding, and I let him control it, let him pull me tight against him and thread his hand into my hair, let him take the kiss deeper and deeper until I'm a mess of need.

He pulls away, tracing his lips along my jaw.

My chest heaves and lavender surrounds us. I need him to knot me, lay me out on this counter until I can't think. That horrible feeling of not belonging that had faded over the summer is nearly gone again, pushed aside by his scent and body. He grinds into me, not caring at all that my thighs are wet with my slick and messing up his pants. I palm his neck and play with the ends of his hair.

He trails his mouth down my throat, letting his teeth scrape my skin. I arch into him, gasping, and his mint blends with my own scent, cocooning us. All rational thought drips away. His teeth bite into my shoulder, hard enough I cry out.

He grunts and pulls me closer to the edge, undoing his jeans before wedging an arm under my leg and tipping me back just enough to let his dick brush my slick-soaked panties.

"Pull them to the side, or I'm tearing them," he mutters against my skin.

I skim my hand down his chest before doing as he instructs. He bites me again, right over top of the last one, and I cry out a curse. His tip teases me, just barely easing in.

"Ethan," I gasp, begging, and close my eyes. "Please."

He pushes forward, just a hairsbreadth of movement.

"Ethan." Caleb's voice is grim.

I open my eyes to find Caleb grabbing the iced coffee from the fridge and pouring it into a travel cup nearly identical to the one Ethan had pulled. He's dressed in dark jeans and a black shirt that stretches across his chest. Lavender floods the kitchen in a new wave. Ethan kisses the stinging skin of my shoulder as he sighs. He pulls away from me, tucking his dick back into his jeans, and fixes my panties before looking over his shoulder.

"What happened?" he asks.

I wiggle on the counter, trying to find relief from the pent-up mess he's made me. He grabs both my knees, forcing me still.

"Got called in. That nasty one down in Boise broke free. They've been having awful winds all week." He snaps the lid on the cup and tosses the empty cold brew pitcher in the sink. "I called Mom and she's fucked all week. School started Friday, so Miranda's back to weekends only."

"Mom's in Jackson since it's Wednesday." Ethan grabs his phone and sends a text. After only a minute, he curses. "Emily's seasonal help is back to school, too. She's running the rides this week, splitting them with Melissa."

He holds out his phone toward Caleb.

"Damn," Caleb mutters.

The euphoria brought on by Ethan's touch fades away. I grab the mug of tea and take a sip. Caleb grabs a string cheese from the fridge, runs a hand through his hair, and then curses again.

He says, "My Dad might be able to take him. I can call—"

"I can watch Cam," I offer in a quiet voice.

Both men freeze, the kitchen going so quiet in a heartbeat that you could hear a pin drop. Their combined gazes are enough to have heat shooting through me again, and I perfume. I force a swallow and then take another drink of the tea.

Ethan runs a hand up the outside of my leg and then palms my waist, pulling me close to him again.

"You don't have to," he says.

"Are you sure?" Caleb asks at the same time.

My cheeks heat, and I clear my throat. "Yeah, it's fine. It's not like we haven't spent time together already. He can hang out with me today and tomorrow. And Friday, too, if Lynn's still working on getting her booth caught up."

Ethan frowns. "You really don't have to play babysitter."

The word stings.

Babysitter. The babysitter fucking both dads, maybe. Like a damn porno or something. Is it too soon to be throwing around stepmom? Probably. But having no label is better than *"babysitter"*. Like I'm some random person just hired by them. Something transient.

I drop my eyes to hide my frustration. And then I pull my hair over my shoulder, hiding the new mark from Ethan, when just avoiding his gaze doesn't feel like enough.

Clearing my throat, I say, "We got the new seat for my car already, so it's really no big deal."

Caleb crosses the kitchen and kisses me, pulling me just far enough to the side to avoid Ethan.

"Thank you," he murmurs against my lips.

I offer a small smile and kiss him again, needing his touch and scent and taste before he's gone. After too short a time, he pulls away. Ethan does, too, after squeezing my knee.

"I need to get to the ranch," he says when I grab his hand.

I force my breathing steady as I release him. Both men rush around the kitchen, pulling together the things they need. Ethan grabs the flannel thrown over a chair from yesterday and shrugs it on.

"We'll be done by six," Ethan says.

"I'll call tonight," Caleb offers.

"Be safe," I tell them both. They nod in unison.

And then I'm alone in the kitchen.

Alone and wanting.

Again.

For a moment, I'm in that damn condo in Denver again.

And then I shove the feelings aside before they can swell up and drown me.

Chapter Forty-Seven

BRIELLE

Olivia's smiling when she opens her door. Her gaze takes me in and then the small pair of feet just behind mine. Her smile turns sly, a knowing glint in her eyes.

"Hey!" she says. "Let me just grab my purse, and we can head out."

Camden giggles behind me, his forehead pressing into my back. When Olivia starts past me, Camden jumps out.

"Boo!" he says.

Olivia jumps, pretending to be spooked. Camden cackles and then hugs her.

"Hi Aunt Olivia! I get to spend today with Bri." He starts down the porch. "Nana and Grammy are both busy and Emily has to work at Misty. She has trail rides today."

"I hope you don't mind," I tell her. "I've packed activities and snacks for him in case it takes longer than I'm hoping."

She smiles and shakes her head. "I think it's great he's doing this with you!"

I help Camden into the new seat that's now taken up residence in my Land Rover—on the left side at his request. I hand him the trucks Ethan said were his favorites, and he grins.

"Thanks Mommy Bri," he says.

He garbles the r in my name for the first time in weeks, making it sound like "*mommy be.*"

My breath catches, and I freeze.

"Oh my God," Olivia breathes. "I wish I'd gotten that on camera."

Camden flushes red and ducks his head. "Sorry, Bri."

"You're fine, sweetie," I offer, my voice way calmer than I feel. "You can call me that if you want, all right?"

He smiles, his dimple showing, and hugs me, pressing his cheek into my stomach.

"I'm so glad you live with us," he whispers.

I run my hand through his hair, letting him hug me as long as he needs. After a minute, he pulls away and focuses on his trucks.

"To Jackson!" he says.

I climb into the driver seat and start down Olivia's street.

Olivia waits until we're out of town, speeding down the highway, to say anything.

"So the transition is going well?" she asks. She runs a hand down her belly and adjusts in her seat.

"Seems to be," I offer.

Yesterday had been awkward at first when Camden had woken up to find both his dads gone. The call Caleb promised helped a lot, though. And today has been great. We'd made pancakes and then packed a bag of things for him to do while we sit through whatever nightmare pile of paperwork the Council's going to potentially hand me today.

"You read the paper this week?" Olivia asks in a different tone.

I glance over at her and frown. "No," I say carefully. "Should I avoid it?"

She nods. "Definitely. We should probably make sure Caleb doesn't find a copy of it, either. He was fit to be tied with the article Jessica wrote about you and Ethan after the fireworks. And she was mostly nice about you in that one."

"I spent four months being called a gold digging whore by Brett's mistress," I say after a minute. "Honestly, Jessica's probably tame compared to that."

Olivia grimaces. "Yeah, okay. It wasn't quite that bad."

"What's a whore?" Camden asks. "And why does it dig for gold?"

Olivia covers her laugh with a cough. I glance back at Cam. He has that line between his eyes, his gaze focused on the road outside the car. He taps his truck against his leg. I fumble for some way to soft pedal the phrase but don't manage to come up with anything that isn't going to open another can of worms.

"I thought you found gold in rivers," he says when I don't say anything. "Grandpa Mark read a book to me last week about guys using pans with holes to find gold in water."

"Gold digging is a mean term," I say, trying to keep my voice light and calm. "And so is the other word."

Camden frowns. I focus on the road again.

"Why would someone be mean to you, Mommy Bri? You're so nice to everyone."

Camden sounds genuinely worried.

I clear my throat. "There was someone I used to know that didn't like me. She thought I was the reason her life was... not the way she wanted it to be."

Camden purses his lips but doesn't say anything else.

~

Camden circles me, his truck following a route around my thighs as he does. He mutters a race commentary under his breath. My phone pings with a message, and I dig it out of the bag I'd brought. When I see it's Olivia, I set the packet of papers on the counter, keeping my hand over the most sensitive information.

> Cake in hand. Just looking for some champagne glasses that don't cost an arm and a leg. Everything good there?

> Just waiting for a jerk of an Alpha to admit he didn't have an appointment so I can get the paperwork turned in.

> Ugh. Those ones are the worst. World doesn't belong to you just because you grow a knot, you know?

I can't help but smile just a bit.

> If we finish before you, we'll walk down to that bakery at the end of the street. I promised Cam a treat anyway.

> Sounds good. Pray for me. About to attempt Walmart.

I grimace. Walmart is awful on a good day. Walmart after spending the last hour with me while I sorted through the three different check-in processes the Council required to get me into this specialty office? No, thank you.

> Good luck.

When I tuck my phone back into my purse, the Alpha that's been harassing the poor receptionist for the last five minutes has his eyes on me. I drop my other hand to the paperwork, too. The guy's a jerk as it is, and the last thing anyone needs is him trying to hunt me down later. The receptionist, to his credit, keeps his back straight and his chin up as he turns away from the man and focuses on me.

"Finished, Mrs. Ashford?" he asks.

I keep my flinch at the name internal.

Even if this doesn't work, I need to do something about my last name. No way I want to spend the rest of my life being called Brett's name.

With a slightly trembling hand, I pass him the paperwork. He flips through it, double checking I didn't miss anything, and then nods.

"I'll get it into the system." He offers me a smile. "The process should, hopefully, be smooth sailing since you had the bloodwork results with you. Getting those is the part that takes the longest."

He grabs a card and circles one of the four name and number pairings.

"This is the case worker that's been assigned to your case," he says. "He'll send you an email update when everything's been finalized in the system. That should be by this afternoon, but he might wait until everything batches over the weekend to officially send it to you."

He pauses, and I offer a nod.

"And then he should call you once it's been processed and the new information packet is available for pickup. Again, that should happen quickly. Probably by the end of next week barring anything wild happening."

I grab Camden's hand as he circles around me again. He drops his truck, looking up at me with a frown.

"Thank you so much," I tell the man.

He nods.

"Bye," Camden says as we leave the small waiting area. The man smiles and waves at him. Camden giggles. He looks up at me once we're in the hallway. "He was really nice even though that guy was rude."

I nod and beeline for the closest exit. "He was very polite. And you did a great job being patient through all of that. I have one more quick project, and then we'll go get that treat. Want to help me with it?"

He nods and grins. "Always, Mommy Bri!"

"Perfect. Let's go get it from my car."

He skips instead of walks with me to the parking lot, bouncing a bit on his toes as I dig out the small box shoved under the passenger seat. I pull up the address of the thrift store and get it sorted in my phone's map. It's only a couple blocks away. We're halfway down the block when he finally gets curious.

"What's that?" he asks.

He holds out his truck, pretending to drive it through the air.

"It's some things from when I was still married," I tell him truthfully.

The last couple things I couldn't part with when I moved here. The two watches I'd given him and the tickets to the movie we saw on our very first date nearly a decade ago now.

"What are we doing with them?" he asks. Not a moment later, he frowns and looks up at me. "You were married? Like Nana and Grandpa Scott?"

I nod and squeeze his hand. "I was."

"But Papa says you're an Omega." He frowns, and that line forms between his eyebrows. He taps his truck against his leg in thought. "Betas get married. Omegas bond. That's what Papa says."

Nerves tighten my chest. He bounces in place while we wait for the light to change.

"Not all Omegas bond," I manage to say around the lump in my throat. "Bonding isn't something that can be taken back, so it's never done without a lot of thought."

Camden hums. "Like Daddy's tattoos? He says he can't get rid of them, either."

I squeeze his hand and start across the road. "Just like that."

"So why were you married?" he asks.

The thrift store is unassuming, a simple warehouse with a small sign labeling it. It's more rundown than the Artisan Square, but there's still a good amount of foot traffic along the front. I guide Camden around the side, following the signs for the donations drop-off.

"Well," I say slowly, "he was a Beta, so I couldn't bond with him. And I really loved him at the time, so it felt like the right decision to make."

"Do you love Papa and Daddy?" he asks.

I swallow the lump in my throat and force my breathing steady. The employee walks up to us before I can figure out just exactly how much I want to admit to the four-year-old son of my scent matches. I give the employee the box, and he flips it open. His eyebrow ticks up and some of the color drains away from his face.

"Do you need a receipt, ma'am?" he asks cautiously.

I shake my head. "No, that's all right."

He tucks the box under an arm and nods. "Have a good day, ma'am."

Camden waves as we leave. He's quiet as we retrace our steps and start toward the little bakery. Olivia stands outside, a small drink in her hand and a new bag over her shoulder. She waves when she notices us heading toward her.

"Mommy Bri?" Camden asks once we've rejoined Olivia. "Do you love my dads?"

I twist my hand into my hair and breathe deeply. Olivia raises an eyebrow but doesn't say anything. I pin her with a look. She smiles and shrugs.

As I open the door, I tell Camden, "I do, sweetie."

Chapter Forty-Eight

"**I**t was looking hopeful yesterday, but the winds picked up again overnight."

Caleb sighs and runs his hand through his hair. I set the phone against my empty mug and curl up in the corner of the living room's loveseat, burying my face in the hoodie I stole out of Caleb's hamper this morning. It's still mostly covered in his scent, and I breathe it in, letting it soothe the ache of his absence.

The small finches chirp just outside the windows, and I take them in for a minute. The sun is already high, casting shadows on the front yard. Caleb had managed to find a couple minutes to call me during his lunch break between flights. I focus on him again.

"So you're not going to make it home tonight?" I ask.

He shakes his head. "I'm hoping for the middle of the week at this point. If the winds can stay lower, there's a chance of tomorrow or Monday. But..."

He trails off, and I offer a small smile. "I get it."

I can't quite keep the unhappiness out of my voice, though.

His being gone wasn't as bothersome when we weren't living together. Now it's almost like I can live and breathe and *feel* his absence. Maybe I should spend the day at Emily's guest house where I still have my nest set up.

He frowns and murmurs an apology. "I'd hoped to be there yesterday. Did everything... end up all right?"

Between me and Ethan. Between me and the family. Between me and Camden.

Because yesterday had been the anniversary of Kayla's suicide.

Ethan had woken up before me and had Camden halfway out the door for a day of hiking by the time I'd made a cup of coffee. I hadn't been invited. Message received.

I'd spent way too long trying to convince myself I wasn't hurt that he had wanted to avoid me.

"I took a drive up to Jackson," I offer, shoving the awful feelings away before they show on my face. "Ethan didn't seem to want any company."

Given Ethan's obvious desire to avoid me, I'd intentionally stayed away from the town, from the families. It helped that there's a winery on the outskirts of Jackson I'd been meaning to explore for most of the summer. Three hours of wine tasting and a light lunch were enough to have the ever growing pit of worry in my stomach subsiding.

Caleb sighs. "I'm sorry, sweetheart," he murmurs.

Tears well at his easy affection, but I blink them away. I shrug and mess with a strand of my hair.

"It's okay," I say after a moment, making sure my voice is calm. "Grief is complicated. I'm not offended."

Hurt, maybe. But not offended. And isn't that embarrassing, to be hurt over Ethan grieving his bonded Omega?

"I'm going to take Phoebe out this afternoon," I offer, changing the subject.

Caleb smiles. "She'll love that. She missed you last week. Beau said she's been sassy for him."

A chime sounds from Caleb's side of the call. He glances over his shoulder and waves to someone, acknowledging something I don't hear.

"I'll call tonight," Caleb says, focusing on me. "And I'll take you out dancing as soon as I'm back."

I nod and offer a quick goodbye.

"I love you," he tells me, oddly serious.

"I love you, too," I offer, smiling just a bit. "Be safe."

When the call ends, I leave my phone on the table and take the mug to the sink. The pans from lunch have cooled, so I fill up the sink and start cleaning them. I'm rinsing the final piece when the front door opens and a single heavy set of steps cross through the living room.

I swallow my nerves and glance over my shoulder, keeping my body relaxed and the worry off my face. Ethan has Camden in his arms, the boy's head perched on his shoulder. Dirt coats most of his jeans and the boots he slowly toes off and leaves in a heap near the door. Camden's eyes are half-shut, but he perks up when he notices me. Ethan eases him to his feet, and he slowly crosses the room to me.

"Hi Mommy Bri!" Camden says as he wraps his arms around my legs, grinning tiredly up at me.

Ethan stiffens at the nickname. Has he not heard it before? I could have sworn Camden called me that around him the last couple days.

"How was your morning?" I ask Camden, setting aside the pan in favor of hugging Camden.

"It was so fun," he says with a yawn. "We spent time with Nyx. But now he needs to nap. Nana had mac and cheese ready.

It's my favorite." He pulls something from his back pocket, and I can't help but smile. The white daisy is smashed to bits, but the petals have somehow managed to stay mostly intact. "Nana let me pick this from the garden. She didn't have any purple ones."

He yawns again as I take the flower.

"Thank you," I tell him.

He pulls away from me with another smile and crosses the large open space, sprawling on the couch and grabbing a couple of his trucks from the basket of toys beside it. Ethan settles into one of the island's chairs, his eyes locked on his phone. Those nerves flare hot again, but I force them down.

"Did you have a good time?" I ask him.

He glances up before focusing on his phone, tapping a couple times on the screen. He shrugs. "It was fine."

His tone doesn't invite follow-up questions.

I take a deep breath, trying to hold off the emotions that are wanting to consume me. Maybe it's heat drop, and it's just my body trying to rebalance after going through a complete heat cycle for the first time in my life. I can't remember if that's something that happens immediately after surfacing, though. It's not something I've ever worried about happening to me.

I turn back to the dishes, drying the pan and then putting them all away. When that's finished, I clean the sink and then the counters. Anything to keep myself busy. This fear, this unholy concern over Ethan being completely apathetic toward me is probably just me reacting to being so near to both of them all the time now. And there's probably some shit that Brett's left behind that makes it more noticeable, too. Like when Caleb got called to the fire Wednesday morning. I'd halfway convinced myself then that Ethan doesn't really want me here.

A high-pitched whine echoes through the kitchen.

"Brielle?" Ethan's low voice skates over me, but it just makes the emotions swell higher.

Crap. It's me whining again. I swallow the sound and straighten the dish towels draped over the oven's handle. I wait for the soft footfalls that warn me of Ethan's approach, but there are none. Inexplicably, I want to cry. Tears line my lashes, but I blink them back. Mostly. One falls down my cheek, and I brush it aside.

"Caleb should be back in a couple days," Ethan says, his voice suddenly cautious. He's no closer to me, though.

I breathe carefully through my nose before turning around, trying to keep myself together. Camden's asleep on the couch, his mouth slightly open and his truck caught under his cheek.

Ethan's always been about action, not words. Maybe that will be enough between us, like it was Wednesday. Maybe just sitting with him, touching him, will ease the mess that's happening inside me.

I cross the kitchen and press my forehead into Ethan's shoulder, leaning into his side until I can smell him over the lingering cinnamon entrenched in the hoodie.

He stiffens. His scent floods the space around us, but it's stale and sour, carrying his rage and disinterest more succinctly than any word he could utter. I take a step away from him, my heart in my throat.

Just give him time, I coach myself.

His dynamic with Kayla hadn't been anything like the one I'd had with Brett. Grief is messy and unorganized and every person carries it differently. His resistance to me right now probably has nothing to do with whatever we are.

"I'm going to go to the guest house," I mutter. I'm nearly positive there's still something there that smells of him, untainted by his irritation and anger.

His shoulders drop as he sighs, everything about him screaming his relief at my leaving.

Something in me snaps. A piece that had been cracked since

he left Melissa's house the day before I went back to school, a piece that had been frayed and worn by years of mishandling by Brett. A piece that had been slowly healing under Caleb's attention this summer.

It tastes like bile on my tongue.

"Should I even come back?" I ask. My voice shakes as much as my hands. I press them into my stomach. I take another step away from Ethan, ready to bolt.

He looks up at me, his eyebrows furrowed, but doesn't say anything. Doesn't reach for me. Doesn't soothe me with his hands or scent or any of the other innate things Alphas have at their disposal when dealing with a skittish Omega.

I back away from him another step, and he grunts.

"Your stuff is here," he says. "And Caleb will be pissed if you start sleeping at the guest house again."

Caleb.

Caleb will be pissed. Not him, *Caleb.*

"Will you?"

His throat ripples, but he doesn't say anything.

The silence is fucking *deafening.*

Desperation claws at me.

"I don't need perfect," I whisper, the dam inside breaking between one breath and the next. "I lived eight years with a person I thought I had perfection with and it meant absolutely nothing to him. I just need honesty. I just need the person I'm with to want *me* and not someone else. I..." I swallow down the growing whine. "I need to not be fighting with a ghost."

Pain flashes through his eyes.

"Not forever. I can... God, I know how much it fucking sucks to lose someone you love," I say, the words pouring out. "I lost him before he physically died. I cried over him and lost sleep and couldn't eat. I *get* it. I can give you time. But eventually, I need to not be competing with her. I need to hear you admit that this thing between us is more than just a physical entanglement because of a genetic mutation that's marked me as yours."

He doesn't move. It's like he's become a statue.

Something horrid slides through my stomach and up my throat.

God, I want to throw up.

"Just once. I just need to hear it once, Ethan. I'll put up with whatever dynamic you want, whatever you're willing to give me. I just need it once."

He still doesn't say anything, though a muscle flexes in his jaw from how hard he's clenching it.

This time, I can't swallow the horrid whine. It's full of grief and devastation. I sob in the next second, but I blink away the tears. He flinches.

"I..."

Hope swells in my chest for a second, so strong it strangles me.

He shakes his head and lets the sentence die off.

And that piece breaks off completely, slicing through every part of my heart. Before I even realize it, I've closed the gap between us. My fist hits his cheek with a satisfying crunch that's almost loud enough to cover the heart wrenching sob that tears through my throat.

He mutters a vicious curse, wiping away a bit of blood that's pooled on his lip as he stands, towering over me.

"Fuck, I can't believe I let myself be a goddamn piece of meat *again*," I whisper. I catch the tear before it can fall. I *will not* cry over him. Not yet, not when he can see. My laugh is brittle, on the edge of manic. "Just like me to be ready to throw away every single warning sign in the hope the bastard will just want *me*, love *me*. But I've only ever been a replacement, a second-best consolation prize."

The color drains from his face.

"Brielle," he says, rough and anxious. "What the fuck are you talking about?"

"That's all I've ever been," I say.

I blink faster, willing my body to not let the tears fall right now. I wrap my arms around my waist, trying to soothe the awful feeling that's ripping through me like shards of glass. Crap, I might actually throw up.

"Just the pretty Omega with the good body and enough education to override my shitty childhood to come across as the posh trophy wife." Ethan's eyes are wide enough I can see white all the way around. "Fuck, but I just wanted to hear you say it. Just once."

Ethan's frozen again.

"Say what?" he asks, dread filling his voice.

"You know damn well what," I say, my voice cracking. "What I waited three months to hear at nineteen because I was too damn naïve to realize that the best I could ever hope for was a Beta that liked me *just enough* to fake a half-decent marriage."

"Brielle," Ethan mutters. "Princess, calm down."

This time, there's the innate soothing laced in the words. My breathing steadies for a moment. He starts to sit down, his attention sliding back to his phone. The jagged piece cuts through my chest again.

"I deserve to be wanted," I whisper. "Exactly where and how I am. I deserve to be *chosen*."

Ethan flinches.

I swallow the rest of the words building, forcing them to stay hidden away.

Crap, I have to get out of here before I completely lose it.

Another sob boils up my throat, and I don't bother to quell it. It rips through the room as I grab my purse and rush through the front door.

Chapter Forty-Nine

BRIELLE

The moment I've pulled onto the dirt road that leads to the Monroe Ranch, I pull over and let the car idle. Tears flood my eyes and flow down my cheeks, making it impossible to see anything. Can someone die of a broken heart? Because I think I just might.

Pain sears through me, so overwhelming it's difficult to breathe around it. Nausea roils through me, and I don't have the fortitude to resist it. I manage to circle the SUV, heaving into the prairie grass that lines the road. When it finally subsides, I lean against the wheel and try to get my breathing under control.

God, how could I be so damn blinded again?

I close my eyes and let the tears fall unrestrained, too exhausted to move. Time falls away from me, blurring into the background.

A car pulls up behind me, the tires biting over the gravel. I freeze, my breath catching.

"Brielle?" Melissa's voice is soft and cautious.

The last bit of me that had hoped, had held onto a shred of possibility, withers. I surge to my feet and wipe my face, blinking until I can see.

"I have to go," I say. "I... I can't stay here."

Melissa's eyes are wide, her cheeks pale. But she doesn't hesitate. "All right. Let me get you to the guest house."

She opens the driver door and hops into my SUV, waiting until I've closed the passenger door to start toward Emily's place. She doesn't say a word, just watches as I get out of my own car and run to the safety of the small cabin that's become my home, my nest. The second I'm inside, I shut the door. Cinnamon and mint hit me in a singular, overwhelming wave, and I crumple to the floor.

Chapter Fifty

CALEB

My body aches as Sam and I work through the preparation for the last flight for the day. Two hours, and then I can grab some dinner and talk to my son and my Omega. My hands ache with the need to touch her, feel her warmth and curves and the silky strands of her hair. My phone rings, cutting through the near silent hangar. Sam raises an eyebrow as I dig it out of my back pocket. I frown.

Why the hell is Melissa calling me? Did something happen with the ranch? Oh shit, did something happen with Phoebe? Had Brielle gotten hurt while going out for that ride?

No.

No, Ethan would be calling if something like that had happened. I swallow the growl and shove the phone away, trying to focus on my job. I've already been frazzled during this assignment, my head not totally in the game.

The ringing stops. I run my hand through my hair and join

Sam in going through the final checklist. And then my phone rings again.

Sam frowns, too, looking over from where he's running through everything in the copilot seat.

"Take it," Sam says. "I'll finish the walkthrough."

I nod and step down from the plane, answering the call without bothering to find privacy. If something's happened, Sam will have to know anyway.

"Melissa?" I answer, bypassing a greeting.

"You need to get here," she says, her voice full of panic. She sniffles and then stutters in a ragged breath.

Is she crying?

"What's wrong?" I ask, glancing up at Sam. "Why are you upset?"

"It's..." She blows out a breath. "It's Brielle."

My stomach drops. It's like I'm reliving four years ago, getting the call from Ethan that confirmed what I already knew from the broken connection, the lack of feeling in my chest. My hands are clammy, and I tighten my hold on the phone. Ironic that it's literally the day after the anniversary.

August is a shit month.

"Melissa?" I ask, trying to figure out where to start. Fuck, why is this happening again? *How* is this happening again? "Melissa, you need to tell me what happened."

I put as much command as I can manage into the words, and she whines.

"Brielle and Ethan got into a fight, I think. I'm not entirely sure. She... she wouldn't tell me." Melissa's words grow rushed, and they run over the top of each other. "She's packing a bag. Emily's trying to stop her, but she's inconsolable and..." She trails off, and then she sobs again. "Ethan dropped Cam with Mark at the hotel."

He dropped Cam with my dad? Dread sinks deeper into my

stomach, and bile burns the back of my throat. He wouldn't. Losing Kayla that way nearly destroyed us both. He wouldn't do that to me, to Camden.

"With my Dad?" I ask, my voice stark.

Melissa sobs. "He won't answer his phone. Lynn texted Emily about it."

There's a long stretch of quiet.

My mind races and yet stands utterly still in the oddest of paradoxes, a sensation I had hoped to never relive, never feel again. I swallow, trying to wet my mouth. Fuck me, where the hell do I even start this time?

"I... I can't go over there," Melissa whispers, her voice broken. "I'm sorry. I know I should."

God damn it. The last thing our families need is Melissa finding Ethan's body right now.

"No, don't go over there," I say, letting my voice drop into a croon. I rush around the plane, catching Sam's attention. My look must say everything because he nods and waves me out of the building. I'm running before I hit the back door. "I'll be there in a few hours. Get Emily to calm Brielle down."

Melissa's sobs grow louder. I swallow around the lump in my throat, choking on my heart. How in the *hell* could this be happening again? I hadn't even gotten to claim her. Fuck, I should have brought it up this past weekend after she surfaced from her heat. I should have reiterated just how serious I am about her. Especially with Ethan still so resistant to everything. She deserved to have it clear as fucking daylight just how in love with her I am.

I climb into the rental car.

"Melissa, listen to me," I say, pushing as much of that innate soothing into the words. She sucks in a breath, and her sobs quiet. "If she wants to leave, let her leave. Get Emily to calm her down before she does, though. It's nearly dark. I need her to be safe while she drives."

Brett was an asshole through and through, but there's no way I can stomach the idea of her getting hurt the way he did.

"I don't think she'll listen to Emily," Melissa whispers.

"She doesn't need to listen to her for it to work. It's something that Alphas can just do." I tilt my head back and groan. "Emily will know what I mean. Just tell her to calm Brielle down before letting her leave, all right? Don't go to the house. I'll be there in a few hours."

It's nearly four hours after the call from Melissa that I have my plane stowed and I'm rushing to where my truck waits just outside the hangar. It's another hour to town, a little less than that to our place. I drop into the driver's seat and turn on the engine, trying to calm my racing heart. My phone vibrates like crazy the moment I turn it on. I'm bombarded by texts from Melissa.

> She's leaving. Emily can't convince her to stay.

> Emily got her to stop crying. She's calm.

> I'm sworn to secrecy over where she's going.

> She's laying low in Jackson. I didn't tell you that, though.

> Ok. She's where she's staying for right now. She's safe.

Still nothing from Ethan. Lynn has Cam.

A single text from Emily greets me after Melissa's filter through.

He's alive.

There's no way to know when she sent it originally. It must have been after Brielle left for Jackson. An hour, maybe? Two? I toss my phone onto the passenger seat and start the drive toward the house, emptying my thoughts the same way I've done the last several hours.

Or try to, at least. The questions swirl, so loud it's impossible to ignore them.

What the hell happened? They'd been fine. *Better* than fine. She'd been wrapped up in him, sporting his own hickeys, smelling of him when I interrupted them on Wednesday. Hell, they'd been half a second from fucking on the damn island. Even this afternoon, she'd been willing to give him time, had been way more understanding than I'd manage in her position.

Had Camden seen whatever fight had happened? Had he been scared? Or worried? Fuck, he *loves* Brielle. Does he realize she's left?

I need to find her, need to comfort her and calm her and make sure she knows just how much Camden and I love her, *need* her. God, it had felt like something was missing for months, something other than the holes left in our little pack by losing Brandon and Kayla. Just a couple months ago, I'd known in my bones that something needed to change.

And I hadn't told her any of it, hadn't laid it out so explicitly. Sure, I'd given her actions, had given her the small *I love yous*, but so had that bastard who'd cheated on her.

I grab my phone, risking a ticket. I need Melissa to tell me where she is so I can find her. I'll buy a different house. I'll figure out a true co-parenting schedule with Ethan. I'll move anywhere in the world for that woman. Camden's still little, not yet in school. He'll adjust to whatever happens. He's so damn resilient.

Emily's text is still on the screen, though, and it has reality slamming back into me.

He's still alive.

Fuck, I'm getting ahead of myself.

None of that even fucking matters if Ethan's dead. God, I don't want to have to bury another person, another friend that's practically a brother. We'd managed to survive two separate deployments without losing Hudson. If this little town takes both of my brothers by choice, I might just lose it.

I swallow the growl that's building. Fuck, I don't want to have to explain to Camden that Ethan's dead just like Brandon and Kayla.

It's nearly midnight when I finally pull onto our quiet street. My heart hammers in my ears, so fast I'm nearly dizzy. Adrenaline has my hands shaking.

The house is dark and silent. I pull up to the curb, not bothering with the garage at all. I stash my phone in my pocket and grab my keys before heading toward the house. I'm sprinting by my third step, ripping open the front door that hadn't even been locked.

The burn of alcohol hits me first, cutting through all the other mundane smells of our home. There's not a trace of Brielle's lavender anywhere. A near empty bottle of whiskey sits on its side on the island. It had apparently already been mostly used by the time it fell because only a couple drops of the liquid are on the white stone.

Shit.

Ethan hasn't so much as tasted whiskey since Kayla died.

Suddenly, my body is convinced it's four years ago, and I'm

walking into this same damn house after a different emergency flight home. At least Camden isn't crying in his crib this time.

There's a stumbling crash, and I rush for the kitchen, not bothering to take off my shoes. Ethan's sprawled on the floor, facing away from me, wedged between the island and the coffee bar. I take a step closer, and the smell of vomit overpowers the alcohol. I grimace, controlling my own reaction to the awful mix.

He's fucking shitfaced. My Omega is a goddamn mess, hiding somewhere in Jackson, and he's so wasted he can't even move out of his own vomit.

"Ethan," I growl, all my frustration rising to the surface.

He twitches and slowly twists his head.

"She's gone," he says, a wealth of pain and sorrow and agony lacing the words that it brings me up short.

I play ignorant. He might just be remembering Kayla. He's trashed enough, it could be possible.

"Who is gone?" I ask, my voice calmer and softer than it had been.

"Brielle," he mutters, closing his eyes. "My city princess..."

He sobs, and every single ounce of my anger drains away, tucking itself in a box to deal with later. I grab the dish towel and wet it down, using it to get the worst of the vomit off of him. Then I pull him to his feet, supporting him when his legs buckle.

"She needed me to say it, to admit out loud how much I need her, and I..." He sobs again and tears track down his face and into his beard. "I couldn't do it. I love her, but I couldn't say it." He sucks in a breath, and for a second, I'm convinced he's going to throw up again. Instead, he closes his eyes and whispers, "I couldn't lose Kayla like that."

My stomach twists. This is not a conversation we can have until he's sober.

I get him into his bed, and he drops onto it.

"Shirt," I order him. "Before you get vomit on the sheets."

He pulls it over his head and lets it fall to the floor. His jeans are clean, at least, so I don't force him out of those. Which is good, because not a minute later, he's passed out on the bed, nowhere near the pillows.

I turn off the light and head deeper into the house, dropping onto my own bed.

I send a single text to Brielle.

I love you.

The message marks as read, but the dots don't appear. With a sigh, I tuck the phone onto the nightstand and get ready to sleep.

<h1 style="text-align:center">Chapter Fifty-One</h1>

CALEB

My phone chimes, and I grab it, abandoning the half-finished burrito. That awful pit in my stomach gets wider when I see the notification. Every single one has made dread build this morning. A multitude of texts—from Mom, from Lynn, from Melissa, from Sam. But Brielle's name stays the same. No notification, no text. Not even those damn dots that show she's at least thinking about sending something.

Is she all right? Is she scared? God, the idea of her being scared eats at me, but I can't risk calling her and it leading to her running even farther. Jackson, at least, is accessible with only a short drive. If she goes any farther, it'll be a plane ride. And that just doesn't bode well for any of this shit.

I focus on my phone again. This text is from Mom.

> Cam's with us. Lynn mentioned Emily
> needing to do something at Misty. You might
> check in with her.

I send her back the latest update... which is the exact same as the last one.

I'll let you know when I have a plan.

Take as long as you need.

Running a hand across my eyes, I send Lynn the update, too. It's only a few moments later when she responds.

Totally understand. If you need Melissa, she's at her place all day.

I focus on the hall leading to the bedrooms, then the clock on the stove. Nearly ten in the morning. Even completely shit-faced, he should be up by now. With a sigh, I grab the extra burrito and head down the hall. I knock on his door twice and then lean against the threshold, slowly counting to fifty in an attempt at patience.

At thirty-nine, the door swings open.

He doesn't look any better this morning. The vomit is gone, and his hair is damp from a shower I hadn't heard him take. But his eyes are bloodshot, and there's a new layer of stubble along his neck where he typically keeps his beard neatly groomed. I hand him the plate, and he glances down at it like he's not quite sure what to do with it.

"Eat," I tell him. "And then we need to talk."

With a sigh, he brushes by me and walks into the kitchen. He slides into a seat at the island and slowly eats the food. I clean up the dishes, keeping my back to him, while he does.

"Is everything all right with Sam?" he asks as I'm putting away the last dish.

"Not unfixable." I shrug. "Just taking unpaid time off."

Just like four years ago. Hopefully this time I don't have to then fill out a leave of absence to bury my Omega. Just the thought has pain slicing through me and stealing my breath. I grab the edge of the counter to keep from collapsing.

"So since my job isn't on the line at the moment, you get to explain to me why I got a panicked call from Melissa yesterday evening," I say. All my frustration and anger boil right back to the surface. I turn around and cross my arms over my chest. Ethan's food is mostly untouched, his hands hidden under the counter. His eyes are locked on me, though. "A call where she was sobbing and telling me I needed to get here. A call where she implied she thought you were going to attempt to kill yourself."

He flinches. His throat ripples with his swallow. His eyes flutter closed.

"Probably because I was going to," he whispers after a full minute. "Until I remembered what it felt like to be the one finding the person. So instead I dug out the bottle of whiskey you've had stashed for the last two years and drank until I couldn't feel anything anymore."

His stark honesty surprises me. Ethan doesn't talk about shit like this—not without a metric ton of whittling him down and bothering him.

"All right," I say, trying to keep everything about me neutral. "Why did you hit a point where you wanted to do that in the first place?"

The silence is longer this time. I force myself still.

"If I love her, if I admit to it, then I'll lose Kayla," he says. Tortured pain colors his voice. My stomach clenches. "That's how it feels. By moving on, I lose her. I already can't remember the way her roses blended with us. Some days I can't remember the sound of her laugh or the feel of her hand in mine." He blows out a breath. "I'm already losing her. If I let Brielle in, I'll lose the last bits I have of her."

"Ethan," I murmur.

He grimaces. "And even if I can stomach that…" He shakes his head but keeps his eyes closed. "I had her ten years ago. We… fuck, I can't even say we dated. I never took her out. We kept it all a secret. But she was mine for that summer. I gave her every first I still had, and I took…"

He trails off.

It's easy enough to read between the lines.

"You were her first?" I ask. Not really to double check, but to keep him talking. I don't give a fuck who she slept with first as long as it was a good time for her.

He nods and sucks in a sudden breath. He holds out his right arm. "The West Barn."

Yeah, that makes sense. I wonder what other memories those tattoos carry. His eyes are haunted when he focuses on me, tears lining the lashes.

"If I have her now, if I tell her exactly how much she means to me, and I can stomach losing Kayla, then I have to confront the ten years I threw away that summer. I could have had her this entire time. She didn't want to end it, she was ready and willing to figure out a long distance solution."

He shakes his head before dropping it into his hands.

Fuck, I haven't seen him this messed up in years.

I cross the kitchen and sit next to him. He leans his head against my shoulder and sobs. I sift through everything he said, trying to decide where to even start. After a few minutes, I clear my throat and wrap an arm around his shoulders.

"You aren't going to lose Kayla," I say. "Some things fade over time. I can't always remember the way she'd smile. But my body remembers it when my mind can't. Even as you make new memories with Camden and me and even Brielle, you won't lose her. Not if we talk about her and remember her, just like we do with Brandon."

He shudders in a breath and slowly sits up. I let my arm drop.

"And you can't crucify yourself for what you did ten years ago. Neither of us know the future. If you had chosen differently, there's no way to know that she'd still be here with you now." The look he pins me with is tortured. I try to give him more. "And how many other things would be different now even if she had stayed? We wouldn't have formed a pack, you wouldn't have taken over Monroe Ranch. Brandon might still be alive and wreaking havoc on some unsuspecting buckle bunny instead of working with you. Hell, Misty Mountain might not even be Melissa's and Emily's."

My phone chimes, but I ignore it.

"If we spend all our time thinking about the ways life could have been different, we miss out on the life we actually have," I tell him. "We take each day as it comes and make the best decisions we can. We apologize when we get it wrong, and we correct our course when we realize we're nowhere near where we want to be. But we can't keep looking behind us wishing it could change."

After a minute, he sighs. "Yeah, all right." And then, quieter, "You'll make sure I don't lose her?"

My heart clenches. "I won't let you lose her."

When he doesn't say anything else, I grab my phone. Even now, there's a small bit of hope that it'll be Brielle.

It isn't.

I send a quick text back to Lynn.

> I'll be over ASAP. Just finishing up talking with Ethan.

"I need to grab Cam from Lynn."

He wipes his face and dries his hands on his jeans.

"Fuck," he mutters. "I need to talk to Brielle."

That's going to be hard right now. I stop him with a hand on his shoulder when he tries to stand up.

"Do you love her?" I ask him. I'm not about to let him hunt her down if it's for anything less than love. "Maybe not enough to bond her, but enough to love her until you're dead, no matter what happens?"

"Yes," he says without hesitation. "Fuck, I've loved her for a damn decade."

Thank fuck.

"She's in Jackson," I say. "Melissa won't tell me more than that, and Brielle won't text me back."

He frowns and then grimaces. "Fuck, man. I'm sorry."

He runs a hand over his beard and then stretches his neck.

"I need to convince Melissa to fess up," he says, a flinty, unwavering look in his eye.

I cock an eyebrow, but he doesn't waver. Well, at least I won't have to make the drive to Jackson alone. As long as she's still in Jackson by the time we figure out just exactly where to go.

I text Melissa, giving her a heads up.

"I hope you're ready to beg," I tell him. "Because the girls are fucking *pissed* with you right now."

Chapter Fifty-Two

ETHAN

Melissa's standing on the porch of her house, her arms crossed, her eyes blazing with fury. I ease out of the truck, closing the door and tucking my hands into my pockets. Caleb waits until I start walking, staying a few steps behind me.

"You have some nerve, Ethan," Melissa seethes as I stop, one foot on the bottom stair of the porch.

I don't say anything. My head is fucking pounding, and my eyes burn. It feels like I've been run over by a truck and then trampled by a herd of cattle. Fuck, I'd forgotten just how shitty a hangover can be. It doesn't help that I know one wrong word will have Melissa slamming that door on me and refusing to help fix my fuck up.

"If you think I'm going to cover for your stupidity this time, you're *wrong*," she says. She's practically vibrating with rage. "I shouldn't have done it the first time. The only reason I did is because she begged me to."

Caleb pauses behind me.

"I'm not here to ask for you to cover," I say.

I don't even touch the whole subject of my stupidity. That's not a conversation for here and now, not until I manage to convince Brielle to forgive me for it first. *If* she'll forgive me, at least.

I shove the thought away before the hopelessness can swallow me again.

Her eyes narrow, and she crosses her arms. "If you're here to convince me to tell you where she is, you'll need to do better than every single moment of begging in your damn life, Ethan."

I force a swallow and start up the steps.

"All right," I say.

Caleb stays behind me, leaning against the railing of the porch, just to my left. His arms are crossed over his chest, his frown etched deep enough to look like one of mine.

"I fucked up yesterday," I tell her. "And I want to fix it."

"You wanted to fix it so bad you waited an *entire damn day* after I found her crying on the side of the road leading into the Monroe Ranch?" Melissa's words grow rushed, her cheeks a dark red with her anger. "Doesn't seem all that convincing to me."

Anger drops my voice, and I take a step toward her.

"It took an entire day because she was already gone when I made it to Emily's place." I breathe through my nose, trying to keep my hands from shaking. Mint bleeds out of me, soured by my rage and frustration. "It took an entire day because after my sister punched me hard enough to split my damn lip while refusing to tell me where she might be, I got blackout drunk and had to wait until I sobered up enough to form words."

Melissa sucks in a startled breath, her eyes widening.

"You went after her?" she asks. The rage is still coloring her voice even if her body has started relaxing.

I nod once, clenching my jaw hard enough it aches.

"Prove it, Ethan. Beg me on your knees."

Melissa's words are stark, brooking no argument.

I pull up short. Beg her?

I glance at Caleb. He adjusts his ball cap, a single eyebrow cocked. After a minute, he shrugs.

"You want her, then you're going to have to do a lot more than beg Melissa, Ethan," he says. "She's spent the last eight months rebuilding her life after an asshat lied to her and made her feel absolutely worthless."

My stomach twists.

Fuck Brett.

Slowly, I ease onto my knees, letting my hands rest on my legs. Melissa stares at me and then at Caleb.

"You love her?" she asks.

"Yes," I answer, just as quickly as I did Caleb.

God*damn*, do I love Brielle.

Melissa blows out a breath and pulls out her phone.

"She said she was thinking about flying back to Faedra in Denver," she says. "I'll see if I can convince her to stay in Jackson another day."

She taps a couple times, and then mine and Caleb's phones chime in unison.

Denver? Fuck me. I should have just told her in the moment, should have let myself think I'd lose Kayla. Chasing her all the way to Denver sounds miserable and exhausting.

Not that I won't do it. I'll follow her to the ends of the earth if that's what it takes to prove I can't live without her anymore.

Melissa continues, "If I can, this is where she's staying. If you text me when you get there, I'll double check her location in case she decides to go somewhere else."

I surge to my feet and pull Melissa into my arms. "Thank you," I whisper.

She sighs. "I swear to God, Ethan, I'm not helping if there's a next time. She's been hurt enough."

Her phone vibrates, and she glances at it while still stuck in my hug. She turns the screen to me, and some of the coiled worry and fear eases.

> I'm staying. I'll come back in a couple days
> and decide what to do then.

BRIELLE

Despite what I'd told Melissa, I'm ready to climb the walls of my hotel room by Monday morning. I grab the blue sundress that still manages to carry just a hint of Ethan's scent, leftover from its close proximity to my heat a couple weeks ago. Mint wafts over me, nearly indiscernible. The worry eating me from the inside fades to the point I can breathe around it.

It's ironic that it's *his* scent that's kept me the calmest the last two days.

Proof that biologically perfect has no bearing on actual reality.

My phone vibrates, the screen lighting with a message from Melissa this time.

> You're heading back tomorrow?

> Yeah. Going to spend today planning and
> then I'll be back tomorrow.

> All right. Share your location with me if you
> go anywhere so I know you're safe.

Always.

I gather up the embroidery supplies and stuff them into my bag. I stare at the suitcase I'd thrown together and then the dress. The need to keep Ethan's scent intact on it overrides the desire to wear it. Crossing the room, I dig out the yellow sweatshirt I'd worn the day Caleb got called to the fire. I swap out the pieces, pulling on a set of black leggings that smell only of my laundry detergent and then the hoodie, letting the cinnamon wash over me until it's all I can smell.

I bypass the hotel's breakfast, keeping my head low and my arms crossed. It shouldn't feel so vulnerable, walking around in such a small town, but knowing that there's no one to save me makes anxiety tighten in my stomach. It hadn't bothered me when I moved to Creek Falls a couple months ago—not enough for me to notice it, at least.

My phone vibrates again, and I swipe open the message without looking.

I love you, sweetheart.

It's the fifth time he's texted me that since Saturday night. My fingers twitch with the desire to text him back, to let him comfort me in the middle of this mess. I wouldn't feel alone and scared in the middle of this small mountain town if I texted him back. My fingers hover over the keyboard. I close the message before I can break. Panic tries to claw its way up my throat, but I stuff it down.

I can't have Caleb, not if Ethan doesn't want me, too. I refuse —*refuse*—to be a homewrecker like that bitch. I couldn't live with myself if I was the cause of Camden not having access to both of his dads all the time. I breathe as deeply as I can manage, letting the cinnamon scent soothe me again.

I force a swallow to keep from crying again and push the main door open, burying my nose into the hoodie so I can't smell any of the city. I share my location with Melissa before I forget. Jackson is quiet this early in the morning, mostly only tourists who are serious about their hiking and other outdoor sports are out.

Luckily, it's also early enough that it's not too warm for the hoodie, so I don't rush the four block walk to the nearest coffee shop. Instead, I take the long route, trying to ease away the restless energy building in my bones.

It mostly works. By the time I'm standing in the small line, I don't feel like I want to crawl out of my skin—or cry in a huddle in the corner.

My phone vibrates with a new notification. I press on the screen, and then my stomach drops out entirely. The email is innocuous, and yet it might as well be emblazoned with neon lettering.

How has it only been a weekend since I submitted the paperwork?

My hands tremble as I open the email and read through it. My mouth is dry, and I can't quite remember how to breathe.

Of course this is the one time paperwork actually moves efficiently. God, I'm going to have to find time today to go to the office and talk with the caseworker about my options.

The panic roars up again, and it takes every ounce of self-control earned from years working in corporate boardrooms to keep from dissolving into tears.

The barista offers me a smile as she calls me forward. I try to match it, but her face falls. I order a simple mocha and then sink into the chair in the far corner of the small cafe, keeping my back to the door and windows.

My hands still tremble as I pull out the snapdragons I've been working on since Faedra's visit. They're nearly finished now, just a few small details needed before I can decide exactly what to do with them. I start in on them, willing the monotonous work to dull out my thoughts.

The same barista brings me a mug a few minutes later rather than calling my name.

"Here," she says. She sets a plate beside the mug, full of three different pastries. "On the house."

Tears well in my eyes as I glance up at her. She offers another smile, this one more vulnerable than the last. As she turns back to the counter, the lights above us catch on a silver scar just behind her ear, right where my tattoo is.

My breath catches. She pauses, glancing over her shoulder, and I drop my gaze.

Damn, I'm a mess.

I eat one of the muffins even though I'm not particularly hungry. When I go to wipe off my hands to keep them from messing up the embroidery, I find a small note written in the corner of the napkin.

Even the darkest nights end. It'll be okay.

I let my eyes flutter closed and focus on my breathing. God*damn* it, I will not cry. Not yet. After a count to thirty, I grab the flowers and start on them again. I lose track of time, my mind finally quieting.

A small voice has me practically jumping out of my skin.

"'Cuse me," a boy says. "Can I have this chair?"

"Go for it," I say without glancing up.

There's a long pause, only interrupted with the scrape of the chair's legs on the tile floor, and then he says, "Thanks, Mommy Bri."

My gaze snaps up, my composure thrown out the window

when my eyes lock on his bright blue eyes, a kid-sized to-go cup in his hand. I glance around the cafe, but I don't see either of his fathers anywhere. Maybe he'd come with Emily?

"You okay, Cam?" I ask.

He doesn't seem to notice the shakiness of my voice.

Swinging his legs, he says, "Daddy said he's grabbing something and for me to not go anywhere else. Papa promised whipped cream when he gave me this." His tongue sticks out a bit as he works to get the lid off. His grin is huge before he cackles, licking a large piece of the whipped topping off the drink. "There's sprinkles, too. This place is kind of cool."

The bells jingle again, a singular set of steps throbbing like a heartbeat in my ear. The unmistakable mint scent of *him* surrounds me, and my breath catches in my throat, a presence behind me that has my heart racing.

"Brielle," he murmurs, and my heart skips a beat.

Chapter Fifty-Three

BRIELLE

I cling to the fabric, trying with everything I am to keep my hands from trembling. The silence stretches, long and heavy, but I refuse to break it first. Another set of steps cuts through the quiet, and then there's cinnamon, too, mixing together until I'm half a second away from becoming a puddle on the floor.

"Here's the snack," Caleb says. He crouches beside Cam, setting a baked good from the cafe's display on the table beside the drink. Camden smiles and kisses Caleb's cheek.

"Thanks, Papa," he says.

I force a swallow, trying to understand what's happening. He was on a fire. Had he flown back? Why had he flown back? I chance a glance out the windows, still not looking at the man I know stands behind me. Is it better to try and run now or wait a few minutes?

I haven't even decided what to do with the Council's paperwork, with the process I started that's only halfway complete.

Did they happen upon me by accident? Did Caleb force him to come? God, the last thing I want is to have a forced apology, something twisted out of him by Caleb. I'd rather he not apologize at all, not talk to me at all, than have something like that.

I'm getting ahead of myself. There's no way to know that's what they're even here for. My heart races, so loud it drowns out the noises of the cafe. My eyes unerringly focus on Caleb again.

He's dressed in a set of jeans and a shirt that says "Flying for All" in a white font, a circular logo of a vintage plane just below it. It clings to his chest and stretches over his back as he twists toward Camden and runs his hand through Cam's blond hair.

"You all right?" he asks, and Camden nods.

He pulls the muffin from the bag and smiles before he attacks it with the ferocity of a starved hiker, giggling the entire time. It's so endearing, I can't help but smile just a bit. Caleb takes a deep breath and drops his hand, twisting until his gaze focuses on me.

My breath catches in my throat before I can manage to look away. He doesn't say anything, doesn't move from where he's crouched. His gaze roams over me. I know what he sees: his sweatshirt drowning my body, my hair pulled back and unwashed, the circles under my eyes that betray my horrible sleeping. I didn't bother to hide the last couple hickeys fading behind my ears and along the base of my throat. His gaze catches on the one straddling my jaw, just in front of my ear. The last one he'd left. A muscle feathers in his jaw.

I'm struck frozen, unsure what to do. Is this how a deer feels when caught in a trap? Knowing that death awaits and not quite sure if it's worth trying to escape? My hands are clammy. I drop them to my lap, running them along my leggings. Caleb follows that movement, too, and his lips thin.

"Brielle," Ethan says again. This time, though, it's no louder than a whisper, a world of sorrow carried in the two syllables.

Oh, God. He's not here to apologize at all, is he? He's here to break my heart one last time.

Panic tightens my chest. I can't do this here, not in public, not with Camden watching everything. It's one thing to explain to him that the woman he's started calling mom moved away—maybe got a job in a different city or something. It's another for him to watch her walk out of his life. I shake my head, my gaze still locked on Caleb.

"Just listen," Caleb says, his voice a soothing purr. "That's all I'm asking."

My mouth is dry, and I can't manage to remember how to swallow, how to do anything other than sit here and stare at him. His shoulders tighten as I don't respond, a whisper of desperation crossing his face. His Adam's apple moves as he swallows.

"Please, sweetheart," he says. It washes over me, soothing me.

With shaking hands, I tuck the needle into a corner of fabric and drop the entire thing into my bag. I take the moment I'm not looking at Caleb to breathe, to try and remember why I walked out in the first place.

I don't think of the words, of the deafening silence, just the feeling of being second. Again. Of being the woman chosen because she's *safe*, because she's considered the most impressive prize, not because she's actually desired. It doesn't quite work the way I hope, though. Instead of being angry and defensive, I'm just fighting back tears. I'm so *tired* of being the second-best choice.

When I sit back up, Caleb's pulled a chair up beside Camden. I still don't chance a glance behind me.

Not that it matters.

The moment my hands are running down my legs again, trying to dispel the anxious pit in my stomach, Ethan palms my knee. He twists me in the seat, forcing me to look at him, the movement so calm and precise that my heart races again.

His ball cap is backwards, pieces of his hair pressed against his forehead. Even with the dark circles under his red-rimmed eyes, he looks like he just stepped out of a Country magazine photoshoot, right down to his scuffed boots. And despite how he left things, it has my body thinking all kinds of things, heat pooling in my core. The scent blocking lotion covers the spike in my scent, though, so only a tiny taste of it bleeds through.

His eyes are hard, his jaw clenched, that muscle ticking in his throat, but his hands are soft where he guides mine away from where they're picking at imaginary lint along my thighs. His callouses catch on my knuckles with each swipe of his thumbs. Another bolt of heat roars through me, but I do my best to ignore it.

I don't say a word. I'm done begging.

He rolls his lips together and squeezes my hands. After a full minute of silence, he says, his voice cracked and worn, "You were gone."

I frown and try to pull my hands away. He tightens his grip.

"What?" I ask. My voice is surprisingly calm given the knot of dread sitting on my chest. "Gone when?"

"It took me longer than it should have to realize I fucked up," he says. "But when I went after you, you were gone."

My breathing turns to shallow pants as I try to keep calm.

He'd come after me on Saturday? Was that why Caleb was home when he didn't think he'd get released until midweek?

"Emily was ready to rip my heart out." Ethan's lips twist into a sardonic smile with the confession. "It would have been just punishment."

Nerves clog my throat.

This couldn't be happening. Was he actually...

I cut the thought off before hope can swell again.

He squeezes my hands, letting his eyes drop to them before

refocusing on me. That desperation, that longing, is back on his face. I brace myself for the final rejection.

"Fuck, Brielle," he says. He licks his lips. "I'm sorry, princess."

I flinch at the nickname. It slices across my chest, more effective than a blade. His throat moves with a swallow as the silence extends between us. And suddenly, it's like a curtain pulls back. Or maybe melts away.

His eyes soften and gain a haunted look, and his shoulders roll forward. He runs his thumb across the back of my hand. He drops his eyes, focusing on where he holds me.

"He had to beg Melissa," Caleb says into the quiet. "She made him get on his knees before she'd tell us where you went."

Ethan on his knees? The idea is so entirely foreign, I can't even properly imagine it. He's never gone to his knees, not for anything other than getting exactly what he wants from my body. In submission or supplication? Not ever.

"I'd pay good money to see you on your knees," I admit. My voice cracks.

He swallows, his hands tightening around me.

Without saying anything, he sinks to his knees before me, stopping only when our gazes are level. Something lodges in my throat at the blatant desperation in the action, something so close to hope and sorrow and cautious optimism.

"I'll give you more than that if you come home with us," he says, all levity absent. "I'll give you anything, princess."

I swallow around the lump in my throat, trying to dislodge the swell of emotion. Ethan searches my eyes. I'm not quite sure what he sees, but his shoulders relax at whatever must be in my look.

"I've spent the last thirty-six hours thinking over what I'd tell you if you didn't immediately try to deck me."

The giggle bubbles out of me without me realizing.

"Deck you?" Camden asks.

Caleb murmurs, "It means punch."

"Mommy Bri would never punch someone." Cam gasps, shocked. "She's so nice."

Caleb chuckles. "Let Daddy finish talking, bud."

"Sorry," Camden squeaks.

Ethan raises an eyebrow and gives me a flat look. Of all the possible things that could make me blush, it's this that manages to send a flush down my neck and across my chest.

"You deserved it," I say after a minute.

I wasn't going to apologize for a single thing that happened on Saturday.

Ethan nods. "I did. I deserved the punch Emily gave me, too."

The small bit of humor fades away between us, and he squeezes my hands.

"I love you, Brielle," he says, his voice low and fervent.

Tears line my lashes, but I ignore them. How many times had I hoped to hear those words from him? A single tear manages to slide down my cheek, and a muscle feathers in his neck as he watches it track down my face. After a minute, he wipes it away and cups my cheek.

"I've loved you for a decade," he continues, "and have spent most of that time trying to convince myself that you were better off without me, that you'd moved on and were happy and fulfilled."

I shake my head, and he runs his thumb along my cheekbone.

He shudders in a breath before murmuring, "I'm sorry I couldn't admit it to you when you needed to hear it. I thought..."

He glances down and changes the way he holds my hand, lacing our fingers together instead. He brings it to his lips and runs his lips along my knuckles. When he looks up at me again, tears line his lashes. It's the most vulnerable I've ever seen him.

"I thought that by loving you, I was going to forget her, lose her in a way I couldn't bear."

Warmth blooms through me, making me nearly giddy, the switch so fast it's enough to give me emotional whiplash.

"I don't want you to forget her," I whisper. "She was part of your life. She deserves to be part of your pack forever."

He blows out a breath and nods.

"Caleb helped me realize I can love you both."

I manage a half-smile. He kisses my hand again. And then his words are clear and confident, ringing through me.

"I love you so much, Brielle. Even without the scent match. I'll chase you anywhere to be able to wake up with you in my bed every morning."

The thin defenses that I still had crumple.

"You do deserve to be chosen, to be loved exactly how you are without any expectation or desire for you to change," he says. "And I'm choosing you, Brielle. Until I'm old and gray, I'm choosing you. I spent ten years without you. I don't want to miss a single one, now."

I collapse into his lap, crumpling against his chest, and let the tears fall, hard and fast and inelegant. He wraps his arms around me, twisting a hand into my hair and palming the nape of my neck. His lips are soft where he brushes them across my temple. He sits back on his heels, not bothered by my weight or awkward position at all.

"You have never been the second option. Not ever. Not ten years ago and certainly not now."

His voice rolls over me, soothing me in a way it hasn't since I was a teen. My breath hitches. He tightens his arm around my waist and kisses the crown of my head.

"I know I'm shit at saying it, but I'll say it every single second until you believe it's true, princess. I'll spend the rest of my life proving it to you if you'll let me. Every single day."

I breathe in his scent, the woody feel of his aftershave and the mint that's his alone. He doesn't smell like the barn today. I snuggle deeper into him, letting all the hurt and worry drop away.

"Does that sound all right to you, princess?" he asks, his voice dropping and growing husky.

I nod and sit up enough so I can see him again. He runs his thumb across my cheeks, wiping away the tears.

"It sounds like a dream," I tell him. "I always wanted to grow old with you."

My voice is watery, but the corner of his lips tick up in a small smile. He kisses me, soft and gentle without any spark of heat at all. It's simple intimacy, and I settle into it, craving it so intensely it steals my breath.

"Papa, can we take Mommy Bri to the store?" Camden asks. "So we can get her that picture we picked out last week?"

Ethan pulls away from me with an exasperated sigh.

"No such thing as a secret when there's a four-year-old around," I joke. I glance over at Caleb and Camden.

Caleb's gaze drinks me in, and my thighs clench.

"I'll go anywhere if it means I get to be with you," I tell the three of them.

Chapter Fifty-Four

CALEB

"How is this hike *harder* than it was in June?" Brielle asks where she walks a few steps ahead of me. "I've been hiking and riding all summer. It should be easier now."

Her hair swings with her gait, the high ponytail leaving the phoenix tattoo fully visible behind her ear. I eye the longest tail feather. Fuck, my bite's going to look fucking perfect on either side of it. My dick presses against the zipper of my jeans.

Shit, this hike is harder for me, too. When I mutter as much, Brielle looks over her shoulder, an eyebrow raised and her lips pulled into a smirk.

"I'll just politely remind you that this was *your* idea," she says with a laugh.

Yeah, it was. And I don't regret it at all.

This week has been a fucking fever dream. Waking up with Brielle in my home, watching her interact with Camden, getting to see my son fall just as in love with her as I have? They're dreams I didn't realize I had.

And seeing Ethan relaxed and content for the first time in years is a nice change, too.

I did end up taking a leave of absence, not that Sam minded. I had to in order to not be called back out to a fire until September. The proof of our scent match was enough to keep any of the really big problems from landing on my head, at least.

My phone vibrates, and I check it out of habit. Ethan's single text waits for me.

Just finished. Ready for Sunday.

Great. Thanks, man.

Don't fuck it up this time.

As if the last time was actually my fault.

I roll my eyes and focus on the gorgeous woman in front of me again. Her jeans hug her ass in a way that has my mouth watering. She's wearing a simple tee I've never seen on her before, but the dark blue is gorgeous against her skin. She picks over the rocks in the trail, her breathing growing ragged as we work up the worst of the grade.

"Nearly there," I tell her, needing to soothe her.

She doesn't stiffen this time, simply looking over her shoulder with pursed lips.

"Someday I'm going to find a hike that you have to work for, too," she says, full of sass I've never heard from her.

Giddiness floods my chest. I grin and grab her hand, lacing our fingers together.

"Oh, I'm working for it," I say, sliding my phone back into my pocket and readjusting my hard as fuck dick. Her cheeks flush. "Any trail where I'm behind you, I'm working for it."

She shakes her head in exasperation as the trail opens into the small meadow. The creek runs lower than it did in June, and most of the wildflowers are gone, leaving only the longer prairie grasses and low-growing shrubs behind. It makes it more green than before. I soak it in, committing it to my memory. Every single detail of this afternoon with her deserves to be remembered.

I slip my phone out of the pocket of my jeans and take a couple photos for good measure. As I'm putting it away, Brielle turns to me.

"So who did you bribe for this picnic?" she asks, another devious smirk on her lips.

She runs a finger along the backpack's strap on my shoulder. I pull her to me and kiss her until she's breathless and writhing against me, her lavender scent filling the air.

"Mom," I tell her when I finally pull away. "I don't want anyone else to know yet."

Her look softens. "Know what?"

I kiss her nose and then cup her cheeks.

"That I'm claiming you today," I whisper.

Her breath hitches, and her eyes widen. But her scent only grows stronger as she covers my hand with hers.

"Really?" Her voice is a whisper between us. I run my thumb along her cheek, soaking her in. When I nod, she smiles, the movement lighting up her eyes. "Well, at least I won't accidentally drop into my heat this time."

I laugh, and she leans into me, my hips bumping into her stomach. Shit, she's tiny.

"Definitely a bonus," I murmur. And then I'm kissing her again, not pulling away until I'm hard and aching and she's whimpering into my mouth.

"Let's at least get the picnic set up," I say, humor dripping from my voice. "So I can pretend this was romantic and all that."

And to keep me from pushing her up against a tree and taking her hard and fast. But I won't admit to that out loud. She smiles and steps away, walking deeper into the small clearing.

It only takes me a few minutes to lay out the blanket and arrange the picnic, the small containers of food sitting centered between our outstretched legs. Once we've worked our way through most of the food Mom packed, Brielle relaxes on the blanket, leaning back on her hand in the mirror of my own laid-back pose. Her hand brushes mine, and cinnamon bleeds out from me. The forest moves around us, birds chirping and the wind brushing through the trees. The creek burbles, and I close my eyes, relaxing into the feel of it all.

"Strawberry?" she asks. My eyes flutter open to find her grabbing one of the large fruits from the dish.

I'm not overly interested in one, but I won't miss a chance to flirt.

I let my lips brush her fingers as I take a bite, and her breath hitches, lavender swirling around us. Her cheeks flush, and her throat moves with her swallow.

"Caleb," she whispers. It's full of the same breathless anticipation that's making my entire body focus on her. "Knot me."

She doesn't need to ask me twice.

I wrap my hand into her hair, palming the nape of her neck, and pull her to me. Her lips are soft but ravenous, and it's only a few moments before I'm a raging inferno of need.

Her skin, her scent, her whimpers. Fuck, I need them all. I need her slick dripping down my dick while I bond her, claim her like I've wanted to do from the moment I smelled her perfume in Mom's coffee shop. I roll us until she's sprawled on her back, her hair falling out of its ponytail and draping around her, falling over the edge of the blanket.

I strip her out of her clothes in record time—and that's saying something. She forces my shirt higher as I drag my tongue across her clit. Her nails bite into my skin, but I relish the burn of it, the stinging ache it leaves behind.

"So, do I?" I ask before pulling her clit between my teeth. Her hips arch into my mouth, her back bowing with her need.

Brielle moans. "Wh-what?"

"Do I eat you better than he did?"

Probably shouldn't bring up that asshole right now, but the possessive need in me has to know. It's what I've wanted to know since I first brought her to this meadow in June. And that protective, territorial part of me has to take every fucked up thing he did and make new memories right over the top. Just like I'm going to with that phoenix tattoo that covers the flowers.

She shudders, squirming under me as I blow on her clit. She mewls, her nails biting harder into my back. When I run my tongue along her skin, avoiding every single part I know will have her hurtling toward her release, she whines and whispers, "Y-yes. Holy God, yes, you do." She tilts her hips. "Please, Caleb."

"Good."

I scrape my teeth over her clit, and she shatters, her legs tightening around my shoulders as she throws her head back on a desperate cry. Before she's fully come down, I have my jeans low enough to free my dick and I'm easing into her. She grips me like a too-tight fist, and I groan into her shoulder.

"Fuck," I mutter.

I keep a slow pace, trying to draw this out, trying to make it the best moment she's ever fucking had. And yet, the release barrels toward me, the heat building at the base of my spine.

"I'm not going to last."

It's a whispered confession into her skin.

Her laugh is desperate as she twists her hand into my hair, keeping my lips pressed against her throat. I let my teeth scrape along her collarbone, and she arches, her cunt clenching around me. I groan, the sound low and mournful.

"Mark me," she whispers. "I want to know what it feels like."

I drop any pretense of keeping things slow and sensual, claiming her body until she's shaking under me, her cries echoing through the trees and her lavender perfume surrounding us. My orgasm races through me, stealing my vision and making me fingers fucking tingle. I bite her, right over top of that damn phoenix feather, as my knot swells.

Her scream is shrill. I wrap my hand in her hair, keeping her immobile, even as she pants and squirms against me. Her desire, her overstimulation, her love flood my chest, and I groan.

"Caleb," she whispers. Her nails bite into my neck as she tightens again, a third orgasm ripping through her. "Oh God, oh God. *Caleb.*"

I kiss my bite and then trace the phoenix with my tongue, enjoying the fuck out of feeling her come down from the ecstasy of knotting and bonding.

"I love you," I whisper, letting my lips brush the shell of her ear. She shivers and whines under me. "So fucking much, Omega. So fucking much."

Her love rushes through the brand new connection, more intimate than any words she could ever whisper. She covers my hand with hers and kisses my temple.

"I love you, too," she says.

Chapter Fifty-Five

BRIELLE

Phoebe presses her ears back as Ethan rides up beside me, so close he actually manages to palm my thigh. She shakes her head when he and Cottonwood don't move, and he chuckles. I pat her shoulder before scratching her skin. She blows out a sigh and stomps.

"Ease up," he tells the horse. "At least I'm not riding Minthe. And it's not like I'm trying to shoe you right now."

I can't help but smile. I'd gotten to witness Phoebe detesting getting her shoes redone Thursday. Watching Ethan work in the Monroes' private barn was an exercise in delayed gratification. He'd done it all with only a thin white shirt that clung to his chest and faded jeans, his hair tucked under a ball cap. Luckily, I'd had the sense to wear scent blockers, so he didn't realize the extent of me obsessing over him until much later.

Even the memory of it now, three days removed, has me scenting.

Ethan breathes in, his nostrils flaring, before glancing around the open meadow we've just crossed into. We've spent the morning since family brunch riding through the Monroe Ranch, the lands that aren't currently being used as pasture. This meadow is larger than the others we've visited. And it also holds more memories for me.

"I love this meadow," I admit, tightening my hold on Phoebe's reins and adjusting in my saddle, my right leg going a bit numb.

"Daddy does, too," Camden says from his perch in front of Caleb. "He has it on his shoulder, next to my bluebird one."

Caleb glances at me, his eyebrow arching. "Yeah?"

My cheeks heat. Once Ethan told him the memory attached to the West Barn, he'd filled in the gaps of most of the other tattoos, too. Ethan laughs, not at all embarrassed that most of his tattoos are memorials of our knotting. He squeezes my thigh as he looks across from me, focusing on Caleb.

"How about we stop here for a bit?" he asks.

Caleb nods, and Camden claps. Ethan guides us to a small outcropping of trees near the center of the meadow, a small copse of aspens full of bright green leaves. Ethan ties out Cottonwood before turning to Camden, easing him off the double saddle so Caleb can get Maple secured, too. I slide off Phoebe and tie her out as far from Cottonwood since she seems particularly irritated with Ethan's favorite horse right now. I ease the single saddle bag off of her and toss it over my shoulder.

Camden runs through the meadow as soon as his feet are on the ground, giggling, grabbing the few wildflowers still blooming. Before I've managed to walk away from Phoebe, he's back, holding out the small collection of white and yellow flowers.

"Here, Mommy Bri! For the new house!" he says, his grin so wide his dimple is showing.

I take them, smiling, until he's run off again. I turn to the men, my Alphas, and raise an eyebrow while tucking the flowers between Phoebe's saddle and her saddle blanket.

"New house?" I ask.

Caleb sighs, and Ethan digs through the pack attached to Cottonwood's saddle. He pulls a smaller bag and tosses it over one shoulder before holding out his hand to me. I lace my hand in his, and he kisses me.

"Let's go walk," he says as he pulls away.

I take Caleb's hand, too, as the three of us slowly make our way across the meadow. Camden's a hundred or so feet away, laying in the grass, messing with something on the ground.

Once we're in the true center of it, the sun beating down on us, both men pause. Caleb's amusement fills my chest as he kisses my temple. Ethan hands me a folded paper and wraps his arm around my waist.

My curiosity spikes. I thought I was the only one with a surprise today.

My breath catches as I unfold the paper and realize what it is.

"Blueprints?" I ask. "You're building a house?"

Ethan nods, his brown eyes piercing me. "We can still change them if you want to adjust anything."

He points to the front door on the paper, and then turns me until I'm facing the southern edge of the meadow.

"Welcome to the view from your porch, princess," he whispers.

I blink back tears, tenderness and happiness welling up in me in a great wave.

We'd spent the day here, talking about the future, things we wanted, our dreams and hopes. Kids and vacations and houses.

"You remembered," I whisper.

Ethan eases a finger under my chin and urges me to look at him. "I remember everything," he whispers, low and fervent. "And I plan on making every single one a reality."

"Promise?" I ask. Caleb comes up behind me, his hand a hot brand on my hip.

Ethan nods, his thumb pressing into my lips. "Promise, princess."

I breathe them both in, letting my eyes close for a moment, soaking in the moment, the feeling of them surrounding me and the Wyoming wilderness around us all. Then I pull the saddle bag from my shoulder and dig out my own folded pieces of paper. I grab Caleb's hand, easing one of them into his hand, and then give the other to Ethan.

"Brielle," Caleb whispers, his voice shell-shocked.

I twist out of his hold so I can see them both. He looks up from the official announcement, tears in his eyes.

"When?" He swallows. "How? This takes *weeks*. And we just bonded on Friday."

"Princess," Ethan's voice is just as surprised. His knuckles are white, his grip enough that it crumples the paper. His eyes are bright, the vulnerability in them making my breath catch in my throat. I grab his waist, pulling him closer to me. And then I grab Caleb, too. His lips trace his bond scar.

"I did it while you were out on the fire. When Olivia, Cam, and I went up to Jackson," I explain.

"How did you manage to get Cam to keep it quiet for over a week?" Caleb asks, his awe a light in my chest.

I grin. "I distracted him with a bakery."

"Wait," Ethan says slowly, his voice hoarse. "You did this before..."

His question trails off.

I give him a single nod.

He crushes me to him, kissing me so intensely, I'm almost positive I'll forget my own name. My new name.

Lavender surrounds us between one breath and the next, and

his mint joins in. Caleb's cinnamon does, too, the three of them swirling together in a moment of perfection.

"Welcome to Pack Taylor, princess," Ethan breathes against my lips.

Love swells in me, and I laugh as both men cuddle me into them, surrounding me, holding me up in their safety and acceptance. I look out over the meadow where our house will be, and happiness floods through me. Caleb's breath catches, and then he kisses his bond scar. I hold Ethan's hand.

He drops the paper, letting it get caught in the wind. I don't need to see it to know what it says. I'm no longer Matchless. I'm part of a pack, an Omega with a family and a place. Roots of my own.

"I love you," I tell them both.

ONE YEAR LATER

ETHAN

"**M**y dick was literally in your ass last night, princess," I say, and Brielle's cheeks grow dark. It makes her skin glow against the black lace and silk bra that matches her hipsters. Damn, she's gorgeous. "Nothing you do in here is going to scare me off."

She still hesitates, standing in front of her half of the long double vanity, a look on her face not unlike the one she wears when she's worried Phoebe will spook on the trail. My patience wears thin after a few minutes of our impasse.

"Brielle," I growl.

She winces, chewing on her bottom lip, her hands still grabbing the counter as she angles toward me. A whine spills from her lips, and I take a step toward her.

"Oh fine," she mutters, stomping her foot. "That's what I get for wanting to put something together for you."

With a huff, she crosses the room, leaning against the glass wall of the shower, her arms crossed. It makes her tits press together and her nipples show through the thin silk.

Consider me thoroughly distracted. I take a step toward her, adjusting my dick, my jeans suddenly too tight for comfort. Mint fills the bathroom.

Brielle rolls her eyes even as her cheeks darken. "Seriously, Ethan?"

When I smirk, she shakes her head and waves at the vanity, urging me to look at where she had been standing. At first all I see is the mostly finished bathroom. It's missing the final coat of light blue paint Brielle picked, and the mirror is just resting on the counter rather than hung on the wall right now. Lots of small things aren't quite finished in the house, and our room and bathroom have been the lowest on the priority list. My eyes glance over everything again, trying to figure out what has her hiding out in here when the families will be here in just a few hours.

Three small white sticks are lined up in front of the sink, carefully arranged on their corresponding wrappers. I haven't seen one of those since...

My smirk falls away as I shoot my gaze back to her.

"Really?" I ask. I don't even need to see the result. Brielle wouldn't be trying to hide out in here for a negative. And definitely not three of them.

As soon as she nods, I'm crossing the space and sweeping her into my arms, my shout echoing through the room. Her knees bracket my waist as she digs her hands into my hair. Her breath catches as I sweep my tongue into her mouth, kissing her until we're both breathless and her lavender scent drowns out my own and has the bathroom smelling like a damn cottage garden.

"Brielle," I murmur, and she wraps her hands around my neck, pulling me back to her lips, a whine deep in her throat. I nip at her bottom lip, grinning as that whine turns into a full-fledged moan. "Does Caleb know?"

She shakes her head. "I was planning on telling you both tonight after everyone left."

"Fuck, princess," I say. I run my nose along her jaw and kiss the delicate spot under her ear. She shivers in my arms and presses her hips into my stomach. "Tell me this is real, that I get to keep you forever."

She smiles, her face lighting up, her entire being radiant. I'm filled with awe that I'm the bastard who gets to see it. I get to know how she smiles in the morning when she sits on the porch and watches the sunrise. I'm the one that gets to know what her moans sound like, the throaty ones when I'm rough with her the way we both love and the breathless ones when my knot's locking us together or when my tongue is between her thighs. I know how she softens against me when I whisper in her ear when I'm deep inside her, soft little things that asshat never told her. I get all of it.

And now I get another one, this soft moment where she leans against me, her eyes betraying her vulnerability.

"I don't know whose it is," she whispers.

I run my thumb across her cheek. "We don't care, princess."

Her shoulders drop away, and she offers a tentative smile. Her lips are such a damn temptation. I glance over my shoulder, double checking the door to our bedroom is mostly closed. And then I press her against the glass of the shower, grinding into her as I kiss down her neck, biting at the pulse points that make her shiver.

"Let me bond with you," I whisper against her collarbone.

I hadn't planned to ask about the possibility until tonight after dinner. But *fuck* I need to ask her now, need to see if she'll accept my bonding bite knowing that we've put a fucking baby in her. We've talked about it several times over the last year, but neither of us were inclined to rush it. There was so much we needed to rebuild, and I didn't want to look back in another thirty years and worry we'd done everything wrong this time.

Her chest shudders with her breathing, her nails digging into my skin for a heartbeat. She runs her hands along my sides, pushing my shirt up. Her panties are soaked through already, her slick coating her thighs as she pushes her hips into my stomach.

"Is that a yes?" I ask, chuckling as she whines and rolls her hips again. "I'm not about to bond with you without clear consent, princess."

Her throat ripples as she swallows, the lavender of her scent growing again, nearly as powerful as when she's going into heat. Then she nods.

"Bond me," she says, barely more than a whisper.

It races down my spine, straight to my dick.

Yes.

I rip her panties in the next second, more than ready to have her slick dripping down my legs.

"Dad!" Camden's voice echoes down the hallway a moment before the rushing footsteps of his running follow.

Damn it.

Brielle curses, pushing me away and scrambling for the dress laid out over the edge of the tub. I readjust myself again as I watch her slip into the soft green fabric a hairsbreadth before Cam busts into our bedroom. I blow out a breath and turn around, crossing my arms, blocking her with my body. The dress clings to her body, and her cheeks are still flushed.

"Dad, did she like them?" he asks, skidding to a stop at the bathroom door. He bounces on his feet, his blond hair dropping into his eyes.

"Brielle's getting ready. Damn it, Cam, you need to knock," Caleb calls across the house.

His footsteps are softer than our son's but relentless anyway. He comes up behind Cam, putting a hand on his shoulder. He raises an eyebrow as he turns Cam away, running his hand through our son's hair as his gaze soaks in Brielle. Cinnamon overlays the mint and lavender already filling the small space, and Brielle whines, low in her throat. Her body practically vibrates with her need. If she hadn't just gone through a heat last month, I'd worry she was dropping into one.

No, she's just that desperate for us.

The feeling's mutual, and neither Caleb nor I will deny it.

"Since they're still on the island, she probably hasn't seen them yet," Caleb says. His voice has dropped an octave. Brielle's scent grows stronger, and her breath catches in her throat. "Let's give them time to finish getting ready and then we can show her both of them together."

The doorbell rings, and Caleb sighs. Camden's head jerks up, twisting toward the front of the house.

"Nana's here!" he says.

Before any of us can say anything, he's bolting out of the bedroom and back toward the rest of the house, Brielle's reaction to the flowers I'd picked out this morning forgotten.

Caleb runs a hand down his face.

"Don't take eight years, Ethan," he says, already turning back toward the door to our room.

I scoff. "You took an entire day. Everything will keep for an hour."

He chuckles. "I'll hold off your mom that long, at least," he says. He glances over his shoulder as he pauses with his hand on the doorknob. His gaze isn't locked on me, though. He drinks Brielle in again, his cinnamon scent so strong it wafts over to us in the bathroom and blends anew. "Can't promise more than that, though."

He locks the door before closing it behind him.

Not going to complain about that gift.

I grab Brielle and pin her to the glass again, lifting her and moving her legs to grip my hips, groaning at the slick coating her thighs.

"Ethan," she admonishes.

I respond with a hard pull on the pulse point just beneath her ear, grinning against her skin when she melts into me, her gasp making me even harder. She scrapes her hands down my chest, pushing up my shirt before tracing the phoenix that spans my left side. The soft intimacy of the touch has me groaning, undoing my jeans and shoving into her before she can prepare for me.

"Oh shit," she moans, throwing her head back as I work into her, short, hard thrusts that have her legs trembling. I pause when I'm buried to the hilt, watching her pulse flutter and her throat ripple with her swallow.

She's fucking gorgeous.

She tilts her hips, grinding against me, and I adjust my stance with a low grunt.

"Ethan," she moans, pushing into me, her breath catching as she squirms. "Please don't tease me. Your mom..."

I kiss her, not needing to hear anything about my family while I'm inside her. Her chest flushes as I take her hard and fast, the sounds of our skin slapping filling the space, nearly drowning out her moans and curses. I loop my arms under her knees, making the angle more intense. She whimpers, clenching around me.

"Fuck, princess," I say against her ear, taking one hand and twining our fingers together, bringing them above her on the glass. "I meant to make this way more romantic. Take you to your favorite spot and bond you where you don't have to be quiet."

Her laugh is breathless. I push my hips forward, forcing myself even deeper, and she tightens her grip on my neck, her nails drawing blood.

"Tit for tat, Ethan," she says. She bites back a whine and rolls her hips. "I wanted to do the same with telling you about the baby."

How did I get so lucky?

Her moan rips through the room, her body locking, her legs pressing my hips harder into her. God, she's beautiful when she's coming around my cock. Her cunt ripples, gripping me tighter. I let go, burying my face in her shoulder as I empty inside her, my groan blending with her breathless curse. A moment later, my knot locks us together. I already have my teeth biting into the crease of her shoulder, breaking skin as my knot swells. In an instant, her sated desire and unadulterated, smug satisfaction roar through me.

My knees buckle, but I force myself to stay steady, pressing her harder into the glass to keep her from falling.

"I love you," I whisper against my bite. "Fuck, I love you, princess."

She shudders in a breath and kisses the phoenix spread across my chest.

And later that night, when our friends and family are crowded around the large outdoor table she'd commissioned to fit the patio of our new home, she takes my hand and kisses the new tattoo centered on the back of it. A small cabin, nestled against the forest around Emily's house.

"Mommy!" Camden says, running out of the large sliding doors we've opened all the way. "Look what we got you!"

Caleb walks with him, his eyes on our Omega, one of the large bouquets of purple daisies in his hand. Camden carries the other one, the water sloshing in the opaque white vase but not quite spilling over.

"Oh! Mommy, can we grab ours, too?" Iris asks. "Please?"

Jude sighs but stands, crossing the patio to the small bag I hadn't noticed he brought in. Iris and Rose both jump up and grab a small package from their dad. Their eyes are just as bright as Cam's as the three of them approach us.

Brielle chuckles beside me. Her amusement is a warm balm in my chest. Caleb's happiness is fainter but not foreign enough to be odd. I focus on him as he stops in front of the table and sets the vase of flowers on it, just in front of Brielle. It's been a long ass time since I could feel him through a bond.

The thought doesn't hurt, even as I remember what it was like to feel Kayla, feel Brandon. He smiles at me, feeling the surge of emotion. Brielle leans against me, squeezing my hand.

"Okay, girls," Carter says. "You can give yours in just a minute. But let's let Camden give his first."

The girls nod, standing on either side of Caleb as Camden rounds the table and hands Brielle the vase of flowers. She takes them. And then Mom hands Camden the envelope, and his grin explodes. Brielle raises her eyebrow in question, glancing first at me and then at Caleb.

Her hands are steady as she opens the envelope. And then her eyes flood with tears.

"It's final?" she asks.

"Yes!" Camden cheers, raising his hands in celebration. "You're my mommy, Bri!"

Brielle laughs as Camden hugs her, climbing into her lap.

Our friends and family cheer even as a baby cries and Emily rushes into the house. Beau follows her a moment later, clapping Caleb's shoulder on his way past.

"Hey," Brielle whispers, kissing my cheek. "Love you, cowboy."

I wrap my arms around her, pulling her and my son into me.

"Good, princess," I tell her. "Because I love you, too."

Content Warnings

ON PAGE

- Suicidal Ideation
- Significant Alcohol Consumption

OFF PAGE & HISTORICAL

- Death of Spouse
- Suicide
- Car Crash
- Infidelity
- Alcoholism & Rehab
- Death of Parent

Acknowledgments

Every book that gets to this point is its own achievement. You'd think writing these would get easier, but they, in fact, become more difficult!

Thank you to my husband who always manages to keep the house afloat when I'm in the thick of writing. You encouraged me when it felt like this book would never get done, picked me up when I had to cancel it the first time, and listened to me rant about backstories and rodeos and mountain ranching. You're an all-star, and I couldn't do this without you.

Thank you to the best friends a person could ask for. Jian, Djoya, Ande, Gabby: you are each a light in my life and I am so grateful to have a place to drop my random snippets at two a.m. so I can make sure they pass the vibe check.

Thank you to Courtney. Every single week I look forward to our calls, and your calm in the face of my spiraling panic over deadlines is something I will never take for granted. Thank you for being a stalwart support through every iteration of this book.

Thank you to Rachel, Kiki, and Aimee for reading through the book when it was still a dumpster fire in need of a fire extinguisher. Your feedback and support were so incredibly helpful, and I am eternally grateful!

And thank you to each and every reader who has found themselves in my characters. I hope this story serves you, too.

About the Author

Jillian has been crafting stories since she was a young teen. She's always had a soft spot for heroines thrown into the deep end without any prior training. And while she, like most of Booktok, loves the dark-haired love interest, she secretly enjoys the blonde, Golden Retriever heroes. Other secret indulgences include the miscommunication trope, surprise or secret babies, and arranged marriages with age gaps.

Jillian enjoys soaking up the sun in Colorado. She can be found most days keeping the children and animals alive. During the summer, she enjoys testing the limits of her mental health by seeing how far into July she can remember to water the flowers and veggies in the garden. She spends most of the winter chasing after her snow loving children while silently cursing that she lives somewhere that actually gets cold.

www.ingramcontent.com/pod-product-compliance
Lightning Source LLC
Chambersburg PA
CBHW061046310726
48969CB00004B/1098